Television ratings points are equivalent to the number of households with television sets that are turned on. One ratings point represents one million homes.

The share is a percentage of all households in America with television sets who are watching a particular show.

The highest rated broadcast in television history is the final episode of *M*A*S*H* which earned a seventy-seven share.

People have killed and subsequently gotten good ratings. But no one has deliberately killed to get good ratings.

At least not yet.

Praise for
Killer Ratings

"Lisa Seidman weaves together vivid characters, delightful mystery, and the wry wit of a true TV insider to create a delicious tale of reckless ambition and literal and figurative backstabbing that will not only entertain you, but change your relationship with your television forever."

—Sheryl J. Anderson, author of *Killer Heels*

"In Killer Ratings, Lisa Seidman, a television writer herself, provides a thrill ride through the ambition-ridden and ego-saturated world of TV production, where there is more death and drama behind the camera than in front of it."

—Sue Ann Jaffarian, author of the Odelia Grey mysteries and the Ghost of Granny Apples mysteries

"Take an edgy TV production team, add a sprinkling of fierce ambition, and finish off with a large handful of paranoia and you have the perfect setting for murder. TV writer Lisa Seidman, who's been on that set, skillfully does it all in Killer Ratings."

—Annette Meyers, author of the Smith and Wetzon series

"Fascinating. Fast-paced. Fun. Emmy Award-winning scriptwriter Lisa Seidman's debut mystery goes backstage at a TV production company where pride, passion, and peril lead to Killer Ratings. A Killer Mystery!"

—Carolyn Hart, author of the Death on Demand series

"Lisa Seidman's page-turning whodunit, Killer Ratings, perfectly captures the backstage world of a struggling TV series where appearances are deliberately deceiving and ambition can be absolutely criminal."

—Mimi Leahey, script editor, *All My Children*

"The drama going on behind the scenes at a TV show is always juicier than what's on the screen, and Lisa Seidman masterfully combines three of my favorite things: TV, mystery, and a good story well told."

—Paula Cwikly, writer, *The Young and the Restless*

Killer Ratings

Killer Ratings

Lisa Seidman

San Diego

For my teachers,
Louis E. Catron
Fran Kohn
Sandy Pinsker
Joe Voelker
Gordon Wickstrom

And the best teachers of them all,
Mona and Howard Seidman

TEASER

1.

"Your job," said Rebecca Saunders, after taking a sip from her Vodka Collins "is to take the blame for my mistakes." She was gripping the glass so tightly, her knuckles were turning white.

I was so astonished the chunk of cashew chicken I was chewing got stuck in the back of my throat. I started coughing.

Rebecca's baby blues widened. "Are you all right?" she asked in faux concern.

I nodded as I reached for my glass of water, swallowed. "I'm fine," I gasped, still a bit short of breath, due more to her pronouncement than the piece of chicken that was still wedged in my throat. Rebecca's feigned concern evaporated, and she continued as if I wasn't about to asphyxiate in the middle of the Plum Tree Inn dining room.

"Fortunately, I rarely make mistakes, so you won't be working too hard in that department." She offered up a light, tinkly laugh, hoping, I was sure, to sound like wind chimes but reminding me, instead, of shattered glass.

I could only stare at her in silence, not wanting to make a scene in the elegant, pink-damasked restaurant by writhing on the floor, slowly choking on cashew chicken and her insincerity.

Rebecca, however, must have mistaken my oxygen-deprived bug eyes for disbelief because her smile disappeared, and she abruptly pushed aside her mostly untouched steamed vegetable plate. She leaned across the table, looking earnest.

"All kidding aside, you really do have to take better care of me. If I need you to pick up my clothes from the cleaners, you'll do it. If I'm working through lunch, you'll take my lunch order, get the food, and bring it to me. Everything you do for Peggy and Zack, you'll now do for me. And you'll make coffee for me each morning—decaf—and you'll wash out all my mugs and utensils at the end of the day."

If I had been able to get air into my lungs, I would've told her that I didn't know how to make coffee. It was a skill I had never mastered in spite of two years of all-nighters in graduate school.

Rebecca continued, oblivious to my distress. Did the woman not notice I was turning blue? "Oh. One more thing. You'll straighten out my desk each morning before I arrive. Put the colored pages into my scripts. File memos." She paused. "And open my mail." She said the last somewhat portentously, studying my reaction, seeming to think opening her mail—and who gets mail anymore anyway?—should have a deeper meaning for me than it did.

I could hold out no longer. My chest spasmed, and a giant cough erupted out of my throat, dislodging the chunk of chicken and sending it flying across the table . . . straight onto Rebecca's gray silk blouse.

We both stared at the morsel as a tiny piece of half-chewed cashew slid off the meat and into Rebecca's lap. Rebecca glared at me, her blue eyes narrowed and calculating. She reminded me of Mrs. Virgin Mary, the sleek and spoiled Siamese cat owned by the Covellos, my next door neighbors back home on Long Island. Mrs. Virgin Mary, so named by the youngest—and brattiest—Covello, Anne-Marie, had all the sensitivity of a sociopath.

Staring into Rebecca's glittering blue eyes, I could almost hear the snick-snick of Mrs. Virgin Mary's claws flicking open in anticipation of my sockless ankle or unwary bare hand. Although Rebecca was not a Mrs. and she was certainly no virgin, I instinctively moved my hands into my lap and out of her sight.

"I thought I was supposed to work with the two producers," I said, hoping that if I ignored the little faux pas on Rebecca's chest, she would, too.

Rebecca smiled through clenched jaw muscles. She took her napkin and daintily removed the chicken from her blouse, placing it on my side of the table, next to my plate.

"You work for all three of us," she said. "You work with anyone who needs you. That's what television production is all about. Teamwork."

She stole a sip of vodka, as if rationing each swallow.

"Listen, Susan, I like you. I really do. But you're an assistant. Which is only a glorified name for 'secretary.'

And secretaries work for whomever their bosses tell them to."

Whomever. I was impressed. I had been a straight-A student in college. I had a Master's Degree in English Literature from an Ivy League school. I had even won the F. Scott Fitzgerald Award for Creative Writing. So I liked the whomever. But it didn't mean I liked taking the blame for a woman who, in the past two months I had known her, had mistakenly omitted some of the crew's names on title cards, given the post-production supervisor the wrong dates for dubbing sessions, and forgotten to distribute the network's airdate schedules to the writing staff.

As if sensing my reluctance, Rebecca tried a softer tack. "Look, I know you don't want to be an assistant for the rest of your life. In fact, I heard you've written a spec script. I can get it read—maybe get you an assignment on the show. But you have to help me here. We have to help each other."

She smiled again, but it didn't reach her eyes. She took another swallow of her drink, started to call the waiter over for a refill, caught me looking at her and waved him away instead.

"Who told you about my spec script?" I tried to keep the fear out of my voice. If Rebecca found out that my script was already in the hands of one of the show's producers, I had no doubt she'd make sure my dream of becoming a television writer would remain just that—a dream.

"There are no secrets in the office," she said. But her eyes shifted away from mine and I knew she wasn't telling me the entire truth.

She reached for her glass, realized it was empty, and used her hand instead to cover mine, which had accidentally crept out of my lap and back onto the table. I tried not to show my distaste. Her hand was cold and clammy and felt like the skin of the pet salamander my brother Larry and I kept when we were kids. I noticed that she had chewed her nails through the coral pink polish.

"Working for me isn't as bad as it sounds," she said. "I did the same things for my boss when I first started out. Now look where I am. You could be me one of these days."

God forbid. I slid my hand from hers and reached for my glass of 7-Up. I wasn't thirsty, but I didn't want her to feel my skin contracting at her touch. "But the job description said . . ."

"Fuck the job description!" she shouted so suddenly, I jumped in my seat. "You work for me or not at all." Her hand shook as she lifted her glass, remembered yet again it was empty and abruptly put it down on the table. "Are we clear?"

I stared blindly at the other diners, suddenly feeling five instead of twenty-five. I mentally recited the opening stanza of "Dancing Queen" by Abba, my favorite song by my favorite group, until the urge to inflict physical damage on Rebecca had passed. The other diners, who had paused to stare at us, resumed their conversations. At that moment, I wished I had never moved to L.A.

It's not that I didn't want to work hard for my bosses. But when Linda Ramsay, the office manager at Romulus Television, hired me she explained I'd be the writers' assistant, working solely for the two writer-producers on the show. When Rebecca, the associate producer, started giving me tasks, I did them as a courtesy and not because she was my boss. That, however, was obviously changing. And I doubted a salary increase would follow.

Stalling for a reply, I reached again for my 7-Up and wondered with dread how long it would be before I, too, was sucking down vodkas like water. How badly did I want to be a television writer? Badly enough to put up with Rebecca and her petty needs and phony smiles? I thought of returning to New York with my tail between my legs, the pitying looks on my parents' faces as they tried not to say, "I told you so." If I couldn't handle one measly associate producer with a Napoleon complex, then how was I going to survive executive producers and studio executives with God complexes? I could handle Rebecca. I had to handle Rebecca. I just didn't have to become her.

My spine stiffened. As did my resolution. "Yes, we're clear," I said, looking her straight in the eye. "I'm sorry about the attitude. I guess I didn't understand what I was supposed to do."

"Good." She relaxed back into her chair, the anger dissipating. "I knew an open and honest conversation would clear the air." She patted her hair as she admired her reflection in the mirrored wall next to our table. Rebecca had a lot to admire. At thirty-five, she could still pass for twenty-five, with a clear complexion and thick, light-brown hair that curled at her shoulders. I, on the other hand, had a redhead's fair complexion, even though my own straight, shoulder-length hair had more brown in it than red. I freckled violently in the summer, and knew, if I lived in L.A. for any length of time, I'd soon be using sunblock year-round.

Rebecca reluctantly turned away from the mirror. "I can understand things may not have been made clear to you when you first started working for us," she said, the "us" meaning the writing staff of Babbitt & Brooks, a moderately successful hour-long drama series about two women lawyers. "But it's been two months already and you need to realize working in television is not as glamorous as most people think it is."

"The glamour was gone for me the minute I received my first paycheck," I said, surprised I could still joke.

Rebecca refused to smile. "No one understands it's a privilege to work in television. You all think jobs should be handed to you on a silver platter. But TV jobs are hard to get—and in this economy almost impossible. I fought tooth and nail to become associate producer—but I deserved the job. No one worked harder than I did to get it. I paid my dues. Just like you have to if you want to get ahead."

There was an edge to her voice, a defensiveness that I had noticed throughout lunch. She looked at her empty glass, said, "To hell with it," and held it up high to catch our waiter's attention.

When he returned with a new Vodka Collins, Rebecca winked at me before taking a sip. "Our little secret, okay?"

I nodded as I watched her take another sip, her hand shaking. She tried to steady it with the other, and her eyes slid toward mine to see if I noticed. I looked away, pretending ignorance. For a moment I had caught a furtive, hunted look in her eyes, and I realized Rebecca wasn't shaky, defensive, or edgy because she needed a drink. Rebecca was shaky, defensive, and edgy because she was afraid.

2.

Rebecca's fear surprised and puzzled me. She was the associate producer of a primetime, award-winning television series and made a good living, and while she wasn't the easiest person to work with, Ray Goldfarb, the executive producer, seemed fond of her and not likely to fire her. If anyone should be afraid, shouldn't it be me?

I was raised in the middle class town of Cohasset, in Long Island, New York, the daughter of two elementary school teachers who made it clear they wanted me to follow in their footsteps. But I was making up my own stories before I learned how to read, grabbing books out of my dad's hands as he read to my brother and me at night, insisting that I would tell the story, and then promptly doing just that. In my versions, however, the princesses were the ones fighting dragons to rescue their imprisoned princes. (How my brother, Larry, hated that!) When I was old enough, I'd scribble down stories in black-and-white composition books, then on my computer: talking dogs, kids who grew twenty feet tall, people who lived on the moon. Walking to school with my best friend, Nancy Shilay, I'd relate my stories to her and she'd reply with disapproval, "You have such an imagination," like that was a bad thing.

Television was always a part of my life. I'd watch movies with my mom on the cable channels, and to get my brother and me out of the way during her and dad's infrequent dinner parties, she'd go through TV Guide and suggest shows we could watch. Friends. Beverly Hills 90210. Home Improvement. At night I'd dream about my favorite shows, coming up with my own stories to fit the characters and premise. And when I'd wake up, I'd think, Why can't I do that for a living? Why can't I write for the TV shows I love so much?

When I told my high school guidance counselor, Mr. Workman, that I wanted to write for television, he discreetly paused, then pointed out several good liberal arts colleges. And my parents made it very clear they were not going to pay the money to send me to film school.

But I never stopped writing, and when a professor in graduate school bragged about his student who was currently writing for a successful show in Los Angeles, I showed him my spec scripts and he became my mentor. Seeing that I was determined to go to Los Angeles, my parents gave in and Mom flew with me to L.A. and helped me find an apartment. After a year of temping at various companies, I landed at Romulus Television, doing secretarial work for a writer developing TV pilots he and Romulus hoped to sell to a network or cable channel. Linda Ramsay, the office manager, took a liking to me, and when the assistant's job opened up at Babbitt & Brooks, she made sure I was the only qualified candidate to be interviewed. I was still poor, still making spaghetti sauce with cans of tomato soup and eating ramen noodles every other night, but I was working full-time for a TV series. I was on the bottom rung of the ladder, but at least I was on the ladder.

Romulus Television, which produced Babbitt & Brooks, was an independent production company not associated with any of the major studios like Paramount, Warner Bros., or Universal. The show was filmed in a warehouse in downtown L.A., a few miles north of Chinatown, in a no-man's land of littered streets, abandoned warehouses, and greasy taco stands. Although not the lowest-rated series on television, the show wasn't a huge hit, so it was made for as little money as possible, with the exteriors of downtown L.A. used as substitutes for New York City, where the series supposedly took place. Not quite the glamorous movie studio location I had hoped for, but it was better than working as an office temp for an auto paint firm, which had been my first job when I moved to L.A.

Returning from lunch, I followed Rebecca up the narrow cement stairs to the peeling white warehouse which served as the Babbitt & Brooks's offices and entered the unlocked door. Walking rapidly ahead of me, she slipped into her office at the end of the dark, musty hall. A door on my right suddenly opened and Sandy Martin, the executive producer's assistant, took a step toward me.

"Get in here!" she hissed, and before I could respond, she grabbed my arm and yanked me into the room, firmly shutting the door behind her.

"What's wrong?" I asked, rubbing my arm. "What did I do?"

Sandy stood stiffly in front of the closed plywood door, her arms crossed against her almost non-existent chest. She reminded me of a skinny version of those red-and-black uniformed Beefeaters who stood guarding the entrance to Buckingham Palace. Only she wasn't preventing me from going in somewhere; she was keeping me from leaving.

"What did Rebecca talk to you about at lunch?" In her

early thirties, from England, she had an accent that spoke of years spent in tony public schools and Cambridge University.

"How did you know we were having lunch?" Belatedly, I remembered Rebecca telling me how there were no secrets in the office.

Sandy ran a hand through her short brown curls and began pacing her small, windowless office. "Rebecca came to me wanting to fire you. I told her to take you to lunch and explain her problems to you instead."

"She wanted to fire me?" My stomach did a somersault, and I could taste chicken and cashews in the back of my mouth. "Why? I didn't even know I was supposed to be working for her." Queasy, I sank into Sandy's desk chair. It was the only piece of furniture not covered with scripts, memos, or files.

"You weren't. Most associate producers don't have secretaries." She absently pulled on her upper lip, a nasty habit that drew attention to her small, crooked teeth. The British could invent DNA profiling but they couldn't seem to produce decent dentists. I looked away from her mouth to study the memos on her desk.

"So why is Rebecca so privileged?" I asked. Sandy sat on the edge of her desk, blocking my view of the memos.

"Never mind that. What did she say to you?" Totally thrown by the absence of her usually reserved, stiff-upper-lip demeanor, I answered in spite of myself. "Rebecca wants me to take the blame for her mistakes." I briefly summed up our conversation at lunch.

Sandy stared at me in shock. "You're joking."

"I wish."

"No, really. Why do you always have to exaggerate things?"

I stared at her defiantly, angry over not being believed. "I'm not exaggerating. You know her. You don't think she's capable of saying stuff like that?"

Sandy paused then managed an apologetic smile, immediately backing down. "Sorry, luv, I don't mean to sound like Attila the Hun. I was just worried for you."

But her normally cool green eyes darted away from mine, reminding me of Rebecca's secretive behavior at lunch. Wanting something from me but without having to tell me why.

"Do I still have a job?" I asked, dreading her answer.

"I don't know. I mean, Peggy and Zack think highly of you. They've told me how much they like you and what a good job you're doing for them."

"So, why are you freaking me out?"

"Because Rebecca has a lot of power. At least she thinks she does. And if she complained to Ray about you . . ."

I filled in the blanks. "He would fire me? Even though Peggy and Zack like me? Don't they have more of a say in this?"

Ray Goldfarb, Sandy's boss, was Babbitt & Brooks' showrunner. A writer who toiled in the trenches of one-hour dramatic television for years, he created the series, sold it to Romulus and became its executive producer. As showrunner and EP, Ray made the final script and production decisions, including hiring and firing.

Sandy paused. "I thought Rebecca might tell you . . ." She trailed off.

"Tell me what?" Instead of answering, she stood and

began gathering up assorted scripts scattered on her desk, her mouth a thin, prim line.

I stretched out a hand, stopping her. "You're not being fair. This is my job we're talking about. My career, if Charles likes my script. At least let me know if I need to update my resume."

I hoped I didn't have to. I needed to keep my job at B&B since I doubted that any other producer would be as generous as Charles Green was when his assistant, Jennifer, raved about my script to him and he offered to read it and give me notes. Notes I was anxiously waiting to receive that afternoon.

Sandy put down the scripts she was holding, pulling on her lip. "You're right, luv. I'm sorry. It's just that I'm not supposed to tell anyone. Not until it becomes official."

"Until what becomes official?"

"Promise not to tell anyone."

"Cross my heart and hope to die."

Sandy reached across her desk and plucked a piece of paper from the pile of memos she had been guarding. She handed it to me in silence.

It was a memo printed on Babbitt & Brooks stationery, dated that day, from Ray Goldfarb to the writing staff; Cliff Rosen, the president of Romulus Television; and Bob Berg, the executive in charge of production (the Romulus budget man), notifying everyone that as of October 7th (the next day), Rebecca Saunders was being promoted from associate producer to co-producer with all its attendant responsibilities, including at least two Babbitt & Brooks script assignments.

"It's going out tonight," Sandy said. "After Ray leaves

for the day. He's too cowardly to deal with the reaction. He's hoping everyone will cool off overnight."

"Does she know how to write?" was all I could think of to ask. "Does she have a spec script?" Speculation ("spec" for short) scripts were written by beginning writers like myself. They were samples of our work, either based on shows already on the air or written as original screenplays. Spec meant you didn't get paid to write the script.

Sandy removed the memo from my fingers. "I don't think so."

"Then how could she be allowed to write scripts for the show?"

"I think you're missing the point, Susan." But I wasn't missing the point; I was deliberately avoiding it. As associate producer, Rebecca wasn't high enough on the pecking order to fire me. As co-producer, she would be. I tapped the memo Sandy still held in her hands. "This is why she wanted to talk to me."

Sandy nodded. "As co-producer Rebecca is entitled to her own assistant. But the budget can't afford another secretary. So she has to work with you."

"She was marking her territory," I said. "Peeing on me at lunch."

Sandy wrinkled her nose. "Not quite the way I'd put it."

"You weren't at lunch." I kneaded the crease in my khaki pants. "Why does she hate me so much?"

Sandy said, "Hate is a strong word."

I shrugged. "Okay. Dislike. Even when I wasn't officially working for her, I worked for her. Maybe not in the capacity she wants me to now, but I never blew off her requests."

Sandy said, "I don't know, Susan. All I can say is I don't think she likes any of us very much. She's always after me for not doing as good a job as she did when she was Ray's assistant."

"But she's not trying to fire you."

"Maybe she is, and I'm just not aware of it. I honestly don't know what makes that woman tick. I wish I did. It would make all our lives easier."

I nodded then thought of something. "There is one thing I didn't tell you." Sandy looked at me expectantly. "Rebecca's afraid. And she was drinking to hide it."

Sandy dropped the memo back on her desk as if it were burning her fingers. "Of course she is. Rebecca's not qualified to be co-producer. She's not even qualified to be associate producer. She was Ray's secretary before Babbitt & Brooks got on the air. Once this memo is released, the entire writing staff is going to explode. And Rebecca knows it."

"So why is Ray promoting her?"

Sandy merely looked at me.

"Is it true then? About their sleeping together?"

Sandy's voice was sharp. "Who told you? No, you don't have to say anything. It was Jennifer."

She was right but I only asked again, "Is it true?"

"Maybe. In the past. I don't think so now."

"Ray's married," I said.

"When does that have to do with anything?" Sandy replied.

True. "Is my job really safe? Or am I going to come in tomorrow and find my desk packed up?"

"I don't know, luv. All I can tell you is that once the

memo is officially released, the shit—as you Yanks so quaintly put it—is going to hit the fan."

And, as if to emphasize Sandy's statement, a cry of rage and fear barreled down the hall, through the walls of Sandy's small office.

"Susan, get in here. Now!"

Rebecca.

I raced to her office, barely aware of Sandy pounding down the short hall behind me. Jennifer Bardos, the supervising producer's assistant, joined us from the bullpen around the corner. The three of us wedged in her doorway and stared at Rebecca, who stood behind her desk, holding a sheet of paper between two fingers.

"Look at this!" she screamed at me. "Look at this!"

She shoved the paper in my face, and, having no choice, I reluctantly took it from her. It was plain white bond, the kind we used for our company stationery, only minus the Babbitt & Brooks logo in blue script on top.

"Read it," Rebecca ordered unnecessarily since I had already begun scanning the words, which were cut out from various newspaper headlines and then pasted on the page:

roses R ReD

violets R Blu

ALL living things die

And sO will U

Scotch-taped underneath the words was a squashed cockroach, rust-colored stains of dried blood circling it. I could almost hear the sickening crunch it must've made as it was ground under the heel of the psycho's shoe. I shuddered.

Jennifer, reading over my shoulder, took a step back.

"Oh, gross."

I dropped the paper on the desk in disgust, wiping my hands against my pants as if to erase any germs connected with my proximity to the ugly words and dead roach. As long as I wasn't looking at the letter, the crunching sounds in my mind stayed quiet.

"I tried to be nice," said Rebecca, her voice shaking. "I tried to be helpful. No more. You either explain yourself right now. Or I'm calling the police and pressing charges against you."

I looked at her in shock. She was staring straight at me.

END OF TEASER

ACT ONE

1.

"I don't know who you think I am," I told Rebecca, my face flaming with anger. "But I'm not some lunatic who cuts out threats from a newspaper."

"What a joke," said Jennifer. "You're just looking for an excuse to fire Susan."

"I don't need an excuse," said Rebecca, her voice suddenly shrill. "Who else would do something like this to me?"

I ignored the frisson of fear that rippled down my spine, threatening to replace the anger. Inexplicably, I thought of my grandmother, my Buby, who at age nineteen, fought and killed Nazis in the last days of the Warsaw Ghetto uprising. She eventually escaped under the sewers with her thirteen-year-old sister, my Aunt Rosie. Buby stole food from bakeries, hopped trains like a hobo, and hid from the Nazis, eventually managing to acquire two passenger tickets to America under false identities. I would be ashamed to call myself her granddaughter if I backed down now.

"Why do you think it was me?" I asked. "How could you even think I was capable of doing something like this?"

"Yeah. Why are you blaming Susan?" said Jennifer. "What did she ever do to you?" Originally her surfer girl blond looks and body had intimidated me. Now I flashed her a smile of gratitude.

Rebecca's eyes ping-ponged from Jennifer to me. "Maybe you were in this together."

Jennifer snorted. "Yeah. Me. Susan. The CIA and Lee Harvey Oswald."

A small muscle spasmed along Rebecca's jawline. I jumped in before she could reply.

"Now I know why you wanted me to open your mail. This isn't the first threat you've received, is it?"

Sandy and Jennifer, their faces almost comical due to the similarity of their stunned expressions, stared first at me, then Rebecca.

Rebecca glanced at her top drawer then looked away.

"But why didn't you wait to let me open this one?" I continued, nodding to the nasty looking note on her desk. "You were curious, weren't you? You just had to see what it said."

Rebecca slapped her palms against her scratched metal desk with a resounding thwack, her face flushed with rage.

"Enough!" she yelled. My shoulders twitched, but I held my ground, trying to keep a diplomatic smile on my face. Rebecca, of course, completely misread my expression.

"You think this is funny? Why don't I call the police and

see if they think it's as funny as you do?"

I was flabbergasted. I took a step away from her desk, as if to distance myself from her irrational anger. Sandy, fortunately, came to my rescue. She took a step forward, a placating hand held out before her.

"Rebecca, perhaps you should call the police. But I'd want to more carefully examine my reasons for blaming Susan before doing so. There are other people, with better reasons, who might want to upset you."

If my mouth wasn't frozen in place, I would've laughed at Sandy's masterful use of understatement. Instead, I stayed silent, watching the look that passed between Sandy and Rebecca. I wondered if those other people, with better reasons, had anything to do with Rebecca's upcoming promotion. Rebecca might have thought so, too, because she was the first to turn away.

"Forget it," she finally said, sinking into her chair. "Just get rid of . . . that." She waved at the letter in distaste.

"Don't you want to keep it as evidence?" I asked, hoping the question would prove I had nothing to hide.

"No. Dump it." She lit a cigarette with shaking hands.

The thought of touching that letter again made me cringe. I looked at Sandy for help. She read the plea in my eyes and picked up the letter, holding it away from her body. As I turned to leave, Rebecca swiveled toward me.

"Maybe you didn't write the letter," she said, exhaling smoke from her nostrils in a dragon-like gesture, daring me to complain about her smoking inside the office. "But for the sake of your job, Susan, you better find out who did."

I left her office before I lost my temper completely and

said something I really would regret.

Jennifer caught up with me in the ladies' room where I had gone to kick a few stall doors while Sandy disappeared into her office with the letter.

"What's going on with that woman? Why does she hate me so much?" I raged, gripping the edge of the porcelain sink with both hands.

"She's a nutjob," Jennifer said, her blue eyes sympathetic as she rubbed my arm in support and comfort. "You might recall I got caught in the crossfire. She's an equal-opportunity paranoid."

"But why?"

"If someone was sending you death threats, wouldn't you feel the same way?"

"Just because you're paranoid, doesn't mean someone's not out to get you," I said wryly.

"Exactly."

"But who could've sent it?" I asked as Sandy entered.

The door to the ladies' room opened again behind her, and the three of us tensed. Peggy Stevens, one of the show's writer-producers, popped her head in.

"There you are," she said to me, shoving a mass of dark hair off her face. "Charles is looking for you." I hesitated, thinking Rebecca had sicced the cops on me anyway, using Peggy to lure me into their clutches. She noticed my wild eyes, the shredded toilet paper. "Is everything all right?" Her dark brown eyes widened in concern.

"Everything's fine," Sandy answered for me. She gave me a small push toward the door. "Go see Charles, luv. Jennifer and I will hold down the fort."

Peggy held the door open for me, a small, puzzled smile

pulling at the corners of her mouth. As I preceded her out of the bathroom, I looked over my shoulder. Jennifer grinned and gave me a thumbs-up in support. But Sandy had already turned away, tugging at her upper lip, looking thoughtful—and concerned.

2.

"**N**ice script," said Charles Green, casually flipping through the dog-eared pages of my Dress Blue spec script. "Of course you make some choices that aren't necessarily the ones I'd make, but even still . . ." He looked me in the eye and smiled. "I'm impressed."

I could count on one hand the number of times I've been at a loss for words. This was one of them. I stood awkwardly in front of Charles's battered metal desk while he sucked on the stem of his unlit pipe. At forty-two, with thick, dark hair graying at the temples, pipe, and faded corduroy blazer, Charles looked more like my favorite college English professor than the supervising producer of a well-respected—even if low-rated and therefore low-budget—television show.

"If you don't mind, I'm going to give this to Ray. I think he'll like it, too."

I reeled from the news. Charles liked it! He was giving it to Ray! The executive producer of Babbitt & Brooks. Our king of kings. Prince among men. If Charles liked my script enough to give it to Ray Goldfarb, I'd be rich and famous by the end of the year. I was ready to kiss Charles's feet and give him my firstborn child. And second. Maybe even third.

But all I could croak out was, "It doesn't matter that it's Dress Blue—not Babbitt & Brooks?" Dress Blue was a popular TV series about the daily lives of cops working in a nameless Midwestern city. I had written the script out of love for the show my last semester at Columbia instead of a term paper on William Dean Howells and turn-of-the-century New York society.

Charles put his pipe in the misshapen ceramic ashtray his six-year-old son had made for him. "A good script is a good script," he said in his gentle, soft-spoken voice. "I don't think it matters what show it's written for. If you stick with it, you might have a nice little career ahead of you." He moved the script to an uncluttered corner of his desk. "Congratulations, Susan. Maybe you'll get an assignment out of this."

"Thank you," I stammered. "Charles, thanks so much!"

Charles smiled vaguely, returning to the pages of his own script, dismissing me. But I hesitated, risking his annoyance in order to unburden myself.

"Did Rebecca tell you about the note she received?"

Charles barely looked up from the script. "What note?"

"Well, it was kind of a death threat and had a dead cockroach scotch-taped to it."

I had Charles's full attention. "When was this?" he asked.

"Right after lunch. You didn't hear her screaming?"

Flimsy wood walls divided the secretaries' bullpen from the writers' and producers' offices. Everyone could usually hear everyone else's conversations especially if those conversations were loud enough.

But Charles shook his head. "I just got back from lunch five minutes ago."

"Oh." There was a moment of silence between us.

"What did the note say?" Charles asked. He didn't seem all that concerned about Rebecca receiving a death threat. Maybe it wasn't as big a deal as I—or Rebecca—thought it was.

"You know, it was a 'roses are red, violets are blue' kind of thing. 'I'm dead and so are you.' Something like that. And then there was the squashed cockroach." I made a face in disgust.

Charles, oddly enough, smiled, seemingly amused by the news. "And I suppose Rebecca handled it in her usual unflappable manner."

"She thought I sent it." My fists clenched at the memory.

"I wouldn't worry about it." Charles seemed to choose his next words carefully. "Rebecca enjoys attracting attention to herself."

His lips curled, and I realized Charles didn't like Rebecca.

I felt relief—as if his dislike gave my own feelings of antipathy more credibility.

"Rebecca said she'd fire me if I didn't find out who sent the letter."

Charles sighed, reaching for a tin of tobacco on his desk, then pausing, as if remembering the no smoking ban in the workplace. I wouldn't have minded if he had lit his pipe. The smell of pipe tobacco always conjured up memories of my travel agent grandfather, sitting in his Barc-a-lounger by the front window of his and my grandmom's condo in

West Palm Beach, chewing on his pipe stem and booking imaginary vacations to exotic ports of call that he never got to visit himself. He had been dead for three years and I still missed him.

"This show attracts a lot of crazies," Charles said. "They usually write letters to the actors. But some of them focus on the producers. I've gotten a few letters myself. If you want, I'll talk to her."

"No, it's okay." I could tell he didn't want to get involved, and I didn't want to lose his support of my script. "I can handle it." At least I would try.

Charles returned to his script. "Good."

As I was about to leave his office he added, "If Ray feels the way I do about your script, Susan, you won't have to worry about Rebecca too much longer."

Wow. I mean wow. Was it really going to be this easy? I move to L.A., find a job in TV, get my script read, and then become a writer! But yet, it was not that easy. For example, if Rebecca found out, would she really let that happen? Was she despicable enough to concoct phony evidence that I sent her the death threat just to ensure I was never hired as a writer?

Jennifer sat typing at her computer as I made my way back to the bullpen that was our shared office. She looked at my grim face in dismay.

"He didn't like it?"

"He loved it," I said.

"I knew it!" She grinned in triumph, her forest green fingernails flying over the keyboard. They matched her Stella McCartney blazer-and-shorts outfit. I didn't know what to marvel at more: Jennifer's ability to type with those Fu Manchu-like nails or the fact that, although only in her late twenties, she could afford designer clothes on an assistant's salary.

"He's giving it to Ray," I said. "I might get an assignment."

Jennifer whooped then asked, "So why the long face?"

I glanced at the wall of Rebecca's office and leaned in, murmuring, "Rebecca."

"Screw her," she said. "You're on your way, kiddo. I'm calling Charles's agent and telling him he has to represent you."

I stared at her, speechless for the second time that day. In spite of her Baywatch looks, Jennifer was proving to be a terrific new friend.

Sandy strolled into the bullpen. "I heard festive noises. Is there good news to share?"

"Charles loved Susan's script," Jennifer said, blowing blond bangs off her forehead. "I'm gonna get Susan his agent."

"See?" said Sandy, smiling at me, revealing her crooked teeth. "This didn't turn out to be such a wretched day after all."

Rebecca stepped out of her office and entered the fluorescent-lit, windowless room. "What's going on? I could use some good news." A lit cigarette dangled from two fingers, and she acted as if she had never accused me of writing her a death threat.

"Charles thinks your letter is from a crazed fan. He says it's nothing to worry about." I said this quickly, not wanting her to know the real reason for our lifted spirits.

Rebecca stared at me, the smoke from her cigarette

curling up to the ceiling. Jennifer coughed, making a show of blowing smoke away.

Rebecca stubbed the cigarette against the wall. "Maybe." I could tell she wasn't convinced.

"Peggy said Charles was looking for you," she added. "Was it about the letter?"

I wanted to tell her to mind her own business, but while I was thinking of a tactful way to say it, Jennifer jumped in.

"Charles likes Susan's script," she said.

Oh, Jennifer. No.

I held my breath as I watched Rebecca struggle with the news, a flash of—could it be?—vulnerability in her face. "How nice," she said, in a falsely-pleased voice. "I hadn't known you gave it to him. Was it for our show?"

"No, for Dress Blue," I said reluctantly.

"Then I'm not surprised Charles liked it. Since he doesn't know Dress Blue as well as Babbitt & Brooks, I'm sure he wasn't as harsh a critic."

Ouch.

"It's a terrific script," Jennifer said. "Susan's a good writer no matter what she writes." I smiled at her, although I wasn't sure I forgave her for opening this can of worms in the first place.

"I'm sure that's true," said Rebecca, turning her laser beam gaze on Jennifer. "You gave the script to Charles?"

Jennifer nodded. "This show needs good writers."

"Of course it does," Rebecca said. "But you can't bother the producers every time you want a spec script read."

"Charles is my boss. He's always looking for fresh talent. I wasn't bothering him. Especially since he likes Susan's script."

Rebecca looked at the stubbed cigarette then closed her hand over it. "If you want to recommend your friends, go through me first. I'll decide who should be passed on and who shouldn't."

"I don't work for you."

I admired Jennifer's guts but knew she was fighting a losing battle. I braced myself for Rebecca's "television production is teamwork" speech. Instead, she smiled, dropping her cigarette on the carpeted floor.

"You will, starting tomorrow. When I become co-producer."

So much for keeping secrets. I watched Jennifer for her reaction, but she didn't seem all that surprised.

"It's not official until tomorrow," Sandy spoke up. I had forgotten she was there. Sandy had stepped out of Rebecca's eye line when Rebecca first entered the room, plastering herself against the thin plywood wall. As all attention turned to her she stopped pulling at her upper lip, looking self-conscious.

"Doesn't matter," said Rebecca, unable to keep the satisfaction out of her voice. "It still puts me in charge of the three of you. You have any problems, complaints, you come to me. Call me if you're sick, if your car breaks down on the freeway, if you're coming in late. Starting next week, I'm putting you all on a schedule. Who comes in early. Who stays late. And don't go running to Ray about this," she added, anticipating Jennifer's protest. "Like I already told you, I've discussed it with him, and he's agreed with me."

"But Charles hasn't," Jennifer said, standing up so that she and Rebecca were eye-to-eye. "Why don't I talk to him about it?" She started to move out of the bullpen.

"Wait."

Jennifer paused. Rebecca licked her lips. I looked at Sandy who nodded. We both saw it. The fear was back. "Tomorrow," Rebecca said. "This will all be straightened out tomorrow."

Ray wasn't the only one who wanted the writers to cool their heels overnight. But Rebecca had been so busy lording it over Sandy, Jennifer, and me, she had forgotten the more serious implications of announcing her promotion early. Normally, I would enjoy watching her swing in the breeze but that flash of vulnerability earlier — and the fear now — made me wonder what was really driving her anger.

Jennifer stared grimly at Rebecca. "I don't think so," she said. "I think we'll straighten this out now." She turned her back on Rebecca and marched toward Charles's office.

Rebecca took a step after her, almost as if she was going to follow her or try to stop her. But then she stopped. Licked her lips again. As she turned back to her office her glance fell on me, and I watched her regain control with an effort.

"Congratulations again on your script, Susan," she said. "I can't wait to read it."

Innocuous words, but I shivered anyway. Now that Rebecca had two script assignments of her own would she start viewing me as the competition? Would she use the death threat to knock me out of the running? I didn't know, and as a result I felt off balance. Rebecca must have sensed my insecurity because she gave me a final smug smile, the fear and vulnerability banished, before going back to her office and gently shutting the door behind her.

3.

Ten minutes later Jennifer returned to the bullpen, still raging. I looked at her in concern as she slammed into her seat.

"What did Charles say?" I asked.

She reached into a drawer, pulled out her Kate Spade purse, and slammed it on her desk. "He was on the set. I tried to grab his attention but he was too busy talking to Tabby." Tabitha Wentworth. One of the stars of Babbitt & Brooks.

"I'm sorry."

"Why? It's not your fault." She grabbed a compact from her purse and reapplied lipstick. "I'll tell you one thing, that bitch . . ." Jennifer glared at the wall of Rebecca's office, not bothering to keep her voice down, "won't get away with it." She slammed her purse back in the drawer.

"Has something happened to upset my lady Jennifer?" Patrick Hager, the unit production manager, appeared in the bullpen. He held a single, long-stemmed red rose in one hand and a sleeved DVD in the other.

"That's an understatement," Jennifer said, smiling bitterly. He stared at her in friendly puzzlement. In his late thirties and a little over medium height, Patrick was attractive if you liked Nordic-looking men with white blond hair and pale blue eyes. But he was slender to the point of effeminacy, and Jennifer and I often wondered about his sexual proclivities. He turned to me, one blond eyebrow raised, as if looking to me for an explanation of

Jennifer's behavior.

I shrugged my shoulders, pretending ignorance. He pointed the rose in my direction.

"And how doth the lady Susan fare?" he asked, acknowledging me with a courtly bow. The keys attached to his belt loop jingled softly.

For a second I thought he was offering the flower to me. Fortunately, I stifled my instinct to take it. Patrick had a three o'clock appointment with Rebecca; the rose, I realized, was for her.

"As well as can be expected," I answered. "M'lady Rebecca is awaiting you in her chambers."

Patrick bowed his thanks and started toward Rebecca's office. He paused, turned back to me.

"If you see my Lord Raymond, tell him I have the shooting schedule for next week. Mistress Neely actually has Tuesday off."

Gail Neely was one of the stars of the series. She played Alexandra Brooks, the sophisticated, upper class half of Babbitt & Brooks. Because she and Tabitha Wentworth were the stars of the show, they were in every episode and usually filmed every day.

"Gail must be doing somersaults," I said.

Patrick bent his head in acknowledgment. "She's most pleased." He once again headed to Rebecca's office when Jennifer's voice stopped him.

"Great news about Rebecca's promotion, isn't it, Patrick?"

He turned toward Jennifer, his eyes alight. "Yes, it's most pleasing news . . ." He stopped. His eyes narrowed. "I'm not sure I know what you're talking about."

"'Course you do." Jennifer's eyes danced maliciously. "Rebecca's promotion to co-producer." She nodded at the rose. "That's what the flower's for, right? To congratulate her? We're all sooo happy for her."

Jennifer offered him a wide, gleaming white smile. Patrick returned it with a tight one of his own. He rapped on Rebecca's door and entered. I waited until I heard him present Rebecca with the rose and her delighted, throaty laugh of thanks before sidling over to Jennifer's desk.

"What the hell was that all about?" I demanded, speaking low enough so Patrick and Rebecca wouldn't overhear.

Jennifer studied her nails, then reached into her center desk drawer and pulled out an emery board. "I was just having a little fun with him."

"Yeah. But why?"

Jennifer began filing her already perfect nails. "Did you notice the DVD in his hand?" I nodded. "That's his director's reel. He showed me some of it in his office the other day."

The director's reel is for the wannabe director what the spec script is for the beginning writer. A sample of his work, usually a thirty-minute movie, shot at the director's expense, to show off his directing talents to interested producers. For already established television directors, it is simply clippings of scenes from their best work.

"Patrick wants to direct?" I asked, surprised. As unit production manager, his job was to work out budgets, break down locations, and generally ensure the smooth flow of production. Some UPMs became producers. Granted, I was new to show business, but I had never heard of any becoming directors.

Jennifer shrugged, blowing nail shavings from her fingers.

"Everyone in this town wants to be something else. You want to be a writer. Sandy a producer. Rebecca—God."

I stifled a giggle. "So you think Patrick wants to show the reel to Rebecca?"

"Patrick told me he wants a shot at directing a 'Broads with Balls' episode. But associate producers don't hire directors."

"And co-producers do?"

"No. But our newest co-producer would like to. When I saw the DVD in his hand I had a feeling Rebecca had jumped at the chance to tell Patrick about the promotion. She knew that he would bring her his reel and she could recommend him to Ray. Rebecca likes power."

"Do you think that's what the letter was all about? Someone who already knows about Rebecca's promotion and is angry about it?"

"It wouldn't surprise me."

"I guess that leaves Patrick out."

Another throaty bubble of laughter burst from Rebecca's office. Jennifer stared over my shoulder, also momentarily distracted by the laughter. Her gaze focused back on me. "True. If she likes his reel, her promotion benefits him as well."

We fell silent, mulling this over, when Peggy Stevens exited her office from behind Jennifer. She looked dazed. "You don't have any other work pressing, do you?" she asked me, a thick strand of hair coiled in her fingers. I shook my head, hoping she hadn't overheard Jennifer's and my conversation.

"Good. I just got off the phone with Gail. She's got some notes on tomorrow's scene with the drug dealer. We've got to get the rewrite to her ASAP."

"No problem," I told Peggy, relieved she'd been on the phone while Jennifer and I had had our little bitch slap, er, chat. "My computer is armed and ready. Let the rewrites begin."

Peggy smiled, her brown eyes crinkling at the corners. I felt happy that I could lighten the air of sadness that always seemed to surround her. When I first met Peggy, I had thought, "This is who I want to be when I grow up." She made a six-figure salary on a show that was nominated for an Emmy, had received accolades from various women's groups around the country, and lived in her own house in Beverlywood, on the outskirts of Beverly Hills. Therefore I was stunned when, straightening up, her office late one night, I found a note she had written on a torn scrap of paper.

"I'm a thirty-eight-year-old single woman going nowhere," it read.

I recognized Peggy's handwriting. It could've been a line of dialogue that came to her mind suddenly, but deep down I knew it was how Peggy felt about herself. And I couldn't understand why. She had the life I was struggling to build for myself. If—no, when—I finally achieved that life, would I, like Peggy, discover it meant nothing, that I had gone nowhere as well? No, I said to myself. No.

Unaware of my thoughts, Peggy returned to her office, unconsciously pulling at the bulky white sweater that reached mid-thigh to her jeans, hiding her curvy figure.

The aura of sadness seemed to once more settle like a heavy cloak around her shoulders.

We worked on the revisions long into the night, my mind half on the rewrites and half on who might've sent Rebecca the threatening letter. While Peggy rewrote the drug dealer scene for Gail in her office, I plugged all the changes she e-mailed to me into the computer, asterisking line changes, making sure we had enough blue paper with which to run off the new pages. (All changes are made on different colored paper: starting with blue, going to pink, green, yellow, etc. If, God forbid, the changes exceeded the number of colors allotted, we started back at the beginning with white.)

Gradually, the rest of the staff made its weary way out the door, stopping first to commiserate with Peggy, who was probably looking at an all-nighter. Ray, leaving earlier than usual, told her to e-mail him the changes before giving them to Gail. Sandy was supposed to e-mail Rebecca's promotion memo to everyone after Ray left. She told me he planned to let all messages go to voicemail.

Ignorant of the bomb waiting to explode, Charles left soon after Ray, giving Peggy an ironic smile.

"Cheer up," he said, "Think of all the money you're making."

Zack North, the other writer-producer, exited his office, briefcase in hand, looking preppie in a Ralph Lauren polo shirt, pressed jeans, and loafers. Peggy had left her own office to hand me more rewrites she had printed out and marked-up to plug into my document, and he put down his briefcase and began giving her a shoulder massage. She closed her eyes and rotated her head in pleasure.

Zack finished his massage. "Better?"

"Much," she said. "Thanks."

"Anytime." With a quick good-night to me, he was off.

Peggy stared after Zack in yearning. I couldn't say as I blamed her. Although he wasn't good-looking in the conventional sense, being on the short side with thinning brown hair and hazel eyes, Zack, in his mid-thirties, had a killer grin. It was boyish and charming and promised fun days at the beach and romantic picnics in the park. I wondered with some envy whether Peggy had ever been a recipient of that grin's promise. Judging from the soft look in her eyes, I guessed she had.

However, she wasn't the only one. After I printed out the script changes, I crossed to the copy machine in the hall, next to the front entrance of the warehouse. The door was propped open to let in some of the cool October night air, and as I fed the pages into the copier, I heard a familiar bubble of soft, throaty laughter.

I moved to the door. In the graveled parking lot, next to her Cadillac Escalade, stood Rebecca. Bathed in the yellow glow of a nearby street lamp she lifted a cigarette to her lips. I saw a tiny orange flame as the cigarette lighter flicked open. Rebecca bent toward the flame, her eyes meeting those of the person lighting her cigarette. The man was Zack North.

Rebecca took a deep drag, then theatrically expelled the smoke off to one side. Zack handed her back the lighter, said something to her, and she laughed again. Her slim throat gleamed in the moonlight. Zack cupped a hand to her face and kissed her. Apparently, kissing a woman who had just filled her mouth with tar and nicotine didn't bother him in the least. The kiss looked like it might last for a while. I quietly removed the prop wedged under the door before closing it behind me.

I wanted to pound the copy machine in anger, feeling betrayed on Peggy's behalf. But should I be surprised? Just because Peggy had a thing for Zack, it didn't mean Zack had to reciprocate. Right? And why not kiss Rebecca, who was an extremely attractive woman. Despite her animosity toward Sandy, Jennifer, and me, she clearly had another side, a sexual side that Zack obviously found appealing.

But still, I hurt for Peggy and was unable to look her in the eye when I handed her the completed changes. At home I took a long, hot shower, trying to scrub away the memory of Rebecca's sexy laugh, Zack's killer grin, and Peggy's look of unrequited longing.

Unfortunately, I did not succeed, and the images haunted me as I tossed and turned in my lumpy studio bed throughout that endless night.

4.

A week before my twenty-fifth birthday, I had walked in on my law student boyfriend, Peter Williams, in bed with his fellow classmate, Casey Bitterman, in the apartment Peter and I shared, underneath the quilt my grandmother had made for me as a college graduation present. Before the first explanations or recriminations could be uttered, I whipped Grandmom's quilt off their naked bodies, leaving Casey Bitterman frantically trying to cover her breasts and Peter looking embarrassed—not because I caught him in flagrante

delecto, but because I was in full view of his quickly
deflating, condom-covered you-know-what. (A tumescent,
throbbing flower of manhood, it wasn't.) Bundling the
quilt under my arm, I had stared at both of them for a
silent, judgmental heartbeat before throwing them both out
of the apartment and forcing the naked Casey to retrieve
her clothes in the hallway.

A few weeks later, I defended my thesis and,
accompanied by my mom, took the next plane west
without waiting to hear whether I had passed my orals. (I
had.) Long hours, hard work, and low pay at my series of
temp jobs helped push the memory of Peter and Casey
Bitterman to the back of my mind. At least until I caught
Zack North kissing Rebecca in the parking lot of Babbitt &
Brooks's warehouse, knowing an unwitting Peggy was
crushing on him inside her office.

As the images of Peter and Casey collided with those of
Zack and Rebecca, stealing my sleep and peace of mind, I
finally threw back the covers at six a.m. I needed to distract
myself with work. If I still had work with which to distract
myself. Realizing that it was Rebecca's first day as co-
producer, I decided to alleviate my own guilt for wanting
to hurt her by fulfilling one of the conditions of my new
job description given to me by her: cleaning up the mess
she had left behind in her office the night before.

Once I arrived at the office, I straightened her desk and
washed out her coffee mug, letting my memories slide
down the bathroom sink along with the used coffee
grounds. I found a stray check made out to a Michael
Keller among the pile of production reports, revised script
pages, and pink telephone message slips, and clipped it to

her desk calendar to remind her to send it out. Several bottles of vodka, empty and full, were stashed in the credenza behind her desk. I debated tossing the empties into the glass recycling bin for the rest of the staff to see. But I decided my job was more important than one brief, smug moment of humiliating Rebecca. I slid the panel shut, leaving the bottles untouched.

I also found my script. It sat on Rebecca's desk, with a narrow, white buck slip paper-clipped to the title page. The buck slip had the blue-scripted Babbitt & Brooks logo on top and Raymond Goldfarb, printed in small, red letters on the bottom. In his looping, careless scrawl, Ray had asked Rebecca to read the script and give him her thoughts.

I remembered the look of vulnerability in her eyes when she learned my script had already been given to Charles. From the little I knew of Rebecca, I doubted support for one's assistant was high on her list of virtues. I picked up the script, ready to lock it in my desk drawer, and let Rebecca think she had lost it.

Looking down, I noticed her center desk drawer, and remembered Rebecca's guilty glance at it when I had suggested she had received a prior death threat. Just a quick peek, I promised myself, and then I'd leave. I slid the drawer open gently, almost reverently.

Inside: another death threat. I was right, although I didn't feel like gloating. I didn't want to read it, but couldn't not read it, like rubbernecking an accident on the freeway. I looked at the note out of the corner of my eye, as if that would somehow make it less threatening.

Violets r bLu

Roses r reD

Take **a WRONG** step

& u R d**E**ad

The same white-bond stationery. The same pasted-on newspaper headlines. One letter was creepy enough but two were downright chilling. Even though the threats weren't directed at me, I felt a coldness in the pit of my stomach, suddenly convinced the sender was in the room with me.

I quickly looked up and saw Sherman O'Dell staring at me from Rebecca's doorway. I took a step backward, my breath drawn in so suddenly, it clogged in my throat, and I was unable to scream.

"Hey, Susan, you okay?"

I found my voice. "Sherman, you scared me."

"Sorry." He smiled apologetically, shifting the plunger he held from his right hand to left. Sherman was the production's night watchman/janitor. "I was just surprised to see you here. You're an early bird today."

"New job description," I said. I laughed shakily, still not recovered from my double scare. "Rebecca's maid."

Sherman nodded in understanding, his long, black dreadlocks bobbing at his shoulders. "It's just that you looked like you'd seen a ghost. And Lord knows no one's mistakin' me for a dead white guy."

I smiled in spite of myself and picked up the second death threat, walking it over to him. Sherman read it, his angular face creased in concentration. He was only in his late twenties, but his ebony skin typically folded into dozens of lines around his mouth and eyes when he smiled. He wasn't smiling now.

"It's the second one," I said after he finished and handed the letter back to me. He rubbed a bony hand against his white T-shirt. The late, great reggae singer Bob Marley graced its front. "Rebecca thinks I'm sending them to her."

Sherman snorted in disbelief, which made me glad.

"Do you have any idea who could've sent it?" I asked.

"Pick a number and stand in line," he said. "The woman is one large ball of misery. And she needs to share the pain." I wondered what she did to Sherman to make him come to that observation, true as it was. But I didn't have the nerve to ask. He began to move into the bullpen, seemingly as unconcerned about the threats as Charles was. But I was concerned—and scared—and, needing his reassuring presence, I said, hoping to stop him, "Rebecca's being promoted to co-producer. Starting today."

Sherman paused. Like Patrick, he wore the keys to the warehouse attached to his belt loop. But, unlike Patrick, who only carried those to the production offices and sets, Sherman had the whole schmear: a thick bundle of keys to every door in the building. They clanked heavily together at his sudden stop. His chocolaty eyes looked thoughtful.

"Is that what you folks in the biz call 'failing upwards'?"

I smiled at the term. "I hadn't thought of it like that. Next time someone asks me why television is so bad, I can tell them it's because all the incompetent people are failing upwards."

"Yeah. You think if I start missing notes on my sax, club managers will start hiring my band for more gigs?"

As Jennifer said, everyone wanted to be something else. Sherman played tenor sax in a struggling rhythm and blues band.

I shook my head. "If the news of Rebecca's promotion had already gone out, I'd think someone was sending her the threats out of spite. But obviously someone hates her without even knowing she's being promoted."

Sherman said, "You know there are no such things as secrets in this town. Maybe word of her promotion already leaked. Who knows about it here?"

"Sandy, Jennifer, and me. And of course Ray. And Patrick. But I don't know when she got the first letter. It could have been before Ray even decided to promote her." Something was bothering me, but I couldn't put my finger on it. "Anyway, it wasn't Sandy."

"How do you know?"

"Because it just wasn't." I sounded irritable. I looked up at him to see he was smiling at me, teasing. "You're jerking my chain, aren't you?"

"Maybe." He continued to smile at me. Fondly. Like big brother to little sister. It made me squirm. I already had a brother, thank you very much, and I wasn't looking for another one.

"You don't seem to be taking this very seriously," I told him.

"Far as I'm concerned Rebecca, deserves everything she gets. If this makes her lose a night's sleep, more power to the sender." He saluted me with the plunger before sauntering down the writers' corridor, turning the corner, and disappearing from view.

I watched him go, once again wondering what had happened between him and Rebecca that made him dislike her so much. I realized I was still holding the letter and turned around toward Rebecca's office to put it back on her desk.

But just as I was about to enter, the front door opened, and Rebecca appeared. Since this was Promotion Day, I expected to see a smug smile, triumphant eyes, maybe even a huge frosted cake with "Congratulations to Me" inked on top in cherry frosting. But her lips looked dry and cracked, dark Jackie O glasses covered her eyes, and instead of a cake she clutched a cigarette. She stumbled into her office and slammed the door behind her so hard the plywood walls vibrated. I decided not to return the letter. In her mood, she would call the police, and have me in cuffs and thrown in county jail before I could scream, "I'm innocent!" I put the note in a folder in my desk, instead, deciding to replace it later, when she wasn't in the office.

I was aware of its presence all morning, feeling as if it was burning a hole in my desk. I showed it to Jennifer as soon as she walked in.

"I was right," I said. "She had received another threat. I found it in her desk."

"If I were you, I'd throw it out," said Jennifer. "Burn it even."

"You don't think I should give it back to her?"

Jennifer shrugged. "How badly do you need this job?"

Before I could answer, Peggy, Zack, and Charles

entered the bullpen. I put the note back in my desk, reluctant to show it to them behind Rebecca's back. As they entered Ray's office, I suddenly remembered I had forgotten to take my Dress Blue script from Rebecca's desk. What did she plan to do about it? Was she reading it even as I gnashed my teeth? The cockeyed optimist in me hoped she would overcome her prejudices and read the script on its own merits. But the resident pessimist in me laughed in scorn.

I surfaced from my fog of worry to realize that the writing staff seemed to have taken Rebecca's promotion surprisingly well.

They had arrived to work with their usual cheery "Good mornings;" there were no fireworks, no angry debates in Ray's office, no Rebecca looking superior. Something was up.

I found Sandy in her office and asked what was going on. She placed some folders in a file drawer and shut it with a bang.

"Ray called me from his car last night. He told me not to send the e-mail." Her eyes didn't meet mine.

"I don't get it. It seemed like such a sure thing. And half the staff already knew about it. What made him change his mind?"

Sandy looked annoyed. "I don't know, Susan. Maybe Cliff Rosen told him to hold off. Cliff wasn't all that crazy about Ray promoting her to associate producer."

Cliff Rosen was the president of Romulus Television and Ray's boss.

"Why not?"

"Because she's not qualified. She was Ray's assistant."

"I'm an assistant. Does that mean I'm not qualified to become a staff writer?"

Sandy waved her hand impatiently. "That's different."

I opened my mouth to ask another question but she jerked her thumb toward the wall that separated her office from Ray's. "This is not a good time to talk about it."

But I had a funny feeling she was only using the thin walls as an excuse not to talk about the memo at all. I debated telling her about the other death threat, but she seemed eager to have me leave, so I left without saying another word.

I told Jennifer what Sandy had related to me. Jennifer listened intently, tapping one pointed nail against her teeth. "Just because Ray changed his mind now, doesn't mean he won't change it again later," she said when I finished.

"Are you still going to talk to Charles about it?" I asked.

"I don't know. Let's see how things shake out. If Rebecca still thinks she can lord it over me, I will. But I'd just as soon not stir things up. At least not yet. But I am glad she's not getting the promotion."

I was glad, too. If Rebecca read my script, there was no way she would treat it fairly now that she was denied her own writing assignment. I was right. Charles called me into his office that afternoon. "I just heard from Ray about your script," he said. "I'm sorry, Susan, he didn't like it as much as I did."

A cannonball of lead dropped into my stomach even though I knew I shouldn't be surprised. I stood rooted to the cheap green carpeting and nodded dumbly.

"He didn't believe in the characters," Charles said. "I

don't think he likes Dress Blue very much if that's any help. Maybe because they won the Emmy over us."

I worked up the nerve to ask, "Did he read it? Or was that Rebecca's opinion?"

There was a pause then Charles spoke, sounding very tired and very sad. "Let's not get into that. I honestly don't know. I'm sorry."

I nodded again. "Thanks anyway," I managed to choke out before exiting his office and heading for the front door. As I passed the closed door to Rebecca's office I was tempted to flip her the finger but really, what would be the point? She hadn't gotten her promotion and so took her anger out on me and my script. I had worried success wouldn't be that easy to attain and I was right. But it still didn't make me feel any better.

Once outside, I paused as I noticed Jennifer turning away from the dumpster on the other end of the parking lot. I stood back from the door, not wanting her to see me, but she trotted up the ramp in the middle of the warehouse and entered the large barnlike double doors without looking in my direction. As soon as she disappeared inside, I headed toward my car.

I sat in my 2005 Honda Civic, window rolled down, gulping drafts of warm, polluted air that smelled faintly of tar. I popped in a DVD of Abba's greatest hits and closed my eyes, blocking out the sight of the peeling facade of the warehouse, while practicing my Emmy acceptance speech. With the pulsing beat of "Waterloo" pounding through me, I thanked Rebecca for her lack of belief in me, which had only served to motivate me to keep going despite the odds. Rebecca sat in the audience looking humbled and ashamed, and eighty pounds overweight.

Feeling much calmer, I opened my eyes and smiled. Success really is the best revenge.

5.

When I returned to the bullpen, Charles stood at Jennifer's desk, talking into the phone. He did not look happy. Jennifer was nowhere in sight.

"Let me explain it to you this way," he started to say, but the person on the other end cut him off. "Uh-huh," he said instead, listening impatiently. And again, "Uh-huh."

Charles glanced at me in irritation, and it took me a second to realize he wasn't annoyed at me but with whomever he was speaking.

"Look," he said, "I'm not at my desk. Let me take this in my office." But again he was cut off. As he stood there and listened, a burst of laughter rocketed out of Rebecca's office. Something about it struck me as odd until I realized Rebecca had been unusually quiet all morning. Charles looked up sharply. "She said what?" He glared at the wall of Rebecca's office. Did he feel her laughter was an inappropriate interruption?

"Gail," Charles said, and I thought, Uh-oh, trouble on the set. "Gail, look, why don't I come to location and straighten it out with you there?" He looked at his watch. "Ten minutes, okay? Good, I'll see you then."

He hung up the phone, his face pale with anger, and turned to me. "Does Rebecca have someone with her?"

"She doesn't have a meeting scheduled," I said. "But I can hear someone in the office with her."

Charles nodded, jaw set. "Tell her . . ." He changed his mind. "I'm going to location to talk with Ms. Neely. I'll go home from there."

He didn't wait for my nod of acknowledgment. He threw one last angry look at Rebecca's office before striding down the hall to his own.

Jennifer tore into the bullpen about five minutes later, Sandy right behind her. "It's bullshit," Jennifer said. "Pure bullshit."

"Jennifer, promise me you won't—" Sandy stopped when she realized I was sitting at my desk, typing Zack's first draft of his own script assignment into the computer.

Ignoring me, Jennifer dropped into her chair, angrily blowing her bangs out of her eyes. "You can't let her get away with this."

"Not now," Sandy hissed, looking at me.

"Do you want me to leave?" I asked. Sandy heard the hurt in my voice. Her face softened. "Oh, luv, it's not about you."

Her face crumpled, and she fished out a tissue from the pocket of her dress and dabbed at her eyes.

With phone to ear Jennifer asked me, "Know any hitmen?"

"Jennifer!" Sandy frantically pointed at Rebecca's closed door. We heard the murmur of voices inside.

"I was kidding." Jennifer turned back to me, stabbing at the intercom button. "Where's Charles?"

"He went to location. There's trouble with Gail."

Jennifer put the phone down. "Good. I can go home early." She looked at Sandy. "Unless you want me to stay?"

Sandy shook her head. "No, I'll be all right. I have a dentist appointment anyway." I nodded at Rebecca's office behind me. "What'd she do?" Sandy and Jennifer exchanged a look. In a low voice Jennifer said, "Rebecca's trying to get Sandy fired."

I looked at Sandy. "Why?"

Sandy shrugged, still dabbing at her eyes.

"Rebecca claims she's received a ton of complaints about Sandy," said Jennifer. "About her phone behavior, relaying messages incorrectly, not getting work done on time."

"She couldn't get me fired so now she's going after you?"

Sandy looked away, still struggling for control. I had a sudden, horrible thought. "Did Rebecca go to Ray about this?"

"Of course," Jennifer said. "Why do you think we're so upset?"

"But Ray has to know it's not true."

Sandy spoke up. "He put me on warning." She sounded bitter. "Ray believes whatever Rebecca tells him."

"Why does she hate us so much? Is she really that insecure?" But before either Sandy or Jennifer could answer Peggy popped her head out from behind her office door.

"Susan," she began. But I never did find out what Peggy wanted. Just then Rebecca's door opened and out strolled Vampire Woman with Zack, both laughing, Zack's arm around her waist. She seemed to have fully recovered from not getting promoted. Maybe trying to get Sandy fired was an acceptable substitute.

Zack, however, took one look at Peggy and dropped his arm.

"Peggy," said Rebecca, seemingly unfazed, "you've got to hear this joke Zack just told me."

"Maybe later," said Peggy. "I-I have an appointment. I have to leave now."

Rebecca put on a concerned look. "Is everything all right?"

"Everything's fine," said Peggy. Her voice cracked. She withdrew into her office and shut the door behind her. Zack and Rebecca still stood next to one another, but the easy camaraderie was gone.

"How's Act Two coming along?" Zack asked me, as if to alleviate the awkwardness.

"Fine," I said, unable to look at him. "I'll be done in a couple of hours."

I couldn't believe my voice sounded normal. Inside, I was seething. Zack's face morphed into ex-boyfriend Peter's face, morphed back to Zack's face. I was getting vertigo.

"Great. Thanks." He grinned shakily at Rebecca before heading back into his own office next to Peggy's.

Sandy and Jennifer stood transfixed, their own problems forgotten. I could tell what Jennifer was thinking. Turn the cameras around! The action's much more exciting behind the scenes! But all she said instead was, "I'm outta here." She tucked her purse under her arm and headed for the exit.

Rebecca grabbed her. "What do you mean? It's not six-thirty yet."

Jennifer looked pointedly at Rebecca's hand until

Rebecca dropped it from her arm. Then she said, looking Vampire Woman straight in the eye, "If you ever touch me again, I will sue you." To Sandy and me, cheerfully: "Hasta la vista, babies." She swung down the hall and out of our sight.

Way to go, Jennifer! I wanted to shout. But instead I quickly turned back to the computer screen as Rebecca's speculative gaze fell on me. For a minute I thought she was going to blame me for Jennifer's act of defiance. But instead she said, "I'm meeting with Patrick Hager tomorrow at ten." Pointedly she added, "He called while you were away from your desk." Geez, a girl's gotta pee every once in a while, I wanted to say, but instead I penned in Patrick's name in the ten o'clock time slot on my desk calendar.

Sandy left shortly after Jennifer, Peggy following on Sandy's heels. Neither woman looked well and both left without their usual good-nights.

I continued to plug Zack's script into the computer as Zack packed his briefcase and prepared to leave. But first he stopped off at Rebecca's office and asked if she was leaving any time soon.

"I've got some things to do for Ray," I heard her say.

Zack nodded. "I'll see you tomorrow then." He looked like he wanted to say something else, but changed his mind. He gave her a brief nod instead and exited the building.

As soon as Zack left, Rebecca headed for Ray's office across the passage. She carried several scripts as well as a DVD. Patrick Hager's director's reel?

The writing staff, although paid a hefty weekly salary,

was also paid the standard Writers Guild fee of approximately thirty-five thousand dollars for every script they wrote. To prevent the staff from hogging all the scripts, the Guild required that a certain number of freelance writers be brought in to write scripts, and Ray (although he was not a writer), Charles, Zack, and Peggy dutifully held meetings for mostly hopeful, all very nervous writers who came in and pitched story ideas for the show. These writers were found through the scripts their agents submitted, either spec scripts like mine or paid writing assignments from other shows. Judging from the stack of scripts under Rebecca's arm, I gathered she had read them all and was now reporting back to Ray. I wondered who else's career she was in the process of destroying and decided to come in early the next morning and read the scripts myself. I wanted to see if she was being fair or if her judgment was biased.

I finished Zack's second act, printed it out and proofed it before e-mailing it to him. Now all I had to do was wait until Ray and Rebecca left before I could go home.

A woman appeared at the entrance to the bullpen. In her forties, she was dressed in a business suit, rare for our production office, and carried herself regally, almost arrogantly. She was tall, with straight, blunt-cut brown hair, a thin-lipped mouth and only a hint of makeup around the eyes.

"Can I help you?" I asked.

"I've come to pick up Ray."

Pick up Ray? She sure didn't look like one of the Teamsters who occasionally gave Ray a lift home when his Mercedes was in the shop.

I reached for the phone. "Shall I tell him who's here?"

For all I knew she could be a crazed fan with a gun. It wouldn't be the first time someone burst onto a studio lot, looking to blow away his or her favorite movie star. But this woman merely smiled at me, full of confidence, as she walked past my desk.

"Don't bother. I'm his wife."

Oh, I thought. Winifred McCauley. Winifred was one of Romulus Television's lawyers, and she had helped put together the deal for Babbitt & Brooks. She and Ray had met over bagels and danishes in the company's conference room, and the rest, as they say, was history. Of course, they had to divorce their respective spouses first to make that history. But who cared? Things like that were supposed to happen in Hollywood.

Just as Winifred reached the door to Ray's office, Rebecca stepped out. The two women almost bumped into one another, and Winifred took an immediate step backward. She looked like she had just come face to face with a boa constrictor. Rebecca didn't look all that thrilled herself.

"Hello, Winifred," she said.

Winifred nodded icily. "Rebecca. How are you?"

There was less frost on the trees in Montana in February.

"I'm fine. Thank you. And you?" Rebecca's smile looked like it had been pasted on crookedly by a demented artist.

"Good. Good." The two women stood there, dislike a palpable tension between them. Was it my imagination or did Rebecca look longingly past Winifred's shoulder, into her own office, at the closed door of her vodka-laden credenza?

Ray's voice boomed out. "Winnie, is that you? Have you come to take me away from all this?"

Winifred's voice became lighter, younger. "As always, my love." Without giving Rebecca another glance she brushed past her and headed into Ray's office, closing the door in Rebecca's face. I decided I liked Winifred McCauley Goldfarb.

Rebecca stood there, the snub taking about three seconds to catch up to her. When it did, her smile faded, and for just a moment she looked like a four-year-old girl who had lost her favorite teddy bear. Then she turned and caught me watching her.

"Why don't you go home?" she said quietly.

And so I did.

6.

When my alarm went off at six the next morning, I nearly hit the snooze button to go back to sleep. But I knew I'd never forgive myself if I didn't get to the warehouse early to see if Rebecca had read and torpedoed the other writers' scripts. I had to know if she was gunning for me (and Sandy) only, or if she was an equal-opportunity career crusher. Because if this was personal, then I had to find out why. No way was I going to let that woman sabotage me and my determination to become a TV writer.

I lived in West Lost Angeles, a pleasant community of small stucco homes and apartments, located west of UCLA and the more upscale community of Westwood. My apartment was part of a small, two-story, twelve-unit complex, lined with ancient, shedding palm trees that blocked the sunlight, and fronted by cracked cement parking spaces for which the landlord charged extra. The building was across the street from the V.A. hospital on Wilshire Boulevard, and every once in a while a confused and ailing vet would knock on the door, asking for money. Not the safest location for a single woman, perhaps, which was probably why the rents were slightly less than normal and made the place affordable for me.

The overhead light illuminated a two-room apartment as depressing as a prison cell. Everything about it was beige. The cinderblock walls. The worn and stained carpeting. Even the two built-in studio beds and sagging armchair covered in a matching beige-flowered fabric. I had pinned brightly colored 1930s-style Harper's Bazaar and Vogue posters to the walls for contrast. But, instead of making the place cheery, the posters, filled with the holes of previous thumbtacks and dog-eared at the corners, only added to the loneliness of the room's decor.

The low-flush shower regulator the landlord installed to save money barely woke me up. But after a brisk toweling and a bolted-down breakfast of Cheerios and banana, I was on the road in an hour.

Traffic on the 10 Freeway was just starting to slow down, and I stopped and started my way east then north on the 110/Harbor Freeway. Circumventing the skyscrapers of downtown, I made it to work in forty-five minutes, shaving fifteen minutes off my usual commute and arriving earlier than the rest of my colleagues. The cast and crew were on location that day, and the parking lot was empty of the usual trucks, trailers, cables, and other paraphernalia that clutter up a TV series in production.

Sherman had already unlocked the front door, although the writing staff all had keys of their own, and I headed down the corridor toward the bullpen. I stowed my shoulder bag in my desk, grabbed the coffee pot, rinsed it out in the bathroom sink and made fresh coffee. Jennifer had shown me where the coffee and filters were—relieved, I think, to be done with the chore herself.

Then, with the coffee brewing, I took my keys and headed for Rebecca's office. The agent-submitted scripts, I knew, would be sitting in an untidy pile on her couch.

I stuck the key in the lock and turned the knob, but the door pushed open of its own accord. Funny. Maybe Rebecca forgot to lock up when she left last night.

But the door wasn't locked because Rebecca had never left. I swung the door open and took two steps inside. Rebecca was slumped over her desk, her head almost unrecognizable because of all the blood. I also couldn't help noticing the blood-spattered walls before backpedalling out of the office and shutting the door behind me. I was shaking and my palms were sweaty. I wiped them down my pants, took a deep breath then raced off in search of Sherman.

His tiny office was in a corner next to the bathrooms, down the hall from the writers' corridor and around the corner from a basketball court–sized area used to hold production meetings. A portable TV droned softly on Sherman's battered metal desk. The Today Show. Willard Scott was announcing the birthdays of fragile-looking, smiling centenarians. Sherman wasn't in the office. I turned around, and the warehouse spun with me. I will not throw up, I vowed. I will not throw up.

"You're here early again," Sherman said, exiting the men's room, holding a bucket and mop in each hand. "Don't make it a habit." He smiled at me, his keys clanking at his side.

I swallowed. "Sherman, will you come with me to Rebecca's office?"

My voice was tight and small. Sherman looked at me more closely and his face filled with concern. He set the bucket and mop down on the cement floor.

"What's the matter?"

"Rebecca . . ." I trailed off, too traumatized to finish.

"What about her?"

"Can you just . . .? Her office . . . Oh God . . ."

I started to shake and without another word, Sherman headed through the bullpen. I followed him, we stopped in front of Rebecca's office. I nodded at the closed door.

"In there," I said.

Sherman started to get the picture, but he didn't hesitate. He twisted the knob and stepped inside. I turned away and stared at the closed door to Ray's office. Sherman can make fun of me later, I thought. But I wasn't going back in there for all the script assignments in Hollywood.

Sherman came back outside. His expression was unreadable.

"So?" I asked.

"She's dead," he said. "It looks like someone bashed her head in with a baseball bat." He picked up the phone on my desk and dialed 911.

END OF ACT ONE

ACT TWO

1.

It was not a baseball bat, in point of fact, but Rebecca's Women in Television Award. A triangular-shaped object made of crystal, the award sat on a heavy wooden base, inscribed to "Rebecca Saunders, associate producer, Babbitt & Brooks, for her contribution to the image of women in television." Rebecca prominently displayed it on her shelf above the couch, and every time I entered her office, I had a strong desire to turn the award around so that it faced the wall. The associate producer's job was to handle post-production: deal with the film editors, the background musicians, set up dubbing and looping sessions. It was the least creative and most nuts and bolts job on the producer pecking order. Not that associate producing wasn't important, but compared to the other producers and writers, Rebecca should've been low person on the totem pole. Charles, Ray, Peggy, and Zack had also received Women in Television Awards, the only difference being their awards were deserved.

"Susan Kaplan?"

I looked up. Two detectives stood by my desk. One was Asian, dressed in a suit and tie, the other was black, and wore a black T-shirt and windbreaker. I nodded up at them, having been peripherally aware of activity taking place in the warehouse after the arrival of several black-and-white police cars. Serious-looking men and women went in and out of Rebecca's office. I could hear a camera click, voices murmuring to one another. The detective in the suit and tie continued.

"I'm Detective Albert Lu. This is Detective Mike Wagner. Officer D'Amato tells me you found the body."

Again, all I could do was nod. Believe it or not, I used to fantasize about what it would be like to be involved in a murder investigation. As the prosecution's expert witness I would be articulate, intelligent, and observant. The sexy detective involved in the case would be impressed and fall in love with me. The reality was, not only was there not the least bit of chemistry between Detective Lu (mid-forties, leathery skin, black hair the consistency of shoe polish) and myself, but I also didn't feel particularly observant or intelligent. In fact, the experience reminded me of when I was ten years old and wishing I were sick so that I could stay home from school and watch cartoons and reruns of The Brady Bunch on TV Land. Then I came down with the flu, threw up for three days straight, and wondered endlessly what my classmates were doing and whether my best friends were making new friends without me. Like my ten-year-old self, now that I got a dose of my fantasy, I no longer wanted it.

Perhaps the detectives sensed some of this, because Detective Lu's expression softened and his voice seemed gentler.

"Is there a private room where you can give a more detailed statement to Detective Wagner?"

It took me a second to get my brain into gear.

"An office?" I asked. "Maybe Charles Green's office?"

Even though I'm sure neither of the two detectives had any idea who Charles Green was, Detective Lu nodded encouragingly.

"Why don't you lead the way?"

I got up from my chair and crossed the bullpen, heading for the corridor that led to Charles's office. Detective Wagner followed me, and as I passed into the corridor I heard Detective Lu say, "Sherman O'Dell? Is there somewhere you and I can talk in private as well?"

Charles's office was locked, but I was still clutching my key chain and I used the master key to open the door and step inside. I turned to Detective Wagner, not sure what I needed to do next. He nodded to Charles's black leather couch, and I sat while he pulled over one of the desk chairs and sat down himself.

I kept my legs together, hands folded politely in my lap, overly conscious of my posture and trying hard to sit up straight. The room was stuffy and Wagner shrugged off his jacket, dropping it onto the chair next to him. His black T-shirt revealed weightlifter's muscles. I stared at the puckered patch of skin in the shape of a crescent on his upper right arm. A scar from a knife fight? Bullet wound? Birth defect? I slid my eyes back to Wagner's face, uncomfortably aware of staring at his arm longer than was polite.

But Wagner didn't seem to notice. Not once had he cracked a smile or looked at me with anything remotely resembling warmth. When he pulled out a notebook and pen and looked me in the eye, I felt overwhelmed with guilt. Even though I had nothing to do with Rebecca's death, I believed myself to be in some way responsible. And I was convinced Wagner thought so, too.

"Why don't you tell me how you found her?" he asked, not taking his eyes off mine.

I had already explained everything to the uniformed officers who had arrived first, but I didn't have the nerve to tell that to the detective. So, with another brief glance at his scar, I said, "I came into work early. I wanted to read some scripts that I knew were in Rebecca's office. I went to unlock the door, but it was already open."

I stopped. Wagner looked at me expectantly. I felt I had to be specific.

"I don't mean it was open open, I just mean the door was already unlocked."

"Is that unusual?" he asked.

"Normally I'm the last one to leave. So I usually lock up the office for her. But last night she told me to go home early. She was still in her office when I left."

"What happened after you found her? Did you examine the body? Touch anything beside the doorknob?"

"No. I took maybe two steps into the room. I kind of knew what happened. I mean, I sort of figured she was dead."

Could I sound any more like a blithering idiot if I tried?

My stomach cramped. Oh please God, don't make me sick now. I had the Weiss stomach, inherited from my mother through my grandfather. It would go sour on me at the most inappropriate moments. Like now. I crossed my legs, wondering if the detective would let me get the roll of Tums out of my bag in my desk.

"And then you ran and got . . ." Wagner checked his notebook. "Mr. O'Dell."

I nodded. Wagner's continued silence, his expressionless stare, was, I knew, a ploy to keep me talking. I obliged.

"I knew what I saw," I said. "But part of me was hoping I didn't . . . You know what I mean?"

Wagner continued to stare at me. My eyes slid back to his scar. It was a startling white-grey against his dark skin. My stomach cramped again, and I could feel beads of cold sweat forming at my hairline. I felt guilty as hell, and I knew Wagner was already picturing me on death row. Suddenly, having a vivid imagination didn't seem like such a great thing after all.

He turned back to his notebook. "Do you normally come in to work at . . ." He looked back up from his notebook. 'What time did you say you came in?"

There it was . . . The question I had dreaded all morning. I came in early because I hated my boss so much I had to see if she was ruining not only my career but everyone else's who wanted a shot at writing a Babbitt & Brooks script.

Faintly, I said, "Eight o'clock." My stomach bubbled with gas. Maybe I had an ulcer.

"And normally you arrive at . . .?"

"Nine-thirty."

My stomach cramped again. This'll make a great story for the grandkids, I thought. If I ever live to have grandkids. "Why'd you come in an hour and a half early then?" I bolted upright from the couch. "Excuse me," I said, and I could hear the panic in my voice. "I really have to go to the bathroom."

Without giving him time to stop me, I ran out of Charles's office, hitting the ladies' room in five seconds flat.

2.

I washed my hands and blotted my face with a paper towel. My face in the speckled mirror looked pale beneath the blush I wore the Plumberry Collection for winter complexions. I had no idea what a winter complexion was; all I knew was that I didn't want to leave the bathroom and face that detective again. I didn't want to have to explain to him why I came in early, how much I hated Rebecca, but, no, not enough to kill her. My stomach still felt queasy and I was terrified of having to run back into the stall. Wouldn't Wagner view that as a sign of guilt?

When I left the bathroom, he was sitting at one of the cafeteria-style tables that lined the basketball court. Great. He probably heard me in the bathroom. This was definitely not the sexy detective scenario I had constructed for myself. I made my way toward the table, sliding onto the bench opposite him.

"Are you all right?" he asked.

"I am now," I lied. I tried not to look at his scar, but did anyway.

"Why do you keep staring at my arm?" he asked.

Oh great. Caught in the act. "I just wondered what that scar was on your arm." Might as well be honest.

Surprisingly, he made a face. It was the first human expression I had seen from him since we met.

"Stupid," he said. "Fraternity initiation. We all got tattooed. Six years later I realized how dumb it was. Had it removed."

"Oh," I said, taken aback by his honesty. Maybe he wasn't such a bad guy after all.

"When is everyone else expected in today?" he asked, all business. The real Mike Wagner, lurking under the mask of "Detective" was gone as quickly as it had appeared.

I looked at my watch. Could it only be nine in the morning?

"In about thirty minutes or so," I said.

"How many people work here?"

"Lots," I said. "It's a television production company." I added with a note of pride, "We're filming the show Babbitt & Brooks."

Wagner looked like he didn't recognize the name. I shouldn't have been surprised. In spite of the high praise from critics and women's groups, the male demographic sucked.

"You actually film here?" he asked.

I nodded. "But the cast and crew are on location today. Yesterday, too."

"So who was here yesterday? And who do you expect

today?"

"Ray Goldfarb, the showrunner slash executive producer. Sandy Martin, his assistant. Charles Green, supervising producer. Jennifer Bardos, his assistant. Peggy Stevens and Zack North, writer-producers. And I'm their assistant."

"Anyone else?"

I paused, remembering Winifred McCauley's visit last night. I also remembered how much Winifred seemed to dislike Rebecca.

Suddenly, I felt completely out of my depth. Could one of these people have killed Rebecca?

"Susan." Wagner brought me back to the present. I noticed he called me by my first name. Was it to put me at ease, like my gynecologist back home on Long Island tried to do, when I was lying naked on the examination table, feet in the stirrups, legs spread? Somehow, I felt just as exposed, fully dressed, sitting across the scarred Formica table, staring at this T-shirted detective with the tattoo removed from his right arm.

"Rebecca received two death threats," I blurted out.

Wagner's brown eyes narrowed, his gold Cross pen paused over his notebook.

"Explain," he commanded.

And so I did.

I told him everything, even about Rebecca initially blaming me. I looked away as I told him that, convinced he'd suspect me of her murder as well, but fearing worse consequences if I said nothing and he learned of the accusation from Jennifer or Sandy instead. He kept his eyes steady on me throughout, only occasionally glancing down to jot a note or turn a page in his notebook.

"I never returned the first threat to her," I said in conclusion. "And she never asked about it. She was kind of quiet yesterday." Because she didn't get the promotion? Was that something I needed to tell Wagner?

Without looking up from his notebook, Wagner asked, "Do you still have those letters?"

"The one I found should still be in my desk. Sandy Martin took the other note to her office. She may have thrown it out."

"Let's take a look."

We walked down the writers' hallway to the bullpen. I opened the lower right hand drawer of my desk and removed the folder in which I had kept the letter. It was gone. I stared blankly at the empty file as if waiting for the note to magically reappear.

"Are you positive that's where you put it?" Wagner asked.

"I thought I did. But maybe in my rush to put it away, I misfiled it." I looked through my other files. Nothing. Then I searched the rest of my desk. The note had vanished. I looked at Wagner helplessly, feeling my face flush, convinced he thought I was making the whole thing up. "Maybe Sandy held on to the other one," I said, hoping that would appease him.

We headed toward Sandy's office around the corner, passing Rebecca's on the way. I tried not to stare into the open door, but I couldn't help catching a glimpse of the body-bagged figure as the coroner's attendants strapped it to a gurney. I felt shocked—and scared. Wagner placed a hand on my shoulder and steered me away. I shook off the feeling of doom and entered Sandy's office — and stopped in surprise. It looked like a hurricane had hit — or maybe an earthquake that only jolted this particular room. Papers were everywhere, in disorganized heaps not only on her desk, but on top of file cabinets, even on the floor. Sandy was not known for her neatness — but she did have an uncanny ability to find a particular memo or contract in a particular pile. I had been in her office the night before to place some phone messages for her on her desk. Although her office was not neat then, it definitely had not looked like this. Wagner, of course, noticed my surprise. I told him what was wrong.

"Can you tell if anything is missing?" he asked.

I surveyed the room once again, this time more carefully. Sandy's computer still sat on her desk, but I had no idea where to look for the death threat. Which is what I told Wagner.

"Then we'll just have to wait until Ms. Martin comes in," he said.

"Do you know why anyone in this office would want to send Ms. Saunders death threats?" he asked as we walked back to the table in the basketball court.

I shook my head, not because I didn't know, but because I couldn't believe this was happening. Everything felt so unreal. Was Rebecca really dead? Had she actually received two death threats? Had I hidden one away? A philosophy professor in college once asked the class if we really knew the difference between sleeping and waking. He suggested that maybe when we thought we were dreaming we were actually awake. And when we thought we were awake, we were really dreaming. At that moment,

I wanted to believe him. I wanted to believe I was asleep and dreaming.

"You know of no one who would send her those notes?" Wagner asked again as we slid across from each other on the cafeteria benches. I pulled myself out of my reverie. If I was actually awake, I had better start dealing with it.

"Rebecca wasn't well-liked in the office," I said. "But is one of my coworkers capable of sending her threats? Of killing her?" I shook my head again. "These people are my friends. She could've antagonized a crew member. An actor. I wouldn't know."

I hoped that answer satisfied him. I didn't want to accuse people without justification. "Okay," said Wagner, and I could see him shifting gears. "When did everyone leave last night? Do you know?"

I nodded, relieved at the change in subject. "Charles Green left to go to the set," I said. "That was about five o'clock. Then Jennifer left about ten minutes later. Sandy Martin had a dentist appointment. She left around five-thirty. Peggy Stevens left soon after, followed by Zack North. Ray Goldfarb's wife picked him up."

"And what time did they leave?" Wagner asked.

"I don't know," I said. "They were still in Ray's office when Rebecca sent me home."

"Is that usual? You mentioned earlier that you normally leave after her."

Once again I forced myself not to look at Wagner's scar. Why did I want to stare at it as a way of avoiding difficult questions? Why couldn't he put on his jacket and put me out of my misery?

"My work was finished for the day. I think Rebecca was about to leave soon after me."

"But she didn't."

I shook my head. "I guess she didn't."

Then I paused, staring at Wagner as I just remembered something. "Rebecca's car isn't in the parking lot," I told him.

"Are you sure?"

"She has her own space. All the staff does. The lot was empty when I drove in this morning."

"Which is her space?"

"Right in front of the building. It has her name on it. You can't miss it."

"And where does she keep her purse? And her car keys?"

"Her keys are in her bag," I said, pleased that I remembered this from the day she drove me to lunch. "And she keeps her bag in her lower right hand desk drawer." Wagner nodded and rose. "Stay right here. And don't talk to anyone." He crossed the huge, empty room, disappearing down the corridor back to Rebecca's office.

Who in the world was I going to talk to? No one was in. And where had that other detective taken Sherman? I remembered my stomach. The cramps and queasiness had passed, maybe because the murder had suddenly become less personal. If whoever killed Rebecca stole her purse and car, then perhaps this was just a robbery gone wrong, or some crazy person who wandered into the unlocked building last night and found Rebecca alone and vulnerable. Maybe the death threats were practical jokes, not to be taken seriously, just something someone wrote to rattle Rebecca.

That would've made me feel better except for the disappearance of the note in my desk. And the building should've been locked. I knew whose fault it was if it hadn't been. Not, I decided, that I was going to say anything to Wagner. Nevertheless, I was more than a little nervous when he returned a few minutes later.

"We can't find her keys or her purse," he said. "However, we did find this."

With the tips of his fingers, he carefully removed a script from a paper bag and placed it in front of me. Spots of dried blood sprinkled the top of the title page. Dress Blue, I had typed neatly about a quarter of the way down the page. Then, two spaces underneath, "A Stitch in Time," the title I had chosen for my story. "Written by Susan Kaplan" four spaces below that. Scrawled diagonally across the page in blazing red ink in Rebecca's bold, sprawling hand, were the words, "Let's get a real writer in on this."

I sucked in my breath sharply. The knife in my gut reappeared, twisting deeper, and I was distressingly aware of Wagner looming above me. "Is that the victim's handwriting?" he asked.

The victim. Did he choose those words deliberately to remind me of what exactly had happened to her? If he had, it was unnecessary. I nodded and spoke so quietly Wagner had to lean in closer to hear. "Yes, she wrote this."

"Did you see this before her death?"

I wasn't too shocked to realize that Wagner was gently trying to get me to admit I had—and it was that which had set me off and caused me to kill her. But I could only admit the truth.

"No. I didn't know about this. Until now."

I kept staring at those words, repeating the phrase over and over in my head, knowing I would never forget them. I hate you. Rebecca. I hate you. I'll make you eat your words. I will. To my utter embarrassment, a tear slid down my cheek and splattered onto the script.

Perhaps Wagner took that single tear as a sign of remorse. He sat down next to me and asked in a gentle voice that invited confession, "Are you sure about that?"

How could I tell him that even in death that woman had the power to wound me? How could I tell him that I was still hurt and angry by her actions, that her death wasn't enough for me to forgive her? But I had to try because, underneath my shock and hurt, there was a part of me that knew Wagner thought of me as a suspect. Her words on my script had been my motivation to kill her.

I looked him straight in the eye, mentally giving him permission to probe my psyche and discover my innocence.

"Charles Green read my script," I told him. "He liked it and gave it to Ray Goldfarb." Wagner stared at me, his brown eyes warm and compassionate, ready to be the best listener I ever had in my life. The guilty deserved no less. "But Ray gives everything to Rebecca." I faltered, looked away. "I saw the script on Rebecca's desk. But that was before she wrote . . . this." Spitting the word out, not even able to look at the red-inked phrase. "Rebecca wasn't going to like it no matter what—I knew that. An assistant couldn't be a better writer than she was, couldn't be a better anything. Especially her assistant." Especially me.

Wagner didn't say anything, and I forged wearily ahead, knowing I was talking too much, but needing to tell my side of the story.

"Charles told me yesterday that Ray didn't like the script. I asked him if that was really Rebecca's opinion, but Charles wouldn't say.

"Last night Rebecca had a bunch of scripts and DVDs she reviewed with Ray in his office. Maybe mine was one of them."

"But you already told me Ray rejected your script."

"Oh, yeah, that's right." I shook my head as if to shake away the cobwebs. "She must've just told Ray about it and kept the script on a pile with the others on her couch."

Wagner's voice was still gentle as he said, "We found your script on her desk." That's why it's got blood on it, you dummy, I suspected he thought.

"If I knew she had written that on my script, I would've taken it with me."

"When?" asked Wagner.

"Whenever I found it. But I didn't."

Wagner merely looked at me.

"I didn't do it," I said to him, trying to convince him of my innocence. "I didn't kill her." Tears started running down my face unchecked. "I wish you'd believe me." I hunched further into myself, hands covering my face. The tears spattered onto the script and Wagner gently removed it from the table, for fear, I was sure, that they would run and blur the ink of Rebecca's final, vicious commentary on me.

3.

Wagner didn't arrest me. Even I knew the evidence against me was circumstantial at best, and he needed either a confession that I wasn't about to give, or proof like my fingerprints on the murder weapon. After I calmed down, he asked if anyone had seen me the night of the murder, after I left the office for the evening. I told him about my next-door neighbor taking me out for ice cream at Baskin-Robbins. The detective asked for my neighbor's address, so I knew things really were serious.

"Do I need a lawyer?" I asked, my voice tight with fear and anxiety.

"Not yet," Wagner answered. He reached into his inside jacket pocket and pulled out his card. "But if you remember anything else pertinent to the case, give me a call."

I took the card with ice cold, shaking fingers, too crushed with anxiety to look at him. What did he mean by not yet? What was wrong with a simple no?

Wagner stared at me a moment longer, his expression unreadable, before rising from the table and exiting the room.

Jennifer and Sandy dashed into the basketball court a few minutes later.

"There you are," said Jennifer, her blond hair slightly mussed as if she'd been driving to work in a convertible with the top down. She slid onto the bench across the table from me. "What happened?"

Sandy sat down next to her, concern knitting a sharp vertical line between her eyes. She absently pulled on her upper lip. "Rebecca's dead?" Despite the shock I knew she felt, her upper-class British accent made her sound like she was really saying, "And can you pass the crumpets, please?"

I took a deep breath and nodded. "I'm the one who found her." There was a pause as Jennifer and Sandy absorbed this piece of information.

"I thought Sherman might have found her when making his rounds," said Sandy. Jennifer nodded emphatically.

"No, I came in early and . . . and . . . there she was . . ." I trailed off, suddenly overcome.

Sandy moved to my side of the table, rubbing my back in sympathy.

"What happened?" asked Jennifer. "The cops wouldn't tell us anything. They just took our names and said they'd talk to us in a few minutes."

I imagined the figure in the body bag, strapped to the gurney, the struggle to fit her through the narrow door leading out of the warehouse. Here in the basketball court, we had huge sliding doors that opened onto the loading dock that enabled the crew to bring in large pieces of camera and lighting equipment. I wondered if I should tell that to the police, in case they were still struggling with Rebecca, when Sandy interrupted my thoughts.

"What about the writers? And Ray? Have they shown up yet?"

I shook my head. "Not that I know of. You didn't see their cars in the lot?"

"No. Jen and I drove in at the same time. We saw your car and all the police cars. And several cops mucking about Rebecca's parking space. Susan, what happened?"

"I found Rebecca with her head bashed in when I went into her office this morning."

Sandy and Jennifer's jaws dropped simultaneously.

"God," said Jennifer. "We knew she was dead, just not why . . . I just didn't believe she was killed. I mean, I guess I knew she couldn't just drop dead from natural causes, but murder . . ." She stared at me, her face pale under her tan.

"Do they have any leads?" Sandy asked.

My voice quavered as I explained about the missing car and purse, and Sandy looked at me more closely.

"What's going on, Susan?" she asked. "What aren't you telling us?"

I took a breath and told them about Detective Wagner finding my spec Dress Blue and what Rebecca had scrawled on the cover. "I think . . . I think he suspects I killed her in anger."

"That's ridiculous!" Jennifer said, "It had to be a thief or crazy person."

"Or the nutter who wrote the death threats," Sandy added.

Jennifer nodded. "Or even a homeless person who wandered in after discovering the door was unlocked. There was no way it was you and if you want me to tell him, I will."

Her defense of me lifted a weight from my shoulders and I smiled at her in thanks.

"There's another thing," I said. "The second death

threat is gone."

I realized I hadn't told Sandy about it so I started to fill her in when she interrupted, "You mean the one you found in Rebecca's desk?" I must've looked surprised because she added, "Jennifer told me about it."

I looked at Jennifer accusingly. She shrugged, affecting nonchalance. "Sorry. I didn't think it was such a big secret."

"Did either of you tell Rebecca I took it?" I asked.

Chewing out Jennifer, I knew, would be an exercise in futility.

"No," Sandy said. She paused, as if knowing I wasn't going to like the rest. "But I did tell Ray. Don't worry," she added hastily, forestalling my objections, "He didn't believe you had sent them. He agrees with Charles, that they're probably from some lunatic."

Thank God for small favors.

"Did he take the letter then?"

Sandy shook her head no.

"What about the first one? The one you took."

"I threw it out."

"Sandy, that's evidence!"

"But I didn't know it at the time," she said. I couldn't argue with her logic.

Jennifer started to say something, but paused as both she and Sandy suddenly looked up. I turned around. Detective Wagner was walking across the basketball court toward us, his face again expressionless.

"Ladies," Wagner nodded briefly at us. Jennifer eyed him speculatively. I knew what she was thinking. Those muscles . . . I wanted to kick her under the table for staring.

At least she wasn't ogling the puckered scar.

Sandy's reaction was different. She studied the table top, giving the detective a quick, jerky nod when he asked if she were Sandra Martin.

"And you're Jennifer Bardos," he said, turning to Jennifer. Jennifer gave him a two hundred megawatt smile and held out her hand. I stared in shock as he took it and gave her a smile back. Wow! Jennifer was flirting with the detective on a murder investigation! I didn't know whether to slap her silly or applaud in appreciation. Instead, I sat silently in awe.

"It's nice to meet you," said Jennifer then she paused, flustered. "Well, I guess not under these circumstances."

Wagner seemed unfazed. I realized that people like us, with our silly reactions, were nothing new to him.

Jennifer kept smiling as she said, "And if you think Susan killed Rebecca, you're nuts."

Although Wagner didn't react, I wanted to kiss Jennifer.

"I need to take your statements," he said, as if she hadn't spoken. "And I'd like you to examine your office," he said to Sandy. "Do you still have the second threat sent to Miss Saunders?"

"No. I just told Susan. I threw it out."

Wagner nodded, accepting this setback calmly. "I'd like you to take a look at your office anyway. Susan thinks someone may have been through your things." If he still believed in my guilt, he gave no evidence of it.

Sandy gave a start of alarm. "Was anything stolen?" she asked, looking at me.

"I don't know," I said. "The room is a mess. Papers everywhere."

Sandy relaxed a bit, even managed to smile. "That's how I left my office last night." She turned to Wagner. "I'll take a look, but I'm almost certain that's a mess of my own making." But I could tell by the way she held herself, she was still tense.

"I don't think so," I said, "I was in your office last night after you left. It didn't look anything like what it does now."

"No, you don't understand, Susan," she said. "I came back after my appointment."

Wagner, Jennifer, and I all stared at her. Was that why she was so tense? Did Sandy know something about the murder she was afraid to tell us about?

I'm sure similar thoughts were running through Wagner's mind. "What time was that?" he asked.

Sandy shrugged. "Seven-thirty. I had a dental appointment at six. When I got out, I started to feel guilty about some of the work I had left untended. So I came back here. But I wasn't able to catch up on everything, as you can tell."

She smiled, but it was weak, and I knew something else was going on.

So did Wagner, because he loomed over Sandy. "Why don't we check out your office anyway," he said. And you can tell me whether Rebecca was still here and whether you and she had a violent argument that ended in her death, I suspected were his unspoken thoughts. Not that I wanted Sandy to be guilty, but I wouldn't have minded him thinking someone other than me could be a suspect.

Jennifer and I watched Sandy and Wagner cross the warehouse and disappear into the corridor. Even though

Wagner was not touching her, Sandy's shoulders were hunched as if anticipating—and dreading—physical contact with him.

"Do you think she did it?" Jennifer asked in awe.

Normally I'd be scandalized at such a question about a mutual friend. Now I needed to know everything Jennifer knew.

"Why do you ask?"

Jennifer paused. I could see she was desperately worried.

"Sandy told me she was going to have a talk with Rebecca about the probation thing," she said. "Last night. Just the two of them. With no one around to interrupt."

4.

Sandy returned fifteen minutes later. She looked pale and shaken but managed to give us a smile that was meant to be encouraging. "Zack just arrived," she said. "The police are questioning him now."

"What did you tell Wagner?" I asked.

Sandy didn't look happy. "I'm afraid I got Zack in a bit of trouble. But I had to tell the truth."

"Which was?" I tried to keep the urgency out of my voice.

"He was here last night. Rebecca and he were arguing." Jennifer and I looked at her in shock.

"But I saw him leave," I said.

"He had come back," Sandy said. "I was working in my office. I knew Rebecca was still here. Her car was in the lot and she was making phone calls from her office. But I kept my door closed so she wouldn't know I'd come back."

I snuck a peek at Jennifer. Didn't she just tell me Sandy had wanted to talk to Rebecca? Was Sandy lying to us? Or did she have second thoughts once she had calmed down?

"So Zack didn't know you were here, either?" Jennifer asked.

"Zack didn't see me. He walked right past my office, but as I said, my door was closed."

"Then how did you know it was him?" said Jennifer.

"I told you. I could hear them arguing. Which made me realize he had returned."

"The fight was that loud?" I said.

Sandy nodded glumly. "Was it ever."

She stopped and stared down at the tabletop, possibly reliving Zack and Rebecca's fight. She didn't seem inclined to continue, so Jennifer pressed her.

"What were they arguing about? Did Zack kill Rebecca?"

"I don't know," she said unhappily. "I couldn't bear to hear them arguing, so I snuck out before he left."

She looked so miserable I put my arms around her. I knew what she was thinking. If Zack didn't kill Rebecca, Sandy had gone and made him the number one suspect.

"Sandy, we know someone stole Rebecca's car," I said. "I don't think her death had anything to do with Zack. It had to be someone who just wandered in off the street."

Sandy managed a hopeful smile. "And Zack's not really the murdering type."

"Right," I replied. Although that's what everyone says about murderers they know personally.

"So what were they arguing about?" Jennifer's one-track mind returned to the heart of the story. "C'mon, San, if the police already know, what difference does it make?"

Sandy hesitated, then said, "Care to take a guess?"

"Peggy," I automatically answered.

Sandy looked at me in surprise. "How'd you know?"

"You were there last night. When Peggy saw the two of them together. I think Zack and Rebecca were having an affair." I told them about the kiss I inadvertently witnessed in the parking lot. "I bet Zack felt bad about Peggy finding out or at least suspecting something."

Sandy nodded. "It began with Peggy. How Zack didn't want to see her hurt, blah, blah, blah. You know, the usual male bullshit."

Jennifer and I nodded. We knew all about the usual male bullshit.

"I really couldn't hear everything, just the gist of things. Not until they really started arguing. And it was mostly Zack doing the shouting."

She took a deep breath. I almost wanted to tell her to stop. Gossip was fun in the telling, but afterward you felt dirty and guilty. And neither Jennifer nor I were very good at keeping secrets. But I wanted to stay out of jail, so I kept my mouth shut and waited for Sandy to continue.

"Zack wanted the relationship out in the open. No more hiding, I think he said."

"So they were really screwing each other?" asked Jennifer, wide-eyed.

"I don't know," Sandy said. "They were obviously involved. Zack wanted more of a commitment. Rebecca didn't."

"Well, that's a switch," said Jennifer. I knew she had

been trying to get her boyfriend Steve to propose marriage for a year with zero success.

"So why was Zack shouting at Rebecca?" I couldn't help myself. I was getting as involved in the story as Jennifer.

"She kept laughing at him. Not taking him seriously," Sandy said. "I couldn't quite hear what she said, but I did hear her laugh."

That throaty, ultra-feminine laugh. Strange to think we would never hear it again.

"So he tried to shout her into a commitment?" asked Jennifer. "I don't understand."

"I told you, he wasn't shouting at first. But the more Rebecca laughed, the more upset he got. She just refused to take him seriously. And then he . . ."

She paused. By this time both Jennifer and I were hanging onto every word.

"And then he what?" Jennifer demanded.

Sandy shook her head. "It was getting pretty tense in there so I left the office and drove home."

She spoke directly to the table top when she said this, and I studied her closely. She was lying. But why? I opened my mouth to ask her, when suddenly Charles Green appeared.

"Sandy."

Even though her name was spoken gently, Sandy practically jumped out of her seat. Charles put a placating hand on her shoulder.

"Sorry. Didn't mean to scare you."

He had entered the basketball court with Peggy, a frightened-looking shadow, behind him. He moved around to the head of the table, his pipe sticking out of his jacket.

"I was just with Ray. He wants to know whether you talked to the police."

Sandy nodded. "Zack's with them now."

Charles and Peggy looked at one another; Peggy turned three shades of pale.

"All right, I'll tell him. Look," and Charles directed this to all three of us, "don't say anything more to the police. Ray is calling our legal department right now. He wants a lawyer with us when we make our statements."

I was glad legal would be involved. But I wish they'd been there when I'd answered Wagner's questions. "I already made my statement. I was the first one in . . . I found the body . . ." My voice trailed off.

Charles and Peggy swiveled their heads in my direction.

"Do they have a suspect?" Peggy asked. She looked nervous, and I wondered if she was concerned for Zack or for herself.

"Susan says Rebecca's car was stolen," said Jennifer, "and her purse. Maybe it was a drug addict. Or some homeless person."

"Okay, look, I don't know anything more than you do," said Charles, taking command. (Something he never got to do when Rebecca was around, a devilish voice within me said.) "Stay here and don't say anything to anyone. I need to tell Ray about Zack. You'll be okay?"

The three of us nodded.

"Good. I'll be back."

He strode out of the room. Peggy threw us a brief, reassuring smile (though I felt I should be the one reassuring her) before following quickly after Charles.

"Damn, I forgot to tell him about Sherman," I said.

"What about Sherman?" Jennifer asked.

"He disappeared with some detective ages ago. I want to know what happened to him." I stood up and climbed over the bench.

"Susan, where are you going?" Sandy asked in alarm.

"I just want to check out Sherman's office. My rear end's numb from sitting on that bench all morning."

I strode past the bathrooms and made for Sherman's office. I shoved open the door. Sherman was inside, sitting at his desk, head in hands. For a horrified moment I thought he was crying.

"Sherman?"

He looked up, tried to grin at me, but failed.

"Hey, Susan," he said.

"Sherman, how long have you been in here?"

He shrugged. "I don't know. What time is it?"

I looked at my watch. It was ten o'clock (only ten o'clock?), and I told him so.

"Do the police know you're here?" I asked.

He nodded. "That detective . . . Lu, was it? He asked me a lot of questions."

"So, how did it go?" I asked. It was a rhetorical question. As soon as I saw his hunched figure sitting behind his desk, I knew how it had gone.

"I found cocaine in her office a couple weeks ago," he said, sounding tired. "And I was stupid enough to tell them about it."

5.

"**S**he had a baggie of the stuff right on top of her desk," Sherman said, sitting at the cafeteria table next to Jennifer and across from Sandy and me. I had convinced him to join us, hoping that our company would make him feel better, knowing his company made me feel better. "I was cleaning her office after she left for the night. It was underneath one of the scripts, and her big mirror was sitting flat on the desk, with a little powder still stuck to it."

I knew that wall mirror. It usually hung above the credenza behind her desk, really just a face mirror, bordered with some sort of yellow, flowery stripe, and at the bottom, in flowing script, were the words, "Smile. You look gorgeous." I always thought Rebecca kept it to tell her who "the fairest of them all" was. I never dreamed she used it as a surface to snort cocaine.

"When was this?" Jennifer asked.

Sherman shrugged. "A couple of weeks ago. Maybe last month."

"What did you do?" I asked.

"I thought about throwing the stuff out and letting her stew about it. But then I thought she'd blame me for taking it, so I left her a note instead." He smiled grimly at the memory. "I wrote it on one of those little yellow stick-on pads. Basically I said, 'If you don't want me calling the cops, find someone else to clean up after yourself.' I stuck it on the baggie and left. She never said a word and I never went into her office again. Until this morning."

"You told the cops this?" Jennifer asked, bug-eyed.

Sherman nodded. "When the detective asked me if I knew anyone who wanted to kill her, I must've had some kind of giveaway reaction. He was all over me after that."

"Why?" I asked. "Just because she snorted coke?"

"Because maybe he thought I was her dealer," he said bitterly. "And killed her over drugs."

"Why would he think that?" Sandy said.

Sherman's eyes narrowed and his lips flattened into a thin, straight line. Suddenly, I was staring into the face of a stranger. "Baby, they see a black man, they hear about drugs, they see motive and opportunity."

Sandy spoke into the appalled silence that followed. "Sherman, that's your perception. It's not necessarily theirs. They won't send you to prison just because you knew about the cocaine."

Sherman was bitter. "Were you ever stoppped by the police because of your skin color?" Into the silence, Sherman added, "Welcome to my world."

How does an "I'm sorry" even adequately make up for the pain and bitterness I saw on Sherman's face? Jennifer turned to me.

"Susan, did you ever see anything in her office?"

I shook my head. "Before our lunch, I didn't even know I was supposed to be working for her. I rarely went in." I looked at Sherman. "I'm sorry."

"Not your fault, Susan." Sherman gave me a faint smile.

"I wouldn't be surprised if others knew about her . . . little hobby," Sandy said.

"Did Ray know?" I asked.

Sandy made a face. "He hated that stuff. He may have

known what she was up to, but he probably overlooked it. She was too valuable in other ways."

"Yeah, like flat on her back," Jennifer said.

"Jennifer, I don't think we should be talking about this right now," Sandy said.

"That would explain her promotion," I said. I thought of Ray Goldfarb's wife, Winifred McCauley, and how clearly she detested Rebecca. What if Winifred found out about Ray and Rebecca? Certainly, she had an excellent motive for murder.

Jennifer said, "And then Ray and Rebecca broke it off and Rebecca moved on to her next conquest.

"Zack," I said.

Sandy hid her face in her hands, as if disavowing all of us.

Sherman yawned. I raised my eyebrows in surprise. My first thought was the man's just told us he thinks he's being implicated in Rebecca's murder and now he's yawning? Then I thought, of course he's yawning, he's been up all night. That's his job. Which led me to speak my third thought out loud.

"You were here when Rebecca was killed."

Jennifer and Sandy looked at me in astonishment. Then they looked at Sherman. I think we all felt stupid for not remembering this in the first place.

Jennifer asked him, "Did you hear anything?"

Quickly followed by Sandy's, "Maybe you know something you don't realize you know."

Sherman said, "The cop asked me that first thing. 'What did you see? What did you hear?'" He shrugged. "I was in my office all night. I didn't hear or see anything."

Which wasn't surprising. Although sound traveled easily in the bullpen, with its thin wood walls and open areas, it would have to travel through the corridor and along the vast basketball-sized court in order for Sherman, back in his office, to hear even something as loud as a shout or a scream. The three of us slumped in disappointment.

I had one more question to ask, and I debated whether to voice it in front of Sandy and Jennifer. I hadn't said anything to Detective Wagner, not wanting to get Sherman in trouble, but I knew it was going to come out eventually. I tried to look and sound as non-threatening as possible as I turned to him and asked, "Did you lock the front door last night? When I got in this morning, it was open."

As I said earlier, we each had our own keys, but Sherman's job was to lock up after eight o'clock at night, no matter who was still left in the building. If he had locked up, the murderer would have to have his own key. If he hadn't, the police—and Romulus Television—might decide Sherman was responsible for Rebecca's death, even if he hadn't been the one wielding her Women in Television Award.

But Sherman didn't seem to take offense, much to my relief. "I already told the police about that," he said. The three of us looked at him expectantly. "Rebecca told me to keep the door unlocked. She said she was expecting someone. But I don't know who."

6.

The lawyer from the Romulus legal department finally

arrived close to lunchtime. On the way over, he'd given his okay from his cell phone for all of us to be fingerprinted so the cops could compare our prints against the ones in Rebecca's office. (Though we did find out that the Women in Television Award had been wiped clean—surprise, surprise.) The writers and producers were herded into the main area along with Sandy, Jennifer, Sherman, and myself. Zack looked desperately ill; his eyes were red, his face white and puffy, and even his brown hair seemed thinner, as if Rebecca's death was responsible for his encroaching baldness.

Peggy didn't look much better. She hovered around Zack, who, shocked and grieving, didn't seem to notice. Ray, when he finally made his appearance, was even more remote and imposing than usual. He chomped on an unlit cigar, absently fingering the bright red suspenders that held up his baggy khakis, standing at the head of the table, and looking down on the rest of us like Captain Ahab scoping out Moby Dick.

"It's important that you do not say anything more to the police until Ed Gruzcak arrives," Ray told us. A uniformed cop watched dispassionately, perhaps making sure we didn't hatch a plan that would destroy any evidence—or maybe even hoping one of us would say something that would give us away. "I'm certain this was a burglary gone tragically wrong, and I want to ensure everyone's safety and peace of mind as much as possible."

Our "protector," the Romulus lawyer Ed Gruzcak, was not one to inspire hope. Short, balding, with thin arms and legs and a paunchy stomach, he was the complete opposite of those dynamic and sleek TV attorneys seen on any given night during the ten-to-eleven time slot. Another romantic fantasy goes down the drain, I thought, as I sat in the wooden, straight-backed visitor's chair in Sherman's office. Gruzcak took a seat across from me, behind the desk.

Gruzcak, chin down, eyes focused on me over his large bifocals, had me tell him everything I could remember about my conversation with Wagner. He listened to my recitation in silence, and when I finished, he passed his hand over his forehead, as if brushing back nonexistent hair. He had probably not yet adjusted to the fact that he was going bald.

"Truthfully, Susan, I don't think the detectives consider you a person of interest. Despite what Rebecca wrote about your script, she . . .," he paused, as if unsure whether to continue, "she had problems. Problems that had nothing to do with you." I nodded. "So, relax a little. I'll give you a heads-up if I hear the police are looking at you more closely." Gruzcak must have seen the relief in my face because he squeezed my shoulder in support before leaving the office.

The forensics team and detectives were gone when I returned to the bullpen. Yellow crime scene tape slashed across the door of Rebecca's office. There was no sign of Jennifer.

Thinking she might be with Sandy, I walked around the corner, and saw Ray, sitting behind his desk. He looked up and our eyes locked. He blinked at me in surprise.

"Susan, you're still here."

"Where is everyone?" I asked.

"I sent them home," he said. "I didn't think we'd get much work done today. I'm going out on location. I need to talk to the cast and crew about Rebecca's passing before the media does."

"I'd like to go with you," I said. "Maybe I could help."

Ray considered then said, "Fine. I might need you to make calls for me on the way."

The heat felt good for the first five minutes as it baked out the basement-like chill of the warehouse, and I took a moment to enjoy it before joining Ray as he headed for his yellow, SL-Class Mercedes convertible parked in the lot.

The sun was warm on my skin and the air smelled of fried beans, cooking oil, and cilantro from the corner taco stand. Ray drove in a casual, reckless manner, his right arm lightly guiding the steering wheel, his left resting on the driver's side door, doing fifty in a thirty-mph zone. Although he was practically bald, the fringe around his head was a dusty red, and I noticed his arms had a redhead's freckled complexion. The hairs on his arm were golden and he had strong, long-fingered hands.

Ray was quiet, apparently, not needing me to make calls for him after all. To fill the silence, I asked, "Do the police have any idea who might have killed Rebecca?"

He stared out the window. We had crossed above the sluggish, metal-colored Los Angeles River and were heading south on Broadway into Chinatown. "It's obvious, isn't it?" he said. "A mugger. One of those crazies that hang out on street corners looking for easy cash."

He glanced at me, perhaps looking for agreement. When I didn't respond, his voice softened.

"I'm sorry you were the one to find her."

I shrugged. "It wasn't that bad." Liar, liar, pants on fire.

"You came in early this morning?"

Traffic stalled as a vehicle signaling left in the middle of the intersection held up cars in our lane. The signs on the elaborately ornamented buildings were written in Chinese characters, and the few gawking, camera-snapping tourists stood out like aliens among the predominantly Asian inhabitants.

"I came in at eight this morning," I finally said, tearing my gaze away from a grocery store that displayed what looked like giant chickens' feet in a tray in the window. There was no way I was going to tell him I arrived early to see who else's career Rebecca was deep-sixing so I lied. "I needed to update the website."

"What about last night?" he asked. "I didn't see you when I left."

In spite of his casual tone the hairs on the back of my neck stood on end. I started to feel kind of weird, sitting in Ray's Mercedes, driving through Chinatown. Maybe it was his lack of emotion with regard to Rebecca's death. Especially if he had been her lover. Or was Ray just putting on an act for my benefit? Was he actually shattered with grief and successfully hiding it? Somehow, I couldn't believe Ray was that good an actor.

I said, "Rebecca sent me home before you left. Your wife had just arrived to pick you up."

Ray looked vastly relieved and I wondered why. Certainly, he and Winifred hadn't ganged up on Rebecca and bashed her head in, had they? I tried to imagine the two of them, expressions frozen in a rictus of hate, and I wanted to laugh at the ludicrousness of it. But then again, whoever killed Rebecca must've hated her as much as my imagination portrayed him—or her. Maybe even more. It was not a pleasant thought and I shuddered as I stared out the windshield while we crossed over the 101 freeway into downtown L.A., wondering how I could find out what Ray did last night without making him suspicious.

Ray and I both jumped when his cell phone started ringing, playing the Babbitt & Brooks theme song.

Ray put the phone to his ear, ignoring the fact that hands-free devices were the law in California.

"Hello," he barked. If it had been me on the other end, I would've hung up in fright. The other person was braver because after a pause, Ray, still sounding unhappy, said, "Winnie, what do you want?"

Not the warmest greeting to one's wife. Ray moved his left arm to the steering wheel and cradled the phone with his right.

I could see his profile but I could still tell Ray was not a happy camper. Because he didn't want to speak to his wife or because I was in the car listening to every word?

"Winifred, I really can't talk now. Susan and I are driving to location." A pause. "Susan Kaplan, one of the writers' assistants."

Another pause. "She works—worked—for Rebecca." He stole a sidelong glance at me, but I was pretending deafness as I stared out of the car.

"You did? Already? Well, I'm not surprised. I'm sure it's all over the company by now." Ray paused. "Look, Win, I can't really talk about this. I'll call you when I get back from location . . . I don't know when." He moved the cell a couple of inches away from his ear as if to let his wife rant without his having to listen. We were at another stoplight, and I could hear, quite plainly, Winifred saying,

"Do the police know you didn't come home with me last night?" With a startled glance at me, Ray jammed his cell back to his ear.

It took every ounce of self-control not to whip my head around and stare at Ray. I kept looking out the window, pretending I was engrossed in the movie theater across the street. "Girls! Girls! Girls!" read the marquee. In a perfect world, I would've changed it to "Women! Women! Women!"

"Winifred, we will talk about this tonight. I promise. I have to go. Good-bye."

The light changed and he stamped on the gas pedal so hard I thought I'd get whiplash.

So Ray hadn't left with Winifred last night. But, then, where was he? Shtupping Rebecca? No, he couldn't have. Sandy had returned at seven-thirty and heard Zack talking with her. Had Ray made a quick escape? Or was he just biding his time in his office, sitting silently while Zack and Rebecca thrashed out their relationship, waiting for an opportunity to shtup Rebecca—or maybe even kill her? Or did Ray hear Zack kill her? If so, why wouldn't he tell the police? Did that mean Ray murdered Rebecca? Was I sitting in a two-seater Mercedes convertible with a murderer? No way! Not Ray. Then I asked myself, Why not? I shivered despite the heat.

"You know," Ray said, his sudden intrusion into my clandestine thoughts almost causing me to leap out of the car in shock, "Charles told me you wrote a pretty good Dress Blue spec script."

I looked at Ray in surprise. Aiming for casual, I shrugged. "He seemed to like it."

"He liked it enough to recommend you for an assignment."

I uttered a silent thank you to Charles. "He's a great guy."

Ray nodded. "We prefer working with people we know. It would be nice to give someone like you a script."

Since when? Since Rebecca died? Since you suddenly have no alibi? Since you probably lied to the police about it? And since only your wife and I now know the truth— and your wife can't be forced to testify against you, but I can? Couldn't you have done this with a little more finesse, Ray? I couldn't help myself: I had to yank his chain for being such a slimebag. "But Charles told me you didn't like the script."

Ray blinked, confirming what I suspected. He hadn't read it, had just given it straight to Rebecca.

"Well," he said, "I'm not too crazy about Dress Blue and I read your script superficially, with all my prejudices intact. Let me read it again. I respect Charles's taste. If he says you're talented, the least I can do is give your script a second chance."

Why did I have a feeling my spec script could be worse than Attack of the Killer Tomatoes and Ray would still give me an assignment? The question was, how badly did I want my shot at fame and fortune? Badly enough to accept the script assignment and look the other way with regard to Ray's alibi? What if Ray had killed Rebecca? Was it worth his going free just so I had a great script credit and thirty-five thousand dollars in the bank? Would my whole future now depend on telling a lie?

Now I could be a mensch and tell Ray to screw his

script. In that case, I was going to the police. Or—a nasty
little voice whispered—I could take the money, write the
best damn Babbitt & Brooks of my life, and forget what I
heard Winifred say on the phone. To survive, that voice
told me, I had to play by Ray's rules. But to live with
myself, I knew, I had to play by mine. I felt like I had a
white-robed angel sitting on one shoulder and a red, fork-
tailed devil sitting on the other. Both were persuasive, but
by the time Ray drove up to location, I still hadn't made up
my mind which one to listen to.

7.

Magic is often the word used to describe film-
making. Magic hour. Magic time. Movie magic.
"Let's make some magic!" directors say, right
before they yell "Action!" But the reality is, it's repetitious,
tedious, and boring. The actors sit around and wait more
than they're actually acting. The crew members rush
around like crazy setting up a shot, then sit around and
wait while the actors act. It takes longer to light a scene
than it does to film one. The days are long, with crew
members and actors arriving at five in the morning and not
finishing until seven or eight o'clock at night. Behind-the-
scenes jobs are usually passed down from father to son
(there are few women in crew jobs) and the stars, once you
meet them up close, have little glamour. The women are
often thin to the point of anorexia, and both the men and
women smoke too much and drink too much, and then
spend more time at the gym than they do with their
families. If there's any magic to be found in film-making,

it's that glamour is so convincingly created for adoring audiences who are unable to see the reality of the tired and anxious-looking people underneath the makeup and expertly coiffed hair.

But for me, driving up to location with Ray, it truly was magical. The crew was filming at the old St. Regis Hotel on Wilshire Boulevard, across from MacArthur Park (originally made famous by the song sung by Richard Harris in the sixties), about ten minutes from the heart of downtown and now closed. The area, once art deco heaven in the twenties and thirties, had now fallen on hard times, and the streets and park were havens for drug addicts, the homeless, and prostitutes. Only the St. Regis, with its graceful art deco columns and tall, thin, red stucco towers, remained a monument to L.A. in its movie heyday, when Clark Gable and Carole Lombard, Humphrey Bogart and Lauren Bacall graced its halls.

The security guard waved Ray into the cast and crew parking lot that used to hold the Packards and Reos of the hotel's guests back in the thirties and forties. Now it contained the makeup trailers, actors' dressing rooms, and equipment trucks, painted in blue, with the Romulus logo displayed prominently on the sides. The lot was also filled with pick-up trucks and battered vans (the crew members' cars, I assumed), interspersed with the occasional Mercedes and Porsches (the actors' cars).

Ray strode down the lot, and I hurried to catch up. The guard semi-saluted as Ray and I passed. "Coming to check things out?" he asked.

Ray smiled. "Just making sure they can run things without me."

The guard smiled back, and Ray and I crossed through an open wire gate to the pool area which in turn led to the back entrance of the hotel. Dead leaves rattled around the bottom of the empty swimming pool, where I could still make out the faded mural of a nineteen-twenties-looking mermaid cavorting among the art deco-type flora and fauna. Extras, costumed to resemble the seedy inhabitants of nearby MacArthur Park, lounged around the pool, reading, sunning, talking among themselves, completely oblivious to the faded, but still beautiful surroundings. Despite the outcry from preservationists, the St. Regis was slated for demolition in another couple of months by developers who wanted to build yet another expensive, high-density condominium in a city already filled with them. Every production company in town was using it as a location before it was destroyed. I looked up at the intricately carved moldings that bordered the windows of the now empty hotel rooms before walking inside with Ray.

A crowd of people stood in the vast, echoing lobby, shouting orders at one another, efficiently moving lights and cameras, or sitting in directors' chairs, reading magazines. Those who noticed Ray nudged their neighbors, concern on their faces. During the long breaks, they had probably checked their e-mails and the Internet on their smartphones, most likely having heard rumors of Rebecca's murder. No one approached Ray directly, although when he greeted various crew members as he walked by, they smiled or nodded in return.

The director, Mack Daniels, was sitting in his chair near the marble counter of the registration desk. Mack had directed several Babbitt & Brooks episodes that season and was often on the writers' side of the warehouse, meeting with Ray during pre-production. Tall, craggy-featured, and in his late forties, he was Ray's good friend and contemporary. Sandy had told me Mack and Ray both started out as gofers for low-budget movies, working their way up through the ranks together. Mack looked up as Ray approached, a large frown creasing his features.

"Is it true?" Mack said, glancing at me, trying to remember who I was, I'm sure, before turning back to Ray. "Some of the crew's been hearing rumors."

Ray nodded curtly, leaning close to Mack, speaking in a murmur. "You and I need to talk." He steered Mack toward a quiet corner of the lobby.

I knew what he was telling Mack, and I had little interest in following them. I stayed where I was, soaking up the sights and sounds of the velvet-curtained, frescoed lobby.

None of the actors seemed to be in sight, much to my disappointment. I wanted to find a place where I could watch everything and still be out of harm's way. I also realized I was starving, having skipped lunch while stuck in the warehouse. I had noticed a trestle table back in the parking lot, covered with a red-checked plastic tablecloth and bowls of what I hoped were food. Since nothing of interest seemed to be happening on the set, and since Ray was still in intense conversation with Mack, I decided to head back to the parking lot and get myself something to eat.

The catering truck—or roach coach, as the crew affectionately called it—was nowhere to be found, lunch having been over for several hours. Fortunately for my empty stomach, snack food remained on the table, and I shoved my steno pad in my purse, grabbed a paper plate and piled it high with potato chips, pretzels, cheese doodles and an apple for dessert. The long tables with folding chairs used by the actors and crew at lunch were still present, and I saw Patrick Hager conversing with some of the drivers at the head of one of them.

I sat down at the table closest to the food, facing the parking lot entrance, in order to keep an eye out for Ray in case he came looking for me. The dressing room trailers lined the entrance to the lot, and I also hoped I'd catch a glimpse of the actresses. I gobbled down the chips and pretzels and decided to help myself to seconds. I was too skinny from poverty to worry about my weight. Patrick looked up from his conversation, spotted me, said a few words to the drivers and strolled over.

"If it isn't my lady Susan," he said. "What brings you to our humble midst?"

Had Patrick not heard the news about Rebecca? It seemed strange given the attitude of the director and the crew.

"I'm with Ray," I said, cheeks bulging with potato chips. "Sandy left for the day."

"Is she all right? There has been gossip about Lady Rebecca, but surely it cannot be true?"

"Um . . ." Suddenly, I had lost my appetite. Concern flooded Patrick's features and he dropped the noble liege act.

"It is true? She's . . . dead?"

"Ray's talking with Mack Daniels," I said, feeling

uncomfortable. "Maybe you should talk to him."

"Where are they? Show me."

I tossed the half-eaten apple into a nearby trash bin and moved back toward the hotel. "This way."

But as we neared the building I saw Ray cross the pool area and approach us from the opposite direction. Head bent, walking hurriedly. I think he would've walked right past us if Patrick hadn't hailed him.

"Susan, just told me. What happened?"

Ray looked up, taking a couple of seconds to focus on us.

"Patrick," Ray acknowledged. "How's it going? I'm on my way to talk to Gail and Tabby. I understand they're in their trailers."

"Yes, they are," said Patrick. "So, it's true?"

Ray took a step closer and lowered his voice. "Rebecca was killed sometime late last night. I want to tell Gail and Tabby in private, and then I'm going to make an announcement to the rest of the cast and crew. I've already told Mack, but he's not going to say anything to anyone else. I'd appreciate it if you'd do the same. They've all heard the rumors, but I want the facts to come from me."

"Of course," Patrick said. His mouth hung open in a semi-gape, and I knew there were a zillion questions he wanted to ask. But Ray abruptly turned and headed toward the actresses' trailers. Patrick and I watched him climb the metal steps to the first dressing room and knock sharply on the door.

"Gail, it's Ray. Can I come in?"

Ray must've gotten a reply in the affirmative, because he opened the door and disappeared inside. Patrick turned to me.

"What happened, Susan? Is Rebecca really dead?"

I'm gonna get you for this, Ray, I thought as I looked up at Patrick and nodded. "I found her this morning," I said.

"Oh my God, Susan... How...? What...?" His papery skin looked paler than usual.

I said, "Someone bashed her head in with her Women in Television Award. They stole her car and her purse." More wishing than believing, I added, "It could be a robbery gone wrong."

Patrick stared at me, ignoring a white-blond cowlick that fell across his forehead. "Do they have any suspects?"

I shrugged. "If they do, they're not telling me."

"My God . . . It was you who found her?"

Again I nodded. "I came in this morning, walked into her office, and there she was."

Patrick took my hand and squeezed it hard. "I'm really very sorry."

He released my hand as quickly as he had taken it, staring, unseeing, at the extras sitting around the empty pool.

"Poor Rebecca," he said. He sounded so genuinely sad and lost I wondered if maybe his flirtation with her had been more serious than I thought. Without the showy facade, Patrick was almost cute and definitely more masculine. Maybe he wasn't gay after all.

"Are you okay?" I asked. "Do you want to sit down or something?" Patrick gathered himself together with an effort and smiled crookedly at me.

"I'm fine," he said, although he didn't look it. "We've got time on our hands before Ray makes his announcement. You ever been on location before?" I shook my head no. Patrick forced a smile. "Then I'll give you the fifty-cent tour if you're up to it."

"Only if you want to," I said, feeling bad at how bad he was responding. She's not worth it, I wanted to tell him. Don't mourn for her. I doubt she would have mourned for you. But, instead, I kept my mouth shut and waited for Patrick to make the next move. He crooked his arm and said, "Then come, my fair Dorothy. Let me introduce you to Oz."

8.

Patrick took me back into the lobby where electricians and grips and best boys were crawling on ladders, hooking up lights and moving cameras, all under the guidance of Rick Froehlich, the director of photography, who stood in the center of a graceful, curving staircase, reading numbers off his light meter. One male and two female stand-ins stood patiently next to Rick as the camera assistant measured the distance from their chins to the camera. The lobby had been "dressed down" to resemble a once graceful hotel now serving as a shelter for the homeless. Looking at the threadbare, faded royal blue carpet and the once ornate sofas now scarred by cigarette burns, I realized the St. Regis did not have to stretch a whole lot in order to play the part.

There wasn't much room between the registration desk and staircase, and burly crew members kept pushing past me with an offhand, "Sorry, sweetheart" or a "Be careful, honey." The show itself might have promoted a feminist viewpoint, but that didn't necessarily extend to the people who worked on it. After about the fifth guy told me to "Watch it, hon," I tugged on Patrick's sleeve.

"Okay. I've seen enough," I said, trying to lead him back outside.

As we crossed back to the pool area, an unshaven derelict with unkempt brown hair bore down on us. He wore a tattered and stained trenchcoat and looked like he had a six pack a day habit. To my surprise he held out his hand to Patrick.

"Patrick," the derelict said, "Jesse Mendez."

To my further surprise, Patrick shook his hand.

"Of course. We've talked on the phone." Now Patrick was friendly but businesslike. I wondered what he was like at home with no one to perform for.

"That's right." Jesse looked pleased Patrick remembered him. "So, did you get to see any of the scene?"

Obviously, this was an actor, which made sense, given the location was being used for a derelict hotel. In fact, I had probably met him myself. Actors auditioning for guest starring roles on the show always waited in the bullpen before their auditions, which were held in Ray's office. I loved casting day because I always got to meet at least one actor who was recognizable from guest-starring roles on other TV shows.

Patrick smiled. "I saw some of it," he said. "Looking good."

Jesse turned serious. "You think so, man? You know, they started with Gail and Tabby's close-ups first and, hey, I don't mind, they're the stars, right? But sometimes, you know, you do it once for the master, then off-camera for the ladies, and by the time it's your turn you get in a rut. I just hope I pulled through for you guys."

Was he for real? Were Gail and Tabitha this insecure even on their worst days? But Patrick seemed to take it in stride because he clapped Jesse on the shoulder in support.

"Jesse, you were terrific. Seriously."

"Well, you know, man, I try. Hey, who knows? Maybe the ladies will run into my character again, you know? I could be like a semi-regular, always with information they need about their clients and stuff."

"You never know," said Patrick, who really didn't know since he wasn't in on the story meetings.

Jesse smiled, encouraged, and his eyes flickered over to me.

"I'm sorry," Patrick said. "Jesse, this is Susan Kaplan. Susan, Jesse Mendez. Susan is one of the writers' assistants."

"Hey, no kidding?" Jesse said, his brown eyes alight with more interest than my humble job warranted. "That's really great." He held out his hand and I tentatively shook it. "Nice to meet you, Susan."

"Nice to meet you, too," I said. "Didn't you guest star on Dress Blue?"

Before Jesse could answer, Patrick squeezed my arm and said, "I've got to go. See you later." He headed back toward the lobby.

Jesse stared at me like he had just found the Holy Grail. "Yeah, that's right," he said.

"You played that gang member. Muñoz."

Jesse was thrilled. "You remembered!"

"Sure," I said. "You stood out because of that scene you

had with the rival gang leader. The one where he wants you to sign the treaty but you don't and your sister and her baby get killed."

"That's the one." Jesse said. "You really liked it?"

"I thought it was great. Dress Blue is one of my favorite shows."

"It's a great show, isn't it?" Jesse agreed. "But so is Babbitt & Brooks. It's been a real honor working for you guys." Honor isn't exactly the word I would've used, but then, what did Jesse know? As Jennifer would say: He's only an actor. "So, Susan," Jesse said, "How long have you been working here?"

"Not long. Only a couple of months," I said, suddenly wary. I knew where this was going.

"And you work for the writers?" Jesse said.

I nodded, mentally searching for an excuse to leave. I glanced at the actors' trailers, but there was no sign of Ray. Damn.

"So, any more plans for my character . . . you know, in the next couple of scripts?"

And there it was. The million-dollar question.

"Gee, I don't know, Jesse. I'm not in on the story meetings."

"But you get to see the scripts, don't you? Before everyone else?"

"Sure." Stupid me didn't know when to keep her mouth shut. "I type them into the computer."

"No kidding? That's terrific!"

"It has its moments."

"So, you'll know if I make a reappearance in the future?"

"I guess," I said. I was not feeling very good about this conversation and realized that Patrick had deliberately taken off on me— and for good reason.

"Well, maybe I can give you a call sometime and you could let me know."

It was definitely time to cut and run. Although my mother taught me never to be rude, she had also never spent any time with an actor.

"Sure, Jesse, you do that," I said. "It was nice meeting you. I have to go now. I think Ray's probably looking for me." I turned around and started to walk away from him.

"I'll give you a call," he said to my back. No wonder Jennifer and Sandy made fun of actors. I used to react in surprise at their scathing remarks about Gail, Tabby, and the other regulars. Now, I realized, their attitudes were not completely unjustified. Jesse wasn't even a star and he was self-centered and self-absorbed. Well, maybe he wouldn't call. I didn't think the writers had any plans to bring his character back, so, I hoped, that would be the end of that.

Thankfully, Jesse didn't follow me as I made my way back toward the parking lot. I decided to wait near the trailers for Ray, still hoping to catch a glimpse of Gail or Tabitha—or any of the other Babbitt & Brooks stars.

I was immediately rewarded. Ray exited Tabitha Wentworth's trailer; Tabitha, wearing a worn pink robe over her dress, followed him. Small in stature, with a cloud of dark brown hair and wide, hazel eyes, she looked her usual aloof self, and I couldn't tell how the news of Rebecca's death had affected her. As they passed Gail's trailer, Ray lightly ran up the stairs and knocked on Gail's screen door.

"I'm doing it now, Gail," he said through the door. "Tabby's coming with me." He didn't wait for a reply, just descended the stairs and rejoined Tabitha. The door slowly opened and Gail stepped out.

"I'm coming, too," she said. Her short, golden-blond hair shimmered in the afternoon sun.

Ray nodded and waited for her as she joined him and Tabby. Gail was dressed in a flowered Japanese silk robe and fluffy pink slippers. She took Ray's right arm, Tabitha took the left, and off they went. I brought up the rear, and if any of them noticed me, they made no sign of it.

The security guard tipped his hat at all of us, but only I smiled and nodded back. We continued past the pool area and entered the lobby as Carrie Benson, the second assistant director, came rushing up to us.

"The scene's not ready yet," she told Ray in near-panic. "They're still lighting."

"Don't worry," Ray said. "I need to make an announcement. And I'd appreciate it if you could get everyone to stop working and come over here."

Carrie looked at him blankly for a second, blinking rapidly, then nodded. I assumed she knew what the announcement was about because she calmed down and said, "Sure. Okay. No problem." She disappeared into the crowd and I could hear her yell, "Hey, everyone. Ray has an announcement to make. People! Please be quiet! Ray needs to speak."

Poor Carrie. The second AD's job was probably the worst in show business. After taking a rigorous test given by the Directors Guild, the second AD started off as a trainee, working his or her way up the ladder to first AD, some becoming UPMs like Patrick, others—with a bit of luck—branching into directing or producing. Carrie, with her thin blond hair and watery pale blue eyes, always seemed on the verge of panic, and Jennifer told me Babbitt & Brooks lost as many second ADs as they did assistants for Rebecca.

But gradually Carrie got the place calmed down and managed to direct everyone's attention toward Ray and the two actresses.

Ray was a tall man, and Gail and Tabitha seemed dwarfed next to him. He had his arm draped protectively around Gail's shoulders as she took a last nervous drag on her cigarette and ground it into the carpet with her bedroom slipper. As if demanding equal attention, Tabitha (Sandy said working out their billing for the opening credits had been a producer's nightmare) reached out a thin, blue-veined arm to Mack Daniels, who had worked his way up to the head of the crowd. He clasped her fragile hand in his huge paw, then enfolded her comfortingly in his arms. I was sure the crew, which held its collective breath waiting for Ray to speak, feared Armageddon: cancellation.

Ray, in command, head held firm, eyes steady, addressed the fifty or so people who had gathered around him with a clear, deep voice.

"I'm afraid I have some bad news to share with you," he said, and you would've been able to hear a pin drop if it had fallen from the wardrobe mistress's pocket to the floor. Beyond the lobby doors, on Wilshire, we could hear cars whooshing past, the occasional shout of a kid on a skateboard, a car honking. It seemed like another world, another lifetime.

"I'm sure you've heard the rumors." Several crew members nodded. "Late last night, after everyone had gone home for the day (Everyone? Or did you wait in your office, biding your time for the right moment, Ray?), our associate producer, Rebecca Saunders, was killed in her office—we think by a thief." Who just happened to send her two death threats in advance?

Someone gasped. All eyes remained concentrated on Ray, but the atmosphere was no longer filled with tense expectancy. We weren't being cancelled. That was the most important thing.

"I know you were on location yesterday," Ray continued. "But if any of you have any information pertaining to Rebecca's murder, please speak to me or the detectives in charge of the case. Call my assistant, Sandy, or talk to Susan over here." He nodded in my direction. "They have the names and numbers of the detectives in charge."

"Will the police want to question us?" asked an older woman with cropped grey hair. I had seen her earlier, sitting in a beach chair, reading a magazine, a hand mirror lying on top of a makeup case next to her. For some reason she looked nervously at Gail when she spoke, although Gail avoided her glance and seemed to shrink further into Ray's embrace.

Ray noticed and held Gail tighter as he answered the makeup artist. "Not at the moment, Irene," he said. "The case seems pretty cut and dried." It does?? Where were you when Rebecca was murdered, Ray? "However, I think we should all be available for questioning if the police need us, and if you are called in, Romulus will provide legal counsel to accompany you."

This didn't seem to make people feel any better, and they shifted uneasily, looking like they were ready to break ranks and relocate to Wyoming. I noticed Jesse Mendez standing at the head of the crowd, head up, ears practically twitching, as he stared at Ray. I wondered if his intensity had more to do with figuring out the best way to approach Ray for a continuing part than it did about the murder.

"Are there any more questions?" Ray asked. One of the electricians, a fat guy with a skull and crossbones tattoo on his right arm, spoke up. "Is production gonna shut down because of this?"

Murmured conversation ceased as everyone stared tensely at Ray.

"I don't know," Ray said. "Gail and Tabitha have expressed a willingness to finish filming for the day."

Tabitha put on a brave smile as if waiting for applause to follow this noble gesture, while Gail stared blindly over everyone's heads, looking like she needed a cigarette. "I've been on the phone with Cliff Rosen, and we'll decide about further filming later this afternoon. You'll all know for sure before we wrap tonight."

I had a feeling that whatever decision the president of Romulus Television and Ray came to would be based on the good of the show, rather than out of respect for Rebecca.

"Well, if you don't have any more questions, why don't we try to wrap this sucker so we can go home to our families?"

Ray was sounding a little "Let's win one for the

Gipper"-ish, but he didn't get any corresponding cheers or high-fives. The crowd slowly broke up and returned to their jobs. Tabitha moved off, still clutching Mack. Patrick hovered nearby, and Ray turned to him. "You and I need to talk in case we shut down."

Patrick nodded. Ray turned to Gail, his voice gentle.

"Why don't you go back to your trailer? It's going to be a while." Gail nodded, but didn't move from under Ray's arm. "Would you prefer some company?" he asked her. She nodded again, blue eyes staring vacantly over his shoulder, and Ray caught my eye.

"Susan, go back with Gail. Whatever she needs, take care of it for her."

I looked at him for a second. Was he really asking me to take care of Gail Neely? And would Gail Neely really want me to take care of her?

Gail didn't seem to mind one way or the other, because she moved out from under Ray's arm and shuffled off like an old lady, heading back outside to her trailer. I started off after her. She crossed from the pool area to the parking lot, walked up the stairs to her trailer, opened the screen door, and stepped inside. I hesitated at the bottom of the steps, took a deep breath, then followed her in.

The trailer was gorgeous. Everything was decorated in pinks, greens, and yellows. A double bed covered in a rose-patterned Ralph Lauren quilt took up the far left end of the room; a fully equipped, galley-sized kitchen took up the right. In the middle was a half-opened door that led to the bathroom as well as an open closet filled with clothes. I thought of my dreary studio apartment and practically drooled in envy.

Gail was at the narrow kitchen counter, fumbling for her Winstons, yanking out a cigarette, and lighting it with shaky fingers. Was she really that affected by Rebecca's death? Or was she playing the role of bereaved coworker for my—and the crew's—benefit?

"Can I get you anything?" I asked, still not convinced she wanted me in her trailer.

"A scotch would be nice," she said, taking a deep drag off her cigarette and sinking into one of the chairs next to a table by the counter. "No ice."

She leaned her head back against the window and blew smoke into the air above her. "Bottle's in the cabinet above the sink."

I walked into the galley kitchen and reached for the cabinet above the sink. Gail seemed to have every kind of liquor ever invented, and it was amazing to me that she could drink all this and still get up at four o'clock each morning to be at the makeup trailer by five, to look as elegant and beautiful and sophisticated as she did in front of the camera.

I snuck a glance at Gail, who still sat at the table, smoking and staring into space. "Glasses are in the cabinet next to the booze," she said, without looking at me.

I reached for the Johnnie Walker Black, grabbed a glass and poured the golden liquid halfway full.

I handed her the drink and hovered nearby while she flicked ash from her cigarette into a crystal ashtray before taking a sip from her glass. She nodded at the chair opposite the table from her.

"Have a seat."

I complied, still not believing I was now sitting in Gail

Neely's trailer. Gail and Tabitha usually shared a personal assistant, grudgingly paid for by Romulus. The assistant was invariably fresh off the farm, starry-eyed and young, who cheerfully accepted the minimum wage salary for the privilege of working with two television stars. However, when the assistant discovered that the job was more about getting Tabitha's sunglasses fixed or picking up Gail's sweaters from the dry cleaners, she would immediately quit and go in search of better paying and more glamorous jobs. Their last assistant had left two weeks ago and Gail and Tabitha had not yet been able to find a replacement. As excited as I was about sitting in Gail's trailer, I wouldn't want to be doing it for the rest of my life. Especially since working for her also seemed to entail breathing Gail's cigarette smoke fourteen hours a day.

"Ray tells me you found her body," Gail said without any conversational preliminaries.

"Yes," I said.

"She was a good person. A good friend," Gail said, sounding like she meant it.

She stared at the smoke that rose to the ceiling, clinging there like a thin, white fog. The trailer smelled more like a sleazy cocktail lounge than it did an actor's dressing room, but then again, how would I know what an actor's dressing room smelled like? This was the first one I'd ever been in.

"Do you think she suffered much?" Gail asked.

"I don't know," I lied. Of course she suffered. The woman had her head bashed in repeatedly by a crystal, rectangular object, not Monty Python's Spanish Inquisition soft pillow. Hadn't Ray given her any of the details?

"It was nice having a woman of some power on the show," Gail said. "Men write the scripts. What do they know about women?"

I kind of agreed with her but had to be fair. "Peggy's on the show," I said.

"Yeah, but she's completely intimidated by Ray. She does whatever he asks her to do."

I didn't know if that was true or not, but even if it was, it didn't stop Peggy from being a good writer. But I wasn't about to get into an argument with one of the stars of the show.

"That's too bad," was my noncommittal response.

"And Charles," Gail made a face, mashing her cigarette in the ashtray. "He knows fucking diddlysquat."

Now we were getting into dangerous territory. Not only was Charles my champion, but I truly thought he was the best writer on staff.

"Don't you think he's a good writer?" I asked.

Gail laughed. It was not a pleasant sound.

"I'd love to know where Ray dug him up. Do you know that Rebecca and I used to go through all his scripts line by line? She could really point out the groaners. Like yesterday's scene. With me and that judge in front of City Hall? I made Charles come to location and rewrite it."

I flashed back to yesterday when I had returned from my car to find Charles on the phone at Jennifer's desk, talking to Gail about her scene.

"Did Charles know Rebecca went over his script with you?"

"You better believe it, kid," Gail nodded, smiling grimly. "Hand me those cigarettes, will you?"

I moved to the counter where her pack of Winstons lay. But as I grabbed them, I was remembering Charles throwing an angry look in the direction of Rebecca's office. Maybe it hadn't been her laughter that was bothering him; maybe it was the fact that he had just learned Rebecca was egging Gail on over his writing.

I handed the cigarettes and book of matches to Gail and sat down again.

"I bet he wasn't too happy about it," I said.

"Who frigging cares whether he was happy or not? I'm the star of the show . . . not him or his sexist writing."

I suspected Tabitha Wentworth would have something to say about that, but I kept my mouth shut. And Charles's writing wasn't sexist by any stretch of the imagination. If Gail thought it was, I wondered if it was because Rebecca had planted that notion in her head. Rebecca . . . It looked like mine wasn't the only career she was trying to sabotage. If Charles knew that, would he have come back to the warehouse to have it out with her? Was he the visitor Rebecca was expecting last night?

"What time did Charles leave location yesterday?" I asked.

She shrugged. "What does it matter?" She paused, looking at me strangely. "You think he left here and killed Rebecca?"

"I don't know," I said. "I can't really picture Charles as a murderer."

"Oh, I don't know," Gail said, lighting another cigarette. I was never going to get the stench of cigarette smoke out of my clothes. "He's a man. And men are capable of doing anything. No exceptions."

Normally, I would've agreed with her; however, I liked Charles. But was I defending him because I thought he was incapable of murder or because he tried to get me a script assignment?

"So what time did he leave last night?" I asked.

"I told you—I don't know," Gail said, suddenly sounding edgy. "We worked on my scene, made some changes. I don't remember seeing him after that."

"Do you think he hung around to watch the scene being shot?"

I could see Gail was not thrilled with my persistence, but I couldn't understand why. The question had nothing to do with her, and if it got Charles in trouble (which I most certainly hoped it didn't), wouldn't she be that much more eager to answer? Instead, Gail looked annoyed and flustered, as if she were suddenly handed a new script which she hadn't memorized yet.

"Look, sometimes the writers hang around to make sure we say the lines the way they wrote them. And sometimes they don't. I got the changes I wanted, I said them word perfect, and that was the end of it. He didn't come up to me and say, 'Nice job, Gail,' so maybe he did leave, I don't know."

"What time did filming wrap last night?" I asked, trying to see if the timing would have fit.

"Seven forty-five," was Gail's prompt reply. Well, it was perfect timing. Sandy had left, Zack had probably left, Charles would have reached the warehouse around eight just when Sherman would usually be locking the door. Sherman wouldn't have needed to keep the door open for him because Charles had a key. Except he was notorious for losing his keys. Not only had Jennifer told me that, but I'd seen Charles turn his office inside out looking for his car keys on more than one occasion. If he couldn't find the key to the office, had he called Rebecca and told her he was coming and ask that the front door be kept unlocked? If Gail had made his life miserable on the set, and I suspected she probably had, Charles may have been out for Rebecca's blood. Literally. The only problem was I didn't want to believe he had killed her.

"He's a patronizing son of a bitch," Gail suddenly spoke up. "Thinking I don't know what's best for my character. Let's see him put on those goddamn heels and walk around in them all day."

Gail sounded more concerned over Charles's inability to write for her than she did over the possibility of his having killed one of her best friends. Jennifer would roll her eyes and call that typical. I was beginning to understand why production people referred to actors as children or cattle. They really did seem to operate on a different wavelength from the rest of us. Unless, deep down, Gail knew Charles wasn't the murderer. But that's ridiculous, I told myself. How would she know that?

There was a brief rap on the screen door, and then Ray walked in. I sat up straighter and Gail set down her cigarette, looking at him expectantly.

"They're ready to shoot the scene," Ray told her.

Gail nodded. "And I'm ready to be shot." She stood up and shrugged off the housecoat. Underneath she wore a beautifully tailored aquamarine suit that complimented her blue eyes and made her blond hair shine. She reached under the table, brought out a pair of blue suede high heels and put them on. Standing before me was the sophisticated and stunning Alexandra Brooks.

Gail noticed me staring at her, and she winked at me.

"Hard to believe, isn't it, kid?" she said as she started to walk toward the door. She passed Ray and patted him on the cheek. Ray caught her hand, staring at her in concern.

"You gonna be all right?"

She took a deep breath, smiled and nodded. "I'll be fine," she said, then stepped out the door.

"Let's make some magic here!" she shouted as I watched her move to a hovering Carrie and sling an arm around the surprised second AD's shoulder. Ray and I stood by the screen door and watched as Gail crossed the parking lot, suddenly surrounded by people fixing her hair, retouching her makeup, brushing the lint off her suit. Gail paused, eyes closed, face turned toward the sun, patiently holding still during these ministrations, acting like they were her due.

9.

The media was waiting for us by the time Ray and I returned to the warehouse.

"Damn," Ray muttered, as he signaled a turn into the parking lot. We could see them jostling for room by the gate leading to the lot entrance, their camera trucks and vans lined on both sides of the narrow street. As soon as they saw us, they came running over, and I think Ray would've spun the wheel and raced out, but they were already hanging over the car, shoving microphones and cameras into our faces. Ray had no choice but to pull into the first available space he could find, both of us trapped in the roofless car as the reporters pelted us with questions.

"Debra Chandler, Channel Eight News. Is it true, Mr. Goldfarb, the deceased was your associate producer?"

"No comment," growled Ray as he opened his door and slammed it into someone's knees. Debra Chandler must've adroitly stepped aside because the "Fuck" I heard in response was distinctly male.

"Did you work with the deceased?" a hair-sprayed Anderson Cooper wannabe asked me, a microphone swooping into my line of sight so quickly I reared back for fear it would knock my teeth out.

I don't know if I would've answered his question under other circumstances, but I had forgotten the location of the door handle and was preoccupied with groping around for it.

"Do you work here?" the Anderson clone persisted. "Do you know anything about the murder?"

Ray was already out of the car and heading for the front entrance, a pack of reporters baying close at his heels. He either had forgotten about me or assumed I could make it on my own because he flung himself up the steps and through the door without looking back.

With Ray gone, the reporters again fell on me, firing questions like the rat-a-tat-tat of machine guns.

"What's your name?" "What's your connection with the murdered woman?" "Do you work for Romulus Television?" "What is your relationship to Ray Goldfarb?"

I was so angry at Ray I was tempted to grab a microphone and announce to the six o'clock news that Ray and I were lovers and had been since I was thirteen.

Suddenly, a hand reached into the car and I drew back with a gasp. I stared helplessly as it reached for the door handle, pulled it up, and opened the door—or at least as far as it would open with a horde of reporters crowding around it.

"Come on, Suze, let's get you out of here."

I looked up. Sherman held his hand out to me, and I gratefully grabbed it as he practically dragged me from the car.

The reporters, of course, now spotted fresh meat, and went after both Sherman and me with renewed enthusiasm. Sherman put a protective arm around me, and we zigzagged through the melee, Sherman swinging open the door and steering me inside.

I paused, trying to catch my breath. Sherman and I both ignored the reporters who continued to shout questions at us through the door.

"You okay?" he asked.

I nodded, unable to speak for a moment.

Sherman looked like he wanted to take me in his arms and murmur, "There, there." But if he did, I knew I'd start bawling, so instead I turned away from him and started walking down the hall to the bullpen. "If they're still here when you're ready to leave," he said following me, "I'll sneak you out the back way."

I nodded my thanks, still trying to catch my breath.

"You know, I always believed in free press and freedom of speech and all that jazz, but this is ridiculous." Sherman smiled, trying to cheer me up. I smiled back weakly.

"After all," I said, "does Rebecca really deserve all this attention? She wasn't the nicest person in the world."

"Should I go back out there and tell them that?"

"I don't think her parents would appreciate it," I said.

"Or Ray."

Speaking of Ray, where was he? Sherman and I were standing right outside his office, and I feared Ray had overheard every word we said.

"He's in the men's room," Sherman said, reading my mind. "I saw him come blasting across the room, cursing about the media. I went to take a look and saw you still in the car."

"Thanks for rescuing me," I said. "You are truly my hero."

"Anytime."

"Have you heard any more from the cops?" I asked as Sherman walked with me back to my desk.

"Nothing. Though I wouldn't be surprised if they checked around my apartment building, looking for Rebecca's car."

"No! You really don't think—" I started to say, but stopped as Ray strode into the room.

"Susan, good," he said. "You made it all right."

No thanks to you, bud. Out loud I told him, "Sherman rescued me from the devouring hordes."

Ray nodded, his mind already moving on to other things. "Check for messages. I'll return the most urgent calls and then we can get out of here."

I stared after him as he turned the corner and went into his office. We still had to work? After the day we just had? The man must be out of his mind!

Sherman patted me on the shoulder. "You want me to kill him for you?"

"That's not funny," I said, sounding sharper than I meant to. I was immediately contrite. "I'm sorry."

"No, you're right. Especially if the cops bugged this place. Which wouldn't surprise me." On that comforting thought, he left.

I typed up a list of the messages left on voicemail and took it with me into Ray's office. Larger than the others, the room was also windowless. The teak furniture was new and the paneled walls were covered with framed photos of Ray's other television credits. The digital clock on the DVD player blinked 12:00, 12:00, 12:00, and the TV stand was surprisingly clear of the usual stack of dailies and directors' reels.

Ray sat behind his desk, talking into the speakerphone, simultaneously checking his e-mail on his iPhone. I hesitated in the doorway, but Ray nodded to a black-cushioned chair in front of his desk. I sat down.

"No, it was definitely a robbery," Ray was saying. "Her car's gone; so is her purse."

"What happened to the night watchman? Isn't he supposed to keep the doors locked?" I recognized Cliff Rosen. The president of Romulus Television's voice sounded tinny and distant on the speakerphone.

"He's supposed to," said Ray. "But he didn't."

Because Rebecca told him not to, I wanted to shout at the two men. I knew I couldn't do that; Ray would be furious and Cliff would be offended that Ray had put him on the speakerphone while someone else was listening in.

"Damn shame," said Cliff. In the meantime, I had grabbed a pad of paper and started scribbling a note.

"I know." Ray sounded sad, serious, and there was a

moment of silence between the two men. I pushed my note over to Ray. It said, "Rebecca told Sherman not to lock up." Ray read it, nodded, then crumpled it in his hand.

"So," Cliff spoke up again. "What should we do about production? Are the ladies willing to go on?"

"They're holding up like troupers. They say we should keep going."

"You crunch numbers with Patrick if we closed down for a week?"

Ray nodded at the speakerphone. Wasn't he going to tell Cliff about my note? "We lose a hundred thou a day for every day we're not filming."

Silence so thick you could poke holes through it.

"Then I think we should keep going," Cliff said. "It's what Rebecca would've wanted."

"I agree," said Ray. I tried not to laugh. What did Cliff Rosen know about what Rebecca would've wanted? Rebecca would've wanted the show closed down permanently as an eternal memorial to her. I remember Sandy telling me that Cliff fought bitterly against Rebecca's promotion to associate producer, forced to hire a post-production supervisor to do the work Rebecca's secretarial background had not trained her for. Her death would save him quite a lot of money—which made me wonder if Cliff had an alibi for the night of Rebecca's murder.

"Okay, so we'll just keep on rolling. You want to make a statement to the media or shall I?"

"I'll do it," said Ray. "They're waiting outside right now. Might as well give them something for the six o'clock news." He had the nerve to wink at me. Did he think we were compatriots because we battled the media blitz together? Remind me not to share a foxhole with this man during the next world war.

Cliff and Ray exchanged closing pleasantries then hung up. Once they had made their decision that the show must go on, neither seemed too concerned about keeping up the pretense about caring for Rebecca or her fate. Ray even smiled at me as he said, "Get me Patrick Hager at location."

"But, Ray, what about Sherman?"

"What about him?"

"Rebecca told him to leave the door open. So it wasn't his fault that she got killed."

"We'll see," was all Ray would say.

I remained sitting in Ray's office while he spoke with Patrick and told him that production would keep filming. I worried about Sherman. Should I warn him about the misconceptions floating around the office? Would it only serve to make him more angry, or would he be able to constructively use that anger to defend himself? I didn't know, and I was still gnawing away at it when Charles appeared in the doorway.

"Ray, we need to talk." Ray looked up from the phone in annoyance. "Now." Charles's face was paper white, his fists clenching and unclenching at his sides.

Ray spoke into the phone. "Patrick, we'll continue this later. Something's come up." He hung up the phone and stared at Charles.

"Have you been here all this time?"

"It doesn't matter where I've been." Charles stepped further into the office. "Susan, please excuse us."

I looked at Ray, who nodded. I got up and walked past Charles; I could almost feel the heat of his anger pulsing from his body. I exited the office, deliberately leaving Ray's door open. If something interesting was about to take place, I wanted to hear every word of it. Unfortunately, Charles closed the door firmly behind me. Rats.

In resignation I checked my computer for messages. I needed to distribute copies of yesterday's production report and tomorrow's call sheet, which listed the scenes being shot, their locations, the number of pages per scene, the actors needed for the day, and what times they had to be in makeup. I placed copies of both the production report and the call sheet in Zack's and Peggy's offices, noticing that the production coordinator who e-mailed them to me had already deleted Rebecca's name from the distribution list.

I sat back at my desk, straining to catch something—anything—from Ray's office, but could only hear Ray's and Charles's muffled voices. I picked up my copy of the production report for lack of something better to do. It listed the minutiae of the day's production: when shooting started and stopped, how many feet of film was used, how many camera set-ups were needed, and the times of the actors' arrival and departure from the set. Gail was right, production had wrapped at seven forty-five. I looked down at her initials, placed next to the time she had finished for the day. Then did a double-take. Gail had signed out at seven-fifteen, thirty minutes before filming had wrapped.

Had Gail lied to me? I tried to remember what I had

asked her. We were talking about Charles and when he had left the set. Gail said she didn't know, but she did know, rather promptly, what time the day's shooting had ended. I had just assumed she wrapped when production did. Gail hadn't exactly lied to me, but I had the distinct feeling she purposely misled me. I remembered how she didn't like my asking her questions about when Charles had left. Could it be she didn't know because she already had gone herself? But why not tell me the truth? Why act like she had something to hide?

Maybe Gail did have something to hide. Or maybe I was making mountains out of molehills. I had asked Gail when production wrapped and she had told me. But how would she know if she had left beforehand? Easy. She looked at the production report just like I was doing now. But why would she care when production wrapped, especially after she had already gone for the day? Or had she really gone? Had she stayed? And if she had, so what?

I shook my head, trying to convince myself none of this was important. But my instincts were telling me otherwise. I remembered Irene the makeup lady asking Ray if they were to be questioned by the police—and looking at Gail when she asked it. Did Gail have something to hide and the makeup lady knew it? Was she afraid she was going to have to lie to the police on Gail's behalf?

Did Gail leave at seven-fifteen, come here and kill Rebecca? Then learn what time production wrapped to mislead the cops? But they could read the production report as clearly as I could. I stared at Gail's hastily scrawled initials. Tell me what's going on, I begged the silent letters. But they remained obstinately mute.

"That's bullshit!" Charles suddenly shouted, and I jumped six feet out of my chair, swiveling my head in the direction of Ray's office door. "She was blackmailing you!"

"The hell she was!" Now Ray was shouting. "How dare you come in here and dictate to me!"

Charles's voice dropped again, much to my disappointment, and all I could hear was, ". . . you and Rebecca."

Ray's voice grew equally muffled; I heard a vehement, "That's not true," and then nothing.

Charles said something I couldn't make out, then the door flew open and he stormed out of the office. He looked neither right nor left, and if he knew I was at my desk, he made no acknowledgment of it. He turned the corner and left the building. Rebecca's office across from Ray's stood silent witness, the yellow police tape glowing like an eerie grin, the nameplate on her door, a single, blind, metal eye.

I wanted to get out of the building and I wanted to get out right then and there. But Ray was still in his office, although I heard neither the rattle of paper nor his voice on the phone. The bullpen seemed suffocating and claustrophobic as night descended, and the overhead fluorescent lights flickered and fizzled. I squelched my rising panic and turned back to the work on my desk. I picked up the production report, which I had thrown atop my desk calendar when I heard Charles shouting. I glanced at the calendar as I shoved the papers into some sort of pile to file at a later date. Something gnawed at the back of my brain—like the name of a movie I wanted to recommend to a friend but couldn't remember, seeing images, seeing the actors, while the name itself slipped elusively from the clutches of my memory. What was it? What was wrong?

Then Ray exited his office, and I lost the thought completely. His face was gray, eyes sunken.

"Go home, Susan," he said. "I'll deal with the phone calls tomorrow."

Without waiting for my answer, he started to turn back inside, pausing as his eyes swept past the door of Rebecca's office. After a momentary hesitation, he re-entered his office and quietly shut the door.

10.

I refused to check my messages while driving home, a firm believer that if anyone were to get mowed down by a 12-ton tractor trailer on the Santa Monica Freeway while texting it would be me. Peter used to joke that I was an old lady living in a young woman's body. Maybe that's why he slept with Casey Bitterman, a young woman in a young woman's body, instead.

With superhuman effort, I did not go on my Facebook page to see what Peter had posted about him and Casey today (yes, they were still together) and instead played back my phone messages. Twelve new messages. A new world record for my voicemail, which was used to getting one message a week and that from my mother who always sounded tense and nervous as if waiting for my smartphone to somehow reach through the digital miles and bite her. All my friends, of course, texted me or wrote me on Facebook.

"Hi, Susie-Q." My mother. Sounding cheerful, nervous,

and concerned, all at the same time. "Daddy and I just heard on the news about your boss. Just want to make sure you're all right. Give us a call when you get a chance. Love."

Well, Mom, I wasn't all right. I found my boss's dead body. Maybe I'm a suspect, maybe I'm not, and several colleagues seem to have a secret about the night of Rebecca's murder. But to tell her or my father any of that was simply not part of the game plan.

"Susan, it's Grandmom. I heard on the news that someone on your show got killed. I called your mother and she told me the same thing. Call me and let me know you're all right. Bye."

Good old Grandmom. I pictured her, sitting on her peach-and-green couch in West Palm Beach, eating leftover chicken from some Early Bird special while watching Brian Williams talk about Rebecca's murder. A wave of nostalgia and a sudden longing for her comforting presence washed over me.

"Hello? Susan? Are you there?" A pause. I recognized the Yiddish-accented voice immediately. My Fascist-fighting Buby, who lived in a one-bedroom apartment in Queens, over the candy store she and my many-years-deceased grandfather used to own. "Hello?" Another beat. She sounded sadder. "You're not home. Call me, honey."

Buby rarely called me in L.A., relying on my parents to catch her up on my news. So I knew the murder had her worried, too.

The rest of the calls were from various friends in New York and from college and grad school. I half-hoped Peter would call; even if he didn't read about Rebecca's murder on the Internet, our social grapevine would've kept him informed. But there was no, "My God, Suze, I heard what happened. Are you all right? I love you, I miss you. I dumped Casey Bitterman, please take me back!" issuing from my phone. I heated up a pot of Campbell's chicken noodle soup, and, after taking three deep breaths, called my parents.

"Susan." My mother didn't even say hello first. "What happened?"

"Someone killed Rebecca. They think it was a burglar or a homeless person." Best to start planting that in their minds early.

"Oh, my God. Brian Williams said it happened at work. You weren't there, were you?"

"No, Ma," I said. "I had already gone home for the day."

"Why can't they film at a regular studio?" my father wanted to know. "Why does it have to be in some dangerous part of town in the middle of nowhere?"

This was a recurring discussion with my father, who had dreams of my waving good morning to the guard at the Paramount studio gate each day.

"You think they'll move you to one of the studios now?" Dad continued. "Maybe you could go to some place like Universal and get the tour for free."

I didn't have the energy to explain that Romulus would have to pay an arm and a leg to rent space at Universal or any other studio for that matter.

"Dad, we're not moving so just forget about it."

"How are you, honey?" From my mother. "This doesn't involve you, does it?"

I was, as Robert Frost would say, at an interesting fork in the road. I could take the right fork and tell my parents that I was the one who found her body and might be considered a suspect. But I guessed my prediction would be they would completely overreact and hop the next plane to Los Angeles to bring me home. Although, on the other hand, sometimes when I've told my parents what I thought was earth-shattering news, they've nodded and said, "Uh-hum," and gone on to talk about something else. I wanted to tell them about finding the body—in fact, I was dying to tell them, but I simply could not predict their reaction. So, I took the left fork instead.

"The cops don't think it has anything to do with us," I said. "And guess what? I got to go on location with Ray and I spent the afternoon talking with Gail Neely in her trailer."

I thought I had made the perfect distracting feint, but instead I got, "That's nice, dear. But what about Rebecca? Who found the body?"

So, it was going to be the right fork after all. My head started to pound, and I squeezed the phone between my neck and shoulder as I poured the bubbling soup into a mug.

"I did," I said. "I found the body. I was the first one into work this morning and there she was."

There was a shocked silence at the other end of the phone.

Then my father spoke up, all business. "We'll get you a lawyer. I'll call Bernie and see if he knows anyone in California."

Bernie was my father's accountant/lawyer, married to

my mother's best friend from college. The last thing I wanted was my parents involving their friends.

"Dad, you don't have to worry. Romulus brought in a lawyer. He's representing all of us during the investigation. He was there when the police took our statements."

Okay, somewhat of a white lie, but I knew it would make my father feel better. And he did sound slightly mollified when he said, "What's his name? Maybe Bernie'll know him."

"Dad, I don't think Bernie knows him. He's with Romulus. He's okay." I sat down behind the kitchen counter and slurped soup from my white ceramic "What? Me stressed?" mug, under the quip, a drawing of a frazzle-haired person. My parents had given it to me as a joke during finals week my senior year of college. At that moment, the mug didn't look so funny to me.

I suspected my father would've pursued the subject of the Romulus lawyer, but my mother cut back in.

She asked, "Are you eating dinner?"

"Yeah. I just got in."

"What are you eating?"

My mother always wanted to know this. I guess she worried that I wasn't eating right—a fear that was usually justified.

"Chicken noodle soup. I have a headache."

Oops. Big mistake. Never, never, never tell my parents I don't feel well.

"Look, Susan, do you want me to fly your mother out to be with you?"

"No, dear, I'm not going out without you."

"We can't both go out. It would be too much for Susan. She'd feel more comfortable with you."

"And I told you, dear" (or, as my Brooklyn-born mother pronounced it, "deah"), "I'm not going without you."

I interrupted before this got out of control.

"Neither of you has to come out. I'm fine. Really. I told you, the cops think it was just a robbery. Her car was stolen. And her purse." Call me a coward, but I figured they didn't have to know about the death threats.

"Oh," said my mother. "She was alone in the building?"

"Yes," I said. "And it was late at night, and the night watchman once found cocaine in her desk."

"Cocaine?" said my father. "She was a drug addict?"

"I guess." Why did I have to open my big mouth?

"Did you know she was a drug addict?"

"No, Dad. But when the night watchman told me about what he found, it made sense. She had a cocaine personality."

"You never liked her anyway," said my mother, as if that made Rebecca's death more acceptable.

"I sure didn't," I said.

"Do the police know that?" From my worried father. Here we go again.

"No, Dad, they don't. Look, I'm really tired. And I want to finish dinner. Do you think you could call Grandmom and Buby for me? They left messages, too, but I think I'm just going to crawl into bed and call it a day. Just tell them you spoke to me and that I'm all right."

"Okay, honey, you go right to bed. That's probably the best thing. We'll call Grandmom and Buby."

"Thanks," I said, squeezing the word past the sudden

lump in my throat. I could treat my mother so horribly sometimes and yet she showed me nothing but love and concern in return.

"You're sure you're going to be all right, Susan?"

"Yes, Dad, I'll be fine. It's great material for my next script."

"We'll call later in the week, just to make sure you're okay," said Mom. In Mom language later in the week meant tomorrow. But I didn't care. I just wanted to get off the phone. In the past, I've begged my parents to text me more and call me less, and while my dad kind of got the hang of it, Mom refused, saying she'd rather hear the sound of my voice.

"Okay, talk to you later. Bye."

We all hung up. I was tempted to slide off my chair and lie on the kitchen floor. Maybe I'll never get up. Maybe I'll spend the rest of my life like this. After the day I just had, it was a pleasant thought.

The floor, however, was cold and dirty, and God only knew what was scuttling around underneath the peeling linoleum. So I stayed in my chair, taking tiny spoonfuls of soup, until someone began pounding at the front door. I looked through the peephole and opened the door to Craig Keefer, my next door neighbor.

"What the hell's going on, Susan? A detective came by to see me this afternoon," Craig said, brushing past me to enter the apartment. "He was asking about you." His blue-green eyes, magnified behind large tortoise-shell glasses, looked concerned as he paced the small room, favoring his right knee, which he had busted three years ago playing football his senior year at UCLA.

I ignored an onrush of anxiety and forced a smile. "Hi, Craig. It's nice to see you, too. How's the book going?"

Craig barely paused in his pacing. "Forget the book. I saw on the Internet that boss you hated was killed. This is serious shi— stuff."

"You can say shit in front of me, you know. I've heard the word used a couple of times before."

"Susan." He removed his glasses and rubbed his eyes, looking so worried, I dropped the act.

"I'm sorry," I said. "I'm trying to pretend I'm not as scared as I really am. Was it Detective Wagner who came to see you?"

"I think so. A black guy?"

I nodded. With a scar on his arm, I wanted to add, but didn't. "What did he want?" As if I didn't know.

"Was I with you last night . . . what did we do, where did we go . . ."

"And you said . . .?"

Craig combed a hand through his thick, sandy-blond hair. "I told him the truth. You came over around eight, we went to Baskin-Robbins for ice cream. He asked if anyone from Baskin-Robbins would remember us. I wanted to know why—I hadn't heard about the murder yet. He pulled a Sphinx-number on me."

I sat down on my sofa-bed, wanting to double over in fear, but refusing to give in to the anxiety. "The Romulus lawyer didn't think I was a suspect. Was he lying to me?"

"Susan . . ." Craig looked at me in concern. I flapped my hand in some sort of "Don't worry, I'm fine" gesture.

"So then what happened?"

Craig sat down next to me, his Levis brushing my

khakis. His blue-and-white striped Oxford shirt smelled of laundry detergent and aftershave. Not an unpleasant combination.

"We walked over to B-R. It was the same teenage kid behind the counter. She said she sort of remembered me because I come in a lot. But she couldn't remember whether I was with anyone or not."

She didn't remember Craig because he came in there a lot. She remembered him because he's cute. Out loud, I said, "Terrific. I feel like the Invisible Woman. What did Wagner say?"

Craig shrugged. "Nothing."

"Do you think he suspects me of murder?"

"I don't know. He gives the term 'poker-face' a new meaning."

"Tell me about it."

"What's going on, Susan? Why is some cop asking about you? Am I your alibi?" His Long Island accent, stronger than mine, seemed even more pronounced. Craig grew up in Great Neck, on the North Shore—a wealthier suburb than my middle-class hometown of Cohasset. But upon discovering we were both from Long Island, with the shared dream of becoming writers, Craig and I struck up a friendship that entailed occasional trips to Baskin-Robbins and intense discussions in the laundry room about writing. During months of rehab for a busted knee, Craig had started writing short stories to alleviate the boredom. When one actually got published in a small horror magazine, he decided to become a horror novelist. He wrote every spare second away from his job as swim instructor at the Beverly Hills Country Club. I found his concern for me thrilling, and as I launched into my story, I studied his expression, hoping to find more visible signs that he was ready to leap from friendship to dinner and a movie on Saturday nights.

I told Craig everything—about Rebecca's death threats, my finding her body, Wagner's apparent suspicion of me, Ray's lack of alibi and his bribing me with a script assignment to keep quiet, and ended with Charles's and Ray's argument in Ray's office. When I finished, Craig slumped against the wall, staring blankly at the built-in closet doors on the opposite side of the room.

"Fuck," he said.

"No kidding."

"So who do you think did it?"

"You mean you don't think it was me?" Although I was joking, I held my breath as I waited for his reaction. Craig turned to look at me, his expression one of utter disbelief. I slowly released the pent-up air, my anxiety lightening a little.

"I don't know who did it," I said. "Maybe her drug dealer. Or someone she thought was a friend." I paused. "Do you think I should tell the cops about Ray?"

"I don't know," Craig said.

"Should I take the script assignment?" I said. Craig once returned a ten dollar bill to a man who had unknowingly dropped it out of his wallet. There was no one more honest—or so I had thought.

"It's not that," he said. "His wife can't testify against him if she doesn't want to. Suppose you tell the cops what she said, but she denies it. The prosecution has no case—unless there's actual evidence that links him to the murder."

"So you're saying it's her word against mine."

"Exactly."

"But wouldn't the cops at least have to investigate Ray's alibi more closely?"

"Why should they if Winifred denies the whole thing? You overheard a cell phone conversation. Who knows what you really heard?"

"So you're saying I should take the script and run."

"No, I'm not. But if you go to the police, Ray will probably have you fired. And if he really did kill Rebecca . . ." He trailed off.

"Ray'll kill me?" I couldn't keep the disbelief out of my voice.

"Why not? He did it once. Who's to say it's not easier the second time around?"

"That's disgusting!" Nonetheless, I shivered.

"What did you expect me to say? I'm worried about you, Suze. You've got to be careful."

I loved the protective tone of his voice.

"The thing is," I said, "Rebecca made a lot of enemies. She didn't only go after me, she had it in for Jennifer and Sandy as well."

"Why?"

I shook my head.

Craig said, "Maybe if you found out, you'd find her killer."

"How do you figure that?"

He shrugged. "You told me once she couldn't keep an assistant for more than a couple of months. Obviously, she treated them as badly as she treated you—and Jennifer and

Sandy."

"You think the assistant I replaced might know something?"

"If Ray killed Rebecca, you could be in danger."

"And if he didn't and I blow his alibi, I could be out of a job."

Craig nodded. "Do you know the name of the assistant before you?"

"Lily something. I'm sure it's in my files."

"Wouldn't hurt to give her a call."

I thought about this. I was curious about Rebecca. Why was she so nasty to Sandy, Jennifer, and me? And was she so nasty to someone else, in a cross-the-line-kind of way, that that person killed her? Maybe her ex-assistant knew something about Rebecca that would prove Ray didn't kill Rebecca. Which means I could accept the script assignment with a clear conscience. I looked at Craig. "Okay. I'll track her down tomorrow."

"If I were you, I wouldn't say anything to anyone else about what you're doing."

"You think . . ."

"I don't know, Susan. For your sake I hope it is a homeless man. But better to be safe than sorry."

11.

I lay in bed that night, listening to my thudding heartbeat and overwhelmed by a sense of doom. I kicked off the covers at five, wishing there were some way I could machete my way through the stifling blanket of anxiety and be the person I was before Rebecca's murder. I jumped in the shower, which only made me feel worse. Maybe it was the hot, suffocating temperature of the water, the billowing clouds of steam fogging the bathroom mirror, or the claustrophobic sense of being crowded in a small area behind a large, opaque curtain. I fully expected Norman Bates to burst in, rip the curtain off its track, and stab me repeatedly with one of the carving knives I kept in my kitchen drawer.

Breakfast was out of the question, the thought of my usual Cheerios and milk made me want to gag. I wanted to get out of my apartment but the memory of finding Rebecca's body the last time I went to work early stopped me from leaving. I checked my smartphone—a graduation gift from my parents—for messages. A friend from back East had sent me a link to Peter's Facebook page and, against my better judgment, I clicked on.

"Congratulate us!" wrote Peter. "Casey and I are getting engaged. Wedding is June 24. Save the date!"

The phone slipped from my hand and my eyes filled with tears. I ran out of the apartment as if I could escape Peter's announcement.

Somehow, I found my way to the studio. I had no memory of how I got there, my mind on automatic pilot. It was amazing I hadn't rear-ended cars on the freeway or run anyone over. If I stumbled across another body at least the horror of it would distract me from Peter and Casey the Bitch's wedding.

To distract myself I checked the files and found the name and contact information of Rebecca's previous assistant, Lily Wainess. I sent her a text, telling her I was the writers' assistant who replaced her and could we talk as I had questions to ask her about the job. No sense in alerting her about my real reason, which was Rebecca.

I paused, thinking I should go into Ray's office and search for any evidence to show he may have killed Rebecca but, suddenly overcome with the news of Peter's engagement, I sat at my desk, with tears running down my face. What was it about me Peter didn't love? Was I too ambitious? Did I not pay enough attention to him? And would I have changed if I had known I would lose him? No, I said to myself. I would never have been happy sacrificing my own dreams to make his happen. But that still didn't make the pain hurt any less.

Afraid Sherman might see my car and come by to say hi, I grabbed a tissue from the box on my desk, blew my nose, swiped my eyes, and headed toward Ray's office. I hesitated at his doorway, feeling guilty about prying through his stuff. But if he was guilty of murder and concluded I might tell the cops he lied about his alibi, my life could be in danger. So I quickly found myself behind Ray's desk, opening drawers, without even being conscious of having crossed the room.

The drawers revealed nothing but loose pens and paperclips, rubberbands, and a half-empty box of Tic Tacs. The top of his desk held production reports and interoffice memos placed in the out tray for Sandy to file. His desk was swept clean of paper and phone messages. Babbitt & Brooks scripts were neatly tucked into black, three-ring binders on the credenza, and I couldn't help but stare at Ray's Women in Television Award, used as a bookend for the notebooks. The triangular crystal sculpture winked at me ominously.

The ceiling creaked overhead. I looked up sharply. Mice? Rats? Or something human?

Above me was a loft-like attic space. It remained unused, even for storage. So why would anyone be up there? I hurried to the bullpen, following the creaks. I was halfway to my desk when the ceiling caved in.

Water from the pipes supplying the overheard fire sprinklers gushed down like Niagara and Victoria Falls combined, flooding my desk and causing my chair to rocket backward against the wall of Rebecca's office with a bang. I screamed—more out of surprise than fear.

Footsteps pounded down the length of the ceiling. I stared up in shock then instinctively followed the sound, until I hit the vast, empty basketball court. The footsteps disappeared.

The stairs to the loft were on the production side of the building, and I wasted several minutes hammering on Sherman's locked door, hoping to convince him to come with me. When he didn't answer, I ran across the plank that linked the writers' warehouse to the production building, following the muted sound of voices and the glow of bright lights until I hit the set used for the Babbitt & Brooks law office.

I skirted around T-shirted men with beer bellies calling to each other from different parts of the room, adjusting Klieg lights from scaffolding above the set and connecting cables that snaked around it on the floor below. Under the harsh glare of the work lights, the set for the Babbitt & Brooks law office looked stagey, forlorn without the actors inhabiting it. Even as I raced past I noticed that the view of the Upper West Side of Manhattan, as seen through the office window, was clearly a paint job. The black leather office couch held someone's well-marked script, and the various antiques scattered around the room were roped off, a sign "Hot set. Do not touch." hanging from the rope.

Ignoring curious glances, I turned the corner and raced up the rickety wooden stairs hidden behind the painted backdrop showing a view of Queens from Hank Babbitt's apartment. I turned the doorknob leading to the attic. It was locked. When I asked nearby crew members if they saw anyone coming down the stairs, they shook their heads no.

To my relief, Patrick Hager and Mack Daniels stood near the law office set in conversation with one another. I pushed past the sound mixer's cart and made a beeline for them.

"The ceiling above my office collapsed," I said, gasping for breath. "Water came gushing down and soaked everything."

The two men gave me the once over, and I realized I had not entirely escaped the flood. My tan khakis were wet with water that had ricocheted off the desk, and my crotch was damp. I looked like I had peed in my pants. I casually put one leg in front of the other, as if that would somehow make the stain less noticeable.

"Let me take a look," Patrick said. Mack looked relieved he didn't have to be involved and turned away to discuss lighting with Rick Froehlich, the DP. I led Patrick back to the bullpen in silence.

The room was soaking wet and there was a huge, gaping hole above my desk where water still dripped. Chunks of plaster hung from the ceiling and lay scattered around the floor. The carpet squooshed under our feet.

"I heard footsteps," I told Patrick who stared in dismay around him. "In the attic. Do you think someone did this on purpose?"

Patrick brushed the cowlick off his forehead. "I doubt it. What would be the point? Looks like a burst water pipe to me."

I walked over to my desk, afraid to get too near my computer should it electrocute me. A small lake had formed in the center of my desk, with yesterday's production report and call sheet clinging wetly to its surface. The papers I had intended to file had been swept off by the tidal wave that had exploded from above.

"Lucky you weren't sitting there when it happened," Patrick said, squeezing my arm in sympathy.

I stood rooted to the damp carpet and shivered.

"I could've been killed."

12.

"They say bad luck comes in threes," Jennifer said, later in the morning, after she had time to absorb the disaster herself. "I wonder what'll happen next?"

"Shut up, Jen," Sandy said mildly as she walked into the bullpen. She carried a yellow legal-sized pad covered with notes.

"What's being done about this?" I asked her. Patrick had gone up to the attic with a couple of the workmen who were knocking the two warehouses together. They discovered that a water pipe leading to the fire sprinklers had, indeed, burst. They were chalking my claim of hearing footsteps to an overactive imagination. I wasn't as convinced.

"The water's turned off until the pipe can be temporarily repaired, so don't use the bathroom." Oh, great, I thought, suddenly feeling a pressure on my kidneys.

"It also shorted out the phone wires for this end of the building so at least you'll have some peace and quiet for a while. If you have to use the phone, use the one in the production office. I called the main office. They said to make a list of what's ruined and they'll deal with the insurance people. They also said not to touch anything electrical."

"No shit, Sherlock," Jennifer said.

"What about my desk?" I asked. "What should I do with the stuff on it?"

"Throw away the papers—unless there's anything desperately important that can't be replaced. In fact, throw away everything. This place is damp under the best of circumstances. We need to avoid mold."

She went off toward her office as Jennifer tossed me a trash bag and told me to get to work. But I felt overwhelmed by the task, the reality of Rebecca's death finally catching up with me.

My chair was too damp to sit on, and I could feel the wetness of the carpet soak through my moccasins. The air was dank and sticky, and I longed to be sitting out in the sun, letting the heat dry me out. Instead, I finally opened the trash bag and, with a sigh, began dumping the soaking wet papers, including last night's call sheet, into it.

"You know, my desk supplies will eventually dry out," I told Jennifer.

"So what? Romulus will get us new ones."

"Yeah. But how long will that take?" The company was notorious for stinting on office supplies.

"True, true," said Jennifer, although that did not dissuade her from dumping her calendar and stapler, three-hole punch and pencil sharpener into the bag with equal abandon. "I'll just go to the supply store and charge it to Charles's account."

I wished I could do the same, but I knew that while Jennifer would easily furnish herself with color-coordinated office supplies, I would be waiting an eternity just for a ballpoint pen. I decided to box whatever of my stuff was salvageable and stow it in the supply closet until it all dried out.

"What am I going to do about Zack's script?" I asked Jennifer as I stared at my electrically lethal computer.

"Borrow Sandy's computer," she said. "Though I'll bet you five dollars Zack isn't going to be writing today."

That was a good bet so I refused to take her up on it. Everyone seemed to be moving underwater, swimming with difficulty through the morning, holding their breath, looking barely able to keep afloat. Ray had left to make calls from his car, which Jennifer and I thought was hilarious—although we did pity Sandy, who had to sit in the passenger seat and dial the numbers for him.

Charles told Jennifer he was going to babysit the set and make sure Gail was happy with her lines. Peggy, probably anxious for something to do, volunteered to go with him, and as I watched them leave I wondered if Rebecca's death

meant less summonses to the set for Charles. Shortly
afterward Zack entered the bullpen and told me he was
going to take a walk. Jennifer and I once took a walk
around the desolate, litter-strewn neighborhood and
counted our blessings we had made it back to the
warehouse alive. But I suppose Zack could defend himself
if the need arose, and I merely nodded as he headed for the
front door, head bowed, shoulders stooped.

I couldn't help feeling sorry for him, although I didn't
want to—not after the way he had hurt Peggy. But he
looked so sad, so pathetic. A small, mean voice in me
wondered if what he really felt was guilt.

"I'm going to get some boxes from the production
office," I told Jennifer, kicking the small, mean voice out of
my head. "Hold down the fort."

Jennifer saluted before sweeping a used bottle of rubber
cement and soggy B&B stationery from her desk and into
yet another trash bag. I walked down the writers' corridor,
pausing before Charles Green's office.

His door was open, the office empty. Knowing he was
on the set, and probably would be for a while, the
temptation to snoop was too much to resist. Especially
after having whetted my nosiness appetite in Ray's office. I
ducked into the room, closing the door partway behind
me. Maybe I could find something that would tell me why
Charles had fought with Ray about Rebecca the night
before.

I began shuffling through the piles of paper on his desk,
sifting through the accumulated call sheets and production
reports, script pages and casting notes. Nothing
incriminating. I pulled his black acrylic wastebasket from

under his desk and went through the papers systematically, smoothing them out, reading them then tossing them back in the wastebasket when they revealed nothing of importance.

I paused at one of the pieces of paper on the bottom of the pile. It had been wadded into a small, wrinkled ball, and when I smoothed it out, my eyes widened as I read its contents.

"What the hell are you doing?"

I was so surprised I nearly fell backwards. Jennifer had pushed the door all the way open and was staring at me in amazement. I straightened up and tried to look calm.

"Are you out of your fucking mind?" She took two steps into the room, glaring at me. "What's going on here?"

"Jennifer." I stopped, my mouth opening and closing like a fish drowning in oxygen.

"This better be good, Susan. Or I start screaming for Charles right now."

I took a deep breath. When I had my thoughts in order, I said, "Charles and Ray had this huge fight about Rebecca. Last night. After you guys left."

"I don't believe you," she said, but I could tell by her expression that she actually did.

"Charles was furious. He stormed out of Ray's office. I had to see if there was anything here that revealed why he was so angry."

"And is there?"

I handed her the crumpled page I found in the wastebasket. It was the memo Sandy had shown me, promoting Rebecca to co-producer and giving her two script assignments.

"The memo didn't go out," I said. "Sandy told me that. Ray changed his mind. So how did Charles get a hold of this?"

Even more important, had Charles learned of the promotion before Rebecca was murdered? And if so, had he bashed her head in during a killer rage as a result? Before Ray had a chance to tell him she wasn't getting promoted after all?

But before I could ask Jennifer she whirled around and fled the office, taking the memo with her.

13.

"Don't say a word. Not a whisper, not a peep," Jennifer hissed at me, as we huddled over the office coffeemaker back in the bullpen. She had taken the memo, ripped it into tiny shreds, and stuffed it at the bottom of one of the Hefty trash bags that held damp scripts and files.

"Jennifer, you're being totally irrational about this," I hissed right back at her. "Just because he saw the memo, doesn't mean he killed her."

"I don't care, Susan. Promise me. You won't say a word to anyone until I figure this thing out."

"Why are you being so protective of him?" I paused, my hand automatically going to my mouth. "You're not . . .?"

She cut in, angry. "We're not fucking. Geez, Susan, get your mind out of the gutter."

It seemed to me Jennifer was the one who usually had her mind in the gutter, not me. Not that I would ever point that out to her.

"So, why the freak-out?"

"None of your business."

"Jennifer, he could have killed Rebecca over her promotion."

"He didn't."

"Do you know that for sure?" I asked.

Jennifer looked away, tearing at the cuticle of a well-manicured finger.

Into her silence, I said, "I like Charles, too. But just because he's your boss, it doesn't mean he's innocent."

The words burst out of Jennifer's mouth. "He lends me money, okay?"

"What do you mean he lends you money?"

"You think I can afford my apartment in Marina del Rey on what I make as a secretary? Steve's T-shirt shop doesn't bring in steady money, especially in this economy. So, Charles . . . helps me."

I stared at her dubiously. "That was very generous of him."

Jennifer glared. "God, Susan, I'm not his mistress. He loves Ingrid." His wife.

I took a step back, held my palms up. "Okay, okay."

She softened. "He and my dad went to college together. They were fraternity brothers. So when I moved out here, Charles hired me. And when my dad died, he left my mom and me without any money . . . and . . . and Charles helps out."

Which explained the designer clothes, I thought. Out loud, I said, "I'm sorry. I didn't know."

"'Cause I didn't tell you."

"So, what are you going to do about Charles and that memo?"

"I don't know. I need time to think."

Jennifer looked close to tears, and I knew she didn't want to do anything. She was hoping that if I kept my mouth shut, the memo would just go away—as if it had never existed.

"You know, Peggy or Zack could've killed her," I said. "They both had motives, too."

But Jennifer wasn't listening to me. All she cared about were the repercussions the memo had against her beloved boss. If Jennifer was this concerned, I wondered if she knew something else that pointed toward Charles's guilt.

"Okay, let's say the worst happened, and it was Charles who killed her," I said. "Why did he have a blowout with Ray about it after she died? What possible difference could it make then?"

"Ray could have been involved in whatever it was that killed Rebecca. Maybe Charles would have killed Ray if you hadn't been sitting right outside the office."

Now there was a thought. I went over the tenor of the muffled voices in my mind, wondering if there was any point where Charles could've grabbed Ray's Women in Television Award and smashed him over the head with it—only holding back due to his awareness of my presence in the next room.

"Nah, I don't think so, Jen. I don't think Charles remembered I was there. He didn't even look at me when he stormed out of the office."

"I hope you're right," Jennifer said.

To make her feel better, I told her about what I

overheard Winifred say to Ray in the car on the way to location. Jennifer's reaction was to hand me the telephone receiver.

"Call Detective Wagner. And you tell him about that right now!"

The decision made for me, I took the receiver from her, surprised to hear a dial tone. The phones were back online. Was this Fate telling me that calling Wagner was the right thing to do?

I fished out his card from my purse and dialed the number printed on it.

"Hollenbeck Division. Detective's room," a gruff male voice answered.

"Detective Wagner, please," I said, suddenly nervous. "It's Susan Kaplan calling."

There was a moment of dead air as I was put on hold. I almost hung up, now rethinking the idea of stirring muddy waters. Then I heard the familiar expressionless voice.

"Detective Wagner."

Too late. I had no choice but to say my piece. I introduced myself again then launched into my reason for calling. "Ray Goldfarb lied about his alibi," I said. I could mentally hear Craig screaming at me, but he wasn't a potential person of interest in a murder investigation.

Wagner, however, didn't seem even momentarily fazed.

"Really," was all he said in reply. The man was infuriating!

"He probably told you his wife picked him up and took him home." Wagner didn't say a word. I sensed his skepticism but marched on determinedly.

"Well, she didn't." I told him what I overheard Winifred say on Ray's cell. "Then he tried to bribe me into keeping quiet by offering to hire me to write a Babbitt & Brooks script."

"He actually told you it was a bribe to keep quiet?" Finally, Wagner was showing some interest.

"Well, no, not exactly." Over the phone I heard a chair squeak and figured Wagner's interest was fading so I quickly added, "But he said he'd read my Dress Blue script again—I know now he really didn't read it the first time—and that he might give me the opportunity to write a Babbitt & Brooks script. And this is right after his wife just blew his alibi to pieces."

"We'll check it out," he said. He didn't seem the least bit excited.

Craig was right; I shouldn't have said anything.

"Thanks," I managed to say to the detective before slowly hanging up the phone.

"What did he say?" asked Jennifer, her eyes huge and her face pale with concern.

Before I could answer Sandy rushed into the room. "I just saw Sherman," she said, as Jennifer and I turned to face her. "He told me Ray fired him last night. He came back this morning to pack up."

14.

Sherman was in his office, wrapping the cord of his tiny TV set, when I knocked on his door.

"Sandy told me," I said. "Are you all right?"

"I'll live." But he didn't look it. His eyes were red-rimmed and his long arms seemed skinny and boney sticking out from the sleeves of his Dodgers T-shirt.

I was furious. "I told Ray that Rebecca told you to leave the door unlocked."

"It doesn't matter, Susan. I wasn't doing my job."

"Even though she told you—"

He interrupted me. "She's not around to back me up." He placed the TV set at the bottom of the beat-up cardboard box sitting on his desk. "Ray said I shouldn't have listened to her. He said I should've locked the door and waited for the person to knock and then let him in."

"And if he had been perfectly acceptable and you had let him in and he'd killed Rebecca, would you have gotten fired then?"

"Probably."

"What are you going to do? Can you sue them for unfair firing or something?"

"I don't want to spend the rest of my life in court," he said as he continued to pack odds and ends into the carton. "I have a friend who knows some people who are looking for a night watchman, and she's going to recommend me to them."

"Sherman, that's great!"

He hefted the carton in his arms. "Yeah, well, we'll see."

He paused, getting ready to say good-bye. I couldn't face that yet, so I said, "I'll walk you to your car."

"You can walk me to production. I have to turn in my keys."

I almost lost it then. Never again seeing Sherman walk across the basketball court, his keys jangling musically from his belt loop. His friendly smile. His never-ending supply of sympathy and support. I looked away from him as I stepped back to let him squeeze out of the office. In silence we walked across the court to the narrow wooden plank that led to the production offices and sets.

When the network renewed Babbitt & Brooks last May, Romulus decided to open their usually tight purse strings and knock the two warehouses together. Workmen were constantly crawling around the two areas, or working in the long, narrow, cement-lined ditch that divided the buildings. The single plank was the only means available to cross from one building to the other without going outside and around.

The plank bowed slightly in the middle under our combined weights. Sherman let me precede him as I avoided the stares of the grimy construction workers in the cement-lined pit below, letting out an unconscious sigh of relief as I made it to the other side.

"Can't say I'll miss those guys," he said, glancing down as we headed over to the production office. I looked at him in surprise.

"They don't bother you, do they?"

He hefted the box more firmly in his arms. "They give me bad vibes."

They gave all of us bad vibes, and I'd be glad when the construction work was done and they were out of our lives. I stopped wearing skirts to work the day I realized the workmen tried to look under them whenever I used the plank to get to the other side.

Miranda Peterson, the production coordinator, was expecting Sherman.

"I heard about it from Patrick," she said, looking at

Sherman from over a mound of paperwork. "Ray Goldfarb's a dickhead."

Sherman and I both looked at her in shock. In her mid-twenties, with baby-fine blond hair and cool blue eyes, Miranda looked like someone who'd never even heard the word "dickhead" much less say it.

"You won't find any argument from me," said Sherman. He set his carton down carefully on the edge of her desk. "I believe I owe you some keys."

He started to unhook them from his belt loop. "I have half a mind to let you keep them," Miranda said, further surprising me. "Then you can come in when no one's around and use the photocopier."

Will wonders never cease? Don't-touch-my-supplies-under-penalty-of-death Miranda Peterson was telling Sherman to just come on in and make himself at home? I almost pinched myself, but I don't like pain.

"Thanks, Miranda," Sherman said. But he handed her the keys anyway, just as her phone rang.

"Production," she said. She paused, paled then said, "Okay. I'll tell him." As she hung up the phone she screamed across the room to Patrick, who was sitting in his office at the computer.

"Patrick, that was Carrie. Gail's having hysterics on the set. No one can control her."

Patrick tore out of his office. "Call Ray," he said as he raced out the door.

Miranda picked up the phone to dial again as Sherman and I looked at one another.

"What do you think?" I asked him.

"It's too good to miss," he replied, and I was pretty sure

he was right behind me as I raced out the door in close pursuit of Patrick.

A crowd of people stood around the set of the Babbitt & Brooks law office. I could hear Gail screaming and crying from halfway across the warehouse. Patrick elbowed his way through the crowd and I followed in his wake. He made straight for Gail, who avoided the comforting words and embrace offered by Mack Daniels. Charles and Peggy hovered nearby, while Tabitha stood tensely behind one of the desks, her mouth a thin, tight line. Patrick put a hand on Gail's arm and she acted as if she had been scalded, jumping away from him, her voice hoarse from screaming.

"Who the fuck did this?" she yelled at Patrick, waving a newspaper in his face. It was crumpled and mashed and tearstained, but even from a distance I could tell it was one of the weekly rags, the National Scoop. Or, as the wits among us called it, the National Pooper Scooper.

"How did this happen? Where did they get this?" As both Patrick and Mack reached out placating hands toward her she screamed, "Don't touch me! Just tell me where they got this!"

She held the newspaper before her, showing it to them, but also giving me a chance to read it for myself: "TV STAR LINKED IN LESBIAN LOVE AFFAIR" blared the headlines. And there, for all the world to see, was a color photo of Gail and Rebecca, eyes half-closed in enjoyment, kissing each other on the mouth.

END OF ACT TWO

ACT THREE

1.

"I knew it all along," Jennifer said, after the fireworks died down, and Ray had led a sobbing Gail back to her trailer. "There were rumors floating around about her and Karen Kearney when Charles and I worked on Karen's show three years ago."

Sandy, Jennifer and I were in the bullpen, huddled around the Scoop, which was spread out on Jennifer's desk. I had managed to grab the paper after Ray walked on the set. Gail had gone straight into his arms, the paper slipping from her fingers onto the floor. As soon as Gail and Ray had left, Mack snatched it up, looking for a place to get rid of it. I approached him and said I'd take care of it. As I tried to fold the paper into some semblance of order, Mack turned to Tabitha and asked her what she wanted to do.

"Can we shoot around her until she calms down?" Tabitha asked, managing to sound sympathetic yet professional.

"That's fine with me, but will you be able to do it?"

Tabitha offered him a brave little smile. "I think so."

But her eyes were cold, and I realized with a start that Tabitha didn't like Gail very much. I wondered if Tabitha thought forging ahead without her co-star was a way of one-upping Gail.

Mack gave Tabitha's arm a comforting squeeze and the crew looked relieved to be carrying on as usual. Tabitha basked in the glow of everyone's approval, and I turned back to look for Sherman to find out what his opinion of all this was.

Only he wasn't there. I searched the crowd of bustling crew members and even glanced in on a few of the other sets. No Sherman. When I returned to the production office, Miranda told me he had grabbed his box full of office stuff and headed toward the parking lot. He hadn't even stopped to say good-bye.

"Do you think this means Ray and Rebecca weren't having an affair?" Jennifer asked, breaking into my train of thought. Sandy made a face at her.

"I can't believe you'd accept this rubbish for the truth," she said.

"I was there when Gail got the news about Rebecca," I said, defending Jennifer. "She was pretty torn up about it."

"Rebecca could be bisexual," Jennifer said. "Plenty of people in this town are."

"Where do you think they got the picture?" I asked, studying it closely. Both women were dressed for some sort of gala occasion; both held glasses of wine. While the Scoop article assumed their eyes were half-closed in passion, one could easily conclude it was drunkenness instead.

"The Women in Television Awards ceremony," Sandy said. "Or perhaps last year's Christmas party."

"But why wait to reveal the picture now?" I wanted to know. "The Scoop wouldn't hold on to something this good for so long."

"Rebecca wasn't important then," Sandy said.

She had a point. The article, while hinting at Gail's possible past lesbian relationships, made a big deal out of Gail being the lover of a murdered woman. "Was Rebecca killed in a fit of jealous rage?" the article asked.

That couldn't be why Gail lied to me, I thought. Or could it? Would Gail have killed Rebecca out of jealousy? But out of jealousy over whom?

"Do you think Gail was jealous because she found out Rebecca was having an affair with Ray?" I asked out loud. Jennifer looked like she thought that was a pretty good idea, but Sandy shook her head. "To tell you the truth I don't think Ray and Rebecca were having an affair at all."

"You don't?" Jennifer looked at her aghast.

"Don't you remember the Christmas party? You and I were standing by the buffet table and Rebecca joined us?" Sandy turned to me to explain. "She was quite drunk, but that wasn't anything new. However, out of the blue she asked us if we thought she and Ray were having an affair."

"You're kidding?" I said. "What did you say?"

"We said yes," Jennifer piped in. As I stared at her in surprise, she added defensively, "Well, at least we told her the truth."

"So what did she do?"

"She broke down and cried," Sandy said. "She claimed

they weren't, that they were more like father and daughter. And I believed her."

"Why? Wouldn't she say that because she thinks that's what you wanted to hear?"

"Of course," Jennifer said. But Sandy looked unconvinced.

"Ray has three daughters by his first marriage. One's more crackers than the next—at least by Ray's standards. None of them are ambitious. Or particularly bright. I think Ray saw Rebecca as the daughter he never had. The one who was going to follow in his footsteps."

"He still could've slept with her," Jennifer said, reluctant to give up her theory.

"Charles thinks Rebecca was blackmailing Ray," I said, referring to the argument I overheard the two men having.

"She could have been blackmailing him over their relationship," Jennifer said, looking defiantly at Sandy.

Sandy sighed, giving up the battle. "Perhaps. I can see her as a blackmailer, I just can't see her as bisexual."

We all stared at the photo. "Maybe that was why she didn't want to get serious with Zack," I said. "But she didn't want to come right out and admit it."

"Do you think Gail will sue over this?" Jennifer asked.

"I doubt it," Sandy answered. "It would only keep this in the news longer, which is the last thing Gail wants."

"She really was bent out of shape about it," I said. "But who really cares? Does anyone believe this stuff anyway?"

"You do," Sandy said. I didn't have an answer to that because I knew it was true.

"Maybe someone's out to get us," Jennifer said. "Maybe the Scoop didn't have this picture on file, maybe someone gave it to them."

"But who? And why?" Sandy asked.

"Someone with a grudge against the show. Or Gail. Even Ray. I mean, how did this rag get on the set anyway? Gail would've had hysterics wherever she saw it. So it had to be lying around. And no one with any ounce of decency would leave this where Gail could find it. Maybe it was deliberately left on the set for her to see."

"So someone first murdered Rebecca to upset Gail and when that didn't work he put this story in the Scoop?" Sandy looked doubtful. "Don't you think that's a bit of a stretch?"

"Why?" I asked. "What if the purpose is to shake up the show? Maybe whoever killed Rebecca hoped we'd close down production—either because Gail couldn't go on, or because Ray would do the compassionate thing."

"So you think someone is really after Gail?" Sandy still looked skeptical.

"Or Ray," I said, remembering Winifred. If Ray didn't have an alibi for the night of Rebecca's death, then neither did his wife.

2.

We heard from Miranda that Gail eventually calmed down enough to resume working, and Zack, returning from his walk, even managed to produce a few pages of Act Three, scrawled in his practically indecipherable handwriting on a yellow legal pad.

Looking tired and drawn, Zack handed the pages to me

just as Ray entered the bullpen. He clapped Zack so hard on the shoulder I thought he was going to stagger over my desk and fall face first into my lap. Fortunately for both of us, he recovered and looked at Ray with a shaky smile.

"Take a break with those," Ray said to Zack, nodding to the pages I clutched in my hand. "We need to talk about the child molestation story. Peggy! Charles!" Ray bellowed down the corridor. "Let's go!"

First Peggy, then Charles, exited their offices and walked into the bullpen, neither of them looking pleased at being hollered at. Ray seemed in an uncommonly good mood considering he had just spent an hour and a half calming down Gail. He rubbed his hands in satisfaction as all three writers joined him.

Zack avoided looking at Peggy, and Charles ignored Ray.

"Come on, people," Ray said. "We've got a child to molest."

He didn't seem to notice the appalled silence that followed this remark as he turned around and headed into his office.

Jennifer and I looked at one another and grimaced. Charles muttered "Asshole" under his breath before following Ray inside. Zack looked sick, and Peggy went to put a comforting hand on his arm, but he twisted his body away from her and followed Ray. Her hand just hung there, frozen in mid-air, before she slowly brought it back down to her side and walked away. I thought she was going to walk right past Ray's office and head down the short corridor that led to the front door and outside. But at the last minute she didn't seem to have either the courage or the desire, because she paused before Ray's door as if gathering her breath, then went inside.

"He's a psychopath," I said to Jennifer.

She nodded. "I think he killed Rebecca."

And I had blown the whistle on his alibi. Maybe Craig was right. Maybe I was in danger. I stared bleakly at the gaping hole above my desk, then at the walls of Ray's office. If that was the case, how was I ever going to protect myself from him?

Jennifer spoke. "He should be fired. Charles is the better writer. If he were the showrunner, the ratings would triple."

Thinking back on my conversation with Jennifer about Charles, I wondered if he was capable of killing Rebecca to save his career, because she clearly had been sabotaging it. And then I had an even more chilling thought. Was Jennifer capable of killing Rebecca to protect her beloved boss? Impossible, I admonished myself. She's your friend. But as I glanced at Jennifer, pouring herself a mug of coffee, I was starting to realize I hardly knew any of my colleagues. As I was learning, they all held secrets. What if Rebecca had found out someone's secret, and that discovery had led to her death? If I continued to ask questions about her, would I stumble on a secret that would ultimately put my life at risk as well?

Leave the investigating to the detectives, I told myself. But as I heard the murmur of voices in Ray's office, as I watched Jennifer check her e-mail on her BlackBerry, I knew I couldn't stop asking questions. Because no matter how hard Wagner and Lu tried to unpeel the layers of Rebecca's life, they were on the outside, looking in.

Whether they liked it or not, I was in the best position to find out what happened to Rebecca. And I would.

3.

B oth detectives showed up at the warehouse later that afternoon while I was typing Zack's Act Three into Sandy's computer. Sandy was straightening her office, deftly avoiding answers to what I thought were subtle questions about Rebecca's life. Another person with secrets. Wagner's soft-spoken, "Susan?" interrupted my unsuccessful interrogation.

Detective Lu stood next to him. I turned to Sandy, who was frozen like a statue in the center of the room, one hand clutching memos, the other grasping the handle of the file cabinet drawer. I realized, with a jolt, that she was just as nervous and frightened of them as I was.

I turned back to Wagner. He was clasping a manila envelope, and his expression, no surprise, was unreadable.

"Yes?" My voice sounded unnaturally high.

"We'd like you to take a look at some pictures. Ms. Martin, too."

"Okay," I said.

Wagner opened the clasp of the envelope and pulled out some colored prints. Sandy peered over my shoulder. I could feel her breath on my neck, coming in rapid, shallow bursts—she was nervous as hell.

There were six photos of six different men, all seemed to look in their mid-to-early thirties, all dark-haired and lean. The men were posed casually: some were standing outside, others sat in living rooms or dens, and two were behind desks in offices. One man, in particular, caught my eye. He had dark, wavy hair, large, wide-spaced eyes, and a lean, oval face. He was lying on the grass of what looked to be a park, propped up on one elbow, grinning boyishly at the camera. He wore jeans and a blue chambray work shirt, opened at the neck, revealing a hint of dark, curly chest hair.

"Do either of you recognize any of the men in the photographs? Have you seen any of them hanging around the office?"

"No, I don't recognize any of them," Sandy said, straightening up to face the two detectives, her face white. I couldn't tell whether she was lying or just nervous about having to identify a possible murderer.

I handed the photos back to Wagner. "I don't recognize anyone, either." Could it be possible they had a suspect? Was that why Wagner didn't seem interested when I told him Ray lied about his alibi? Did he already know who murdered Rebecca? And why were these casual photos and not mug shots?

But neither Wagner nor Lu was much for giving away any unnecessary information so I kept my questions to myself. Wagner asked if anyone else was around who could spare the time to look at the photos. Sandy looked like she wanted nothing to do with them, so I volunteered to take the detectives around. Maybe I could learn something that would prove who Rebecca's killer was.

I led them to Jennifer who was sitting behind her desk updating the Babbitt & Brooks website. She and I took turns inputting information about the series regulars, guest stars and story lines into the show's webpage, which needed to be updated at least once a week. We also had to take a random sampling of fan comments, the good and the bad, and make copies for the writers. Without looking up, she said, "The PR office sent me info on Rebecca's death to put on the webpage. Very respectful. Makes me want to gag."

She looked up, her smile fading when she saw I wasn't alone. "Oops. My bad." She smiled but her eyes went from them to me in quick, nervous flicks.

"I guess it's no secret that none of us liked her," I said to the detectives.

Jennifer snorted. "Oh crap. Let's face it. We loathed her. And she loathed us right back." She held out her wrists toward them. "So if you want to lock me up. Go ahead."

"They just have some photographs they want to show you, Jen," I said in haste. "It's all right. No one's getting arrested." Except for maybe one of those guys in the photos.

Lu stared at the gaping hole in my ceiling but didn't say anything. Wagner once again took out the photos and showed them to Jennifer. "He's cute," she said, pointing to the guy in the park. "Did one of these guys kill her? Rebecca?"

"We don't know that, Ms., uh, Bardos," Lu said. I gave him credit for remembering her last name, and wondered if they went over our names in the car, quizzing each other before walking into the warehouse.

"Well, then, why are you flashing these picture around?" Her charming smile softened the bluntness of her question. Wagner, to my surprise, smiled back. "We just wondered whether any of these men ever came around here . . . or possibly worked on the show in some capacity?" Jennifer shook her head. "Sorry, don't recognize anyone. Why do you think one of these guys was hanging around here?"

Neither of the detectives looked like they wanted to answer that question. It didn't take a genius to figure out why. "You found strange fingerprints in her office, didn't you?" I said, pointing to the photos. "One of their prints. But he doesn't have a record so you don't have a mug shot. These are all casual photos so no witness is prejudiced by a mug shot—and points out the wrong man."

"Perhaps," was all Lu would say. But I knew by the tone of his voice that I was right.

"What about your bosses?" Lu asked. "Are they available?"

"They're in a meeting," I said. "But if you really think this guy worked on the show, Miranda Peterson might be more helpful. Or we could go to the set."

The two cops looked at one another for an unspoken beat, then Wagner turned back to me. "Why don't you show us where Ms. Peterson is? That is, if you can spare the time?"

Was he kidding? I'd give up the rest of my life for these guys if it helped prove none of my colleagues killed Rebecca. I think Jennifer realized this as well because she said, "Go ahead, Suze. I'll watch the phones."

Wagner, Lu, and I headed across the plank and into the other warehouse. The construction workers wouldn't have even dared try to stare under my skirt if I had been wearing one. They recognized the two detectives walking behind me.

Miranda seemed back to her normal self, greeting our presence with the semi-annoyed glance she bestowed upon anyone who interrupted her work. "When are we getting Zack's script?" she demanded before I could open my mouth. The kindness she displayed at Sherman's dismissal had vanished.

"He's writing it, Miranda," I said. "We did have a slight tragedy that delayed us, you know."

For a second I wondered if slight tragedy was the wrong phrase to use, the sarcasm reminding the detectives that I had a valid reason for despising Rebecca and, thus, doing away with her. Miranda didn't notice my sudden, guilty hesitation. "It wasn't my decision to keep production going," she said. "We're two days into prep and everyone's screaming at me for the script."

"I can't write the script for him," I told her. "I've been putting Act Three into the computer all day. If you want to complain, call Zack. Or Ray," I added, feeling meanly triumphant. I knew Ray was the one person on this show Miranda couldn't—and wouldn't—bully.

Miranda's eyes dropped from mine, and I felt a moment of petty victory. Unfortunately, she did have a point. The script should've been finished so that the director could've started reading it and the casting people could have started auditioning actors for the supporting roles. Patrick needed it to break down the scenes and start working on a shooting schedule. But I worked for Zack, not Miranda, and I owed my loyalty to him.

Wagner diplomatically cleared his throat, and Miranda looked up over my shoulder. I had forgotten all about the detectives standing behind me.

"Miranda," I said, "these are the two detectives investigating Rebecca's death. They want to show you some photographs."

"What kind of photographs?" Miranda asked, sounding afraid of having to look at the most fearful array of murderers and molesters, rapists and serial killers.

"We'd like to know if you've seen any of these men before," Wagner said, withdrawing the photos from the envelope. "Take your time. Look at them carefully."

Miranda studied all six photos, but kept returning to the one of the guy in the park, biting her lower lip while drinking in the large, blue eyes, the shock of thick, dark hair, the strong, sharply-defined jaw and cheekbones. I hoped he wasn't the murderer. He was too cute for a life of crime. But, then again, so was Ted Bundy.

Miranda finished her perusal and looked up at the two detectives. "I've seen him around," she said, pointing to the photo of Mr. Cute. "He's one of the construction workers. His name's Michael Keller.

"No kidding?" I couldn't help interrupting. "I don't remember him." But his name sounded familiar. I wondered why.

Miranda shrugged like it was no big deal, but I could tell she was pleased at being able to identify the guy. "He used to come to the office occasionally. To get a drink of water or cup of coffee."

More likely to flirt, I thought, reading between the lines of Miranda's smug smile.

"His fingerprints were found in Rebecca's office, you know." I couldn't help myself. She was acting like it was a privilege this guy had come in here and chatted with her.

Plus, I was upset that I hadn't recognized him myself. But I rarely looked at any of the construction workers the few times I had come across them. I was afraid eye contact would only encourage them to say things like, "Hey, little mama" or "Hi, chickie, chickie, chickie."

"Where would we be able to find Keller?" Wagner asked.

"He's probably working somewhere around the building," Miranda said. "But I haven't seen him for a couple of days. You might want to check with the foreman."

"I'll show you where his office is," I volunteered. Although I had never been inside the trailer, you couldn't miss it—it sat in the far corner of the parking lot, hogging up spaces meant for Babbitt & Brooks employees.

"Thank you, that would be helpful," said Lu while Wagner reached out a hand for the photographs, after having Miranda put her initials and date on the back of Keller's photo.

"Zack's script better be in by tomorrow," was her parting shot at me as I escorted the two detectives back to the other warehouse and through the opened double doors leading to the parking lot and the foreman's trailer.

4.

"I haven't seen Keller around since last week," the foreman told the two detectives as he stared with distaste at Keller's photograph. "Or maybe it was the beginning of this one, I'm not sure."

The trailer was small, hot, and cramped, and the lone

fly buzzing around the tiny window competed with the drone of a portable fan and the stale smell of cigarette smoke to give me the beginnings of a headache. The foreman, who grudgingly introduced himself as Ted Lombardi, was swarthy, with a five o'clock shadow and rings of sweat under the armpits of his grayish white T-shirt. He held the photo by the tips of two fingers, and I couldn't decide whether he thought his fingerprints on the photo would somehow incriminate him in whatever it was the cops wanted Keller for, or if he disliked Keller so much he didn't want to even have to touch his likeness on a photograph.

"Don't you keep records?" Lu asked. I noticed that although both detectives were unflaggingly polite, they treated the foreman with an edge of toughness that had been absent from their dealings with everyone else.

"Not for Keller," the foreman replied. "He wasn't on the company's payroll."

"Then who was paying him?" Lu asked.

The foreman nodded in the direction of the warehouse. "They did. The company that's making this thing. Romulus Television." He didn't look too happy about it, either.

"Why is that?" Lu asked.

The foreman shrugged, clearly not pleased with having to answer any sort of question about Keller. "Got me. We started working and one day I got the word that a Michael Keller was going to work with my guys. He showed up the next day with all the right paperwork, so I put him to work."

"And who told you to hire him? Do you remember a

name?"

"Berg. He hired my outfit in the first place."

"That's Bob Berg," I said. "He's the executive in charge of production. In other words, he holds the purse strings."

Lu jotted the name down in his notebook.

"Yeah, that's the one," the foreman acknowledged. "I wasn't too happy about it. We're a union organization, but Keller had a card and his paycheck wasn't coming out of my pocket."

"How was he to work with?"

"Lousy. He didn't like to work, he wasn't good at what he did. But as I said, I wasn't the one paying him. So I gave him simple jobs and tried to keep him out of trouble."

"Did he seem friendly with anyone on the show or on your crew?"

"None of my guys had much to say to him. And we don't deal much with the TV people."

"Thank you for your time," Lu said holding out his hand, although the foreman looked like the last thing he wanted to do was shake it. Wagner, perhaps sensing this, merely nodded his head, and I scooted out the door first without making eye contact with the foreman at all.

The gravel crunched under our shoes as we walked back in the direction of the warehouse. "Is there anything else I can show you or help you with?" I asked, enjoying my new role as police sidekick.

"You're sure you never saw Keller hanging around the office?" Lu asked.

"No, I'm sorry. But—" Suddenly, I remembered why his name was familiar to me. "Rebecca's office!" I said. "I saw his name in Rebecca's office." The memory had snapped into place and I didn't have a headache anymore.

"She wrote him a check," I continued. "Tuesday morning, when I was cleaning her office, I found it on her desk. I paper-clipped it to her desk calendar so she wouldn't lose it."

"How much was the check for? Do you remember?" Wagner asked.

"A hundred, maybe a hundred and fifty dollars. Was it for drugs, do you think?" Maybe Keller had been the one to supply Rebecca with the cocaine Sherman had found on her desk.

Neither of the detectives answered, and I wondered what the going rate for cocaine was. Then again, it couldn't be that much if Keller needed to moonlight as a construction worker—and a lousy one at that. Maybe the job was a front to fool the IRS, or make contacts to whom he could sell his drugs. But why would Bob "Mr. Straight-Arrow-Vote-Republican-or-Die" Berg insist the construction company hire him?

I wanted to share these thoughts with Lu and Wagner, but before I could open my mouth they thanked me for my help and veered off in the direction of their car, a brown Ford. In script lingo we'd call it the "n.d." sedan, n.d. meaning "nondescript." I figured they were probably heading over to the Romulus main office in order to check out Keller's personnel file—if he had one. Who knew what nefarious means Bob Berg used to slip Keller through the Romulus cracks?

Before I went back inside I checked my messages and saw a text from Lily Wainess. It took me a moment and then I remembered she was the writers' assistant before me. The one I had texted on the pretext of needing help with a work-related matter. She told me to call her, which I did, still standing in the parking lot.

"Hello?" I heard traffic in the background and wondered if Lily was in her car.

"Lily, hi. This is Susan Kaplan. I got your text about calling you back."

"Yeah, hi, Susan. What did you want to talk to me about? Can't Jennifer or Sandy help you with it?"

"Um, well, actually, I really wanted to talk to you about Rebecca." There was silence on the other end of the phone. "Hello? Lily, are you there?"

Lily finally spoke, sounding wary. "If you're calling to tell me she's dead, I already know that."

"No, it's not about that." Jennifer appeared at the front door, glancing around. When she saw me, she made an impatient gesture, telling me to come back in. I spoke quickly into my cell. "I just want to know . . . why did Rebecca hate me so much? And not just me . . . She seemed to have it in for Jennifer and Sandy as well." I held up a finger to impatient Jennifer in a "one minute" gesture.

Lily, unexpectedly, laughed. "She hated you—all of you—because of me."

Jennifer started to head toward me and I spoke fast and low into the phone. "Can we meet? Talk about it?"

There was a pause then Lily, with a weary sigh, said, "I guess. There's a Starbucks in a strip mall on Riverside Drive in Sherman Oaks. Right off Fulton. Meet me there when you get out of work." She hung up before I could thank her. When I turned around, Jennifer was in my face.

"What are you doing out here? The phones are ringing

like crazy and Zack has more pages for you."

"Sorry. You know the photos the detectives were showing us? The good looking guy? He's one of the construction workers here."

"Did he kill Rebecca?"

"I don't know. But Rebecca had written him a check. I saw it in her office."

Jennifer's blue eyes widened. "How did she know him?"

I shrugged. "I guess the detectives will investigate. I thought, maybe, he was her drug dealer."

Jennifer shook her head. "You don't write checks to your drug dealer." She smiled at my naïveté. "Come on, leave the detecting to the cops. Those phones don't answer themselves."

As I followed her back into the warehouse, I realized I hadn't told her about my upcoming meeting with Rebecca's former assistant. And I decided to say nothing unless Lily had anything useful to say.

5.

I found the Starbucks through an app on my smartphone, battling rush hour traffic north, from the Harbor Freeway to the Ventura Freeway, getting off at Coldwater Canyon and continuing west on Riverside Drive. It took me an hour, with stop-and-go traffic all the way, and I was jittery with nerves. The Starbucks was filled with coffee drinkers of all ages, sitting at the tables, their faces staring at their laptop screens, giant lattes clutched in their hands.

When I had found a parking space in the strip mall, I texted Lily, letting her know I was there. I glanced at the women, hoping one of them would look up and acknowledge me. But it wasn't until I glanced at the baristas behind the counter that I locked eyes with a woman in her late twenties at one of the cash registers who said something to the guy behind the neighboring register. He nodded and she moved around the counter toward me.

"Susan?"

I nodded, too stunned to speak. Not because former writers' assistant Lily was now serving coffee at Starbucks but because she was beautiful. I mean drop-dead, she could be a model or an actress beautiful. She had dark, shoulder-length curly black hair, emerald green eyes, and smooth unblemished skin in an oval face. She was my height, which put her at 5'4", and despite the green apron covering her body I could tell she had a figure most women would kill for. I felt hugely awkward standing next to her, embarrassed by my red hair and freckles.

If Lily noticed I was staring she gave no sign. "Let's go outside. I have five minutes. Ten at most."

Without waiting for my reply she headed out the door.

I followed her into the shop next door to the Starbucks, another coffee shop, but filled with trays of sandwiches and salads behind glass counters, which, I imagined, is how it managed to stay in business despite its competing coffeehouse neighbor. Lily and I both ordered Diet Cokes and moved to a small table near the front window. There was one another patron in the store; everyone else, it seemed, was in Starbucks.

Lily sipped from her Diet Coke, staring out the window

at the parking lot crowded with cars, others crawling slowly down the lanes looking for an empty space. She didn't seem inclined toward conversation so I nervously cleared my throat, crumpling the paper my straw came in.

"Thanks for meeting with me," I began.

Lily turned away from the window, regarded me appraisingly. "So, you're my replacement."

I nodded.

"Do the cops know who murdered Rebecca?" she asked.

"If they do, they're not telling me."

She lowered her eyes, sipped from her soda. Her skin glowed in the setting sun. I wondered what it was like to be so beautiful. Did she worry about bad hair days? Zits? Clearly her looks didn't get her everything she wanted, if she was working in a Starbucks. Unless she was writing a novel about a heroine who was a barista and was there for research.

"So, what did you want to ask me?" Lily's question broke into my thoughts.

"You said on the phone that Rebecca hated me—all the assistants—because of you." She nodded. "Why?"

Lily again glanced out the window then turned back to me.

"What will you give me if I tell you?"

I started at her, taken aback. "M-money? I don't have any. You know what those jobs pay."

She smiled without mirth. "I'm not talking about money. I want an audition. On Babbitt & Brooks."

"An audition?" I repeated. "Couldn't you get one when you were there?"

"I tried. But then Rebecca found out . . ."

She didn't have to finish the sentence.

"What makes you think you can get an audition now?"

"Rebecca's not there to stop it," she said simply. Yikes. This girl was cold. Lily must've sensed my hesitation because she added, "How badly do you want to know why she hated you?"

I wanted to know badly enough, especially if it helped me figure out what made her tick, and maybe I would learn if her hate-on for Sandy, Jennifer, and me was related to why she was murdered. "I'd need your headshot and resume," I said, tentatively.

"Done. I've got one back at the shop.

Of course she did. You never know when a director or producer would be walking through the door, ready for his double espresso latte.

"Okay," I said. "I don't know if I can guarantee you an audition, but I can at least pass your headshot on to the casting director."

Lily sat back, smiled. "Good. Thanks."

She didn't look like she was about to say anymore, so I prompted, "About Rebecca?" I hoped Lily wasn't going to wait and spill until after I passed on her headshot. Fortunately, that apparently wasn't the deal because Lily said, "I had an affair with her ex-husband."

Thud. That was the sound of my jaw hitting the table. Lily smiled wryly, amused by the impact her revelation had on me.

I stuttered, "What? When? Rebecca was married?"

Lily took a long sip from her soda before answering. "Years ago. They came out to L.A. together. From the

Midwest. Ohio, I think. He wanted to be an actor. She a singer."

Rebecca could sing? Who was this woman?

"Anyway, Rebecca told me she decided she'd rather be in the audience listening than on stage performing. I think it was the lie she told people instead of admitting she didn't have enough talent to make it big. She got a job working for Ray Goldfarb, as his personal assistant, and never looked back."

"What about her husband?"

"Ex. He did some modeling but never really succeeded."

"So how did you and he . . .?"

"Hook up?"

"Get together."

She smiled, flicking back a dark curl from her face. "He came by the office once. Looking for Rebecca. She was at lunch so he hung around, we got to talking . . ."

"But where were Jennifer and Sandy? They never said a word."

"They didn't know. The show wasn't in production yet, so we all had offices at Romulus. It must've been a day when they were at the warehouse getting it ready for all of us to move in."

The Romulus office was in West LA, near where the 405 and 10 freeways connected. I had worked there as a temp before being hired to replace Lily. By then, the show was in production and the staff had moved permanently to the studio downtown.

"You met him once and started dating him?"

Lily laughed. "I don't know if what Kelly and I did

could be called dating. We were attracted to one another. And it wasn't like he was still married to Rebecca."

"Are you still seeing him?"

She shook her head. "Rebecca found out. That put an end to his ardor."

"Why? Was he still in love with her?"

"I think he was in love with how he could use her. I wasn't the only one who wanted an acting job on B&B."

"So how did she find out?"

Lily shrugged. "Nothing huge like walking in on us while we were doing it. She heard me flirting with Kelly on the phone, got suspicious. She confronted him and he gave it up."

"And she fired you?"

"Well, that was the problem. I mainly worked for Peggy and Zack. So, she couldn't fire me without telling them why she wanted to fire me. And she wasn't about to do that."

"So, what happened?" No wonder daytime soaps are going off the air. Who needs their daily dose of Sturm und Drang when you're living it?

"Rebecca called me into her office, basically told me she'd poison any chance I had at an acting career if I didn't quit. She had already sabotaged my chance at a B&B audition." Lily's mouth twisted and I saw the hurt in her eyes. But, really, was she living in that much of a fantasy world? What else did she expect?

I said, "And, so, Rebecca hates me, Sandy, and Jennifer because she thinks we're going to sleep with her ex-husband? I haven't even met the guy!"

"I guess he's steered clear of the warehouse since our

little debacle." She finished her soda, pushed the empty cup away. "You worked with Rebecca for how long? Two months?" I nodded. "Didn't you see how insecure she was? She didn't have the talent to make it as a singer. And no one had any respect for her as an associate producer, and she knew it. Jennifer is gorgeous, Sandy is very good at her job, and you . . . What are you out here for?"

"I want to be a TV writer."

Lily nodded as if she had already figured that out. "And I bet you're good."

I blushed. "Charles liked my spec for Dress Blue, thought it might lead to a writing assignment on B&B."

"There you go. So Rebecca was sharing office space with three women who were competing with her on some level. She couldn't let any of you screw her over like I did."

"She seemed to get along with Peggy . . ."

"Oh, I'm sure she found some subtle way to stab Peggy in the back."

"I think she was having an affair with Zack."

The corner of Lily's mouth quirked. "Need I say more?"

"But her hatred seemed so . . ."

"Out there? Unreasonable?" I nodded. Lily continued, "The one thing I knew about Rebecca is she was all about control. I'm sorry if my fling with her ex caused you and the other two girls so much pain. But when Rebecca felt like she was losing control, she fought back viciously. She wanted to inflict triple the pain she felt she was caused."

On the drive over Coldwater Canyon back to my apartment, Lily's headshot on the seat next to me, I thought of her words. Yes, Rebecca was vicious. Unreasonably so. And maybe that caused one of her victims to fight back, equally unreasonably. A stupid, dangerous game where control freak Rebecca ultimately and irrevocably lost control.

Five minutes after I arrived home Craig arrived at my doorstep, holding a large, take-out pizza box. I could smell cheese and tomato sauce, and my stomach grumbled in response.

"We may have to warm it up," he said. "You got home later than usual. But I had a feeling you'd had another tough day."

"It could have been better," I said. I decided not to tell him about my ex getting married to the girl he was sleeping with while living with me. Instead, I said, "You were right. I ended up calling Wagner about Ray's alibi and he was singularly unimpressed. But I found out some other stuff about Rebecca that's kind of interesting."

"Do you want to talk about it?"

"Sure." I smiled at Craig, pleased he had come by again, bearing gifts, no less. In jeans and striped rugby shirt, he looked damn cute.

"Can we talk about it now?" Craig said. "My hand's getting stuck to the cardboard."

"Oops. Sorry." I opened the door and let him pass. Craig's hair was damp and he smelled of soap and shampoo. I took in a deep breath of him, trying not to look obvious. He placed the box on my kitchen counter and opened the lid with a "Voila!" gesture. I looked inside. Pepperoni and black olives. My favorite.

"You have just made a bad day good," I said.

Babbitt & Brooks aired that night, and while waiting for the show to start, I filled Craig in on new suspect Michael

Keller, my calling Wagner about Ray's alibi, as well as former assistant Lily's affair with Rebecca's ex-husband.

Craig swallowed a mouthful of crust and cheese. "Whoa. Let's start with your call to the cops. Did Ray find out you told them?"

"I don't know. If he did, he didn't confront me about it. And Sandy said Wagner never called him. So maybe it doesn't matter. Not if Keller is now the prime suspect."

"Get real, Susan," Craig said. "Ray's gonna find out. And whether he's guilty or not, he's gonna get back at you for telling tales about him." He turned toward the TV set and my shoulders sagged. He was disappointed in me. I could've kicked myself for caring so much about what he thought. I conjured up a mental image of my heart and hardened it. All I got in return was heartburn.

But as I silently kissed off any possibility of a romantic relationship, Craig turned back to me.

"I'm sorry," he said. "But at the risk of sounding like your parents, I'm worried about you. I don't want to see you get hurt."

I smiled, pleased by his concern, but before I could respond, Babbitt & Brooks's upbeat yet serious theme song began playing over Gail and Tabby arguing in court, ordering hot dogs from a street vendor, pacing in their law office, Gail looking elegant in an evening gown, Tabby laughing at the dinner table with her family, and ending with the two women, having won their case in court, jumping in the air and slapping their palms in a high five.

Peggy had written the script, which was about Tabitha Wentworth's character, Hank Babbitt, being held hostage in her office by the brother of a client whose case she had lost. The word floating around the office was that the show had turned out incredibly well.

"This is the episode that could win us the Emmy next year," Ray had said after he, Charles, Zack, Peggy, and Rebecca had returned from watching a rough screening. Peggy looked pleased, and I remember Rebecca squeezing her arm and congratulating her. Maybe that was when Rebecca decided to steal Zack. If Peggy had the Emmy for comfort, then Rebecca could have her boyfriend. Too bad Emmy nominations for this season weren't announced until the following August. That was a long time to wait for substitute comfort.

The episode was different from what the show usually did. Ray liked to occasionally break away from the issue of the week to explore major personal crises. The story this time was about how two women, who were best friends as well as law partners, each dealt with a horrific crisis from different perspectives. It was a terrific episode, and I hoped people would remember it eight months from now when it was time to nominate shows for Emmy consideration.

Hank Babbitt was finally rescued with a lot of help and planning from Alexandra Brooks. As the police led the crazed kidnapper off, the two women looked at one another, and Hank said something witty to Alexandra to show that she was perfectly fine; then, just as you thought, that's that, Hank broke down in tears, and Alexandra took her in her arms. Could there be a hint of lesbian lust in that embrace, I wondered, as the frame froze then faded to black. Over black, the words, "In memory of Rebecca Saunders" appeared, held, then faded for "Executive Producer, Raymond Goldfarb."

I felt a twinge of sadness. Rebecca's assistant carried on with her ex behind her back, she lost her promotion, then her life. Why didn't I take the time to understand her? Why was I so quick to judge her? "It sucks," I said. Craig grabbed the remote and turned off the set, an ancient Sony portable inherited from my parents. "What do you mean? I thought it was a good show."

"It was. I'm talking about Rebecca. Her death."

"Feeling sorry for her, Susan?"

"I treated her like she was Stalin. But in the scheme of things, she just wanted what we all wanted. To feel good about herself."

Craig smiled at me, squeezing my knee before standing and stretching. Sitting next to him for an hour on my sofa-bed, wondering if he was going to make a move, had taken half my concentration away from the show. Watching his shirt ride up over his flat stomach took away the last half.

"The show was still good," he said. "Your ratings will go through the roof." He grinned at me. "Maybe Ray'll feel so good about it he'll let you write a script even if you do put him in prison."

Well, a person could dream, but I doubted Ray would give me a script from his prison cell or that the ratings would be as big as Craig predicted. Therefore, I was stunned to come into work the next morning to find the phone ringing off the hook with amazing news.

"Are you ready to hear something incredible?" breathed the voice of Lainie Abbott, our publicist's assistant. Babbitt & Brooks used a public relations firm to handle its publicity needs. One of Lainie's jobs was to call me the day after the show aired to dictate the ratings. The ratings we received first thing in the morning were called overnights and represented seventeen cities, among them New York, Los Angeles, Boston, and Chicago. Later in the day Lainie called with the nationals, which represented the entire country. B&B always did better in the overnights since urbanites seemed to like the show more than Ma and Pa Kettle in Paducah, Kentucky (at least that was the expression Lainie used). We usually came in third to a reality series and sitcom, respectively, barely beating the fourth-place show, which was a news program along the lines of 60 Minutes.

"Yeah, I'm ready for some incredible news," I told Lainie, still not believing it would really be that amazing.

"Okay. Get this." I found a pen and pad of paper. "Chicago, fifteen rating, twenty share."

"What? You're putting me on." Only shows in the top ten got ratings like that, and lately even that had become rarer and rarer.

"I haven't finished yet," Lainie said, and I could hear the huge smile in her voice. "Los Angeles, eighteen rating, twenty-two share."

"Lainie, dream on. What is it really?"

"New York, twenty rating, twenty-five share."

And so on, and so on. Between Rebecca's death and Gail's lesbian allegations, everybody had decided to tune in to Babbitt & Brooks to see what this den of iniquity was all about.

The network—and Romulus—would be ecstatic. Fifteen years ago ninety percent of America watched network shows; now, with the advent of cable, syndication, satellite dishes, Netflix and the Internet, that figure was down to only fifty-five percent. To have snared twenty percent of that audience was to have obtained a sort of Nirvana known only to shows like the final episode of M*A*S*H and the "Who Shot J.R.?" episode of Dallas.

When the nationals came in everyone let out a gasp of pure disbelief. Babbitt & Brooks had garnered twenty-five percent of the audience across America. That was the highest rating a primetime network show had received in years. We were an overnight hit, rescued from anonymity by Rebecca's murder and the Scoop's accusations. There was absolutely no doubt in anyone's mind that when the weekly rankings came out the following Tuesday, Babbitt & Brooks would be the number one show in the country. B&B was a show the critics loved, labeled by TV Guide as "the best show you're not watching." Well, now it appeared that we were watching—a truly remarkable feat.

Ray was overjoyed. The numbers even seemed to thaw the feud between him and Charles, Charles happily accepting one of the cigars Ray was passing out, and Ray slapping him on the back like he was the prodigal son. Baskets of flowers, exotic fruit, and expensive wines arrived from Romulus and the network for the actresses and the writing staff. Peggy seemed to glow in the center of all the congratulatory hugs and kisses she received. Deep down, everyone knew the real reason behind the ratings, but no one was going to admit it. As far as Ray and Romulus were concerned, Peggy had written a superb episode in which Gail and Tabitha shone.

The writers huddled in Ray's office for the rest of the day. Even I was getting concerned that I had seen neither hide nor hair of the rest of Zack's script. Miranda's repeated phone calls were driving me bananas.

"They're changing it around," Sandy told me when I complained to her. "Beefing it up."

"Sleazing it up, you mean," said Jennifer. "Now that we have an audience we have to worry about keeping them."

Sandy didn't deny this. "I overheard Ray talking with the network," she said. "They want to switch next week's teenage pregnancy episode with the housewives turned prostitutes one."

"But Ray hated that episode," I said. "I thought he was going to air it opposite the Super Bowl or something."

"Okay, a) the Super Bowl is on Sunday and b) the network loves it," Sandy replied. "They think it'll be more interesting to our audience than teenage pregnancy. They think that's too depressing."

Jennifer made a rude sound. "And housewives who become prostitutes isn't? This show is going to lose every ounce of integrity it has."

"I wonder if they'll start showing the actresses' bare bottoms," I mused. "Maybe throw in a couple of curse words."

"The only way this show is going to hold on to those ratings," said Jennifer, ignoring me, "is if someone gets killed every week. And you better believe that once Romulus realizes this, they're going to be hiring a hit man."

6.

On Saturday morning I put on a black skirt and white silk blouse to attend Rebecca's memorial service. The medical examiner had concluded that Rebecca had died due to repeated blows to the head that had resulted in severe injury to the brain. Which I did not see splattered on her office walls. I did not.

The service was postponed, according to Sandy, who got stuck making the arrangements, so that Rebecca's parents could fly in from Michigan. But she confided in Jennifer and me later, when no one else was around, that the real reason was so we wouldn't have to close production for even one morning to attend. I debated asking Craig to come with me, but I didn't want him to think I was asking him out on a date—even if it was to a funeral—so I decided against saying anything and to go alone.

Perhaps it was hypocritical of me to want to attend the service, but it was an opportunity to see Ray, Zack, and Gail in a setting outside production. Would all three act grief-stricken? Or would Ray and Gail, at least, tone it down in deference to his wife and the Scoop, respectively? I had thought Gail genuinely mourned Rebecca when we had talked about the latter's death in the trailer. But Gail wasn't an Emmy-nominated actress for nothing, and it was possible she was playing a role for me so I wouldn't question the difference between the time production closed and the time she actually left location. I wondered what kind of role she would play for the Scoop and Rebecca's mourners, and whether it would be as convincing for them as it had been for me.

I also wondered if Michael Keller would show up. Was it de rigueur for one's drug dealer to appear at one's funeral? (If he was her drug dealer. But I had already convinced myself that he was.) Or had the police already arrested him for Rebecca's murder? I didn't think so. With all the media attention her death had been getting, his arrest would've made the nightly news. So, I figured the cops had suspicions, but no proof.

The service was held at the Hollywood United Methodist Church, where there seemed to be more media present than actual mourners. As I got out of my car, I noticed Ray exiting a limo with both Winifred and Gail in tow. The women were dressed almost identically in simple black dresses and pearls, although Gail wore sunglasses and a huge black hat that made her look more conspicuous than if she had gone bareheaded. The press fell on her as she, Ray, and Winifred neared the front entrance. Several clean-cut men dressed in black arrived on the scene to firmly, but courteously, keep the media away.

The procession from the parking lot to the entrance, with its line of limos and celebrities, reminded me of the procession to the Emmy Awards. Tabitha made an appearance with her husband, an ex-actor turned restaurant owner, still recognizable from reruns of his old series, The Force, about a group of rookie police officers. Mitch Barron, the actor who played the detective Babbitt and Brooks were always tangling with on their cases, arrived with a vacant-looking but gorgeous blonde. I also saw Ben Platner, who played Tabby's husband in the series, as well as Ginny Morris, who played the ladies' ditzy yet competent legal secretary. Clumps of people stood at the entrance to the church, ogling the actors as they arrived and, I'm sure, barely restraining themselves from screaming when they recognized Gail, Tabby, and Mitch. Since the church monitors weren't shooing them away, I assumed they were members of Rebecca's congregation or family.

"Are you here to pay your last respects or are you here to gawk?" Jennifer said, approaching from behind.

"I'm here to gawk," I said, turning to face her and a good-looking guy in his late-twenties. "You think anyone else famous will show up?"

"If she screwed them, they might." Jennifer wore an elegant black pants suit consisting of a tuxedo jacket, white silk shell underneath, and fashionably baggy trousers. Her fingernails were a surprisingly modest pink. She introduced me to her companion. "Susan, this is Steve. Steve, this is Susan."

Aha! The mysterious boyfriend. I shook hands with a tall, muscular guy with blond hair, and a wide, white-toothed grin.

"It's nice to finally meet you," I said to Steve, trying not to stare at his body. His was a stunner. He clothed it in pressed Levi's and a white Banana Republic waiter's jacket. The black tee shirt underneath was, I assumed, his one concession to the funereal occasion.

"You, too," replied Steve. We stared at each other, smiling. Apparently Steve had run the gamut of his conversational capabilities.

Jennifer slid her arm through his. "Well, shall we see

what all the fuss is about?"

"Look for Michael Keller," I told her as we strolled three abreast past the reporters and into the church. Jennifer and Steve were so good-looking I could tell people wanted to recognize them but couldn't.

"Rebecca's drug connection," Jennifer confided to Steve just as we passed someone busily taking notes.

I shushed her, mortified.

"No one heard me," Jennifer replied. But her voice was defensive, so I knew she understood—and was probably regretting her social faux pas.

We entered the church. Morning sun slanted through the stained glass windows and people stood in clumps, quietly talking. Knowing this group, they were probably making movie deals. A middle-aged couple stood next to the first pew, and Ray and Gail were speaking to them. Rebecca's parents. They were taking Rebecca's body home to Michigan that afternoon, and I was relieved to see no casket sitting at the front of the church. Not that it would be open if there were. I doubted any surgeon would be skilled enough to stitch Rebecca back together again like new.

Sandy sat alone in a pew, dressed in a black, shapeless cotton dress, with a wide-brimmed, black straw hat on her head, looking a bit like one of the frumpier royals. She was anxiously looking over her shoulder, and, when she saw us, began waving. Jennifer, with Steve in tow, started to join her, but I hung back.

"Save me a seat," I told them. I gave a brief smile to Sandy and went on ahead to greet Rebecca's parents.

Ray was stepping back as I moved forward and he

stepped on my toe, his body bumping into mine. "Oh, I'm sor—" he began to say then noticed it was me. "Susan, I'm sorry. Are you okay?"

I nodded. "Sure, no problem," I said, even though my ankle hurt like hell and I was afraid to look down in case I saw a run in my stocking. Rebecca's mother smiled in polite sympathy as Ray moved off after first squeezing my shoulder in further apology. Gail didn't even notice me as she gave another polite good-bye to the Saunders and moved off with Ray.

"Mrs. Saunders?" I asked. "I'm Susan Kaplan. Rebecca's assistant. We've talked on the phone."

The woman's face lit up in a genuine smile. We had had quite a few conversations, Mrs. Saunders and I. Rebecca didn't have a personal office phone number, so, even though I wasn't officially her assistant until right before her murder, I did take messages for her on the Babbitt & Brooks line. Mrs. Saunders would call Rebecca at the office when Rebecca wasn't answering her cell. Rebecca would tell me to invent an excuse for why she couldn't talk, and her mom and I would end up chatting. To my surprise, I liked Rebecca's mother and couldn't understand how she could spawn a she-devil like Rebecca.

"Susan," she said. "Thank you so much for coming." At the end of every conversation I had with her, there would be an awkward pause before we said our good-byes, and Mrs. Saunders would say, "Tell Rebecca we love her." It always broke my heart. In person, her mother was small and plump, but she had Rebecca's big blue eyes and thick brown hair, although hers was turning grey.

"Frank, this is Susan Kaplan. Rebecca's secretary."

It was obvious Mr. Saunders was not holding up as well as his wife. Tall and angular, he was slightly stooped, his hazel eyes watery. The man turned vaguely in my direction, mechanically offered me his hand, and said, "How do you do?"

He was drunk. The fumes rolled from his breath to my nose in ever-growing waves. I noticed the broken capillaries in his cheeks, the saggy skin under his chin, the deceptive rosiness of his complexion that couldn't quite mask the sallowness underneath. What had looked like grief from afar, I realized, was actually years of alcoholism. Rebecca had apparently gotten her looks from her mother and her addiction from her father.

"It's nice to meet you," I said shaking his hand. His palm was moist, and I forced myself not to wipe my own against my skirt. "Rebecca's told me so much about you both."

Actually, Rebecca had said very little about her parents, but Mrs. Saunders, at least, seemed pleased, and she offered me another tremulous smile. "She was such a darling girl. We're ... we're going to miss her." To my horror, her composure started to crack. I turned to Mr. Saunders for help, but he was gazing reflectively into the pews.

"That Neely girl is not as pretty as she is on TV," he said, loud enough for the people in the first three rows to hear.

"Lower your voice, dear." Mrs. Saunders spoke anxiously as she gently touched her husband's arm. "People can hear you."

"Let 'em," Rebecca's father said, jerking his arm away

from her touch. "What do I care what people think?"

Mrs. Saunders pursed her mouth, the wrinkles edged alongside revealing years of suppressed anger and pain. She slid her eyes away from him and turned back to me.

"He's taking this so hard," she said by way of explanation.

I smiled politely and nodded, said something inane, and moved away. I felt like I had just gotten to know Rebecca a lot better these past few days after her death, and I immediately wanted to bury my new insights. It was getting harder and harder to hate her. Instead, I was starting to understand—and even feel sorry for her.

I tried to listen politely when the minister began his sermon. But it was hard to digest the list of Rebecca's virtues without remembering all the times she was cruel to me—and Sandy and Jennifer. Maybe I had a better idea as to why she lashed out at us but we hadn't been the ones hurting her. I gazed around the church, looking for Michael Keller or anyone else interesting. Patrick Hager sat by himself, looking stylish in a sharply creased black suit that accented his lean figure.

Charles and his wife sat in back; I had noticed them when I first entered the church. Apparently his newly-thawed relationship with Ray didn't include sitting together at Rebecca's service. Or perhaps Charles had made an appearance for form's sake and intended to slip out unnoticed as soon as the minister wrapped things up. Ray, Winifred, and Gail sat in the second row behind Rebecca's parents, and I realized Gail must've heard Mr. Saunders' remark. I wondered if the parents knew of the lesbian allegations between Gail and Rebecca? Had her father's comment about Gail been his way of denying the relationship? Or at least expressing his disapproval of it?

I continued to study them. Rebecca's father nodded his head repeatedly as if agreeing with everything the minister said about Rebecca's wonderfulness, or, more likely, trying not to doze off from the excess liquor he had imbibed that morning. Mrs. Saunders, unlike her husband, sat ramrod straight, her gaze tilted up and unmoving as she raptly listened to the eulogy. The two of them looked harmless and yet I wondered if they were inadvertently responsible for their daughter's death. Their marriage appeared to follow all the rules of alcoholism and co-dependency, and certainly Rebecca had seemed to be following in their footsteps. There was no doubt she had inherited her father's addictive personality, which may have led to her death at the hands of her drug dealer. Or, it could have been the dependency on the men in her life, developed from observing her mother. Having an affair with Ray, who was unavailable because he was married, stealing Zack away from Peggy and then not wanting him when he wanted her, or even sleeping with Gail— forming a relationship that she knew would be frowned upon by both her parents and society—was not exactly a healthy way to live.

The weird thing is, I saw a lot of Mrs. Saunders in Peggy as well. Peggy pitifully hung on to Zack who didn't want her anymore. Now that Rebecca was dead, Peggy seemed to think she might have a shot at getting Zack back. I had a frightening thought: Would Peggy have killed Rebecca if she thought that would bring Zack back to her? I searched for Peggy in the pews. She and Zack were sitting a few rows ahead, next to the center aisle. I couldn't be sure, but it looked like Peggy was holding Zack's hand. Zack was staring down at his shoes, lost in thought. He looked miserable. Even though he had hurt Peggy by dumping her for Rebecca, I realized it didn't matter. In the end he hadn't gotten what he wanted, either: no Rebecca, and now smothered by Peggy. Why had I thought men were invulnerable to hurt? Had Rebecca exposed a particular man's vulnerability which in turn had gotten her killed?

The mourners started to stand and I realized with a start that the eulogy was over. While Jennifer, Sandy, and Steve went off to find the bathrooms, I waited outside the church. We were going to lunch as soon as they came out. People milled around the parking lot, chatting, shaking hands, enjoying the warmth of the October morning, not quite ready to leave. The media had retreated to the street, their vans blocking the right-hand lane of Franklin Avenue, holding up traffic. I saw the detectives, Lu and Wagner, standing unobtrusively near the parking lot entrance, ignored by the mourners, observing everything.

Cliff Rosen was congratulating Tabitha and Gail on the terrific ratings, talking of doing a major two-hour cliffhanger at the end of the season. Tabitha's husband was off to one side, ostensibly chatting with Mitch Barron, but sneaking quick admiring peeks at the blond girlfriend's cleavage.

Ray was immersed in conversation with two men I didn't recognize. I caught odd, meaningless phrases from them: "two hour cliffhangers," "keeping the heat on," "children who kill their parents."

"Ratings, ratings, ratings," Patrick Hager said as he joined me at the side of the church. He rubbed his hand through his white-blond hair. "It's starting to sound like a nasty four-letter word."

"Who are those guys?" I asked, nodding to the three-piece suitors Ray was talking to.

"The network head honchos. I should go over and introduce myself."

I almost asked him why before remembering he wanted to direct. Nothing like networking the network at a funeral. Rebecca was probably turning over in her casket.

"Did those guys know Rebecca?" I asked him.

"They know Ray," Patrick replied, turning his attention back to me. "A vicious rumor has been circling the offices that Zack's script won't be ready for us on Monday."

"It's not a rumor. It's the truth. They're beefing it up for that nasty four-letter word."

Patrick sighed. "I suppose I don't need to remind you that we're already four days into prep."

Prep, short for preparation, was the work done on a script the week before it was shot: holding meetings with the director and production heads to discuss possible problems and answer questions regarding locations, props or costumes; casting guest starring roles; setting up a shooting schedule; and finding locations. Since each B&B episode was filmed in seven days, the scripts normally had a seven-day prep. But because Zack's show was technically four days into prep even without a script, the script would only have three days of real prep time once it was distributed to the cast, crew, and production heads. Patrick had a right to be nervous and concerned. But there was nothing I could do about it.

"Yell at Ray," I said. "I'm only the assistant."

"Yell at Ray for what?" asked Zack as he joined us.

"There's the man of the hour," I said to Patrick. "Talk to him."

Zack looked at Patrick expectantly. He still looked tired, but some of his old sparkle had returned to his eyes. I wondered if it was because he had managed to shake Peggy.

Patrick, I knew, could cheerfully have strangled me, but he turned to Zack with a smile and said as mildly as possible, "Your script. Do you have any idea when we can expect it?"

Zack shrugged. "It's changed since Wednesday. I think you'll have it by Tuesday." Which meant both Zack and I would be working late on Monday. Fun, fun, fun.

"Why does it have to change?" asked Patrick. "I thought the story was perfectly acceptable."

"Ray and the network don't think it will up hold up against the ratings. And it's an important script."

Zack's original script was about a bounty hunter. Sandy said that Ray was looking for a major movie star to play the role which would then possibly spin off into its own series.

"I think this ratings business is getting out of hand," Patrick said. "The show was excellent before. There's no need to change anything."

"I agree," Zack said, sounding unhappy. "I think everyone is forgetting what that twenty-five share is really all about."

Patrick's sympathetic silence was a sign of agreement,

and I realized that these were the only two people who genuinely mourned Rebecca's death. I didn't count Gail. I still didn't know whether I had gotten the truth or the performance of the century from her.

"Do you think Gail is a suspect?" I asked the two men.

"No," Zack answered. "I think that construction worker is."

"You know about him?" I asked.

Zack nodded. "The police came by my house last night and showed me some pictures. Asked if I'd recognize any of them from hanging around the office.

"So did you?" I asked.

"Yeah," Zack said. "One of them was hanging around the office the day of Rebecca's death."

Both Patrick and I looked at him with interest. "What did he want?" I asked.

Zack shrugged. "Beats me. I was talking to Rebecca in her office. The phones were ringing like crazy. We couldn't figure out where you'd gone. So I stuck my head out to look and saw him hovering around your desk. I thought he might have been waiting for you, but as soon as he saw me he took off."

"Did you tell Rebecca?" Patrick asked.

"I was going to say something. But she was answering the phones and pretty upset about it. In fact . . ." But then, inexplicably, Zack trailed off.

"In fact what?" I prompted. Zack was looking at Patrick but I had the feeling he wasn't actually seeing him. It was as if he were remembering something, and it took a few seconds for my question to sink in before he turned to look at me, slowly coming back to the present.

"Nothing. I'm sorry. I lost my train of thought."

"So do you think Keller killed Rebecca?" I asked him.

"I don't know. Maybe not. Look, I've got to go. I'll see you Monday." Zack turned around and walked rapidly to his car.

"Where's Zack going?" Peggy appeared from over Patrick's shoulder, and I wondered whether she had been the reason he had lost his train of thought.

"Home, I guess," I said.

Patrick was also staring after Zack, a puzzled look on his face. "That was curious," he said.

"What was?" Peggy asked.

"Nothing. I'm sorry. I'm being rude." Patrick offered her a friendly, concerned smile. "How are you holding up, Peggy?"

For a minute I thought Peggy's face was going to crumple into tears but she struggled for self-control and managed to offer Patrick a shaky smile in return. "I'm okay. But I'm worried about Zack."

The three of us turned to watch as Zack found his car, a mint condition, 1964 Ford Mustang convertible, and drove out of the lot.

"I hope he's not leaving you behind," I said to Peggy.

"No, I brought my own car," she said.

"Did the police talk to you about Michael Keller?" I asked.

She nodded. "But I didn't recognize him."

"I think he's their number one suspect. But Zack thinks he may not have done it."

"Maybe Zack knows something we don't," Patrick said. Although his tone was light, Peggy looked at him sharply, her eyes wide in fear.

"No," she said. "He doesn't know anything. He can't."

Then Peggy, too, spun on her heel and walked rapidly to her car. Patrick and I stared after her in surprise.

"Is it something in the water?" I asked him.

"It's something," he said.

7.

I related the mysterious reactions of Zack and Peggy to Sandy, Jennifer, and Steve over lunch at the Cat & Fiddle, a dark-timbered, pub-like restaurant located in Hollywood on Sunset Boulevard. No one could puzzle through the reasons behind their attitudes, although the theory was bandied about—mostly by Jennifer—that Zack knew Keller hadn't killed Rebecca because Zack himself had.

"I doubt that," Sandy said.

"Why?" Jennifer asked. "You heard them arguing. What was to stop Zack from picking up that award and zonking her over the head with it?"

"Because he didn't. That's why."

"But you don't know that," Jennifer persisted. "You left the warehouse before he did."

Sandy stared at her Welsh Rarebit. "Look. I just know. So could we please change the subject?"

Jennifer's mouth set into a stubborn line. "That sounds pretty definite. How do you know?"

"What's his motive?" I answered for Sandy. "It has to be Keller. I mean, he was obviously her drug connection. The police found his prints in her office. He had been lurking around the day of her death."

Jennifer shook her head. "Do you really think Romulus would put Rebecca's drug dealer on their payroll? That's crazy!"

"Well, obviously, they didn't know he was her drug dealer," I said, defensive.

"If he was her drug dealer," Steve interjected. He shook his head, smiling. "Man, you ladies like to dish."

Ignoring him, Jennifer asked, "But what about Ray? Susan, you said he didn't go home with Winifred that night. Where was he?"

"I said, change the subject!" Sandy's voice was shrill and a couple of diners at nearby tables stared at us. Even Steve, chomping intently on his bacon cheeseburger, paused in alarm.

"Yes, let's change the subject," I said. "Steve, how are things in the T-shirt business?" I knew that would distract Jennifer's attention. She loved talking about Steve's little T-shirt shop, located on the boardwalk in Venice, just south of Santa Monica. For the rest of the lunch we talked about some of the sillier slogans customers wanted put on their shirts, pretending we weren't the least bit curious as to why Sandy was overreacting to our discussion about the murder.

When I got home, I found Craig standing before the row of apartment mailboxes, reading a letter, grinning to himself. He looked up as he heard me approach.

"Guess what?" he said. "I sold a short story." He waved a check in the air.

"Hey, that's great. What magazine?"

Craig shrugged. "Just a small horror magazine. They

only paid fifty dollars."

"Fifty dollars is fifty dollars. What are you going to do with it?"

Craig looked at me, noticing the skirt and blouse for the first time. His glance turned admiring, and I felt my body grow warm.

"Take you out to dinner," he said. "You look nice."

"Thanks. It was Rebecca's memorial service."

"That's right. How'd it go?"

"Well, if you're serious about dinner, I'll tell you then."

"It's a deal. Feel like California Pizza Kitchen?"

I always felt like California Pizza Kitchen and told him so. I hoped Craig wouldn't be disappointed when I appeared at his door later that evening in jeans and sneakers. I would've been overdressed for CPK in my memorial outfit, but I did put on a bright red blouse that brought out the highlights in my hair.

Craig and I walked to the restaurant, which was across Wilshire and down San Vicente Boulevard, one of the main shopping thoroughfares in Brentwood, lined with upscale boutiques and restaurants. California Pizza Kitchen was on the second floor of an outdoor shopping plaza.

We sat outside, under a heat lamp, the air soft and warm. After our waitress took our orders, I recapped the memorial service for Craig, including Zack's abrupt departure from the parking lot, and Sandy's over-the-top reaction to any discussion of the murder.

Craig sat back, pushing his glasses up the bridge of his nose. "So, what do you think'?" he asked.

I shrugged. "I don't know. I was hoping you'd have some helpful insights."

"Obviously, both Sandy and Zack know something they don't want to share with the rest of you."

"Yeah, but what?"

"If I knew that, I'd quit writing and become a psychic."

"What did you want to be before you discovered writing?" I asked.

"Pro-football player," he answered. "But even if I hadn't busted my knee, I don't think I would've made it."

"Why not?"

He pointed at his glasses. "Bad eyes. And just not good enough."

"Is that the truth or the nasty little voice of low self-esteem speaking?"

Craig grinned wryly. "The truth. 'Cause when the nasty little voice of low self-esteem hammers at me while I'm writing, I can shove it aside to write. I never could when playing football."

"Okay. I accept that answer." I clinked my glass of beer against his.

"What about you?" he asked. "What did you want to be when you grew up?"

"Have I grown up? That's news to me." I smiled then thought about his question. "In no particular order: ballerina, veterinarian, teacher, President of the United States."

"Not too ambitious, are you?"

"Knowing what I know now . . . I should've stuck with wanting to be president. I think it's easier to get elected than it is to get an agent."

"I'll drink to that," Craig said, and we clinked glasses again just as our waitress arrived with our food.

"So when did you begin writing?" Craig asked between bites of Jamaican Jerk Chicken pizza.

"Fifth grade. I had a best friend who wrote short stories and I thought it was the coolest thing. So I started writing short stories, and then I wrote a historical romance in sixth grade, and my parents were so proud they trotted me out at dinner parties and had me read portions of it to their friends. And then I thought, I love TV, I love to write, why don't I combine the two loves and write for TV?" I paused to swallow a couple of strands of spaghetti Bolognese. "Unfortunately, my parents weren't as pleased with my future plans and stopped trotting me out in front of their dinner guests."

"Sorry to hear that," Craig said.

"But here's the funny thing. After grad school, when I told my folks I was moving to L.A., my mom came with me. She helped me find my apartment. And my grandmother—the one in Florida—loaned me money to buy a car." And every month I sent her a check with a letter about my life, since she refused to get e-mail. Mom told me she'd loan me even more money if it meant getting letters from me for the rest of her life.

"So, your family is basically supportive."

"Yes and no. It was really tough when I first came out. Getting temp jobs when I could. I was pre-law in college before I decided to pursue TV writing. Practically every week my dad was on the phone telling me to come home and go to law school. He said . . ." I trailed off, still stung by the memory but determined not to show it, "He said I was going to sell a script like he was going to Cape Canaveral and fly to the moon."

"I'm sorry," Craig said.

"But here's another crazy thing. Each month he sends me a check for a hundred dollars with a note that says, 'Don't tell your mother.' And each week I get twenty dollars in cash from my mom with a note that says—"

Craig finished for me. "'Don't tell your father.'"

I nodded. "Can you believe it?"

"They love you. They don't want you to starve."

"How are your parents taking it?" I asked.

He shrugged. "Hard to tell. My father's so busy with his second family I don't think he knows I'm writing. And my mom's working hard to get my younger sister through college, so as long as I keep sending her some money to help out, she doesn't care where it's coming from."

He said all this in a matter-of-fact tone of voice that brooked no answering pity or sympathy. I put a forkful of spaghetti into my mouth to give me time to think of a response he wouldn't reject. But all I could think of to say was, "Thank God my parents are still married."

Craig nodded in agreement. "Think they'd be willing to adopt me?"

"Sure. And if they won't, I will."

Craig grinned. "I think you already have."

I smiled back weakly, hoping he didn't mean that in the brother-and-sister sense.

Afterward, we strolled down San Vicente, looking through the windows of the clothing boutiques, stopping off at a frozen yogurt place for dessert. We passed the building where Mezzaluna, the restaurant where Nicole Brown Simpson had her last meal before she and Ron Goldman were murdered, used to be. I shivered, reminded of Rebecca and our meal at the Plum Tree Inn.

Craig noticed. "Cold?"

I shook my head, then instantly regretted it, thinking if I had said yes, he might have put his arm around me. "I was remembering Ron Goldman and Nicole Simpson."

Craig checked out the storefront then nodded. "Don't blame you."

When we arrived at my front door, I looked up at Craig. "Do you want to come in? I could make hot chocolate or something."

Oh, to be sophisticated enough to offer him a nightcap.

Craig shook his head. "No, thanks. I think I'm gonna do some more writing."

I tried not to show my disappointment. What did I expect? Craig to jump my bones? And was I really ready for Craig to jump my bones? I mean, wasn't I still recovering from the news about Peter and Casey's engagement? Did I want Craig to be just a rebound? Well, no . . . but who said that's all he had to be? However, there was no way I was going to play desperate and needy so I shrugged my shoulders. "Okay. Another time."

"Sure."

Kind of a noncommittal response, I thought. Maybe he did only see me as his adopted sister. I opened my door and slipped inside, not wanting to embarrass myself by waiting for him to kiss me.

"Good night," I said, trying to sound as noncommittal as Craig. I closed the door and leaned against it, fighting depression. There was a sudden knock on the door. Surprised, I re-opened it. Craig leaned down and gently kissed me on the lips.

"Good night," he said, smiling at me, before crossing to his apartment and slipping inside. This time, when I closed the door, I was smiling, too.

8.

Zack was turning the pages of my Impressionist painters engagement calendar when I walked into the bullpen Monday morning. He looked up guiltily when he saw me approach.

"Susan, I'm sorry. I didn't mean to go through your things. I was just checking out dates on something."

Zack had his own calendar, so I didn't know why he needed to look through mine. I had brought in my Impressionist calendar to replace the office one damaged during the flood. But before I could ask if I could help him with something specific, he thrust some handwritten, yellow legal pages at me. "Here's the new and improved Acts One and Two. I'll have Three and Four for you by this afternoon." He headed back toward his office.

I sat down behind my desk and glanced at my calendar. Zack had left it open at the week of Rebecca's death. Last week.

I again used Sandy's computer to put in Zack's script changes. Sandy flitted in and out of the office all morning, doing chores for Ray, taking down his phone messages, trying to organize her files. She appeared less tense than she had at the Cat & Fiddle on Saturday, but her mind seemed to be a million miles away. I plugged the Act One changes into the computer and sat back to take my seventh-inning stretch. Sandy was at the file cabinet, shelving memos and production reports.

"Your office is a lot neater," I said.

She looked up briefly. "Thanks."

It really was. No more piles of paper on the floor or heaped across her desk. I could actually see the top of her desk and wondered if this new and improved space had anything to do with Sandy's unexpected probationary period, imposed on her by Ray. But wouldn't Rebecca's death have nullified that?

Sandy cursed, and I turned around. She had dropped the papers she was filing, and I squatted next to her to help pick them up.

"Thanks," she said. "I don't know where my mind is these days."

But I think she knew. She just didn't want anyone else to know. I started to hand her the papers I had collected when the top one caught my eye. It was Rebecca's promotion memo. I showed it to Sandy.

"I saw a copy of this in Charles's office. Did you ever distribute it?"

Sandy made a face. "No. He was probably snooping through my things. I had a suspicion someone was. Only the office was always such a mess I could never be sure. That's why I decided to clean it up."

"Do you think Charles read the memo and convinced Ray not to promote Rebecca?"

"Oh, Susan, I don't know. Could we just drop it, please?"

"But, Sandy, don't you want to know who killed her?"

Sandy waved a dismissive hand at me. "It's not our problem. Leave it to the police."

She left the office before I could ask her why she was so disinterested. Was it because she knew who really killed Rebecca and was protecting that person? Who did she care about so much that she would let Rebecca's murderer go free?

I wanted to discuss Sandy's attitude with Jennifer but she was in and out of the bullpen, running errands for Charles, and I needed to concentrate on getting Zack's script to production. I didn't think it was much improved by the changes, or that people would keep watching Babbitt & Brooks just because of this episode or any of the others that were waiting to be aired. In fact, Zack's script now emphasized the bounty hunter over the two stars, perhaps to make the show more interesting to male viewers. I doubted the two actresses would be pleased, and unless the bounty hunter was going to be played by Justin Timberlake or Robert Pattinson and turned into a vampire, I didn't think our largely female audience would stay happy, either.

Zack himself was acting peculiar. He made a lot of phone calls in between rewrites and avoided Ray, Peggy, and Charles. He begged out of the afternoon story meeting in order to finish his script, and yet he had handed me Act Four only a few minutes before the others met in Ray's office.

Zack and I stayed late, getting the script in shape to be distributed the next day. Ray asked to see it before its official distribution. He, Charles, and Peggy had been discussing story for the next episode all day, and I wondered if the script had been assigned yet. Did I dare go into his office and ask? Tomorrow, I vowed. Let's just get

Zack's script out of the way and off everyone's back.

I proofed the final changes I had made for Zack as everyone left for the day. Zack, in his office, was waiting to proof the script himself. I walked into the bullpen on my way to see him, then stopped when I heard crying. Peggy. Sobbing in her office. I didn't know whether to walk away or go inside and offer my help. Her cries were gut-wrenching, despairing, and they made me shiver in sympathy.

To my surprise, Zack's voice spoke above her cries. "I'm sorry."

"What am I going to do?" It was the cry of someone at her wit's end, a plea for help, a despairing demand for an answer she knew she would never get. I stood rooted to the spot, my hair standing on end at such a display of raw emotion.

Zack lowered his voice in an effort, perhaps, to get Peggy to lower hers. I heard him say, ". . . tomorrow" and then, "I'm sorry" again. Peggy continued to weep, and I pictured her crying into a damp and torn tissue while Zack stood helplessly next to her.

"Please go," I heard her say to him. Zack left without another word, fortunately not glancing in my direction as he headed back to his office. Peggy continued to cry, occasionally blowing her nose, sounding too wretched to move.

I returned to Sandy's office and sat down at her desk, blindly staring at the script still clutched in my arms. Zack eventually found me, and I pretended that I had just finished proofing the script.

"Send it to Ray," he said, looking whipped. He barely

glanced at the script, and his eyes were red as if he had been crying right alongside Peggy. "Let him worry about it now."

I nodded and started to send an e-mail to Ray, attaching the computer copy of the script.

"Susan, I'm not coming in tomorrow. There are a couple of things I need to take care of. If anyone wants me, they can reach me at home."

"What about the script? What if Ray has more changes?"

Zack's mouth twisted in bitterness. "Let him make them himself." And with that, he left.

What kind of things did Zack need to take care of? I wondered. Now that he had finished the script was he simply taking the day off to mourn, or did he have another, more secret agenda? I thought of Zack's odd behavior at Rebecca's memorial service and wondered what he had said to Peggy to make her cry. She left shortly after Zack, eyes and nose red, walking swiftly past Sandy's office without saying goodnight. I dreaded going home to my claustrophobic apartment, too strung out by Peggy's outburst to stare at my beige cinderblock walls. Instead, I crossed to the second warehouse, hoping to catch the cast and crew still shooting. Unfortunately, the sets were dark but a light was on in the production office, and as I entered I spotted Patrick behind the desk in his office, playing solitaire. He saw me hovering and beckoned me inside his office with a smile.

"My lady, Susan, what brings you across the moat to my domain?"

"Boredom," I said. "Why are you here so late?"

Patrick's office was also paneled in fake wood, but unlike the offices in the writers' warehouse, he had a single, grimy, wire-meshed window set high against the outside wall. Cheap wood bookshelves held spiral notebooks filled with scripts; production reports and call sheets cluttered his desk, and metal cabinets bulged with dark green Pendaflex file folders.

"I'm waiting for his lordship Zack's script," Patrick said. "Is it almost ready?"

"He's finished. But Ray wants to look at it before it's distributed. You'll have it tomorrow. I promise."

Patrick sighed, putting down the deck of cards he held and motioning me to a wooden chair across from his desk.

"Why don't you keep me company then and prevent me from tearing my hair out?"

I started to sit when I noticed the framed poster behind me. I moved around the chair to get a closer look.

"Where did you get this poster?" I asked. "I loved Knightriders."

"My mentor worked on the movie," he said. "Not too many people know of it."

"I'm a big Ed Harris fan," I said. "He did this before The Right Stuff."

Patrick smiled. "You're a movie buff."

"I love movies. But I'm not a walking IMDB," referring to The International Movie Database, a website that lists every movie and TV series ever made. "Are you a fan of the movie?" I pointed my thumb at the Knightriders poster. "Or of George Romero movies in general?"

"I'm a fan of the movie. Of the idea behind the movie."

"Modern day knights jousting on motorcycles?"

"Modern day chivalry."

I sat in the chair before his desk, fascinated. "What do you mean?"

"I like the idea of people being courteous to one another. Of having a code of honor." He looked away, as if embarrassed at revealing so much.

"I think that's terrific, Patrick. I really do. But isn't that attitude tough to sustain in this business?"

He shrugged. "Treat people well, they'll treat you well in return."

"Or as my grandmother says, 'You catch more flies with honey than vinegar.'"

Patrick grinned. "Your grandmother is a very wise woman."

"She fought the Nazis in the Warsaw Ghetto," I bragged. I had forgotten that at one point Patrick reminded me of an SS officer. He didn't seem remotely like one now.

"She must've been a very brave woman," he said.

"She was. Still is, I guess." I looked over my shoulder at the Knightriders poster. "Is that why you were so nice to Rebecca? As part of that chivalry thing?"

As soon as the words were out of my mouth I regretted them, but Patrick merely shrugged his shoulders, smiled at me with his eyes.

"M'lady Rebecca wasn't all that bad," he said.

"Sorry. I shouldn't have said anything."

He leaned back in his chair, amused at my discomfort. "I caught some of the backstage intrigue between you and Rebecca and the other ladies-in-waiting." He paused, choosing his words carefully. "I think Rebecca was more comfortable around men than women."

"I don't think Charles liked her that much. But Gail seemed crazy about her." I knew I was being indiscreet, but gossip was always my favorite hobby.

Patrick studied the solitaire pattern on his desk. "Charles is a smart man. And Gail likes people who play up to her."

"So, in fact, you really didn't like Rebecca?"

Patrick smiled. "Let's just say I saw the good as well as the bad. Why do you care so much about what I think?"

I thought about this. "I guess I don't want to feel that I was wrong about her. She's like a mosquito bite on my ankle that's driving me crazy with the itching. I think that if I can figure out what made her tick and who killed her, the itching will go away."

Patrick frowned. "Let the police investigate, Susan. That's what we pay taxes for."

"You're right," I said. I started to rise from the chair.

"You're not leaving so soon?" he said. "I didn't mean to chase you out."

"You didn't," I said. "I should get home."

He nodded. "I as well. As long as there's no script for me tonight, I might as well warm up my trusty steed to take me back to my castle." He moved from around his desk, paused by my side to study the Knightriders poster.

"Do you think chivalry is dead?" I asked.

Patrick smiled. "Not as long as fair ladies such as yourself still exist in the world."

His words were corny and slightly embarrassing, but I smiled anyway and preceded Patrick out the door.

9.

The next morning Ray came in, brandishing Zack's script, the pages dog-eared where he wanted changes made.

"When Zack comes in, tell him I want to see him," Ray said, mangling his unlit cigar between his lips.

"Zack's not coming in today," I said. "He told me we can reach him at home."

For a minute, Ray looked like Thor, the God of Thunder, and I expected lightning bolts to flash from above and electrocute me. Instinctively, I ducked my head. Ray growled, "Get him on the phone," before turning his back and heading into his office.

I left a message on Zack's home and cell voicemails. And continued to do so every hour on the hour, per Ray's request. Peggy had arrived to work late but calm, and she actually looked as if a great weight had been lifted from her shoulders. She volunteered to incorporate Ray's changes into Zack's script in order to get the script to production on time.

Ray, frustrated and furious with Zack's lack of communication, finally gave her the go-ahead and Peggy set to work. Not even when Lainie Abbott e-mailed the weekly rankings did Ray lighten up. To no one's surprise, Babbitt & Brooks ranked as the number one show in the country.

A few congratulatory calls came in, although we expected the bulk of them to be made the next day when the week's numbers appeared in the trades. Ray's joy was lessened by Zack's continued silence and the resultant delay in getting the script out. I plugged the last set of changes in as quickly as possible, copied the new script for the writing staff, then made a couple more copies for Miranda and Patrick.

Patrick was pacing in front of Miranda's desk when I hurried in with the scripts. It was the first time I had ever seen him look either ruffled or annoyed. Even his hair stood on end, and, when he saw me, he grabbed one of the scripts from my outstretched hand and hurried into his office, practically slamming the door in my face, our cozy chat the night before seemingly forgotten. Miranda looked equally annoyed. "He's been like that all morning," she said. "He kept calling me on his cell, asking if the script was in. For all the good it would have done since he only came in five minutes ago."

"Well, now he has it and everyone's happy," I said, fleeing her office before she could heap more frosty abuse on me.

"Doesn't anyone wonder where Zack is?" I asked Jennifer when I returned to my desk. "He did say he'd be home all day."

Jennifer shrugged. "Maybe he said it just to get Ray off his back."

Maybe, but that didn't sound like Zack, and I was starting to get worried. He had been acting strange lately, and I wondered how much that had to do with Rebecca—or even Peggy.

I knew a person had to be missing forty-eight hours before you could call the police, and Zack might not even be missing. I decided to ask Ray for permission to leave early to drive to Zack's house and check on him.

Ray looked up from Zack's script as I knocked on his door. "Come in, Susan. I told Sandy to find you."

I paused, confused. "You wanted to see me?"

He nodded. "Have a seat."

My heart started thumping as I sank into one of the chairs across from his desk. I forgot all about asking for permission to leave early.

"It's about the next script."

I looked at him expectantly, but couldn't tell from his expression whether he was about to give me good news or bad.

"Charles thinks you're a very talented writer and I respect Charles's opinion. And now that the show is finally receiving the recognition it deserves, we have to be very careful in choosing writers for the next few episodes."

I nodded, as if understanding completely, although I still wasn't sure whether this was leading to good news or bad.

"I've thought about this very carefully, and although I'd like nothing more than to give you an assignment, I feel we have to hire writers with more experience. At least for this year. Next year, you'll be first on the list." Ray did look very sorry, but I knew firsthand what a good liar he was. There was nothing I could do but swallow my disappointment and nod politely.

"I understand," I told him. "Thank you for telling me."

Jennifer found me in the bathroom. I stood leaning over one of the porcelain sinks, my hands braced on either side, eyes closed. I knew if I opened them I'd only be sickened by the sight of hair, dried toothpaste, and bits of tissue clinging to the basin.

"What did he tell you?" she asked, leaning against the sink next to mine, her arms folded across her chest.

"I'm not getting a script," I said.

"Why not?"

"They can't risk an unknown writer with the ratings as high as they are."

"Do you think this has anything to do with your going to the police about Ray's alibi?"

"I don't know," I said. "Ray didn't mention it. But that doesn't mean anything. Maybe..." I shrugged. "Who knows?"

"So what are you going to do now?"

"Stop feeling sorry for myself. Get on with my life."

After all, there was always going to be something or someone throwing obstacles in my path, whether I lived in Manhattan, Los Angeles, or Oshkosh, Wisconsin.

Jennifer looked at me approvingly. "If I had the week you just had, I'd be in bed for a year. Or put a gun to my head."

I don't know why but suddenly I shivered, as if someone, or something, was crawling over my grave. I looked at my watch. It was only four o'clock.

"Jennifer, would you cover for me if I left early?"

"I thought you said you were going to stop feeling sorry for yourself."

"I want to check on Zack. I'm worried about him."

Jennifer nodded. "Charles and Peggy are as well. I heard them talking about it in Charles's office. Go on. Sandy and I can watch the phones."

I returned to the bullpen to pick up my purse, then

headed outside for my car.

10.

Zack lived in Studio City, a suburb of Los Angeles in the San Fernando Valley. His home was north of Ventura Boulevard, the main thoroughfare in the Valley, which divided real estate values as well as the towns it ran through. South of the boulevard the homes were at least one hundred to four hundred thousand dollars more than the homes north of the boulevard.

I pulled up in front of Zack's modest stucco ranch around four-forty, my growing unease about him replacing my own disappointment about the disappearing script assignment. His house was in the middle of a quiet, tree-lined street, the leaves just starting to turn color and giving southern California the only bit of autumn I'd seen to date.

Zack's home was a depressing brown with an even more depressing darker brown trim. My palms started to sweat when I noticed his red Mustang parked in the driveway. Maybe he just got home. Maybe he was right now calling the office and checking on the status of his script. But I didn't think so.

The neighborhood was quiet. Not even a dog barked as I walked up the stone path to the front door. I rang the bell. I could hear it echoing inside and waited, somehow knowing no one was home to answer. The house felt empty: the blinds were closed tight and Zack's mail still sat in his box. I rang the bell again, then walked to the driveway to peer into his car. The hood felt cool to the touch. I peered through the driver's side window but nothing looked amiss.

The driveway ran past an open, white gate, under an extension of the roof that served as overhead protection for the car, to a two-car garage. Nearing the garage, I could make out more clearly a sound that had provided faint background noise ever since I had driven up. The closer I got to it the more distinct it became. It was an engine running. As I ran up to the huge garage door I noticed the paned windows inset above. They were white with exhaust. I yanked on the garage door handle. It wouldn't budge. Automatic garage door opener, I assumed, running back to Zack's car looking for the battery-operated opener. I glanced through his window and saw it clipped to the visor. Unfortunately, both doors were locked and I didn't know what I could use to smash the window without hurting myself.

Frantic, I ran to the back of the house again, looking for the circuit breaker box and praying it wasn't locked in the garage. Once, when the garage door at home had jammed, my father shut off the circuit breaker and was able to open the door. I was going to try and do the same, not consciously thinking about it, but simply running on automatic pilot, hoping that I might be able to open the door and reach Zack in time.

The breaker box was next to the back porch, and I swung the hinged door open, shutting off the switch labeled garage. Then I ran back to the garage door and once more tried to open it. It slowly, creakily opened, but the exhaust that came rushing out from underneath overwhelmed me, and I shut the door again with a bang.

The fumes were overpowering and I became dizzy and nauseous. I staggered away, knowing I wouldn't have the strength to hold my breath long enough to try again. Desperately trying not to throw up, I called 911 on my cell.

I waited anxiously by the garage until the police and paramedics showed up. They managed to open the door with little effort, coughing as they waded through the exhaust, returning barely a minute later with Zack in their arms. His eyes were closed and his face gray. He lay unmoving and I stared at him in fear, noticing the stillness of his chest. The EMTs made an effort to revive him, but there was little doubt in anyone's mind that Zack was dead and had been for a long time.

END OF ACT THREE

ACT FOUR

1.

God knows I liked Zack a hell of a lot more than I did Rebecca, but I was too stunned to cry. I stood among a growing crowd of neighbors as a forensics team arrived to dust the car in the garage and take photographs of Zack. I had told the two uniformed cops who had arrived about Zack's connection to Rebecca, and within twenty minutes Lu and Wagner arrived, with little notebooks and grim expressions.

After the usual questions about why was I there and how did I come to find Zack, the detectives led me into the garage to take a look at the car in which Zack was found. I had assumed it was his second car, one he used when the Mustang was out of commission or when he didn't want to drive it someplace where it could be stolen. (In Los Angeles, however, that could be anywhere.) The fumes from the car had by now dissipated and I gingerly stepped inside the garage, careful not to touch anything or get in the way of the technicians.

"Recognize it?" asked Wagner as we stared at the Cadillac Escalade. The tone of his voice made me realize that there was no doubt I would.

"It's Rebecca's car," I said, stunned. I didn't know why I was so surprised. If Zack had killed Rebecca, then it made sense he'd take her car to make her death look like the result of a burglary.

Wagner nodded, confirming his own suspicions, and we stepped back out into the sun. Although no police barricades had been set up, the small crowd of neighbors stood slightly away from us, near Zack's Mustang, craning their necks to view Zack's body and stare at the police.

One of the uniformed officers went through the crowd, taking names, asking if anyone had witnessed anything. I doubted people would be helpful. No one would want to get involved or admit they had seen something strange and then chosen to do nothing about it.

"Do you have a key to his house?" Wagner asked me, and I turned back to face him.

"No. I'm sorry." Then felt bad because I couldn't be of further help. One would think identifying Rebecca's car would be enough. "Maybe Zack didn't lock the door because he knew it wouldn't matter anymore."

The detectives didn't answer but they nevertheless turned to the back door and tried the handle, first placing thin, rubber gloves on their hands. The door swung open into Zack's laundry room. I caught a glimpse of a white washer and dryer on one side and dark wood pantry doors on the other. Wagner turned to me.

"Have you been to the house before?" he asked.

"No."

"Stay out here," Wagner said. "And don't go anywhere."

I nodded and stepped away. The coroner's attendants zipped Zack's body up into a bag and then Velcro-strapped him onto the gurney. I watched as they wheeled him down the driveway, cutting through the crowd that quietly, almost reverently, parted for them.

Good-bye, Zack, I said silently. Be at peace. I hoped he hadn't killed Rebecca and then himself out of remorse. But if he had . . ., why now? Was the weight of guilt finally too crushing to bear? Or was he merely acting the gentleman by waiting until after he finished his script? And what was that scene with Peggy in her office about? Was he saying his final good-byes to her? Had he confessed to the murder and told her he was going to kill himself "tomorrow"? If so, why didn't she try to stop him? Why did she sit in her office and cry instead?

Restless and bored, I walked back down the driveway. The crowd was breaking up now that Zack's body had been taken away, but the cops were still taking statements from those who remained.

I walked to my Honda and leaned against it, wanting to leave, to call Jennifer, to do something, but too afraid of the detectives' reactions if they came out of the house and found me gone or on the phone.

A green Prius pulled into the driveway next to Zack's, and a pleasant-looking, middle-aged woman got out of the car holding a canvas bag of groceries. She looked at the black and white police cars, red lights silently flashing, at the police officers, at the crowd of dwindling neighbors, and walked down the sidewalk until she was standing a few feet away from me.

"What happened?" she asked, clutching her bag of groceries to her chest.

"Zack died." I didn't feel right about going into the gory details.

"Oh, my God," she said, staring in horror at the police. "And he was such a nice man."

I nodded in agreement.

"Maybe I should've called the police. But I thought I was being a racist; Zack was entitled to see whoever he liked. And now he's dead."

I turned my head in the woman's direction. I wasn't quite sure I had heard her correctly.

"You saw someone with Zack? Today?"

The woman switched her groceries to her other hand. The package of Fritos sitting on top bobbled slightly then settled down. "This morning." She looked at me, a frown line settling between her eyes. "But just because he was black doesn't mean he killed Zack. And it's not as if I heard sounds of violence or anything like that . . ."

A band of iron started squeezing my chest. I thought I was having a heart attack before realizing my anxiety had come back.

"What did he look like? Zack's visitor?"

But even as she spoke, I already knew what her answer would be.

"He was one of those Rastafarians. You know, with the dreadlocks. Very thin. I thought he was going door-to-door to collect money for something, but he never came to mine."

She looked relieved at the thought, the crease between

her eyes temporarily smoothing out. But then she bit her lower lip as a new thought crossed her mind.

"Do you think I should tell the police?"

"No," I said, without thinking. "He didn't kill Zack. Zack committed suicide." That better be what happened.

"Oh," said the woman, softly, sadly. "He seemed like the last person in the world who would want to do that." We commiserated in silence before she added, "I mean, he had a great job. He wrote for one of my favorite shows. Babbitt & Brooks." She looked at me proudly, as if her acquaintance with Zack automatically made her a part of the actual series.

"Yes, I know," I said. I walked around to the driver's side of my car and unlocked the door.

"You're sure I shouldn't tell the police?" she asked after me anxiously.

"I'm sure," I said. Or at least not right away. Give me an hour's head start. I swung open the door and slid into my seat. As I pulled away from the curb I looked at the woman in my rear view mirror. She was still staring at the police, juggling her grocery bag, and I knew I hadn't really convinced her to not say anything.

2.

I pulled into a parking lot behind a Vons supermarket on Ventura and Laurel Canyon and called Sherman. His cell number was programmed into my phone and he picked up after one ring.

"Sherman, it's me. Susan."

There was a pause as if Sherman was trying to

remember who I was, although my name would have appeared on his caller ID. "Susan," he said. "How are you?"

"I was just at Zack's house," I told him. "He's dead."

There was another pause. A longer one. "I was there, Susan. At his house this morning. But he was alive when I left."

I let out my breath. Sherman couldn't possibly know I had talked with a neighbor who had seen him. His admitting that he saw Zack had to be proof he had nothing to hide.

"The next door neighbor saw you," I told him.

I heard his muttered, "Shit," before hurrying on. "I told her not to tell the police, but I don't think I convinced her. We have to meet. Now."

"Aw, Jesus," Sherman said. He sounded ragged and far away. "Yeah. Okay. Where are you?"

I told him.

"Come over the hill into Hollywood. It'll be faster than if I come to you. You know the Denny's on Hollywood Boulevard and La Brea?" I said that I did. "I'll meet you there in twenty minutes."

I thought it would take me longer to get there than twenty minutes—now that it was the height of rush hour—but I just said, "Fine, see you then," and hung up the phone. Fortunately, no patrol cars seemed to be cruising the streets looking for me. I got back in my car and made a right on Laurel Canyon, directing my straining car up into the Hollywood Hills.

The road was lined with large, nouveau riche, bad taste homes until it crested Mulholland. On the downward slope, Laurel Canyon became narrower, twistier, and steeper, the homes older, the foliage thicker. Traffic was bumper-to-bumper heading back to the Valley, but, heading south, I made good time into Hollywood, too concerned about Sherman to give my usual mental wave at Harry Houdini's deserted mansion.

Ten minutes later, I squeezed into one of the last spaces available in the Denny's parking lot and entered the restaurant. Sherman was sitting in a booth in the back, and he lifted a long, skinny arm to catch my attention.

I slid in across from him. Sherman wouldn't meet my gaze as he stared into his coffee cup as if searching for the answers to Life. A harried waitress appeared at the table with a coffee pot. She refilled Sherman's cup as she said, "What can I get you?"

I hadn't even looked at the plastic menu sitting in front of me. I wasn't particularly hungry. Nevertheless, I didn't think Denny's would let me sit in the booth drinking water for an hour.

"A hamburger," I said. "Medium well. And fries."

She turned to Sherman. "I'll have the same," he said.

The woman nodded and moved off.

"What were you doing in his house, Sherman?"

Sherman didn't seem taken aback by my lack of preliminaries.

"Zack called me. He invited me over for coffee."

Sherman's voice expressed no surprise, no emotion whatsoever.

"When was this?"

"Yesterday. Sometime in the afternoon." Which accounted for one of Zack's many phone calls.

"Did he say what he wanted?"

"Just that he needed to talk to me about a few things. He had heard about my getting fired and said he might be able to help me find another job."

"But why ask to see you in person? That's something he can tell you over the phone. Or in an e-mail."

"That's what I thought, but he also said he wanted to show me something."

"Which was?"

"Rebecca's car."

I sat back in the booth, unable to speak for a moment.

"He actually showed you Rebecca's car?"

Sherman nodded and his fingers were clenched so tightly around his coffee cup I thought the handle would snap. "It was in the garage. He said he found it parked there on Sunday when he came home."

No wonder Zack was acting so weird on Monday. But why didn't he say anything to anybody? And why didn't he call the police? I voiced that last question to Sherman.

"He didn't think the police would believe he hadn't put it there himself."

"Was he blaming you for putting it there?"

"That's what I thought when he first showed it to me. I thought he was trying to shock a reaction out of me. But he had an electric garage door opener. How would I have gotten in there in the first place?"

I explained about the circuit breaker outside the house.

Sherman looked momentarily taken aback, then shrugged.

"It doesn't matter," he said. "Zack acted like he knew who did it . . . and that it wasn't me."

I was glued to my seat, eyes wide, wishing I could suck the answer out of him. "Then who?"

Sherman took a swallow of his coffee, prolonging my agony. When he put the cup back in its saucer, he finally looked at me.

"Zack didn't know that for sure. He also wanted to go over everything I did the night Rebecca was killed, trying to jog my memory."

"And?"

Sherman shook his head. "Nothing. The television was on in my office. I was watching some old movie on TV. I probably even dozed off for a while. Nobody came into the main area—or if they did, I didn't hear them."

I slumped back in my seat. The waitress arrived with our hamburgers, asked us if we needed anything else then moved off when we told her no. Sherman suddenly stiffened, staring over my shoulder.

"What?" I asked in alarm.

"Cops," he whispered.

I turned my head and saw two uniformed officers standing by the cashier. I didn't recognize them from back at Zack's house, and really didn't know whether Lu and Wagner would send an APB out on me—or for Sherman if the next door neighbor spilled her guts. The two cops joked with the hostess and moved off to sit at the counter. I turned back to Sherman, who smiled sheepishly at me.

"Sorry. I thought—"

I cut him off. "Me, too. Don't worry about it."

But I knew we were going to have to deal with the police sooner or later. They were going to want to know why I took off. Either I told them the truth or I invented a plausible excuse. I wondered if Sherman could be convinced to voluntarily talk to them.

"What happened after you told him you didn't remember anything?" I asked before picking up my hamburger and taking a bite.

"Nothing. Zack thanked me for coming by, said he'd work on getting another job for me, and I went home."

"Did he say anything about his argument with Rebecca the night of her death?"

"No. And I didn't ask."

"Do you think he killed her and then covered his tracks by pretending not to know about the car?"

"Could be." Sherman chewed in silence for a minute. "But if that's true, he's a damn good actor."

"But if he didn't, why did he kill himself? Did he look remorseful to you . . . or guilty?"

"No. And who said he killed himself?"

I can't say as I reacted with surprise to Sherman's comment. It had been floating around in the back of my mind the minute the cops pulled Zack's body out of Rebecca's car.

"Do you think Zack invited the murderer over to look at the car—same as he did with you? What if he was testing everyone he suspected?"

"I think it's a possibility," Sherman said. He helped himself to a french fry. "It could be he really didn't know who the murderer was. He may have thought I was a suspect and was asking me questions to see if I'd slip up."

"But who else would he ask?"

"You tell me," Sherman said.

I started to shrug in ignorance, and then I thought of

Peggy who had come in late, looking like a great weight had been lifted off her shoulders. Because Zack was no longer alive to accuse her of murder? Was that what he had done when he made her cry?

"What time did you leave his house this morning?" I asked.

Sherman screwed up his eyes in thought. "Eight. Eight-fifteen the latest."

I told him about my suspicions regarding Peggy.

"What about Charles and Ray?" he asked.

"Charles showed up at nine-thirty, nine-forty-five. Ray at ten, ten-fifteen." I paused, chilled by another thought.

"What is it?" Sherman asked.

"Gail didn't work today. I remember when the schedule was planned, and Patrick told me that Gail would actually have a day off."

Sherman and I looked at one another. "You don't think . . .?" he began.

"I don't know." I shuddered to think what the ratings would be like should Gail be arrested. I almost believed Ray would frame her for both murders if it meant holding on to that twenty-five share. Then I had another thought. "Couldn't the cops prove that Zack was forced into the car? I mean, he wouldn't go in willingly. The killer would have to clunk him on the head first."

"There might be signs of struggle. There was nothing obvious when you saw him?"

I shook my head, not wanting to remember an ashen-faced Zack, dead on the oil-stained pavement of his driveway. Sherman said, "And even if they did find something and that neighbor tells them about me, that brings us back to square one."

We sat in silence, contemplating this, unable to finish our hamburgers. "Sherman, does the name Michael Keller sound familiar to you?"

Sherman shook his head. "No. Why?"

I told him about the detectives flashing Keller's photo around the warehouse, and my theory that he was Rebecca's drug dealer.

"He was also one of the construction workers, hired through Bob Berg. Rebecca wrote him a check; I saw it on her desk."

"Good-looking guy? Slim? Dark hair?"

"Yes," I said, starting to get excited. "You did see him?"

"Maybe. I was cleaning up the bullpen one night. This is before you came on the show. Rebecca was still in her office, but she didn't know I was there. I heard her talking with someone, and he left with something in his hand that could've been a check."

"What were they talking about?"

More silence as Sherman tried to remember. The woman sitting behind me was talking loudly on her cell. I almost turned around to ask her to take it outside but I wasn't sure if she would or only talk louder.

"She was mad at him, I remember that much. She's always gotta chew someone out. She said something like, 'I got you this job. Isn't that enough?'"

"Wait a minute. According to the foreman, Bob Berg got him the job. Do you think she meant the construction job?"

"Susan, I have no idea what she was talking about. I didn't even know who the guy was."

"Sorry," I said. "What else did she say?"

"That's about it, I think. He said something like, 'Don't sweet talk me,' not taking her very seriously. And then he walked out of the office."

"Did he see you?"

"Yeah, he saw me. But he just smiled and went out the front door. He didn't seem to care I was there."

"So he didn't get mad at her at all? For chewing him out?"

"Not that I could tell."

But the last person to be with Rebecca had gotten so angry with her he (or she) had taken her Women in Television Award and whacked her over the head with it so many times there was practically nothing left of her skull.

"Did he seem like a person who would hold it all in until he was at the end of his rope?"

"Susan, I'm not a shrink. I hardly heard the guy say two words to her before he was out the door."

"But we've got to find someone with a motive!"

"Everyone has a motive," Sherman said. "What we need is proof."

Amen to that.

"So what do we do now?"

"I'm moving in with my girlfriend. At least until things cool down."

I looked at Sherman in surprise. I didn't know he had a girlfriend, and I felt a sudden twinge of jealousy. What was I? A walking hormone? I sternly reminded myself to keep my mind on business and pushed that unwanted twinge away.

"Do you think maybe you should talk to Lu and

Wagner?"

Sherman looked at me and laughed without humor. I looked down in embarrassment at the hamburger grease congealing on my plate.

"It was just a thought," I said.

"What about you? What if the cops want to know why you disappeared?"

"I'll tell them I don't remember them asking me to stay."

"And if they ask you about your conversation with the next door neighbor?"

I shrugged. Sherman put down his own hamburger. "You suspect Zack found Rebecca's car, then called a bunch of people who might know something to his house and confronted them with the evidence."

I nodded. "And one of those people killed him."

"Then why put yourself in any more hot water? Call the cops and tell them. Better you should go to them first than they come after you."

"But what about you? Why don't we both go to the police? It might help your case if you come to them voluntarily."

A corner of Sherman's mouth quirked. "Look, Susan, you do what you have to. I can take care of myself."

I wasn't so sure. I wanted to do the right thing—for Sherman and for Zack. I looked at Sherman who had pushed his plate away, glancing at the cops at the counter. "You won't hate me if I call the detectives?"

Sherman shook his head. "Just give me an hour. I need to find a lawyer."

3.

It was too late to return to work so I drove home. I desperately wanted to talk to Craig, but the lights in his apartment were out and he didn't answer my knock. I wondered if he was out on a date, then remembered he worked Tuesday nights, giving swimming lessons to kids at the local Y.

Jennifer had left a message, asking if I had found Zack and to call her whether I had or not. Apparently, word wasn't out yet about his death and I didn't have the energy to call her and give her the news and deal with her reaction. Wagner also left a terse message, asking me to call him at my earliest convenience. I called him back and got his voicemail. Relieved, I left a message, apologizing for taking off and telling him I had some information for him. I then called Linda Ramsay, Romulus Television's office manager. Having started out in the Romulus temp pool, she had worked her way up to her present position and pretty much created her own hours. When I temped in the main office, Linda wouldn't come in until ten or eleven in the morning, but always stayed until eight or nine at night. A night owl, she claimed early evening was the only time she could get any decent work done. She picked up her phone on the seventh ring.

"Hello?" she answered breathlessly. She had probably been down the hall either going to or from the copy room.

"Linda, it's Susan. Susan Kaplan."

"Hi. I've been meaning to call you."

"About what?"

"About everything. Rebecca's death. The flood in your office. The main office is going nuts."

"So are we. That's why I'm calling.

"What's up?"

"You're gonna have to sit down for this one, Linda."

"Okay, I'm sitting." But I could hear a smile in her voice, and I knew she wasn't taking me seriously.

"Zack's dead. I found him in his garage this afternoon." There was utter silence from Linda's end of the phone, and then she broke into a peal of laughter.

"Good one, Sue. I almost fell for it."

I gritted my teeth. I hated being called Sue, and Linda knew it. She had probably done it deliberately as revenge for my "teasing" her about Zack.

"It's not a joke, Linda. I'm sure it'll be on the news tonight. He didn't show up for work today. So I went to his house and found him sitting in Rebecca's car. He probably died of carbon monoxide poisoning."

There was another pause and Linda slowly let out her breath.

"Oh, my God. He killed himself?"

"It looks that way, but I'm not sure." I told her about Sherman's visit to Zack and what Zack had told him about the car.

I knew I could trust Linda; she had found Sherman and his band playing in some rinky-dink club and decided to become their manager. She had also hired Sherman to be our night watchman and was as interested in protecting him as I was.

"What should we do?" she asked as soon as I brought her up to speed.

"Do you think you can get hold of Michael Keller's personnel file? Maybe it explains why Bob Berg hired him."

"I'll try," she said. "The HR director's assistant might help me. She owes me one. I got her the job."

All the assistants at Romulus owed Linda for getting them their jobs.

"Can you go into her office now?" I asked.

"No. All her files are computerized and I don't know HR's password. I'll talk to Gina about it first thing tomorrow. Better yet, I'll call her at home tonight. She can get in bright and early and pull it for me."

"Linda, I owe you big time for this," I said.

"I'll tell you what. If Gina can get the file for me tomorrow morning, I'll swing by with it at lunch time. You can thank me by filling me in on everything over lunch."

"You've got a deal," I replied and we said our good-byes and hung up. I then braced myself and called Jennifer, telling her the news about Zack.

"Oh, my God," she said. "Oh, my God."

"I can't believe the police didn't already tell the office."

"No." Her voice sounded shaky. "Maybe they told Ray. Sandy said he got a call, and tore out of the office, told her he wasn't coming back for the rest of the day."

Before we could really thrash it out, Craig's frantic knocking on my door cut the call short.

Zack's death had made the news. Channel Eight had broken into its regular programming to bring its viewers a Special Bulletin. We watched from my TV, Craig leaving his take-out beef burrito to cool, forgotten, in the see-through plastic container sitting in his lap.

Debra Chandler, the newswoman who had hounded Ray in the parking lot after we drove in from location, spoke sincerely into the camera, standing in front of Zack's now deserted-looking home. "And although his death is an apparent suicide, police are seeking the whereabouts of Sherman O'Dell, a young, African American male seen at the North residence earlier today. He is thought to have worked as a janitor in the warehouse where Babbitt & Brooks is filmed. Is there a connection to the brutal slaying of Rebecca Saunders, the associate producer who was murdered just one week ago? If the police know, they are keeping those thoughts to themselves. Back to you, Chet."

"Damn. Damn, damn, damn!" I buried my face in my hands as Chet Williams, the Channel Eight anchor, thanked Debra and told us to stay tuned for more news at eleven. Craig turned off the TV then looked at me curiously.

"What's the matter?"

I told Craig what I had told Linda. He stared at me, pushing his glasses up the bridge of his nose.

"How do you get yourself into these messes?" he asked.

"I wish I knew. Sherman's hiding out with his girlfriend—"

Craig covered my mouth with his hand. "Don't tell me! I don't want to be an accessory."

His hand was warm and dry. I removed it in order to speak, trying to ignore the physical attraction I felt for him.

"You won't. It's hearsay."

Craig looked thoughtfully at his congealing burrito. "Do you think this will make Sherman come out of hiding?"

"I hope so. He told me he was going to find a lawyer."

"Do you think Zack killed himself?"

I shook my head. "No." Again, the memory of Peggy crying rose before me. "No," I said again, more loudly. "I think he knew something about Rebecca's death. And he told the wrong person. So he died."

"Who do you think he told?"

Images swam before me: Peggy's tear-stained face; Ray's angry mouth mangling his cigar; Charles's lips tightening in anger and disgust at Ray; Michael Keller, good-looking and devil-may-care, as he posed for an anonymous photographer in the park, smiling into the camera.

"I don't know, Craig," I said, liking the sound of his name in the back of my throat. "I wish I did."

"Maybe it's a good thing you don't," he said. "At least you're still alive."

4.

I braced myself for another day of hell. The reporters were lurking on the street as I drove into the studio parking lot the next day. They called to me from the other side of the fence as I walked from my car to the front entrance. What did I know of Zack North's death? Did he kill Rebecca Saunders? Was it a love affair gone wrong? I wondered if the Scoop article about Gail and Rebecca would now be forgotten in light of the new rumor that Zack and Rebecca were lovers.

We walked around the office like zombies. Not many people liked Rebecca, and her death, I thought, was never treated very seriously. Or at least as very real. But Zack was a well-liked, talented member of the Babbitt & Brooks team. Charles sat behind his desk, head bowed, staring blankly at his script-strewn desk. Ray had blasted in, shouted to Sandy that he wasn't taking any phone calls, and slammed his office door shut behind him. Peggy wandered in, looking like death warmed over. Her hair seemed to have turned gray overnight and there were purple shadows under her eyes.

"Hold my phone calls," she whispered to me before shakily crossing the bullpen and entering her own office. The door gently shut after her, and Jennifer and I pretended not to hear her muffled weeping from inside.

The phones rang off the hook, and Jennifer and I wondered at the likelihood of Ray bringing in a temp to help us answer them. In spite of his desire not to take any phone calls, Ray did speak with Cliff Rosen and Bob Berg. Rumors floated around the office that production might close for a week. Zack's script was scheduled to start shooting the next day and still needed more rewrites, and Peggy was in no shape to handle them. Charles had his hands full with a script of his own. The brief hiatus would give the writers time to whip Zack's script into shootable shape as well as repair the disintegrating morale of cast and crew.

Patrick Hager wandered into the bullpen later in the morning. He had Zack's script tucked under one arm and the board under the other. The board was a large square of reinforced cardboard that folded out into two extra sections from the middle: Patrick used it to break down day/night shots, locations, and exterior/interior scenes. His white blond hair fell over one eye, his skin was pinkish white with stress.

"You mean you're actually going to work on Zack's script today?" Jennifer looked from Patrick to the board in disbelief. Patrick shrugged.

"I've been summoned by the king of the land and am at his mercy."

"But I thought production was going to shut down," I said.

"You may be right. But as the court jester, I am always the last to know." He cited the words mechanically, as if thinking that's what we expected him to say, but without actually believing in them himself.

Patrick continued on into Ray's office. When he was out of earshot, Jennifer turned to me and snorted.

"Does he think he's a character in One Flew Over the Cuckoo's Nest?"

"No," I said. "Camelot."

She looked at me, confused, but I refused to elaborate. Patrick's dreams were his own to share or keep secret, and it wasn't my job to give them away. Twenty minutes later he returned, looking whiter and more stressed.

"You're right, Susan. Production's closing down for a week." The mechanical courtliness was gone, replaced by down-to-earth shock. "The writers are going to take the time to polish Zack's script and Ray wants to bring in another staff writer."

Ray's certainly not letting any grass grow under his feet, I thought. But to be fair, shutting down production seemed like the only way of giving everyone breathing room to deal with Zack's death.

"That's going to cost you a fortune," Jennifer said.

Patrick nodded. "At least it's not coming out of my pocket." He slowly walked out of the room, trailing the board after him.

Linda Ramsay called to say she had Keller's file.

"I couldn't help taking a peek," she said. "You're not going to believe it."

"Tell me."

"Uh-uh. Wait 'til lunch." She hung up. I knew it wasn't fair to leave Jennifer stuck with all the phones, but when I explained the purpose of my meeting with Linda, she practically pushed me out the door.

"Just tell me everything you find out," she said before I left.

Linda agreed to meet me at The Oriental Enchilada, a cheap Chinese-Mexican diner not far from the warehouse. I didn't want to take too long for lunch, in case Ray noticed my extended absence and complained. Not that he, Charles, or Peggy were noticing much that day. I took the last table available in the middle of the room. Not very private, but from the sounds of it no one around me was paying attention. Linda arrived ten minutes later, looking hot and out of breath.

"Is it my imagination or does traffic get worse every year?" she asked as she thumped into the seat across from me, blowing strands of silky black hair out of her face. Her large, sapphire eyes smiled at me in greeting.

"Forget about the traffic," I said, feeling my usual pang of envy at Linda's peaches-and-cream complexion and tall, stylish figure. She wore a blue silk shirt that matched her eyes, a black leather miniskirt, and black high-heeled boots. "What's the story with Michael Keller?"

Linda smiled mysteriously and picked up a menu, ignoring the sly glances and nudges of the two men sitting at the table next to us. "What's good to eat around here?"

"Linda!"

She looked coyly at me from over the menu. "Trust me," she said. "This is worth waiting for."

With poorly concealed impatience I waited while she chose the cheese enchiladas with rice and beans (obviously, she was born with that figure) while I opted for the cheap, but filling wor wonton soup.

After Mrs. Huang, the harried owner of the restaurant, had taken our orders and disappeared into the kitchen, I turned back to Linda.

"Okay, okay," she smiled, giving in to my pleading look. She reached into the capacious shoulder bag slung across her chair and pulled out a computer printout. "It was actually easier than I thought. Gina told me she had already pulled the file for the police. She just made a copy of what she had given them."

I wondered if that meant there was nothing helpful in the file that would link Keller to Rebecca's murder. After all, the cops still hadn't made an arrest; in fact, they seemed to suspect Sherman over Keller. Nevertheless, I eagerly scanned the pages; Linda had said there was something interesting in them.

Everything seemed in order. Keller's name, address, social security number. Previous job descriptions. I looked up.

"He must never have been caught selling cocaine," I said, noting where he checked the "no" box after the

"Have you ever been convicted of a crime?" question.

"We don't know he was her drug dealer" was all Linda would say. "Skip to the end."

So I did. And stared in surprise. Under name to be reached in case of emergency, Keller had written, "Rebecca Saunders." After relationship, he put, "Ex-wife."

I looked at Linda, speechless. She grinned broadly at me. "I told you it was good."

"He . . . Oh, God . . . I'm an idiot!"

Linda looked at me, puzzled. "Why? How were you supposed to know?"

I told her about my meeting with Lily Wainess, the former writers' assistant. "She told me she was having an affair with Rebecca's ex. Rebecca found out and that's why Lily quit."

"So, why does that make you an idiot?"

"She called him 'Kelly.' As in Keller. Michael Keller."

Linda's mouth formed a perfect "O." Jennifer was going to roll over and die when she heard this.

"What else did she say? Are they still together?" Linda asked, leaning across the table.

"She said no."

"And you believed her?"

"At the time I had no reason to think she was lying. I still don't. How could you not know Rebecca and Keller were married? Hollywood is a small town."

"They probably got divorced before she started working for Ray," Linda said. I remembered Lily said something to that effect. "Was he at the memorial service?"

"No, he wasn't. And Rebecca's parents didn't seem to miss him. Maybe they didn't approve of the marriage."

"Would your parents—if you had married an out-of-work actor you had to find construction work for?"

My parents wouldn't even approve of my marrying someone who wasn't Jewish. But that was another story.

"Obviously they still kept in touch," I pointed out.

"Rebecca must've talked Bob Berg into getting him this job, and even then kept slipping him money. I wonder why?"

"He still could be her drug dealer."

"But why let him work at the warehouse?"

"Easy. A convenient way for him to deliver the cocaine."

"Did Lily mention if he did drugs?"

"It didn't come up—because I didn't know Rebecca's ex and Michael Keller were one and the same."

"So, the sixty-four thousand dollar question is, do we think he killed her?"

"If he did, he also killed off a source of income."

"But maybe he was too angry to think about that when he killed her."

"And what got him so angry?"

"She decided to stop doing drugs?"

Linda and I looked at one another then simultaneously went, "Nah."

"You know, this is just pie in the sky," Linda said. "We don't really know if he sold her drugs."

"So, if the checks weren't for drugs, but just to tide him over, maybe she decided to stop, and that's what got him mad," I said.

Linda thought about it. "Could be. What else?"

"He was blackmailing her. And she didn't want to pay

any more."

"Blackmailing her over what?"

"Her affair with Ray . . . or Gail."

Linda only looked half-convinced. "Do you think he was the Scoop's source?"

"Why not?"

"But why do that kind of damage after she was dead?"

"They paid him big bucks for the story."

Before Linda could respond, our food arrived. We spent the rest of the meal talking about Zack's death and wondering why Keller, if he was the murderer, would think Zack knew enough to risk killing him.

Neither of us could come up with an acceptable answer, and I returned to the warehouse to fill Jennifer in on the latest news.

5.

Two things happened at once when I got back. The phone rang and Detective Wagner exited Peggy's office. He said, "Susan, I need to talk to you," just as I picked up the phone and answered, "Babbitt & Brooks."

"Is this Susan?" the voice on the other end asked as Wagner crossed to my desk. Jennifer appeared from over his shoulder; she must have run down the hall from Charles's office to answer the phone, not knowing I was back.

"Yes, this is Susan," I said, not recognizing the voice. I was too intent on Wagner, in the pit of my gut knowing why he needed to speak with me and not looking forward to that discussion.

"Hi, it's Jesse Mendez. How are you?"

For a second the name didn't register, so focused was I on Wagner. Jennifer had slid around him to sit behind her desk. From her expression I could tell she was warning me about something but I didn't know what.

"I'm fine. How are you?"

"Great. I was calling to see how the new scripts are going."

I started to ask, "Why's that any of your business?" then paused. Oh, God. Jesse Mendez. Pain-in-the-neck actor.

"The scripts are going great," I lied. Wagner helped himself to a cup of coffee from the coffeemaker on the credenza.

"I heard about Zack's suicide on the news last night. Did he really kill Rebecca?"

What was with this guy? Was life at Babbitt & Brooks his daily dose of soap opera entertainment? I was now so distracted by his call, Wagner's presence, and Jennifer's unspoken warning that I didn't pay attention to what I was saying. "Zack didn't kill Rebecca."

Wagner turned to me so sharply he spilled coffee on the carpet. Jennifer buried her face in her hands and Jesse yelped, "He didn't?"

Too late, I realized my goof. Wagner set his cup down and walked toward me, looking like he was ready to jerk the phone from my hands. Quickly I said, "Jesse, I didn't mean that. Look, it's real busy here and I have to go. I'll call you back."

I hung up before Jesse could reply and stared up at Wagner, looking, I'm sure, like a puppy who accidentally piddled on his master's antique Persian carpet.

"I'm sorry," I told him. "It just slipped out."

"Do you know something you care to share with us, Ms. Kaplan?" So, we were back to "Ms. Kaplan." In spite of his struggle to remain expressionless, I could tell Wagner was angry.

"I don't know anything. Honest." I suddenly remembered my lunch with Linda and our perusal of Michael Keller's personnel file, and my face flushed red.

Wagner didn't look like he believed me a whole hell of a lot. He towered over my desk, his muscles bulging from his dark green T-shirt, looking about ready to burst through his Sons of Anarchy motorcycle jacket. My face flushed even redder and my hairline started to itch. Who needed a lie detector when anyone could just watch the color of my face?

I broke eye contact first and glanced at Jennifer. She looked at me sadly and I read pity in her eyes.

"Can we use Sherman O'Dell's office to talk?" Wagner asked.

Miserably, I nodded my head, still not looking at him.

"Let's go," he said.

Walking down the writers' corridor on the way to Sherman's office was like walking the last few yards to the electric chair. Both Peggy's and Charles's doors were open, and the two writers were in their offices, clearly having overheard our conversation.

I glanced in on Peggy, who sat behind her desk, red-eyed, clutching a tissue. She didn't even bother looking away when our eyes met, and I could read the same pity in her face as I did in Jennifer's. Charles stared at a script, pretending to read it, but I swear I saw his ears twitch.

Wagner sat behind Sherman's desk; I, in the straight-back chair next to it.

"How do you know Zack didn't kill Rebecca?" was his first, terse question.

"I don't," I whispered, staring at my hands clenched in my lap. "I wasn't thinking."

"Where is Sherman O'Dell?"

My eyes flew up to meet his. "I don't know." My face got red again.

"Susan, we can talk about this here or down at the station. Your choice."

I stared at Wagner, my body suddenly ice cold. What would my parents say? The reporters were still outside the building. What if this got on the news?

"Sherman didn't kill Zack," I said.

"How do you know? Did he tell you that? Why did you leave the house when I asked you to stay?" There were too many questions. I shook my head as if to clear them from my mind.

"Can I start at the beginning?" I asked.

"I wish you would."

"The next door neighbor told me about seeing Sherman at Zack's house. I knew you'd think he'd have something to do with Zack's death so I called him and we met. Sherman told me about Zack showing him Rebecca's car. Sherman thought Zack was blaming him for putting it there, but actually Zack was trying to figure out what happened the night Rebecca was killed. He didn't think Sherman killed Rebecca, he just wanted to know if Sherman remembered anything that might give a clue to the murderer."

"And did he?"

I shook my head again.

"Sherman said he didn't hear anything." I paused, suddenly remembering. "He did once see Michael Keller coming out of Rebecca's office though."

Wagner remained expressionless. "How did he know about Michael Keller?"

I again stared at my lap. "I told him," I said.

Wagner tensed. "Susan, you have to learn not to talk about a murder investigation. It could warn the murderer and put you in danger."

I thought of the water pouring out of the ceiling onto my desk and chair. But that couldn't have been deliberate. No one knew I'd be at the warehouse at seven o'clock in the morning.

"What did Sherman have to say about Keller?" Wagner asked, still sounding angry.

"He overheard Rebecca tell Keller she didn't want to give him any more money. That getting him the job was enough. I think she meant the construction job."

"Did Sherman describe Keller for you?"

"Yes. Though he didn't know who he was."

"And Keller's reaction to Rebecca's comments?"

"Sherman said he made a joke out of it, then he smiled at Sherman when he left the office."

"So he actually saw Sherman?" Wagner looked at me with something approaching interest. I wondered, my heart lifting with sudden hope, whether Wagner thought Keller might be trying to frame Sherman.

"Yes. Sherman said he did."

Wagner crossed his leg at his knee, leaned back in his

chair, and regarded me thoughtfully.

"And where is Sherman now? Do you know?"

"Do you promise not to arrest him?" I asked, and then felt silly for asking it. This man didn't have to promise me anything.

"Why are you so convinced of his innocence?" Wagner asked.

"Because I know him. He wouldn't hurt a fly." Then I remembered they also said that about the Son of Sam. I quickly added, "I think Zack was calling a bunch of people to come to his house the day he was . . . the day he died. If you just checked his phone records—"

"Where is he, Susan?" I noticed Wagner wasn't making any promises, but I couldn't lie. I could only hope that the truth would eventually surface. I had a gut feeling that Wagner was a reasonable man. Or so I hoped.

"He's staying with his girlfriend. At least that's what he told me he was going to do."

"And her name?"

"I don't know."

Wagner stared at me, his eyes small and hard.

"I don't."

Wagner looked at me for another second and then reached into the inside pocket of his jacket. I thought he was going to pull out the Miranda warning and begin reading me my rights. I braced myself, placing a hand over my stomach as an ice pick of fear chipped away at my intestines.

Instead, he took out a piece of paper, unfolded it, and handed it to me. My eyes blurred with relief, and I used an arm to wipe the sweat off my forehead. I concentrated on the piece of paper. It was a photocopy of a note. Zack's suicide note.

"I killed Rebecca. I can't take the guilt anymore. Please forgive me."

It was typewritten, no signature.

"That sound like your boss?" Wagner asked.

"I don't know. He was acting funny on Monday."

"How funny?"

I shrugged. "Making lots of phone calls. Avoiding Peggy, Charles, and Ray. He told me he wasn't coming in on Tuesday because he had to take care of some things."

"What things?"

"He didn't say."

"Did your friend Sherman say he sounded suicidal?"

"No. He said Zack wanted to find out who Rebecca's murderer was."

Wagner nodded to himself, as if confirming his own private thoughts. "Did Zack use a computer here at work?"

I nodded. "But he writes his scripts by hand." I paused. "Did you find any evidence that he wrote the two death threats?"

"Why are you asking that?"

"If Zack was murdered, then maybe he didn't kill Rebecca. Or send her the death threats."

Wagner slid the the copy of the note out of my fingers, tucking it back into his jacket pocket. Then he leaned so close, I could smell traces of peppermint on his breath.

"I am not required to answer any of your questions regarding this investigation," he said in a low, flat voice. "People are not innocent just because they're your friends.

How do I know you and Sherman weren't in it together?"

"We weren't." My voice was hoarse with fear. "We didn't kill anyone."

Wagner merely grunted then pushed back his chair.

"We'll see," he said. He stepped aside so that I could precede him through the door. I tried not to touch him, not wanting him to feel—or even sense—my body trembling.

6.

Jennifer, of course, wanted to know everything as soon as Wagner walked out the door. But I had another agenda, and I stalled her pleas for a blow-by-blow by leaving the bullpen as soon as Wagner left the warehouse.

Peggy was still in her office, staring into space, when I lightly knocked on her open door.

"Can I talk to you for a minute?" I asked.

She pulled herself out of her reverie with an effort.

"Sure," she said, not really focusing on me. "Come on in."

I entered the room and shut the door. Peggy's office was the same windowless cubicle as everyone else's, but pretty pink throw pillows brightened the gray couch, and framed posters of exotic foreign cities warmed the dingy paneled walls. I pitched my voice low, knowing Jennifer would be straining to hear every word. "I need to talk to you," I said. "Outside the office."

Peggy looked at me in surprise. "About what? Are you having problems with Jennifer or Sandy?"

"No. It's about what's going on here. Rebecca's murder. And Zack's."

Peggy paled and turned away. She absently tapped her pen against her teeth.

"Peggy, I overheard you the other night, with Zack. When you were crying."

Peggy looked down at her desk. "Oh."

"I was just questioned by the police. They're looking for Sherman. You can tell me whatever happened between you and Zack is none of my business, but if it isn't then I think you should talk to the police."

She put her pen carefully down on the desk and sighed. "Did you tell them what you overheard? Between Zack and me?"

"No," I said. "But I need to have a good reason not to."

She stared at me then apparently came to a decision because she squared her shoulders, her head high, as if ready to face the guillotine with as much dignity as possible. She said, "How about we have dinner tonight?" Now it was my turn to look taken aback. Peggy managed a wan smile.

"I know Romulus barely pays you a living wage," she said. "You've been a good assistant, and I owe you. So, dinner tonight. My treat. And we'll talk."

"Thanks, Peggy."

I hoped she wouldn't regret it.

Peggy chose to have dinner at Philippe's, on N. Alameda, an old Los Angeles landmark, just north of downtown and on the edge of Chinatown, known for its French dip sandwiches. As we gave our orders at the counter, my mouth salivated at the thought of roast beef on French bread, dripping with the slightly salty, au jus sauce.

The restaurant was crowded and noisy, as old men, tourists, and families vied for seats at the long lacquered tables lined with stools in the main room. Maybe Peggy was avoiding this conversation after all, I thought, until she waved me over to a smaller room next to the stairs. It held six tables for four, and only one other group was inside: teenagers too involved with themselves to worry about us. Peggy and I placed our food-laden trays on a table in the rear corner, and I dropped my purse on the sawdust-covered floor.

Conversation, at first, was superficial as we concentrated on our food. Peggy kept up with small talk, although I felt she really wasn't paying much attention. She did react in surprise to my Dress Blue spec script and Charles's interest in it. I told her about Ray first rejecting it, then deciding to take another look, then rejecting it again. She claimed to know nothing about it.

"It's true he's looking for a writer to replace Zack," she said. "But I think he's going to try the writer out on a freelance basis first before he makes a decision."

"Can you and Charles handle the work until that happens?"

Peggy shrugged. "We don't have much of a choice. And with the money they pay us, we really can't complain." She and Charles, I knew, made six-figure salaries, which didn't include the thousands of dollars they'd make in future residuals when their Babbitt & Brooks episodes reran over the summer, and beyond in syndication.

I could tell that, despite the comment regarding her high salary, Peggy wasn't looking forward to the upcoming weeks and probably wondered about Ray, who was so sensitive to the portrayal of women on camera, but basically ignored their needs off. How could he hold on to the high ratings when he burdened his writers with more work and less time in which to get it done?

Peggy stared without interest at her turkey sandwich.

"In a way I envy you," she said unexpectedly.

"Me?" A potato chip paused half-way to my mouth.

She brushed thick hair off her forehead. "I remember when I first started out. Nothing was so much fun as the first script I ever wrote. The words just poured out. I gave up lunch hours to write. Came in early. Left late. I was an assistant district attorney, you know."

"I didn't know," I said surprised. I never much imagined Peggy's life before Babbitt & Brooks.

She nodded. "Burned out by thirty."

She looked down at her plate, lost in thought.

"So you started out writing spec scripts?"

"No. Zack was researching a screenplay he was writing, and mutual friends gave him my name. We talked a couple of times, I helped him out with the legal aspects of his script. He liked what I had to contribute. So we became writing partners."

I took a sip of my Dr. Pepper. "But you don't . . . didn't . . . write together on the show."

"No. Zack thought I needed the self-confidence to write on my own."

"It worked. I think you're a terrific writer." I meant it, too.

Peggy smiled across the table at me. "Thanks. Some days I'm not so sure." She played with her plastic fork, her smile fading.

I chewed and swallowed a rather large piece of roast beef, drenched in dip. "About that night . . . When you were crying . . ."

"It had nothing to do with Zack's suicide. You have to trust me on that."

"The police don't think Zack killed himself," I said.

Peggy's fork clattered against her plate.

"Is that what they told you?"

She looked pale as death and I could see the fine lines a little more deeply etched around her eyes and mouth. I spent a second or two regretting my big mouth, not because she might have been the murderer but because of how this could further hurt her.

"It's only a theory," I hastily said. "But a typed suicide note when everyone knows Zack writes everything by hand doesn't make sense. He even showed Sherman Rebecca's car. Someone—the murderer probably—had parked it in his garage."

Peggy stared at me, not in disbelief, I realized, but in amazement. "How do you know all this?"

"I was there and people tell me things," I shrugged. "And besides, Zack killing himself doesn't feel right."

To my surprise, Peggy nodded. "I'm so glad I'm not the only one who thinks that."

"The police think Sherman did it. And I know he didn't."

"Do you have proof?"

I shook my head. "Just gut instinct."

There was a pause while Peggy considered my answer. "Susan, you have to promise me you won't go to the police with this." She placed a hand over mine, and her skin was hot and dry, as if she were running a fever.

I looked at her blankly. "But if it'll get Sherman off the hook . . ."

Her hand tightened as she violently shook her head. "Promise me!"

"Okay, I promise," I said, not all that confident I could keep it. Nevertheless, I was curious about what she had to say.

Peggy's eyes slid away from mine, and she stared blindly at the laughing teenagers. I thought she didn't believe me (and who could blame her?), but I realized she was just gathering the courage to continue. When she finally turned back, she looked down at her food and avoided my eyes.

"I guess it's no secret that Zack and I were seeing one another," she said.

I didn't say anything—I didn't know what to say, but fortunately, she didn't seem to expect an answer.

"Actually, when we got this job, Zack thought we should cool things down a bit. He thought our relationship might interfere with our work."

I nodded as if I understood, but I don't think she noticed. Now that she had decided to tell her story, nothing was going to stop her from confessing it all.

"I agreed," Peggy continued. "But I really didn't take him seriously. I thought we'd be able to figure it out, and once we settled down it would be like it used to. But Zack grew more and more distant, and then one day I realized he had a thing for Rebecca and had probably been seeing her for a while."

Her mouth twisted into a bitter, self-mocking smile, and

I nodded in sympathy. Zack wouldn't work and sleep with Peggy at the same time, but had no qualms about doing both with Rebecca.

With obvious effort Peggy went on. "But Zack never said anything to me, and I kept hoping it was all my imagination. He was behind in his script. Ray never really liked his last one, so he was under a lot of pressure to do a good job." Peggy looked up at me. "You know how you'll invent any excuse for a man, just so you don't have to deal with the reality of his not liking you more than you like him?"

Oh, yes, I thought. I could relate to that.

"Even after Rebecca died I thought I'd have a chance. That maybe he'd come back to me. Can you believe what an idiot I was? Her death just made him love her all the more. Because dead people don't have any faults." She spoke so bitterly I wondered if Peggy hoped to find a way to kill Rebecca again even though she was already dead.

"What happened?" I gently prompted her, afraid she might lose her train of thought.

"What happened?" Peggy repeated my question ironically, almost to herself, clearly her mind focused back in the past. "What happened is that Zack came to my office. He told me things were over between us. He apologized for not ending it sooner but he was afraid of hurting my feelings."

"Did he mention Rebecca?"

Peggy nodded. "He told me that he cared for Rebecca, although she hadn't felt the same way. But even so, he realized he wanted to move on. He needed some time to be alone. To think about things and where he wanted to go from there. And I . . ." She paused, taking a sip of her iced tea while she composed herself. "I kind of fell apart. Humiliated myself." She continued, quietly, "I'm sorry you overheard that."

"So you're not . . . pregnant?"

Peggy stared at me. "No! That's what you thought?"

I nodded, uncomfortable. "You were so upset. I remember you said something like, 'How do I go on?' I'm sorry."

"He broke my heart, Susan. I was in denial for a long time, and when I realized it was truly over between us . . ." Again, she trailed off, finished her drink in a gulp. I realized she wasn't going to say anymore.

"I think Zack felt awful about it," I said, like that was going to make her feel better. But she nodded in agreement.

"He said he was sorry, and I believed him. He also said he was taking the day off tomorrow, and that I shouldn't worry."

"Did he say why he was taking the day off?" By now, even my dinner remained untouched.

"He said he thought he knew who Rebecca's murderer was, but he couldn't be sure. He wouldn't tell me who he suspected, and to tell you the truth, at that point I didn't care. I was too busy feeling devastated about our break-up."

"Did he say anything about Sherman? About calling him?"

"No, I don't think so. He did say he called Michael Keller, that construction worker."

I looked at Peggy in surprise. "Keller went to Zack's

house?"

Peggy shrugged. "I guess so."

I wanted to shake her until her teeth rattled. "But, Peggy, that means Keller could've killed Zack!"

But Peggy refused to get excited. "No, I don't think so, Susan. Zack said Keller might have some information about the murderer he didn't know he had."

"Yeah, like he was the murderer."

"That's not how Zack meant it."

"Peggy, you have to go to the police and tell them this. I told you they suspect Sherman. They're looking for him right now."

"Susan, I'm sorry. But I can't. And you promised you wouldn't either."

She looked like a spoiled ten-year-old not getting her way instead of the thirty-eight-year-old producer of the number one rated television show in the country. I leaned across the table toward her, almost getting au jus on my shirt. "Why can't we tell the police?"

Peggy looked away from me. Her voice was so inaudible, at first I wasn't sure I heard her correctly.

"Because they'll suspect me."

I sat back in my chair, a roaring in my ears.

"Why?"

Peggy took the bread off her sandwich, crumbling it between her fingers, avoiding my eyes. "When I realized Zack was in love with Rebecca, I went off the rails a bit. I did something I'm not too proud of." I held my breath. "I started following Zack around."

"So?"

"I'd drive to his house early in the morning just to see if

Rebecca came out of it. I'd follow him home from work. To the supermarket. To the movies."

"Peggy, we've all gone a little nuts like that, but I don't think the cops would arrest you over it."

"You don't understand. I followed Zack back to the warehouse the night of Rebecca's death."

I swear my heart stopped beating. I no longer heard the clatter of cutlery or the background restaurant chatter. Everything around me seemed to freeze, and in that sudden, imagined silence I stared at Peggy, having difficulty forming the words that seemed to come out of my mouth in slow motion. "Did he kill her?"

"No," Peggy said softly. "He didn't."

"How do you know that? You were in your car."

"I just know, okay? Zack's not like that."

That was the lamest answer in the world, but I didn't tell her that. Instead I asked, "Did you kill Rebecca? After Zack left her?"

I thought she'd get all indignant on me but she wearily shook her head. "I was too busy following him to go after her."

Maybe, maybe not. But she knew the police wouldn't believe her, which is why she didn't want me going to them.

"So you followed Zack after he left the warehouse?"

She nodded. "He went straight home after that. But just because I said I didn't kill her doesn't mean the police won't think I stayed at the warehouse and killed her myself. I don't have an alibi."

Which is exactly what I was thinking, until I remembered:

"Sandy," I said abruptly.

Peggy looked at me, puzzled.

"She didn't say anything about seeing you when she left that night."

"Why should she?"

"Because she left before Zack did."

"I don't know what you're talking about," Peggy said.

"Sandy said she came back from an appointment to do some work. She overheard Zack and Rebecca arguing, but left before he did."

"No, she didn't. I saw her car there. And believe me, I would've seen her if she had left. Zack came out first and I followed him home. Sandy was still in the office."

7.

West Hollywood, where Sandy lived, is a predominantly gay community located between Beverly Hills to the west and Hollywood to the east. It's an upper middle class neighborhood filled with brightly painted bungalows, flowered gardens, and trendy shops and restaurants to the north, on the Sunset Strip.

Sandy's apartment wasn't exactly on my way home, but somehow I found myself getting off the freeway at La Cienega Boulevard and taking it north until I reached Sandy's street. I had never been there before, but found the address easily enough through my GPS app on my cellphone. When I had asked Peggy why Sandy hadn't gone to the police, knowing Zack may have been the last person to see Rebecca alive, she shrugged.

"Maybe Zack wasn't the last person to see Rebecca

alive," she said.

"Do you really believe Sandy killed her?"

"You know her better than I do. Did Rebecca hurt Sandy in some way?"

I leaned back in my chair, remembering that Rebecca was probably the reason why Ray put Sandy on probation. But was that enough to cause Sandy to batter Rebecca to death in a fit of rage? I didn't know and I was certainly not going to share my concerns with Peggy until I spoke with Sandy.

I pulled up in front of Sandy's green, three-story apartment house, and stopped for a moment with the car engine idling. The exterior lights highlighted palms trees and thick beds of red, white, and blue-colored pansies and begonias. The lighted parking garage was located underneath the building, and thick shrubbery separated the apartments from a small, fenced-in pool. If I found a parking space nearby, I promised myself, I'd go in to see her. If not, I'd wait until tomorrow.

Not twenty feet away, someone in a Toyota pulled out. Fate had decided for me, and I slid into the suddenly vacant space.

Sandy's voice sounded tinny and garbled as she answered the intercom next to the glassed-in front doors. "Ye—? Wh—i—t?" sounded like, "Yes, who is it?" and I answered promptly.

"It's Susan," I shouted into the speaker phone. There was a pause, and then a buzzer sounded, unlocking the front door.

Sandy stood by her opened apartment door as I exited the elevator and walked down the brown-carpeted hall.

She had a puzzled smile on her face.

"This is a pleasant surprise," she said as she stepped aside so I could enter. She wore a green plastic Harrods apron over her jeans and red sweatshirt, looking a little like a Christmas tree ornament.

The apartment, furnished with white overstuffed chairs and couches, smelled of cheese, tomatoes, and garlic. My mouth started watering even though I had just eaten.

"I was washing up the dinner dishes when you called," Sandy said. "I decided to cook in for a change."

"Smells good."

"Lasagna," she said. "I have some left over if you want."

"Thanks, but I've already eaten."

Sandy shut the door after me, and I followed her into the kitchen. She moved to the sink which was half-filled with soapy dishes. The rest were drying on a pale blue Rubbermaid dish drainer. I had one just like it—only in beige—in my apartment.

Sandy indicated the sink. "Do you mind if I finish?"

"No, go ahead." I leaned against the Formica counter, watching as she scrubbed a tomato-flecked baking dish.

She didn't look up as she asked, "Is something the matter? Or is this is a social visit?"

"I don't know what to call this." I shifted uncomfortably against the counter. Sandy noticed and looked at me.

"What is it? Something is wrong."

I didn't know how to begin so I figured I might as well dive in feet first. "I had dinner with Peggy tonight. She told me she followed Zack back to the warehouse the night Rebecca was murdered. She said Zack came out of the building before you did."

Sandy carefully set the baking dish onto the drainer. When she finally looked back at me, her expression was unreadable. "And you believe her."

"Why would she lie?"

"Because perhaps she murdered Rebecca and is trying to blame someone else."

"You don't really believe that," I said.

"And I don't believe you! You'd take Peggy's word over mine!"

Sandy's sudden, angry outburst startled me. "I'm not taking anyone's word over anyone else's," I replied, equally upset. "I just told you what Peggy said."

"And if you didn't believe her, you wouldn't be over here right now accusing me of Rebecca's murder!"

"Sandy, that's not true! I just wanted an explanation."

"Not that you deserve one, but here it is. Peggy lied to you. She probably didn't have an alibi herself so she thought she could blame me. And that's all I'm going to say about it."

Sandy and I stared at each other, breathing hard, as if we had just done ten rounds with a referee. I couldn't believe we were fighting, or that she would overreact like this. My eyes felt hot, and I realized my fists were clenched so tightly my fingernails were cutting into my palms.

"Fine," I said. "I'm sorry I bothered you."

"I'm sorry, too." Without another word, she led me back to the front door and barely waited until I stepped out into the hall before slamming it behind me.

Driving back to my apartment, I went over our brief conversation in my mind. Was my tone belligerent? Had I been too accusatory? Had I automatically assumed Sandy was guilty? But no matter how I replayed our argument, I still couldn't discover where I had gone wrong. And, yes, I did believe Peggy was telling the truth. Which meant Sandy had to be lying. Because she killed Rebecca? No way! My mind simply refused to accept that.

As I opened the door to my apartment I checked my cellphone messages. I had spoken with my parents at work that afternoon and once again convinced them it wasn't necessary to fly to Los Angeles to stand guard over me. I also resisted their attempts to lure me back to New York with their offers of a free trip to Europe to follow in my brother Larry's footsteps. I told them that the show needed me more than ever, and just because I kept stumbling over dead bodies didn't mean the next one I'd stumble over would be my own. They promised to call my grandmothers and reassure them as to my health, safety and well-being, and I hung up wondering if the rest of my life would be filled with such exhausting telephone conversations.

The messages on my cell were from the usual concerned friends in New York and graduate school. I thought about calling Jennifer and telling her about my I-don't-know-how-it-happened fight with Sandy, but was afraid Jennifer might take Sandy's side. What I needed, I decided, was a plan. Too many people were getting hurt, and if I found Sandy's behavior suspicious, then Detectives Lu and Wagner would, too. If I could find out what she was hiding maybe I could help her.

I went into work early the next morning to make a phone call I didn't want anyone else to hear. I would've called from my apartment but the number I wanted was back in my desk, and I hoped no one had been through my drawers and taken it away as they had with the death threat. Sure enough, there, in my top center drawer, was Michael Keller's phone number. Although Linda was happy to help in my investigation, she had reluctantly given me a copy of his personnel file, knowing she could get fired for doing so. I promised I wouldn't show it to anyone—including Jennifer.

Dialing quickly so as not to lose courage, I waited while the phone rang four times, and then went into voicemail.

"Hello," said a warm, masculine voice. "You're here, but I'm not. So leave a message and I'll get back to you." Beep.

Keller's voice sounded exactly as I imagined it would. Cute.

"Hello, I'm calling for Michael Keller. This is Susan Kaplan, Rebecca Saunders' secretary. I was cleaning out her office this morning and discovered a check written out to you. Do you want to swing by the office and pick it up? Let me know." I gave him the office number and got off the phone.

There. Too late to go back now. No one had to tell me I was playing with fire. There was no check and for all I knew Keller might ask me to mail it. I could only imagine what Wagner would have to say if he ever found out. But I knew Keller held the key to a lot of important information, and even if he was the murderer, I thought it would be worth meeting him just to see what I could find out. And if he did kill Rebecca then why was Sandy protecting him? Unless she was mistakenly protecting someone else? Ray?

Charles? And if so, why would she sacrifice herself for them?

That matter having been initiated, I then moved on to the next chore on my list. Rebecca's office. Ray had asked me to pack it up but I had been avoiding it up to now, too creeped out to enter. The yellow police tape still blocked my way, but I peeled it off the door and, shoving my reluctance aside, stepped inside. Romulus had not yet brought in a crew to clean the office (too cheap, I supposed), and I averted my eyes from the stains on the wall near her desk (not her brains, of course they weren't her brains), and moved to the couch opposite. While the cops had removed everything from her desk, the pile of scripts and DVDs she had stacked on her couch still remained. I went through each script and tape, but none of the names were familiar. None of the scripts, I noticed, had Rebecca's handwritten notes on the cover page—only mine had been awarded that honor. At the top of the stack was a brief note written by Rebecca on a personalized Babbitt & Brooks buck slip. It read, "Tell agents thanks, but no thanks. R." Easy enough to translate. Rebecca wanted me to return the scripts to each of the agents with a polite, but firm rejection letter. I had done this for Rebecca before, only signing Peggy's or Zack's name to the letter since no agent would understand why an associate producer was reading— and rejecting—submissions.

But the directors' reels were a whole different ballgame. Sandy usually wrote those letters for Ray, but there was no corresponding note to Sandy from Rebecca. I supposed Rebecca wouldn't dare give Sandy orders, or perhaps she tried and Sandy had put her foot down. Which may be why Rebecca had complained about Sandy in the first place. Again I thought about Sandy left alone in the warehouse with Rebecca after Zack left; I thought about her barely concealed fear whenever the detectives showed up; and I searched through Rebecca's office all the more carefully, looking for something—anything—that would point to Rebecca's murderer and, I hoped, exonerate Sandy.

The top of the desk was empty—the cleanest and barest I had ever seen it. The police had bagged as evidence everything that had been on the surface at the time of her murder; and the desk must have been foot deep in paperwork because, fortunately, little blood or gore had seeped onto the shiny, metallic surface.

The handles were still sticky with fingerprint powder and I used the edge of my shirt to open the drawers. Nothing. Not a forgotten scrap of paper jammed in the corner or an incriminating message slip or even the name of the murderer finger-painted in blood. I slammed the last drawer shut with a sigh of disappointment and exited the office just as everyone else straggled in to work.

Sandy wasn't talking to me, although she was careful not to make a point of showing that in front of the others. Which made me realize all the more that she must have been lying about when she left the warehouse. If my accusation had truly been unfair, she would've gone straight to Jennifer and cried on her shoulder.

Jennifer, in the meantime, was still miffed at me for not confiding in her about my meetings with Linda Ramsay and Detective Wagner. So the three of us spent the day being icily polite to one another, and I mournfully

LISA SEIDMAN 287

wondered whether the murderer had killed not only Zack and Rebecca, but my burgeoning friendship with Jennifer and Sandy as well.

There was one benefit to Jennifer's anger, at least. She refused to answer the phones, which ensured that I would be the one taking Michael Keller's phone call. But I also had to deal with every crank and crazy who called about Zack's death. And so I was, therefore, running out of patience when I was forced to abruptly end one call to pick up another left ignored by a studiously indifferent Jennifer, who was reading the fan forums on the Babbitt & Brooks website, copying their comments for Charles to read in his spare time.

"Babbitt & Brooks," I snapped into the receiver.

There was a pause, then a voice said, "Susan Kaplan, please."

I recognized the voice immediately as the one on the voicemail message, and my stomach lurched. Somehow I managed to say, "Speaking."

"Susan, this is Michael Keller calling. I got your message about the check."

Through the receiver I could hear cars whooshing past and an occasional honking horn. Keller sounded as if he was calling me from the middle of the freeway.

"Yes," I replied, my throat suddenly dry. "Would you like to stop by for it sometime today?"

"Yeah, I could do that. Is seven o'clock too late?"

"Seven is fine," I said. "Do you know how to get here?" I already knew the answer of course but figured I'd best play dumb. Keller assured me he did, and we hung up. I was relieved he hadn't asked me to mail the check, then wondered if it was because he knew the cops were looking for him and was staying as far away from his place as possible.

The phone rang again, and I turned to Jennifer in exasperation. "That was Michael Keller," I said. "And if you help me answer the phones from now on, I promise to fill you in on what's going on."

Jennifer blinked at me in surprise then picked up the phone. I felt slightly guilty, not because I was going to give away state secrets, but because I needed Jennifer as part of my plan with Michael Keller and knew that divulging information would be the only way to get her to comply.

She answered the phone, efficiently dealt with the person on the other end (it sounded like a professor, wondering if Charles would appear as a guest lecturer in his/her class), then hung up. Leaning over with her arms crossed on her chest, she looked me square in the eye. "Now give. Tell me everything."

So I did, keeping my voice down so that Peggy, Charles, and Ray, who were meeting in Ray's office, wouldn't hear. I told her about Zack finding Rebecca's car in his garage, about his asking Sherman to his house to talk about the night of Rebecca's death, and about Peggy's confession of following Zack, ending with Sandy's lie about when she left the warehouse that night. I hesitated about telling Jennifer the last part, afraid she'd side with Sandy against me, but Jennifer merely sat back in her chair and absentmindedly rubbed the bridge of her nose.

"What a mess," she said. "Do you think Sandy killed Rebecca?"

"No," I said sharply.

"Neither do I," she agreed. "I know she was angry with Vampire Woman, but I don't think she had it in her to kill her."

"So why do you think she lied?"

"She must be covering for someone," Jennifer said.

I nodded. "I think she might have overheard the murder," I said. "I think she knows who did it and is afraid to say something."

"But who would she cover up for? No one here is worth it."

"Ray?" I spoke tentatively, still not sure what protecting him would gain her. Unless she thought a new showrunner would bring his or her own assistant. Would Sandy really let a murderer go free to hold on to her job?

"And why is Michael Keller calling you?" Jennifer asked. "You're not going to do anything stupid, are you?"

I took a deep breath. Of course I was. And I needed Jennifer's help to do it.

"He's coming here tonight," I said, and told her about my luring him here with my lie about having a check for him. "I'm going to try and get some answers from him. Zack thought he was important, but he didn't think he was the murderer. I want to find out what he knows."

"Susan, let the police deal with it. Who do you think you are—Nancy Drew?"

Maybe. She had been one of the heroines of my youth. But I avoided directly responding to Jennifer's question.

"The police think Sherman killed Zack. Which means they probably think he also killed Rebecca. I need to get to Keller before the police find Sherman and decide Keller isn't important anymore."

Jennifer shook her head. "You're absolutely nuts. Why don't you call that hunky detective Wagner and tell him Keller is paying you a visit? Let him handle it from there."

"No. Wagner would just yell at me for interfering in police business. And you better not call him behind my back," I warned.

"I wasn't thinking any such thing," she responded indignantly. "But I don't like the idea of you here alone with Keller."

Which gave me the opening I needed. "I won't be if you stick around with me. Romulus hasn't hired a new night watchman to replace Sherman. I don't want to be here alone."

Jennifer paused, her mouth opening and closing a few times. Then, surprisingly, she smiled. "You devious little bitch," she said but there was no venom in her voice. "That's what you wanted all along."

"Will you stay?" I asked. "Please?"

"Why should I? It would serve you right if he was the murderer and killed you, too."

"Then you'd be the only one answering the phones." That got her.

"What do you want me to do?" she asked in resignation.

"Just hide out in Sandy's office. If things start to get ugly, call the police."

Jennifer agreed, although we both knew—but did not say—that if things got ugly the police might not arrive in time. It was certainly not a foolproof plan, but deep down I felt I was in no danger. Which only goes to show you how stupid I could be.

8.

At six-thirty, Peggy and Charles exited stiffly from Ray's office, both looking pale and drawn. Peggy's hair was in disarray, gray predominating over brown. Ray looked equally grim when he left the office, Sandy following shortly after, still not talking to me. When the office was quiet again Jennifer and I looked at one another from across our desks.

"You still want to go through with this?" she asked.

I nodded more confidently than I felt. Actually, I was having major second thoughts, but kept quiet as she disappeared around the corner and into Sandy's office.

Michael Keller arrived at seven-fifteen. I heard the front door open and close and I started to itch with nerves as I waited for him to walk around the corner. I pretended to look busy when he appeared in the bullpen.

"Susan Kaplan?" he said, and I looked up. His photograph didn't do him justice. His thick black hair was slightly curly and longer than in the snapshot. His eyes were an even more intense blue in person, and the lines of age and sun around his eyes and mouth only served to enhance his sex appeal. I wouldn't have expected anything less from an ex-husband of Rebecca's.

I stood awkwardly, leaning against my desk for support, not sure whether I should shake hands with him. "Yes," I said. "You're Michael Keller?"

He nodded as he did a quick survey of my body, although there wasn't anything remotely sexy about my blue trousers and white and blue over-sized blouse from the Gap. I instinctively folded my arms across my chest.

Keller smiled slightly. I had a funny feeling he knew I was embarrassed by his quick physical judgment of me and was amused.

"You have a check for me?" he asked. I nodded clumsily, my head feeling heavy and unbalanced on my neck. This was the tricky part.

"In her office," I said and started to lead the way. Keller fell into step next to me; he smelled of soap, a pleasant, clean smell that reminded me of Zack's aftershave. My stomach briefly knotted, and to distract myself I said the first thing that came to mind. "What did you think of the Scoop article about Rebecca and Gail Neely?" Not the most delicate of opening conversational gambits but it was too late to take the words back. Fortunately, Keller seemed more amused than angry.

"I thought it was very funny," he said. "Obviously those people never met Rebecca."

We paused at Rebecca's door, and I looked up at him curiously. "Why do you say that?"

"Rebecca was a lot of things, but a lesbian she wasn't."

He stared at the police tape dubiously. "The check's in here?"

I nodded. "I found it stuck inside one of her desk drawers. I guess the police missed it."

I removed the tape and stepped inside the office. After a moment's hesitation, Keller followed me in.

"How do you know she wasn't a lesbian?" I asked.

Keller glanced around the office, not paying much attention to my question. "Because she wasn't. And neither is Gail."

I walked behind Rebecca's desk as if planning to open a drawer and take out the check. Keller obviously didn't like being in the office: I only hoped it wasn't because he had killed Rebecca in it.

"How do you know Gail isn't a lesbian?" I persisted. I tried to make my voice as casual as possible, although my palms had started to sweat, and I resisted the urge to scratch my neck. "Do you know her?"

"You sure like to gossip, don't you?" he asked. But he smiled at me to show he wasn't upset. I shrugged noncommittally in return.

"When you work with people you wonder about them," I replied lamely.

Keller looked at the cheap wood paneled walls. "This is where she died, isn't it?"

"Yes." My voice cracked and I nervously cleared it. I tried to muster up a smile as I said lightly, "Any idea who did it?"

"Ray Goldfarb."

I almost started to smile until I realized he wasn't joking. "You're serious."

Keller lazily slid down onto Rebecca's white nubbly couch. He put his hands behind his head and crossed his foot at the knee. He looked at me through half-closed eyelids.

"You like to gossip, there's the gossip."

I wasn't sure, but I thought Keller might've been flirting with me. In Rebecca's office where she had been brutally killed, no less. I thought of every true-life crime novel I had read and suddenly remembered that all the killers were male, intelligent, good-looking, and sociopathic. He killed her. He killed her. My mouth went dry and I sank into Rebecca's desk chair.

"Why do you think Ray killed her?" I asked, fully convinced I wasn't going to believe a word he said.

Keller smiled, as if he knew a good secret that made him superior to me. "Because Ray was having an affair with Gail Neely. Still is, I imagine."

I stared at him in shock, my fear momentarily forgotten. "How do you know that?"

Keller's smile broadened. He knew he had me hooked.

"Rebecca told me. She caught them going at it in Gail's trailer one night after work. I myself prefer fragile-looking brunettes."

I thought at first he was referring to Tabitha Wentworth, but the way he smiled at me made me realize he was talking about me. Without thinking, I touched my reddish-brown hair, then blushed and self-consciously returned my hand to my lap. No wonder Rebecca had married him and Lily Wainess had had an affair with him. This man hadn't just kissed the Blarney Stone, he had swallowed it whole.

Well, I was not going to buy into it. I sternly reminded myself he might be Rebecca's drug dealer, and possibly even her murderer. It was time to get back to the subject at hand.

"Why would Ray kill Rebecca over that?"

"The price he paid for her silence," Keller said, still grinning at me. No matter what his past relationship with Rebecca, he didn't seem broken up about her death. Did I dare point that out to him? He seemed harmless enough, sitting on the couch like he had all the time in the world, grinning that infuriating smile. But who knew what went on in the mind of a sociopath? Any simple question could set him off, and I knew I was not going to be able to defend myself against him.

So instead I asked as innocuously as possible, "Why didn't you go to the police with this?"

"I have my reasons."

Like maybe you have no proof and the police would be more interested in you, I thought.

"So how about my check?" he asked, and I took a second or two to remember that was the real reason for his visit. I licked my lips nervously, tempted to write him a check from my own account just to be done with him. But I couldn't think of an adequate explanation to cover that so I opted for the truth instead and hoped for the best.

"I'm sorry," I said, "but I did a really awful thing to you."

Keller raised his eyebrows but remained silent. I plowed on.

"There is no check. I used it as an excuse to talk to you."

"No check?" Keller said, almost in the same way a little boy would respond to being told he wasn't going to get ice cream for dessert. "I don't understand."

I prayed Jennifer had her finger poised above the telephone. "I know you're Rebecca's ex-husband. But I also know you didn't kill her," I added hastily. "But it's just that a friend of mine is in trouble, and I hoped you could tell me something about Rebecca's murder."

"You did, did you?" Keller still looked at ease, but his violet eyes narrowed as he stared across the room at me. I shifted my gaze away.

"I'm sorry," I said again, uselessly.

"Who appointed you deputy?"

I shook my head; I didn't know what else to say. Keller slowly uncoiled from the couch, and I stared at him, mesmerized, as he took three steps to where I sat.

"You didn't happen to notify the cops that I was coming, did you?"

Again, I shook my head, too frightened to do anything else. Keller continued to stare down at me, his face void of expression. I don't know what he would've done next, but just then Jennifer appeared at the door.

"Susan, you're still here," she said in an artificially surprised voice. She glanced at Keller. "Oh, I'm sorry, I didn't realize you had company."

Keller smiled crookedly at her, and I saw him do the same quick appraisal of her body as he had with mine. Jennifer just stood there and smiled at him before glancing back at me.

"Steve's arrived and we're going out to dinner. Want to come?" She said it so convincingly I actually, briefly, believed her.

"That'll be great," I said, relieved. But I remained seated in Rebecca's chair, not willing to make any sudden move. Keller still stood too close for comfort.

"Well, uh, thanks for coming," I told him.

Keller looked down at me.

"You bitch," he hissed through clenched teeth, so softly, I almost didn't hear him. It was so unexpected I started to smile, as if he had wished me a pleasant good night. But after two seconds, the words caught up with my brain, and the muscles in my face froze.

"I'm—I'm sorry," I whispered. I wanted to turn to Jennifer for help, but I couldn't pull my eyes away from his. Keller's nostrils flared slightly, and I realized his body was trembling in anger.

"We're all sorry," he said. "That was a fucking stupid thing to do." He took another step toward me, fists clenched at his sides, and I cowered back in Rebecca's chair, tensing my body in preparation for the blow I was sure I was about to receive.

"Steve," Jennifer suddenly called, her voice unnaturally high and shrill. "We'll be right there."

Keller looked at Jennifer in surprise, as if he had forgotten she was there. I watched as he deliberately relaxed his body, unclenching his fists in order to run his hands through his hair. He still stood rooted to the carpet, however, and I wasn't sure what his next move would be. But then he took another quick look at Jennifer and smiled grimly.

"It's not a good idea to play with matches, ladies," was all he said before exiting the office, deliberately brushing past Jennifer so that his arm touched her breasts. We waited until we heard the front door close before relaxing.

"Creep," Jennifer said.

"He could have killed Rebecca," I replied, feeling drained of blood and adrenalin. Jennifer took a quick look around Rebecca's office, shuddered and moved away. I followed her back to the bullpen.

"Did he admit it?" she asked.

"No, but you saw him. He was going to kill me."

"I would, too, if you pulled a stunt like that on me."

I didn't respond, half-heartedly agreeing with her, but

also vividly remembering his angry face, and his tightly-coiled body looking ready to attack. If Jennifer hadn't stopped him, would he have punched his fist through my face? Would he have beaten me until I was dead, my brains splattered against the wall like Rebecca's? I had no answer, though every trembling nerve in my body was saying, Yes. Yes. Yes.

We sat behind our desks in silence, both of us needing to catch our breath, calm ourselves down. When I was finally able to look Jennifer in the eye, after spending what felt like an eternity staring at the worn and stained pukey green carpet, I found Jennifer studying me.

"What?" I asked her.

"Did he tell you anything interesting?"

I must have looked at her in shock because she added, "Well, c'mon, Suze, I practically saved your life. Didn't he have any dirt to pass on?"

I had to think for a second and gather my thoughts. I had been so scared by Keller's threatening posture at the end of the meeting I had almost forgotten what he said at the beginning.

"Gail and Ray are having an affair. And Rebecca knew."

Jennifer stared at me wide-eyed. "No shit," she breathed.

I nodded, feeling stronger for being able to talk about something other than Keller's menacing presence. "Which probably explains why Rebecca was so upset with you and Sandy at the Christmas party. Everyone thought she was the other woman when it was Gail all along." I wondered if that also explained why Ray looked so smug after the hour and a half he spent with Gail "calming her down" over the Scoop article.

"Do you think Sandy knew?" I asked.

"If she did, I can't imagine why she didn't tell us," Jennifer said.

"I think it's time I paid her another visit. Maybe now she'll talk to me."

"I'm going with you," Jennifer said. "Maybe the two of us can bully her into the truth."

I followed Jennifer to Sandy's apartment, although the way she drove, recklessly weaving in and out of lanes, tailgating slower drivers, giving the finger to anyone who dared to cut in front of her, made me wonder whether she would make it in one piece. She also got the only remaining parking space left within four blocks of Sandy's building; I ended up parking on Sunset Boulevard, my Honda barely tucked in next to the parking lot entrance to the Chateau Marmont, the ultimate in celebrity hang-outs.

While waiting to cross Sunset, I craned my neck to stare at the hotel, hoping to catch a glimpse of someone famous. Daniel Craig would be nice. Or even one of the two Ryans: Gosling and Reynolds. I wondered if I would ever rate an invitation to dine there among the rich and famous.

I was surprised when Sandy buzzed us through the door, since she still seemed so angry with me when she had left the office earlier in the day.

She stood by her opened door and watched as Jennifer and I exited the elevator and crossed down the hall to her.

"My, my, a delegation," she said as she stepped aside to allow us to enter.

"Susan told me everything," Jennifer began without preliminaries. "And I think it sucks you would freeze her out when she's been nothing but a good friend to you."

Sandy's mouth tightened in defensive anger, and I caught my own breath in surprise. This was not how I planned on handling things at all.

"Jennifer," I warned.

"No, I'm sick of this." She cut me off with an impatient wave of her hand and turned back to Sandy. "Who are you protecting?"

"What is this, good cop, bad cop?" Sandy reached for the door handle. "Who the hell do you think you are?"

She tried to yank the door open to throw us out but had forgotten she had reset the deadbolt once we were all inside. The door didn't budge, and the look on Sandy's face—utter, childlike surprise—inexplicably made me laugh.

Jennifer and Sandy looked at me like I was from outer space, which made me laugh all the harder. Then Jennifer started to smile, then guffaw, then out and out crack up, and it must've been contagious because suddenly the three of us were doubled up in laughter, tears in our eyes, holding on to each other for support.

Abruptly, Sandy's tears of laughter turned to pain, and she leaned against the door, sobbing. Without any hesitation, Jennifer took her in her arms. I ran into the bathroom and grabbed a wad of tissues from the Kleenex box, then headed back into the living room, waving them in Sandy's face as if they were tokens of my friendship.

Sandy broke away from Jennifer to take the tissues. She covered her face with her hands, shoulders hunched and shaking, avoiding Jennifer who once again tried to take her back in her arms.

"I'm s-s-sorry, I'm so s-s-sorry," was all Sandy could say. Her obvious distress made me want to cry myself; instead I went into the kitchen, grabbed a glass from the drain board, and filled it with water.

"Here, drink this," I ordered as I handed it to her.

She obediently took a gulp then made a face.

"I thought you were giving me brandy," she said.

"Since when does brandy look like water?" Jennifer asked.

"Or come in a Fred Flintstone jelly glass," I pointed out.

Sandy took a closer look at the glass in her hand then smiled. "I must be losing my mind."

But she seemed calmer, and she wiped away tears with a fist clenched full of tissues.

"I'm sorry," Jennifer said quietly. "I didn't mean to come on so strong. It was an act to scare you into confessing."

"You've been watching too many detective movies," Sandy said, but she didn't seem angry anymore. The tears, I suspected, had been bottled up for so long their release was having a cathartic effect. She sniffled a couple of more times, but the flood seemed to be over. She finished the water in one, long gulp then looked at Jennifer and me.

I'm sure our faces were mirror images of concern because suddenly Sandy smiled. "It's all right. I promise not to lose it again tonight."

"What is it, Sandy? What's going on?" I asked gently, and her mouth started to quiver again, belying her attempt at calm.

"We only want to help," Jennifer said. "Idiot Susan over here lured Michael Keller to the warehouse tonight. He told her about Gail and Ray."

Sandy looked infinitely relieved. "You know."

Jennifer and I nodded simultaneously. "How did you find out?" I asked.

"I knew almost from the beginning," she said. She walked over to her overstuffed white armchair and sat down. Jennifer and I followed suit on the matching couch. "It began last year. When Gail and Tabitha went on a national tour promoting the show."

That was before my time, but Jennifer nodded as if knowing what Sandy was talking about.

"Ray had me call the florist he uses. He wanted a single, white rose in every hotel room Gail was staying at. But not in Tabitha's. At first I thought it was because Ray was mad at Tabitha. She wants to have a baby, you know, and Ray won't let her. He doesn't want to work it into the show."

I didn't know this and was rather surprised Ray could have that much say in Tabitha's personal life. I would've commented on it, but Sandy was still in confessional mode, and I didn't want to interrupt.

"But then Ray decided to fly to New York for the last part of the tour. Winifred didn't go with him; she had too much work to do at Romulus. His cell was turned off and I needed to speak with him rather urgently, so I called his hotel room. He didn't answer the phone. But then he called me two seconds later; he told me he was calling from his room and had been there all night. But I could hear Gail's voice in the background and knew he was calling me from her room instead."

I opened my mouth to speak, but Sandy forestalled me. "Why would he lie to me about being in the room if he wasn't doing something he shouldn't have been?" she asked, anticipating my question.

"And I'm sure there was more," Jennifer said.

Sandy nodded unhappily. "Lots, I'm afraid. When they returned, Ray couldn't stay away from her. Always inventing excuses to visit her in her trailer. Having me order flowers for her dressing room. Calling her late at night in the office, not realizing I could hear everything from mine." She ran a hand through her short, curly hair. "It was all quite horrid."

"Does Ray know you know?" I asked.

"I think after a while he guessed, but he was too infatuated to really care. He used to make me lie to Winifred if she called when he was visiting Gail in her trailer. I'd have to say he was in a meeting or on the set. As the executive producer he had every right to be with Gail. But because it was for all the wrong reasons he felt he had to totally lie."

"Why didn't you tell us?" Jennifer asked in concern. "We didn't have a clue."

"Because if Ray heard that I, or you, spilled the beans in some way, I might've lost my job. I was too afraid to say anything."

I thought about what a good actor Sandy had been, pretending like nothing was wrong pretty much up until the time of the murder. I also couldn't reconcile my image of the aloof, gruff Ray as an infatuated, adolescent-behaved lover.

"Winifred suspected Ray was having an affair," I said. "She just suspected the wrong person."

Sandy nodded. "I'm not sure how Rebecca found out,

but she also knew."

"Michael Keller told me she walked in on them late one night."

"That makes sense. Ray and Gail often stayed late after shooting finished. I always had to tell Winifred he was in a late story meeting or had some sort of business dinner."

"Do you think that's why Gail misled me about when she finished work the night of Rebecca's murder? Was it because Ray came to the set and they were doing it in her trailer?"

Sandy's head dropped into her hands. "I wish that were the reason," she said, speaking almost inaudibly from between her fingers.

Jennifer leaned over to her. "What was the reason?"

We waited tensely for at least thirty seconds, although it seemed like thirty years, before Sandy looked up at us, her expression bleak. "Peggy was right, Suze. I'm sorry for yelling at you. But I didn't know what else to do. Zack did leave before me. And he didn't kill Rebecca."

I held my breath and I could practically feel the tightening of Jennifer's skin, as she waited expectantly next to me. I think both of us were afraid to speak and possibly break the mood. I could hear the apartment elevator whirring as it made its journey to another floor, and the gentle tick-tick-tick of Sandy's kitchen wall clock.

Sandy stared at the torn and matted tissues still clutched in her hand, looking like she wasn't sure how they got there. As if hypnotized, she said, "I had come back to the office to confront Rebecca about Ray putting me on probation. I went into my office to work up the nerve, and then Zack came back and started arguing with her. I couldn't move. I was too afraid they'd hear me. So I just stood in my office, not even breathing, wanting to sneeze so badly I thought I was going to die. Zack finally stormed out, but she was still alive. I swear she was still alive."

I waited to hear what came next, but somehow I knew before Sandy spoke what she was going to say.

"Of course I couldn't go in then and face Rebecca. I thought she would leave, and I waited and waited. Then the front door opened again, and I heard footsteps walk past my office. I heard Rebecca say, 'I thought you already left.'"

"It was Ray," Jennifer said, staring at Sandy, horrified.

No more little girl, wide-eyed wonder. This was real. And very terrifying.

Sandy nodded in confirmation.

"He killed her," Jennifer continued softly, making it a statement and not a question.

"I don't know," Sandy said in despair. "As soon as I heard his voice, I panicked. I got out as quickly as I could."

"Did they hear you?" I asked.

"I don't know," Sandy said again. "But Gail saw me."

Jennifer and I stared at her in shock.

"She was with him?" My voice was barely a squeak.

"She was sitting in her car. She must've driven Ray back from the set."

"But how did he get there in the first place?" I asked. "Winifred came to the warehouse to take him home."

"I suspect Ray told her he needed to take care of business on location and asked her to drive him there. Then he probably sent her home. Winifred knew he could always get a ride home with one of the drivers."

"But if she suspected he was having an affair . . .?" Jennifer looked confused.

"With Rebecca." I interrupted. "Winifred thought Ray was sleeping with Rebecca. That's why she hated Rebecca so much."

Sandy nodded. "I think you're right. And Rebecca knew. So she blackmailed Ray into promoting her to producer. And letting her write two scripts. In return for her silence."

"But Ray didn't promote her," I said. "You told me he changed his mind."

Jennifer looked from me to Sandy, her head swiveling back and forth as if watching a tennis match. "Because he decided to kill her instead?" she asked in some awe.

"That's what I think," Sandy said. "Ray didn't tell the police he had returned to the office. As soon as I heard Rebecca was dead, I knew he had killed her. Or at least I suspected it."

"But why protect him?" I asked. "He's not worth it."

"Because I don't have any proof!" Sandy wailed, starting to lose it again. "And what if I accuse him and he's innocent?"

"And if he's guilty? And he killed Zack as well?" Jennifer asked. I shot her a dirty look. She didn't have to be so tactless about it.

"Don't you think I know that?" Sandy said, the tears spilling down her face once again. "Don't you think I've lost sleep over this, wondering, afraid, feeling responsible? But I just don't know what to do!"

Jennifer and I watched helplessly as Sandy cried into

the remnants of the tissues I had given her.

"I'm sorry," Jennifer said quietly. "If it were Charles, I probably would've done the same thing."

Why? I wondered. Why were we so loyal to our bosses? Because their continued employment of us kept a roof over our heads and food on our tables? Because they had the power of our future in their hands: one word from them and we got a raise or a script assignment or a promotion. And in return we said nothing to the police if we suspected them of murder. Was that the price of our souls? A script assignment? A weekly paycheck?

"I can't go to the police, I just can't!" Sandy sobbed. "What if that only makes them suspect me?"

Something was wrong about this; something Sandy had said earlier that didn't make sense. I stared at the kitchen clock trying to figure it out when it suddenly fell into place.

"Ray may not have killed her," I said, and both Jennifer and Sandy looked at me sharply.

"Why do you think that?" Jennifer asked.

I turned to Sandy. "Tell me exactly. What did Rebecca say to Ray when he came back to the office?"

Sandy looked at me, not understanding. "I told you. She said, 'I thought you already left.'"

I told you. Where had I heard those words before? Why did my body stiffen as if they were important? I told you.

Sandy and Jennifer were staring at me.

"What's wrong?" Sandy asked.

I pulled myself together with an effort. "'I thought you had already left.' Those were Rebecca's exact words?"

Sandy nodded. Like I told you. "Why?"

"Don't you remember what Sherman said? Rebecca told him not to lock the front door because she was expecting a visitor. But from what you just said, she wasn't expecting Ray."

Comprehension started to dawn on Sandy, and I could practically see the weight of anxiety and guilt lift from her shoulders. "No, she wasn't expecting him. I'm sure of that."

"Could someone please translate this for me?" Jennifer asked, looking annoyed. "What am I missing here?"

Sandy turned to her, the words spilling out of her mouth. "If Rebecca was expecting someone, what happened to him? If he had shown up and found her dead, why didn't he call the police?"

"Unless she was still alive when Ray left and the visitor came," I added. Like I already told you, Rebecca had said.

Jennifer looked from me to Sandy. "Then what I want to know is," she said, "who the hell was her visitor?"

But I was no longer paying attention. I had figured out who had sent Rebecca the death threats. And why.

9.

Since Jennifer and I had come directly to Sandy's from work neither one of us had eaten dinner. Jennifer suggested we stop at Chin Chin's, on the Strip, and, desperately needing to talk to her away from Sandy, I agreed, saying nothing about what was on my mind regarding the death threats.

We sat outside, facing Sunset Boulevard, heat lamps keeping the night chill away. Cars cruised the Strip—

Porsches, BMWs, Mercedes—looking for parking places near The Roxy and The Viper Room, or maybe just looking.

"Jennifer, I need to ask you something," I said as soon as the waitress had taken our orders and left.

Jennifer unfolded a white paper napkin and put it on her lap. "Shoot."

"Remember the day Charles told me he liked my spec script? Rebecca was in the bullpen, giving all of us new job descriptions?"

"Yeah." Jennifer smiled faintly at the rugby-shirted guy sitting at the table next to us. His girlfriend frowned back.

My mouth felt dry and I took a sip of water. "Well, remember when Rebecca told us she was getting promoted, and how things were going to change?"

"Sure. And I said, let's see what Charles has to say about that. And Rebecca freaked."

"But before that. When she was giving us our new duties. She said to you, 'Like I already told you.'" Suddenly, I had Jennifer's full attention. "What did she mean by that?"

"How am I supposed to know? That was last week. I don't remember what I did two hours ago."

"Rebecca told you about her promotion before she told me. Didn't she?"

Jennifer impatiently blew her bangs off her forehead. "So what if she did?"

"You didn't say anything to Sandy and me. Why?"

"Rebecca told me to keep it a secret. Look, am I under interrogation here? What's the big deal?"

"The big deal is none of us can keep a secret. And since

when do you listen to what Rebecca tells you to do? Unless you thought of a way to get even."

Jennifer's blue eyes glittered. "And how, pray tell, did I do that?"

"You wrote those death threats to Rebecca, didn't you?"

The words hung between us, and I wished I could snatch them back. What if I was wrong? What if I had just wrecked a promising friendship?

Jennifer started shredding her napkin. "What's your proof?"

"You threw out the proof. I saw you toss a bottle of rubber cement into the trash after the flood. And bond paper. The same kind the death threat was written on."

Jennifer sniffed in disgust. "The whole office can get their hands on rubber cement and that stationery."

"But you knew about the promotion before the rest of us. With the exception of Charles—maybe. But he doesn't keep glue or stationery in his desk. You also saw me hide the threat I found. You could've taken it out of my desk." A memory came back to me. "I saw you at the dumpster in the parking lot. After Charles told me Ray didn't like my script. You were throwing it out, weren't you?"

Jennifer looked away, studying the cars cruising past on Sunset.

"I'm not going to the police with this," I said. "And I won't tell another soul. But if you did send those notes, I have to know."

The waitress arrived with our food, but I could only stare at my plate of spicy Thai noodles. Jennifer didn't even bother looking at her Chinese chicken salad, but when she finally turned toward me there were tears in her eyes.

My stomach closed into a fist and for a moment I had forgotten how to breathe. I reached for my glass of water and rolled it against my cheek, the coldness forcing air back into my lungs.

"Why'd you do it?" I said when I felt I had my voice under control.

Jennifer shrugged. "I thought it was a good idea at the time. She was so goddamned smug. About being a co-producer. About getting to write a couple of scripts. I thought I was gonna puke. Or scratch her eyes out."

"But, Jennifer, . . . death threats? A squashed cockroach?"

"Okay, okay, it was pretty sick. But, Suze, I was so mad at her. All I could think about was wiping that smug smile off her face. I loved that she was so terrified."

I stared across the table at the face of a stranger. Jennifer's eyes were gleaming in memory, her mouth curled upward in a satisfied smile. I shuddered. Who was this person I called a friend? Was she also a murderer?

As if reading my mind, the corners of her mouth turned down. "And, no, I did not kill our dear Miss Vampire Woman. I'm not that psycho."

"Why'd you take the first note out of my desk?"

"I didn't want you showing it to anyone else. Someone might've gotten cute and decided to check for fingerprints. Look, it was a stupid thing to do and I apologize. Okay?"

"Jennifer, Rebecca suspected me!"

"But she didn't really. Sandy convinced her it wasn't you. C'mon, Suze, don't you see the humor in it?"

I stared at Jennifer in disbelief. "You scared that

woman. You got me in trouble. And you think it's funny?"

"Well, if she hadn't died, it would've been."

I scraped my chair back against the pavement. "I'm sorry. I don't have much of an appetite."

I stood up. Jennifer looked at me in shock. "You're leaving?"

"What do you expect me to do?"

"Eat your dinner. We'll talk this out. It's no big deal."

I shook my head. "I can't."

I threaded my way past the other tables, remembering too late I hadn't paid for my meal. It would serve Jennifer right to get stuck with the check. I got into my car, turned west on Sunset, and drove aimlessly past the gated mansions of Beverly Hills. I didn't know if I could be Jennifer's friend again, didn't know if I wanted to be. Yet, a part of me still liked her. It's easy to remember the good things about a person when you don't want to think about the bad. I thought of her sense of humor, her breezy, "What, me worry?" attitude, the way she stuck up for me when Rebecca tried to denigrate my Dress Blue script.

Maybe I could rationalize her sending the death threats. Hadn't I, after all, wanted to send Rebecca threats when I saw her kissing Zack in the parking lot? But hadn't I also been thoroughly disgusted with myself for even thinking those thoughts? Jennifer had acted on her impulses, had even enjoyed doing so. Wasn't that crossing the line between sanity and psychopathy? Unable to figure out a way to forgive Jennifer, I turned on the radio as loud as I could and headed home.

10.

Starting in high school, when boys became more interesting than just those pains in the neck who knocked your books from your arms in middle school, my friends and I made a vow that we would deal with the opposite sex as straightforwardly as possible. "No game playing," we solemnly promised ourselves; we would not be like Bobbie Walz, head cheerleader, who flirted with every guy on the football team, or Caryn Panzarino, who made a career out of playing hard to get when the reality was anyone who wanted her could have her.

Since boys never seemed to show much of an interest in me, game playing was not too difficult for me to avoid. But most men, at least on a superficial level, I felt, really liked the games, the flirtation, the hard-to-getness, the reassurance that their opinions were more important than mine. I had decided that in order to get the information I needed to solve both Rebecca's and Zack's murders, I was going to have to start learning to play that game. So, Friday morning found me studying the clothes in my closet, choosing the shortest skirt, the highest heels, the sheer black stockings and a seductively unbuttoned blouse. May Gloria Steinem forgive me, I prayed to my feminist God, as I surveyed myself in the full-length mirror behind my bathroom door. Pretty Woman I wasn't: the skirt not being all that short, the heels not really that high (since I was unable to walk gracefully even in sneakers) and the blouse, after cowardly consideration, not too far unbuttoned. But it was also a far cry from the khaki pants and tailored shirts of my normal self, and I hoped that the change would be enough to get the answers I needed.

I drove into the warehouse parking lot around eight that morning knowing that the construction workers would have been there since seven. I examined myself in the rearview mirror, brushing my wind-blown hair back into place, reapplying my lipstick, and smoothing out the blush on my cheeks. I stepped out of my car, unobtrusively straightening my skirt, and teetered on my heels over to the foreman's shack in the hopes of finding Ted Lombardi alone and willing to talk.

Unfortunately, he was not alone. Three sets of male eyes stared up at me from a plan of the warehouse lying spread out on a table, as I quietly entered and shut the door behind me.

"Can I help you?" Lombardi asked politely, almost indifferently, as the other men silently dissected me. Clearly, the foreman didn't remember me.

"I work on the show," I told him, my gaze sliding to the other two men. They wore jeans and work shirts, although I didn't recognize them from the site. "I need to talk to you about some insurance information for Michael Keller. In private." I smiled shyly to show that I was a sweet, harmless young thing just doing her job.

Lombardi didn't look too thrilled with my request, and if he decided to call Bob Berg for confirmation, I was in trouble.

Nevertheless he nodded curtly and turned back to the other two men.

"Why don't you start and we'll get back to this later?"

The men nodded and moved past me to the door while Lombardi rolled up the warehouse blueprints and set them aside. He didn't ask me to sit down. The trailer smelled of cigarette smoke, but the weather had turned cool and fallish overnight, and the air wasn't too stale and stifling.

"What do you need to know?" he asked, barely looking at me. I sat down on a metal chair next to the table, pretending not to notice his obvious reluctance to deal with me.

"It's for the production company," I repeated, trying to make him understand that this had nothing to do with me. "They need a record of Michael Keller's last day of work."

"I don't keep records of Keller's hours," Lombardi said. "He wasn't on the company payroll."

"I know. I was with those two detectives when they questioned you about him."

Lombardi looked at me more closely. "Oh, yeah," he said. Then, almost as an afterthought, "Sorry."

"That's okay." I waved away his offhand apology. "You see, I remember you told the police that Mr. Keller didn't show up for work the day after Rebecca Saunders' death. The insurance company needs something more specific than that."

I smiled my own apology as if to say I was sorry for wasting his time over this but what can I do? I crossed my legs and stifled an impulse to yank the skirt down over my knees. Lombardi didn't even look, and I supposed it served me right.

"Look, Keller came and went. Romulus hired him, let them worry about the insurance."

"They are. That's why I'm here," I said pleasantly.

"You're sure you don't remember whether Keller disappeared on Monday or Tuesday?" To jog his memory, I added, "On Thursday the water pipe broke in the bullpen."

Lombardi's face cleared. "Was that when it happened?" I nodded. "Okay. Then it was Thursday. Because Keller's job was to check on the sprinkler system in the attic. He's probably the reason why the pipe burst in the first place."

"What do you mean?"

"He was up there. You had your flood. I went to talk to him about it and couldn't find him. Haven't seen him since."

"Do you think it was his fault the pipe burst?"

"Probably. Keller shouldn't be in construction. I doubt he even knows how to change a light bulb."

"Then why did you let him work on the sprinkler system in the first place?"

"The orders didn't come from me," said Lombardi. "Keller said the boss asked him to check them out."

He didn't have anything else to add, not knowing whether the boss meant Bob Berg or someone else. Normally, I wouldn't be surprised if Keller had meant Rebecca, since she threw her weight around like a boss. But Rebecca had died on Tuesday, and I couldn't imagine why she would order her ex-husband to check out the sprinkler system before she got her head bashed in. I thanked Lombardi for his time and returned to the warehouse, more confused than ever.

I had a particular reason for wanting to know Keller's whereabouts around the time of Rebecca's death. Since Rebecca had been expecting a visitor who clearly did not have a key to the front door, the most logical person had to be Michael Keller.

If he had killed her, he might have taken off Tuesday night and not come into work on Wednesday, knowing the police would be after him. But the foreman's remarks had only served to muddy my thinking. If Keller had killed Rebecca, why would he come in two days later claiming someone had ordered him to look at the sprinkler system? Unless he hadn't killed Rebecca after all. Maybe he had truly disappeared, at least at first, because he screwed up on the job.

I called Bob's assistant, Estelle, as soon as I got back to my desk. Even though most employees didn't show up until nine-thirty, I knew Estelle—a brusque, flinty-eyed older woman who'd been with Bob for years—would be at her desk, trying, like Bob, to think of new ways to slash money from the various Romulus budgets. Sandy had once told me that it had been Estelle's idea not to authorize money for toilet paper for the construction workers during the show's hiatus last spring. As a result, the men used anything they could get their hands on, clogging the toilets and costing the company more to fix the plumbing than it would have cost them in toilet paper. Way to go, Estelle!

She answered on the third ring, sounding her usual grouchy and impatient self. "Bob Berg's office," she said, and I could hear her unspoken thought, "What do you want, and this better be good."

"Hi, Estelle, it's Susan Kaplan at Babbitt & Brooks.

There was a pause as Estelle tried to place my name with a face. "Yes?" she replied in a neutral, although no less gruff, tone.

"We're trying to get a fix on who broke the water pipe in the warehouse."

"Oh, yes." Estelle sounded more perky. Fixing the pipe had cost the company major bucks, and Estelle wasn't going to quickly forget it.

"Anyway, I was just talking to the foreman of the construction company and he thought that maybe Bob had ordered one of the workers to take a look at it before it broke."

"That's ridiculous," Estelle said. "Bob had nothing to do with that."

"You're sure?"

"Of course I am. What does Bob know about water pipes?"

"Well, you see, Bob hired Michael Keller to work with the construction crew and since it was Keller who might have broken the pipe in the first place . . ."

Estelle cut me off. "Bob hired him as a favor to Rebecca. That's all. Bob would not make it his business to tell him what to fix. That's for the construction company to decide."

"Okay, Estelle," I said meekly. "I was just checking. According to the foreman, Keller told him the boss gave him orders to take a look at it, and I naturally thought . . ."

"It wasn't Bob," Estelle said firmly. "And, besides, he and Keller never even met. This man had no reason to call Bob the boss. Is there anything else you wanted to know?" Her tone implied there better not be.

"No, that's all," I assured her. "Thanks for your help."

Estelle muttered something that sounded like "Hmph" before hanging up the phone. I hung up more slowly, feeling like I was back at square one.

Who else would Michael Keller call the boss? Ray came to mind first, but why would he care about the sprinkler system or have anything to do with Keller? Charles could also logically be considered a boss, but the same question arose: Why would he ask Keller to check on anything? Of course, Charles could have been Rebecca's visitor— arriving after Ray's visit. But what did that have to do with the burst water pipe? Were Rebecca's death and the flood connected? But how? Did the murderer think the flood would somehow destroy evidence not already discovered by the police? And not realize that Keller in his incompetence would accidentally destroy the bullpen, instead of Rebecca's office? But what would that evidence be? I had already been in Rebecca's office and had found nothing of interest. Or had I missed something? I was halfway out of my chair to check again when the phone rang. Lainie Abbott was on the phone with last night's show's overnight ratings.

The housewives-turned-prostitutes episode of Babbitt & Brooks had aired the night before, and I watched it in my apartment with Craig, having given him a murder update during the commercial breaks. Craig, initially sympathetic regarding l'affaire Jennifer, became angry when I relayed the Michael Keller escapade. Which made me decide not to tell him that I planned to talk with Keller's foreman the next day, not wanting to completely jeopardize my chances of receiving another good-night kiss.

The episode, written by Zack, was only so-so. The story, about bored housewives who turned tricks for extra spending money, had been based on an article Ray read in a magazine. Zack hadn't wanted to write it, and as a result his efforts were mediocre. Ray hated the final cut as well and had strongly recommended the episode be buried in the middle of the season. But since Rebecca's death had generated so much publicity for the show, the network thought it would be a good audience grabber and decided to air it early.

At the end of the episode, as the screen faded to black, the words "In Memory of Zachary North" appeared where only the week before Rebecca's memorial had been placed.

"I feel like I'm watching a jinxed show," said Craig, as the words slowly faded to be replaced by "Executive Producer, Raymond Goldfarb." "Who's going to die next week?"

"Don't even think that." I shuddered. "Not that anyone feels the way you do—especially agents."

Ever since the press had reported Zack's death, agents had been calling, recommending their writer clients to fill his slot. It reminded me of living in New York, where people combed the obituaries looking to see who died and left a desirable apartment behind. But, true to his word, Ray was not rushing into anything. Appointments were made to meet various writers, and in the meantime Peggy and Charles continued to shoulder the writing burden.

Either the networks had made a wise decision, or Rebecca's and Zack's deaths continued to keep the audience tuned in. Lainie's breathy voice informed me that the overnights were just as strong as the ones from the week before. The show was assured of another twenty-five share—and a first-place ratings finish.

As a result, I didn't have much time to worry over the

identity of Keller's anonymous boss or how I was going to behave around Jennifer. The phone rang continually with a mixture of congratulations and crank calls, and Jennifer and I were too busy to deal with the awkwardness of our own situation.

Although Ray, Charles, and Peggy all looked pleased with the ratings, their faces did not reflect the elated happiness of the week before. I couldn't help remembering Jennifer's earlier comment about Ray hiring a hit man to keep the ratings up, and I'm sure everyone was aware that the ratings were more a product of Zack's death than of a natural interest in a quality show.

At one, Winifred arrived to take Ray out to lunch. Peggy and Charles had disappeared into Charles's office to work on the rewrite of Zack's script; Ray must've figured he had some time to spare.

Winifred didn't look all that well: her face seemed thinner, and she had lost some of that haughty self-assurance I remembered from the first time I met her. Ray looked equally tired and unhappy, which I had chalked up to overwork, but wondered now if it had to do with juggling his affair with Gail and his marriage to Winifred. Before leaving Sandy's apartment the night before, I had asked her why Ray didn't simply get a divorce from his wife to marry Gail. Sandy shook her head and smiled at me as if she couldn't believe my naiveté.

"Community property," she told me. "It'll kill him."

"But they haven't been married that long. How bad can it be?"

Jennifer answered for her. "Ray owns a piece of the show. Winifred helped put the deal together. If "Broads with Balls" continues as the number one show, or even manages to remain in the top ten, that could be a hefty chunk of change. Ray probably doesn't want to part with any of it, even if it means sneaking around behind Winifred's back."

The phone calls petered out during the lunch hour, and Jennifer and I contemplated each other from across our desks.

"I tried calling you last night," she finally said. "You didn't pick up the phone."

"I know." I had let her calls fall into voicemail, not knowing how to deal with her.

"Are you going to hate me for the rest of your life?" she asked.

"I don't hate you," I said. "I just . . ." I trailed off, wearily shaking my head.

"How many times do I have to say I'm sorry?" Her voice broke, and for a horrified moment I thought she was going to cry.

"Jennifer—" I half rose from my chair.

She rose, too, holding up a hand as if to ward me off. "Just stay the fuck away from me." She ran out of the room just as Sandy entered.

"What's wrong?" she asked. "What happened?"

I didn't know how to answer around the lump in my throat. It felt like granite.

Sandy looked at me more carefully. "Susan, did you two have a fight?"

"I don't know what we had," I said. I didn't know whether to tell Sandy about Jennifer's and my aborted dinner the night before. Would telling her about Jennifer sending the death threats be appropriate? Or would it just label me a gossip?

Sandy looked at me strangely. I couldn't blame her. My face must've looked as confused as I felt. But all she said was, "I'll be in my office if you need to talk."

Jennifer slid into her chair as soon as Sandy disappeared in the opposite direction. "Why didn't you tell her?" she asked.

I looked at her in surprise. "You were listening?"

Jennifer nodded. "I wanted to hear what you'd say. But you didn't say anything. Why?"

I shrugged. "Got me. It's hard to stop liking you, I guess."

Jennifer grinned. "I know. It's that ol' black magic."

I grinned back. But inside I still didn't know how I felt.

"Let's have lunch to celebrate the renewal of our friendship vows," she said.

But I couldn't. One of us had to stay and answer the phones. "You go," I said. "I brown-bagged it today. Another time."

"Promise?"

I nodded. "I promise." But I didn't know if that was a promise I could, or wanted to, keep.

11.

When Jennifer returned from lunch, I decided to share my new knowledge of Michael Keller and the burst water pipe with her. I needed to talk to someone and thought confiding in her would bring me a step closer to seeing her, once again, as a friend.

But Jennifer only shook her head in despair at my determination to get to the bottom of the murders, although she did react with interest when I told her about Keller referring to the person who gave him the orders as "the boss."

"It has to be Ray," she said after I told her Estelle denied Bob Berg's involvement.

"But why would Ray want him to mess with the water pipes?"

"You know Ray. He walks around here like he owns this place. He must've known Keller's connection to Rebecca and asked him to do a little handiwork on the side."

"I don't know," I said.

"Your problem is you're trying to link the flood to Rebecca's death. I don't see why there has to be any connection."

"To destroy evidence," I said, but without much conviction.

"Are you seeing conspiracies everywhere, Susan?" Charles stood at the entrance to the bullpen, clearly amused. I flushed with embarrassment, grateful I hadn't brought up his name in connection with Rebecca's anonymous, keyless visitor.

Fortunately, Charles didn't seem to expect an answer because he moved further into the room and handed Jennifer some pages.

"Script changes," he told her. Then turned back to me. "Peggy's in her office working on the second two acts. She'll have them for you soon."

I nodded, sick at heart, because I realized that if Peggy

were back in her office, then she must've overheard me, too.

"Everyone heard you," Sandy told me later when I went back to her office for a brief visit to fill her in on what happened.

"Ray and Winifred came back for lunch just as you were spouting off to Jennifer about broken water pipes and destroying evidence. I could even hear you in my office."

My heart sank further. I hadn't noticed that Winifred and Ray had returned from lunch, although Patrick had shown up a few minutes earlier, claiming he had a meeting with Ray. I could hear the low murmur of their voices from the wall separating Ray's office from Sandy's.

"I guess I should've just taken out an announcement in the Hollywood Reporter. Or. maybe Nikki Finke could write something up on Deadline Hollywood."

"And maybe the murderer will step forward and apologize for causing everyone so much trouble and turn himself in."

There was nothing I could say in response so I gloomily trailed back to my desk.

"It has to be Michael Keller," Jennifer told me. "He was a pretty creepy guy."

There was no denying that, but Zack, according to Peggy, hadn't believed in Keller's guilt. What had he known that the rest of us hadn't? The police never mentioned whether Zack's house had been ransacked prior to his "suicide," and I wondered if Zack had been killed because he had undeniable proof of the murderer's identity. But what was that proof and how did he get it? And more importantly, if the murderer didn't find it, was it still lying around somewhere?

Taking my courage in hand, I approached Ray toward the end of the day. I tentatively asked him for permission to pack up Zack's office, afraid he'd see through my excuse and realize I wanted to snoop around looking for clues to Zack's death—and possibly his knowledge of Keller's innocence. But to my relief, Ray thought packing up Zack's things was an excellent idea and told me to go ahead.

I waited until everyone went home in order not to arouse suspicion and to be able to take my time. I unlocked Zack's door with my master key, turned on the overheard fluorescent, and stepped inside. Jennifer had told me that Detective Wagner had made a cursory search of the office the day after Zack's death while I was having lunch with Linda Ramsay. But as far as she knew, Wagner had found nothing. The office looked exactly as Zack had last left it. Old drafts of his script lay on his desk, new lines of inked-in dialogue squeezed between the old, laser-printed ones. On Zack's couch—a horrid, clashing plaid that Linda had dug out of Romulus's storage room—sat several scripts submitted by agents, an abandoned umbrella and an orange nerf ball. Zack had a toy basketball hoop clipped to the back of his door. I knew he liked to shoot hoops while working out a scene in his head. It looked lonely and abandoned, and I felt a pang of sorrow for Zack, suddenly missing his presence in the office.

The bookcase behind his desk housed three-ring binders filled with Babbitt & Brooks scripts starting from the year before. I flipped though several at random, but found no mysterious notes, veiled threats or revealing clues tucked between the pages. With a sigh, I shoved the last notebook back onto the shelf and turned to rummage through his desk. I went through each page of paper, scrutinizing the corrections, trying to translate Zack's doodles. I put the old script pages in some kind of order and stacked them on a corner of his desk. Technically, they were useless and could've been thrown in the recycling bin, but I was too afraid I might miss something that would come back to haunt me later.

Zack's drawers held the usual office detritus. The top one housed loose paper clips, rubber bands, ballpoint pens without caps, and script brads. The middle drawer held neatly stacked pads of yellow legal-sized paper on which Zack used to write his scripts. The third drawer was empty, and I studied it contemplatively, wondering if it had once held the alleged missing clue.

But, eventually, I closed it with a sigh, although I have to admit that I did check for secret cubbyholes and false panels. Zack used an ordinary metal desk, dented and worn from use over the years but without the hoped-for Gothic accoutrements. In searching for a clue, I had inadvertently straightened out the desk. The piles of script pages sat neatly in one corner, a Babbitt & Brooks coffee mug, which held pens, pencils, and magic markers, sat in another. In the center were a three-hole punch, stapler, and Zack's engagement calendar. Like me, Zack was a technophobe, preferring the old-fashioned method of writing dates down rather than plugging them into his smartphone. I slid the calendar across the top of the desk to look at it more closely. I remembered catching Zack looking at mine the day before his death and finding it turned toward the week of Rebecca's murder. I flipped through Zack's, wondering what entry he thought mine had that his didn't.

There were no incriminating names or phone numbers listed on the day that turned out to be Zack's last. Nothing the day before— or even the week before. A lunch with Peggy, notations of various story meetings under particular times. No coded entries. No breakfast dates with a murderer (unless Peggy . . .? Nah!). If he had dined with Zack, wouldn't the murderer have taken Zack's calendar? Would Rebecca have put down a meeting that turned out to be with a murderer? But she always told me what meetings she was going to have, and I always penciled them in my calendar. No one had stolen my calendar. It was too badly damaged by the busted water pipe.

Suddenly I froze. I hastily turned Zack's calendar back to the day after Rebecca's death. But, of course, he didn't have the entry I was looking for. Only my calendar had that.

I sat in Zack's chair, not wanting to move. In spite of all my questions, in spite of all my searching, I realized I absolutely did not want to know who the killer was. Not this killer. Because I knew this person. This was not some abstract evil that had swept down and snuffed the life out of two people I knew. This person was real. This person had talked to me. And now this person might possibly want to kill me.

Stiffly, I rose from my chair and exited the office. I crossed the now deserted bullpen. I moved toward the storage closet near the front entrance, opened the door, and yanked on the cord that turned on the bare, thirty watt bulb. My carton of damp desk supplies still sat in the center of the room where I had placed it after the flood. My desk calendar sat on top of the pile, the pages crinkled from water but the writing still legible. I grasped the calendar by its center metal rings, and took it back with me to my desk. I sat down and stared at it, not wanting to read the page, praying that what I knew I would find there would somehow not be on it.

The calendar page staring up at me was the day of Rebecca's death. After the trauma of finding her body, being questioned by the police, then going to the set, I had never turned it over to the next day. I did so now. The ink had run a little but the name was still legible. I stared at it, realizing I had missed a clue in Rebecca's office when I had gone into it before Keller's arrival. I remembered when Zack first started acting funny and finally understood why. He had just realized who the murderer was but needed proof. But was my battered, crinkly, ink-stained calendar enough proof to send a murderer to jail?

I sat there and wondered, and then the lights went out.

END OF ACT FOUR

ACT FIVE

1.

It was just like in a horror movie, but of course I didn't think that at the time. I actually didn't think much of anything at first, too frightened to move. Granted the construction workers had been messing with the electrical system for months, creating havoc with power surges, but they always left at five, and now it was past seven. I knew this was not the construction company. This was Rebecca's and Zack's murderer. There was absolutely no doubt in my mind that this person was now coming after me.

The bullpen was pitch black; the natural light from the window in the front door didn't penetrate the gloom of the office. I thought about rising from my chair and feeling my way down the corridor and the exit, but just as I was about to make my move, I sensed a presence materialize in the hallway between Rebecca's and Ray's offices.

"Susan," a voice said, and I almost screamed in shock. Then, surprisingly, "I'm sorry." I heard the soft jingle of keys as he moved into the bullpen.

Patrick Hager. I didn't need to see his face to know that it was him. The calendar gave him away. Patrick must have known that as well, because he didn't try to disguise his voice. Which did nothing to reassure me. It meant I would be dead before I could call the police.

And yet, I still couldn't move. In all those mystery books I liked to devour, the heroine was always able to keep the murderer talking while she figured out a way to escape. But I forgot how to talk in those first, frightening seconds. If I opened my mouth at all it would be to take great, gulping gasps of air because, suddenly, I couldn't breathe.

"Susan?" he said again. I remained at my desk, head bowed, unable to look at him.

"What happened to chivalry?" I finally managed to say. My voice sounded resentful, as if I couldn't believe he had the nerve to betray my belief in him.

"Give me the calendar, please," Patrick said, ignoring my question. Even though he asked politely, I shook my head no. I still felt mad that this was happening to me—and from someone I had actually liked!

"Susan?" I realized Patrick couldn't have seen me shake my head. He was probably as blind as I was. So instead of answering, I curled my fingers over the center metal hooks that kept the calendar pages in place, and slowly stood up. A part of me that had conveniently removed itself from the emotions of the moment noticed that my hands were shaking.

Patrick must have sensed my movement because his shadow detached itself from the corridor entrance. I could hear his heavy breathing and knew that if I didn't do something quickly, I would be dead before I hit the ground. My first instinct was to slide under my desk and curl there fetus-like until Patrick went away. But this wasn't a nightmare in which I could just wake myself up to make the bogeyman disappear. I felt Patrick's warm breath on my hair, and without thinking, I abruptly swung the calendar in his face.

Contact! I heard Patrick's surprised grunt of pain and then I ran. My aim was to reach the writers' corridor and the basketball court beyond, but I still couldn't see anything and my nose slammed into the wall of Peggy's office. I grunted in pain myself, tears springing to my eyes. I could hear Patrick knock aside my desk chair and come for me once again. The corridor was only a few feet to my right, and I rolled around the side of the office and ran like hell. Patrick was right behind me.

The basketball court was somewhat lighter since high, dusty windows were set above the huge double doors. But, unfortunately, the sun had set and there wasn't much reflection from the moon. The double doors, I knew, would be locked, the only other exit being the narrow plank that led to the other warehouse. I skidded on the slippery wood floor, my high heels almost causing my ankle to twist and spill me to the ground. I couldn't run very quickly in my short, tight skirt, and I had to pause to take off my shoes in order to keep going in my stocking feet.

"Susan," Patrick said again, as he exited the writers' corridor. "It's over."

"No," I said out loud, and shot out my arm as if to wave him away from me. I forgot that I was holding one of my shoes, and I could feel the heel hit Patrick's eye. I guess the calendar in his face hadn't been sufficient warning to stay away from my waving arms.

"Shit!" he said. "Oh, fuck!"

I had never heard him curse before and the words brought back my sense of unreality. I shot off toward the plank leading to the other warehouse.

Enough light came from above to show me the plank and to prevent me from falling over the side. Unfortunately, Patrick had been in this warehouse many more times than I had and probably knew its ins and outs in his sleep. I wasn't thinking too much about where I was going or what I was going to do once I made it to the other warehouse. I suppose I thought I'd try to find an exit, but aside from the twin set of double doors I really didn't know of any other escape routes.

I ran past the production offices, supposedly closed and locked for the week's unexpected hiatus, but now open. Patrick must have hidden there, waiting until everyone else went home, and I knew his office would not be a great place to hide. So I made a quick turn and found myself in the large, open area that served as the show's soundstage. Patrick had since recovered from the clunk in his eye, and I could hear his running footsteps behind me. I found myself next to the set of the Babbitt & Brooks law office, and, following my earlier instincts, I ran behind one of the sheet-covered desks, crawled under the dust cloth and curled up in the dark, comforting space of the desk underneath.

I needed a plan. I knew that if I were to survive, I would have to control my panic and be craftier than Patrick. Which might not be as hard as I thought, in spite of my scattered thoughts and numbing fear. Obviously, his goal had been to count on my frozen surprise once the lights went out and kill me on the spot. My panicked, unthinking flight had unnerved him and left him without a back-up plan. Or so I hoped.

But the bottom line was I was stuck in a warehouse most of which was unfamiliar. I couldn't imagine fumbling around the sets, seeking an exit, without making a sound and subsequently getting killed. I had to get back to my side of the building and the front door. While Patrick could have locked it on the inside with a deadbolt key in order to trap me, I was counting on his not having done so.

As unit production manager, Patrick had a key to every lock in the warehouse. But he kept the set belonging to the writers' side in his desk. If Rebecca was expecting Patrick on the night of her death, then of course she'd ask Sherman to keep the front door unlocked—so that Patrick could get in.

But I didn't have time to put all the pieces of the murder jigsaw together, even though I knew what most of them were. While I was trying to master my breathing and control my panic, the rest of me had been on the alert for any sound of the killer. I had heard him dash across the plank after me—the keys on his belt an incongruous musical accompaniment—but I had turned the corner and ducked under the desk before he had time to see me. However, he must've stopped in his tracks the instant I disappeared because all was quiet around me. Even the night time sounds of creaking walls and settling floorboards were mysteriously absent, and with a shudder I imagined Patrick creeping around the sets, listening as carefully for me as I was for him. I prayed that he would make some sort of sound, trip over a loose nail, bang his shin against a piece of cloth-covered furniture to clue me in on where he was and how I could safely get away.

My breath rasped in my ears and I had to pee. My heart had slowed from its initial adrenalin rush, but I was still too afraid to crawl out from under the desk. For all I knew Patrick was right in front of me, waiting for me to make the next move. I could easily have stayed under the desk overnight, waiting for daylight and my returning coworkers. Except the next day was Saturday and not even the cleaning crew would show up until Monday morning. I had to make my move sometime between now and then or face death from a burst kidney and/or dehydration. Neither thought was any more pleasant than my death at the hands of —

A sound! The soft jingle of keys, sounding fainter and fainter until it finally stopped. Either Patrick had taken the keys off his belt loop or he was too far away for me to hear them anymore. In any event, the keys had sounded far enough away for me to make my move. Patrick had probably counted on my heading for the double doors and had moved deeper into the warehouse than I had actually gotten. I slowly poked my head out from under the cloth and looked around. There was hardly enough light to see three feet in front of me, but fortunately, my night vision had checked in and I could look around me with more confidence.

Large pieces of furniture loomed over me from the darkness but nothing looked remotely human. I quietly rose from under the desk, brushing away pieces of dust and lint from my skirt from force of habit. Although my skirt was black, I wore a white blouse with matching black trim and knew the white probably made me visible from miles away. But there was no way I was going to take off my shirt and run through the warehouse in my underwear. So I crossed my fingers in the hopes I wouldn't be seen and, still clutching my shoes, moved quietly out of the lawyers' office, walking smack into a light pole.

Both the pole and I lost our balance and crashed down together with a mighty thunk. I had walked into a thin, steel, movable pole that the electricians used to string up lights. Normally sandbags kept the poles in place, but I supposed the departing electricians hadn't thought that necessary for the week's unexpected hiatus. I had clunked my forehead pretty hard into the pole and still lay dazed on the ground when in the distance I heard the pounding of footsteps and the clanking of those damn keys.

Patrick arrived as I staggered to my feet, and he paused to regard my plight. I thought he would say something like "Gotcha," or "I'm sorrier about this than you," but instead he said, "Is milady Susan terribly injured?"

Patrick's face was a pale, formless blob above me, but I could tell by the tone of his voice that he had lost his mind.

"Patrick," I began. But he interrupted me.

"What did you do with the calendar, milady?"

My head throbbed from where I had beaned myself, but the pain was remote, something I noticed impersonally while I tried to breathe around my hammering heart.

"I left the calendar under the desk over there," I told him, motioning toward the piece of furniture I had just hid under. It was a lie, of course. I actually had no idea where the calendar was. After hitting Patrick with it back in the bullpen, I must have dropped it during my pell-mell flight down the writers' corridor.

"I would be very honored if you would retrieve it for me, milady."

Patrick, completely in Cloud Cuckooland, started to make one of his wide, sweeping bows. I bent down, picked up the light pole, and swung it at him. The pole was unwieldy and heavier than I expected, but I managed to crack him in the knees with it. I heard his "Ugh!" as he folded neatly to the floor. I dropped the pole like a hot potato and took off once again for the more familiar terrain of my warehouse and the front door, still holding onto my shoes as if they were sacred talismans.

I ran back in the direction of the basketball court, having finally found my voice and screaming my bloody lungs out, although no one, except Patrick, was around to hear me.

I suspected Patrick was merely stunned, and that I had only bought myself a matter of seconds. He'd catch up to me before I made it to the front—and if he didn't, I had no idea whether the door was locked or not, and if it was, whether I'd have time to find my keys, unlock the door, and run out before he grabbed me. There was only one chance left, and although I knew that too many aspects about my plan could go wrong, it was the only thing left I could think of to try.

Still screaming for help, I raced for the writers' warehouse. But instead of crossing over the plank, I carefully dropped down from it into the pit below. The drop was a little over five feet and I sat down on the plank and used my arms for leverage to move into the pit. I landed with knees braced and bent, my head barely reaching the top of the newly-built cement walls. Now I screamed deliberately to cover the sounds of my slowly removing the plank from its perch. A six foot, narrow piece of plywood, the plank wasn't very heavy, and it was easy enough to lift into my hands and maneuver into the pit with me. I tried to hold it like a battering ram, although, like the lighting pole, it was heavier and more unwieldy than I expected.

I still kept screaming, deliberately alerting Patrick to my whereabouts. I didn't think about the consequences if my plan failed. I only knew that I would fight until my last ounce of strength was gone. Still holding the plank, I backed a few feet down the pit, the cement floor damp and hard against my stockinged feet. Groping around the floor while I screamed until my voice was hoarse, I found what I needed, and although it felt like hours, it must only have been seconds before a shadow appeared in the basketball court and raced toward me. I immediately clammed up, gripped the plank awkwardly with one arm, and threw a screwdriver left behind by one of the construction workers onto the floor of the other warehouse. It made a clattering sound far enough away for Patrick to think I had crossed to the other side of the building. I could only hope he'd be too determined to kill me to notice that the plank was missing.

I hoped correctly. As soon as he heard the rolling screwdriver, he raced toward the edge of the warehouse, looking too late for the plank, and falling head first into the pit. He tried to brace himself, but he landed painfully on his knees. I heard a crunch and a sharp intake of air before he fell over on his side, his arms wrapped around both knees. I stood frozen in place, the plank still clutched between my hands, my heart twisting at the sound of his sobs.

Amazingly, he tried to crawl toward me, still intent on killing me. Enough already, I thought, more angry than frightened that this man was acting like The Terminator, refusing to quit until he killed me. It was that anger that helped me grasp the plank firmly in both hands and deliberately slam it against Patrick's head. I heard a soft, almost surprised, "Oh," before he finally slid into unconsciousness.

2.

It was, of course, the engagement calendar that gave him away. The day of her death, Rebecca had been forced to answer the phones because I was sitting in my car, angry over not getting a script assignment, and Jennifer was in Sandy's office listening to Sandy tell her she was on probation. Patrick had made one of his usual appointments with Rebecca for ten o'clock the next day, which Rebecca reported to me and which I recorded in my calendar. Zack had overheard the conversation, having been with Rebecca at the time, and it was the memory of this, during our conversation with Patrick at Rebecca's memorial service that tipped him off and led to his death.

Because Patrick never showed up for that appointment. He knew Rebecca was dead. He didn't even call to cancel but remained instead on location, away from the central focus of the investigation. A cooler murderer would have claimed to have forgotten the appointment, although I might still have been suspicious, since Patrick never forgot any of his meetings with Rebecca; he always called to cancel if he couldn't make it.

Of course, unlike the murderers caught in the detective novels I loved to read, Patrick didn't confess a thing. Even when the police and ambulance arrived, as well as Craig, whom I had called from my cell once I was safely out of the warehouse, Patrick remained mute. At the time, the cops could only arrest him for assault, even though Patrick was the one who was physically assaulted. I had survived the ordeal shoeless, trembling, and with a bump on my head from my crash into the light pole. But the evidence, now that the police knew where to look, was soon to follow. I was able to piece the story together on my own, which I was happy to share with Detectives Wagner and Lu, who arrived on the scene shortly after the uniformed cops and ambulance. We spoke in the parking lot of the warehouse. Patrick had cut the wires of the electrical system which were located right next to the supply closet, and the forensics team was examining the damaged wires to include as additional evidence. Craig, who had raced into the parking lot in his mud-stained Jeep Wrangler, refused to leave my side, which was heartwarming—although I suspected his real motive was to prevent me from getting into any more trouble. We all stood under one of the parking lot lamps so Lu could take notes of my explanation of the events leading up to the two murders.

"It was common knowledge Patrick wanted to direct an episode," I began, trying not to look at Wagner who was staring at me. "I even saw Rebecca bring his director's reel to Ray the night of her death. She was giving Ray a rundown of all the possible directors and scriptwriters for the show."

"Yeah, I remember you telling me this," Wagner interrupted. Lu briefly rubbed his eyes, his face a sickly yellow underneath the streetlamp. Craig's looked just as bad, and I suspected mine looked no better.

"Anyway," I went on, "I went back to her office a couple of days later, and Patrick's DVD wasn't among those on her couch. But I didn't notice. I just realized I didn't recognize any of the names on the DVDs or scripts. Patrick must have taken his DVD when he came back to the warehouse and killed Rebecca."

"Is that really proof?" Craig asked. I answered his question before the cops could.

"Maybe not that he killed her," I said. "But since I saw her going into Ray's office with the DVD, and then there was no DVD after she died, it's proof at least that Patrick saw her at some point during that time and took it with him."

"Unless of course it's in Goldfarb's office," Lu said.

"No." I turned to him. "I was in Ray's office the day after her death. There weren't any DVDs around, not even dailies. I'll lay odds that Patrick's reel is either in his office or at home."

The cops found it in his office later that night, and the DVD turned out to be a key piece of evidence in Patrick's case, but at the moment the detectives were concerned about other things.

"Why would Hager suddenly come back to Ms.

Saunders' office, kill her, and steal his own DVD?" Lu
asked, still skeptical.

"When Rebecca met with Ray about possible directors
and writers, she probably deep-sixed Patrick. Ray actually
went to location instead of straight home. Like I told you
all along," I said, glaring at Wagner who didn't even have
the grace to look embarrassed. "I'll bet you anything Ray
told Patrick about not using him as a director. Everyone on
the show knew Rebecca made those decisions for Ray; it
was the reason Patrick was kissing up to her in the first
place. So Patrick probably called Rebecca, told her he
wanted to talk to her, and Rebecca told Sherman not to
lock up because she was expecting a visitor. Patrick has
keys to all the locks, but he doesn't need to carry a key to
our front door with him since he always uses the entrance
to the production side of the warehouse."

Wagner and Lu exchanged one of their unfathomable
glances. "We know about Mr. Goldfarb going to location,"
Wagner said. I looked at him in surprise and he actually
smiled back at me. "You thought I wasn't listening to you.
But as soon as you said Goldfarb lied about his alibi, we
did some checking. It was easy enough to discover he
hadn't gone straight home."

"Then why didn't you say something?"

"Because, as I kept trying to tell you," he explained
impatiently, "this was not your case."

"She solved it for you, though," Craig said, and I looked
up at him gratefully. He had not only placed his UCLA
letter jacket around my shoulders to protect me from the
cold night air, but he'd loaned me his thick white socks to
wear over my shredded stockings so that the graveled

parking lot didn't cut into my feet.

"We would've gotten there eventually, Mr. Keefer," Lu said.

"Then you know about Ray and Gail," I said to the two detectives.

Wagner answered. "We know that they left the set together. The make-up woman confirmed it. But we couldn't trace their whereabouts after that."

"They were here," I said. "Sandy Martin can vouch for that."

Wagner raised his eyebrows. "She can?"

I snapped my jaw shut. I would do my friends a world of good if I kept it permanently wired.

"That's not important," I said. "What is, is that Patrick killed Rebecca in a fit of rage because she wouldn't go to bat for him about the directing gig. Then he killed Zack because Zack figured it out." I explained about Zack's realization after Rebecca's memorial service. Both detectives nodded thoughtfully.

"Now that we know what to look for," said Wagner, "fibers from Ms. Saunders' car will probably match fibers from what Hager was wearing on the days he killed her and Mr. North."

Craig spoke up once again. "And don't forget his trying to kill Susan. If that doesn't tie him into the murders, I don't know what does."

I squeezed Craig's arm, and he looked down at me, concern so evident in his eyes, I caught my breath. Could it be possible his feelings for me had grown? But before I could examine that further, Lu interrupted my thoughts.

"And what are you doing here?" Lu asked.

Craig looked at Lu without flinching. "Susan called me after she called you." Then, simply, spoken more to me than to the detectives, he added, "I was worried about her."

He put an arm around my shoulders and held me close to his body. I could smell the scent of his aftershave, feel the thrumming of his heart through his sweatshirt. I wanted to cry . . . with happiness and relief. Then I caught Wagner's amused glance, and blushed.

"How did you get out of the warehouse?" Unlike Wagner, Lu was not interested in a blossoming romance in the midst of murder.

"Easy," I said, happy to change the subject. "After I whacked Patrick on the head, I couldn't climb out of the ditch. So I ran down it and found a sheet of plastic hanging between the two buildings. I just went behind it and found myself outside."

What I didn't tell them was how I had broken down and cried, after calling the police and then Craig, sitting on the front steps, until the first cop car arrived.

Which reminded me . . .

"Patrick probably stole Rebecca's Escalade after he killed her," I told Lu and Wagner. "Zack made a lot of phone calls the day he died—when he started to suspect that Patrick was guilty of Rebecca's murder. I bet if you check Zack's phone records, you'll see Patrick was one of the people he called." "Patrick drove to Zack's house in Rebecca's Escalade the Sunday after the memorial service. He knew Zack suspected him of killing Rebecca. He planted the car in Zack's garage to frame Zack. Maybe he hoped to knock out Zack and kill him then. But maybe he didn't get the opportunity. So he went back on Tuesday. Miranda told me Patrick was on the phone with her in his car the morning of Zack's death when he should've been at work. So he doesn't have an alibi."

Lu jotted this down and Wagner nodded. "Thanks. That should help."

3.

E vidence slowly came in implicating Patrick in both murders. Crew members spotted him leaving location as production wrapped which, when timed out, put him at the warehouse just after Ray and Gail had left. Fibers in Rebecca's car matched the jacket Patrick wore when he killed her. A cab company had a record of picking up a passenger matching Patrick's description on Ventura Boulevard, close to Zack's house, and dropping him off on Wilshire Boulevard in West Los Angeles, near Patrick's condo. We even learned that Patrick planted the lesbian article in the Scoop, having taken the picture of Gail and Rebecca at the show's Christmas party, then giving it to the paper in order to disrupt the show and confuse the murder issue even more.

Michael Keller, when finally tracked down, admitted that Patrick had asked him to "fix" the sprinkler system so that a pipe would burst over my desk. Patrick paid him in cash, claiming it came from the B&B discretionary budget and promising him a job on the set, which is why Keller referred to him as "the boss." Not wanting to simply steal my desk calendar, with the incriminating ten o'clock appointment, Patrick hoped the flood would destroy it in a way that wouldn't cause me to think twice about his missed meeting. It was unfortunate for him that I had decided to save the calendar instead of throwing it out.

Zack's autopsy revealed a slight bruising above his left ear that proved he was hit on the head before being placed in Rebecca's car. To avoid the death penalty, Patrick unexpectedly pleaded guilty to one count of manslaughter and one count of murder. He made a full confession that confirmed my theory of the events leading up to both Rebecca's and Zack's deaths, and was given a life sentence, due for parole in fifteen years.

Jennifer tackled Charles about his argument with Ray that I had overheard in Ray's office the day after Rebecca's death. Charles admitted that he knew about Ray's affair with Gail as well as Rebecca trying to blackmail Ray into a promotion. Charles had demanded that Ray stop seeing Gail, feeling it was destroying the morale of the show. Ray adamantly refused.

When confronted by the police, Ray admitted to seeing Rebecca the night of her death. He said he had told her he had decided not to promote her because Gail and he had decided to go public with their relationship. Wagner told me this, unofficially, as a thank you, I suppose, for inadvertently speeding up the process of catching Patrick.

"Besides," he grumbled to me as I sat across from him in an interview room at the Hollenbeck station, giving him my official statement, "you'd have found out anyway and ended up telling me. This way I get to one-up you."

He smiled at me and I couldn't believe I had once found him frightening or without personality.

Ray eventually hired two other staff writers, a man and

a woman, to help take over the writing load. Although the show never again received a twenty-five share, it still remained in the top ten. The media eventually found out about Ray's and Gail's affair, Winifred sued for divorce, and Ray moved in with Gail.

I stayed on at Babbitt & Brooks, and, encouraged by Charles, who seemed to want to be my mentor, started writing a B&B spec script about the ladies being stalked by a murderer. Charles's agent called to say he liked my Dress Blue spec and looked forward to reading the one for B&B when I finished it. In the meantime, he'd treat me as a "back pocket" client, which meant he wouldn't sign me to a contract, but would send my scripts out to any show that seemed appropriate.

To offset my joy at this piece of good news, Jennifer and I never really got back to our old, easy friendship. It was my fault. Like learning your partner has cheated on you, I could not forgive and forget Jennifer's sending the two death threats. Jennifer realized what was going through my mind, but let it rest, mainly, I think, because I never told anyone else about what she did. Patrick, of course, denied sending the threats, and since the detectives never found evidence that he had, they eventually dropped the matter. It stayed between Jennifer and me, unspoken, but always in our minds. Sandy remained friends to us both and wisely never interfered.

Sherman checked in briefly to say he found another night watchman job and that his band was practicing for a major gig at Harvelle's, a blues club in Santa Monica. He promised to let me know the date so that I could come, but he never called me again.

My parents eventually got over the shock of my having been chased by a murderer (giving them the G-rated version of that night helped enormously), and Craig and I . . . well, we're taking things slowly. Craig did finish his book, which he showed to me. It was pretty good, and he's currently rewriting it before taking it to New York to try and sell it. My Florida grandmother sent me some money to "tide me over," while my Nazi-fighting Buby didn't seem the least bit surprised when I told her I had successfully defeated a murderer.

"Of course you did," she said. "You have my genes. We're good at things like that."

THE END

About the Author

Lisa Seidman began her television career writing for the primetime serials *Falcon Crest, Dallas,* and *Knots Landing,* as well as *Cagney & Lacy, Murder, She Wrote,* and *Scarecrow and Mrs. King.* For five years, Lisa was the head writer on the phenomenally successful, award-winning Russian prime-time serial, *Poor Anastasia,* as well as *Sins of the Fathers, Talisman of Love,* and the Russian adaptation of *Betty La Fea* (*Ugly Betty* in the U.S.). She received an Emmy nomination for her work on *Guiding Light* as well as Writers Guild nominations for *Guiding Light* and *Sunset Beach.* After a year writing for *One Life to Live,* she returned to Moscow as the head writer of *One Night of Love,* which was nominated for an International Emmy Award.

Lisa spent two years as an elected member of the Writers Guild of America, West Board of Directors and wrote for the daytime serial *Days of Our Lives* for which she was awarded an Emmy. She is currently teaching TV writing at USC's School of Cinematic Arts and most recently wrote for *Hollywood Heights,* a teen soap for Nickelodeon.